The Fall
of the Two Trees

Jeg er ansvarlig for meg selv. (I am responsible for myself.)

MERSAIDEE SOULES

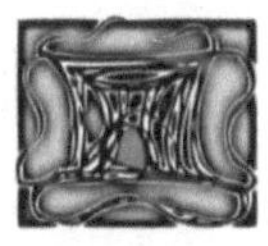

Published by Jaydd Publishing.

Jaydd Publishing is an Imprint of Jaydd Production, 398 E Main St, Suite 218, Tupelo, MS, 38804.

Front/Back Cover Graphic Design by Matthew Ladner

Editing by Dana Isaacson

Photo of Two Trees by Dom Chung

Photos & Images by ©JayddProduction.com

First Print and Electronic Edition: Mar 2026

Digital Edition ISBN: 979-8-9928098-3-1
Paperback ISBN: 979-8-9928098-5-5
Hardcover ISBN: 979-8-9928098-6-2
Audiobook ISBN: 979-8-9928098-7-9
LCCN 2026935283

Published by Jaydd Publishing an Imprint of Jaydd Production, LLC 398 E Main St, Suite 218, Tupelo, MS, 38804.

D ear Reader,

To unlock a glimpse of the books promo & trailer for A VIOLA TED SAGA, please go to the website below. All actors are human. All sets and props are real. Made by human hearts and hands.

———————

This book is for mature readers only, as it contains mature themes that may be upsetting for some readers. A non-exhaustive list of potentially upsetting content may be reviewed on the authors website.

www.mersaideesoules.com

Anyone who believes such content may upset them is encouraged to consider their well-being when choosing whether to continue reading. Please remember that depiction is not the author's endorsement.

In the quiet of your soul, an ancestor stews.

Words cannot teach what you feel to be true.
Words in a book can be misconstrued.
If you lie to yourself, what's the worst it can do?
Shhh, child, only love can give love to you.
Stop wasting time, love is easy to choose.
Your footprint is yours, without manmade shoes.
Kick them off, walk on grass, make this moment new.
Pretty soon, only grass will grow above you.

— Mersaidee Soules, 2026.

-..Chapter 1-. .-

Tuesday, July 7, 1992

It's like a desert in her mouth. What drug did they give her? She feels like she's been sleeping for weeks. Her head is throbbing. It's quiet. Too quiet.

Viola stretches her toes. Her left arm skims the bed she's on, feeling for the edge. She swings her legs over. Her eyes adjust to the light shining through the window across the room next to the door.

Cautiously, she stands, off balance. She opens the door and is blinded by the sun for a moment. She steps onto the porch. She could swear that she heard a baby cry, her baby, Zee...He's gone!

Why did I call that number? I should have known they'd never let me go if I'm as valuable as Jason said I am. Why did I get in the van? I did what she told me to do. I'm scared, not for me, for him, for my baby boy.

A trickle of a tear starts, then stops in the middle of her cheek. She wants to cry, but no tears come. She's dehydrated.

I will get through this. I have no choices left. I have to play their game. My son's future depends on it.

The sound of an acorn hitting metal echoes above her. The acorn rolls down and off the roof, and with a thud, lands on the ground a few feet from her. A steel box containing dried mud sits on the porch to her left. Down two dark grey concrete block stairs in front of her is a fire pit in the middle of an abandoned kids' camp. She peers out at four brown cottages, all of them smaller than her larger white unit.

If her family didn't have the connections they have, Viola would have gone straight to the police and put a stop to her brother and father's madness. Why did Uncle protect them?

I have to keep Zee away from his daddy, Zack. He will purposely wreck Baby Zee's future. Mom used to say that we need checks and balances to make sure no branch of government has too much power. I don't know how many branches there are in this family. Where is Uncle on the branch?

Viola wonders how far her family reaches. How many people are on the family's payroll? They obviously don't know who the Eastmann's really are. Did Mom call the police before her murder? Was that covered up? Probably.

It's clear to Viola now that her mother, Priscilla, knew the two of them were trapped in Telega. Mom tried though, she tried to get them out. Mom's rule number one: "Don't call the police!" Rule number two: "Don't tell anyone about the rules."

The tone of Zack's voice echoes through Viola's thoughts. The drive home with Zee from Jes's place the night before Viola ran away solidified that she had to get Zee out. Viola could smell *her* in the front seat of his car, whoever Zack *had* while Viola was visiting at Jes's. He wanted Viola to smell the other woman on him. He wanted to get a reaction from her.

"I take it you had a good time with your best friend tonight," Zack said.

"I did. Thanks for taking me."

Zack's hand reached out to move a hair from her face. Viola smacked it away, making him snicker.

"You will not touch our son until you wash your filthy Sea Lamprey hands."

His fawn eyes appeared for a split second. Did he feel guilty? No! That's how they trick you into believing they care, but they're incapable of such feelings. An unfeeling predator knows a kind person who will always take the bait...until they won't.

"If you want me to love you, Zack, you don't make it so obvious that you just screwed someone else. That doesn't make me love you. That's why I didn't choose you, and I chose Jason. I don't want our son to grow up thinking for one minute that this is normal behavior."

"My son will live with me when he turns five, Princess."

They stared at each other with venom in their eyes. She didn't dare speak.

"It's the law, Princess!"

There's no bloody way on this planet I'll ever allow Zack near Zee as he grows up. Not as long as I live and breathe. That's why Mom said, "It takes a monster to create a monster." She was warning me. I'm changing this narrative.

It was Viktor Frankl who said, "When a man can't find a deep sense of meaning, they distract themselves with pleasure."

Viola knows it's the same for a female.

Uncle had tapped Morse code on Viola's arm the day before she ran: *"Trust Jason."*

Good, stay with me. I made the right decision to leave with Zee. I know I did. Jason... Jason will never forgive me for running. I wish he'd been raised like I was. I must seem like an enigma to him.

Viola's hand slides down the doorframe. She drops to the ground with it. The pain in her chest is excruciating. She rests her cheek on the wooden door jamb.

Viola scans her surroundings and tilts her head toward the stretch of forest to her right, which is divided by a dirt road with tire marks, running for miles in the distance. She was at a campground like this before with Zack. This place has been here for a long time. These are the tallest pine trees she's ever seen, and aside from nature's symphony, all around her is the serene hum of silence.

"I'm not near a main road."

She looks over her shoulder. A double bed is in the middle of the room, a nightstand on one side. A kitchenette is directly across from it. One metal chair is in the far corner, next to the bathroom. The bed she was lying on has a brown wool blanket pulled across it.

This place is old, but it's been recently painted. She can smell the fresh paint as the breeze flows in, and out of the doorway, awakening invisible particles within the room. Her purse sits on the tall nightstand next to the bed. Her baby bag... gone.

Viola grips her stomach.

"Zee."

-..Chapter 2-. .-

Viola forces herself up to cross the room. She lifts her purse and a dirt-stained burlap bag—drawn tight around whatever is—within falls to the floor with a thud. Viola picks up the heavy sack and messes with its folded flap. Inside is another thick treated animal skin, generously coated in wax. A waterproofing. Inside of that, she finds a hand-bound book. It looks ancient, with a deeply stained green leather cover. She opens the back cover first, hoping to find a message from her mother. She reads the script on the last page—handwritten by whom? It's not Mom's handwriting.

"From sea to see, The eye in thee, Will rest in peace
The me must fall, Two rooted trees, One sets rammaz free
Stay or leave, Ashes or dust, So shall you be
Black wears the truth, white the lie...choose wisely!"
Black wears the truth, White the lie.

A French woman said this to Viola when she was four years old. She spoke of *le mouton noir*. (The black sheep.)

Viola's stomach rumbles. She places the old book on the bed, leans over to open her purse on the other side of the bed. Her eyes lock on baby Zee's pacifier, his favorite.

"No!"

Viola falls to her knees, devastated. Empty. Sad.

When will I see my baby again?

As Jill put the blindfold on Viola, she felt the needle prick. Jill never told Viola where she was going. Viola closes her eyes to clear her thoughts.

Mom, did this happen to you? Were you put here, too?

She holds her tummy.

I swear I had baby crackers.

Viola continues to rummage through her purse, pushing to one side her driver's license, playing cards, lip gloss, a book of matches, and the baby nesting doll.

They took the crackers, not his binky—Really?

She sets her purse on the blanket next to the book, gets up, and heads toward the small bathroom, turns on the tap. She's relieved to find there's running water.

Viola splashes her face. She drinks from the faucet. Well water. She remembers a similar rusty taste from camping with Zack. She shuts the door before sitting on the toilet, producing only the slightest trickle. After she rinses her hands, she scans the bathroom. Nothing. It's clean and empty. The linoleum floor in the bathroom smells new. There's peeling paint on the ceiling above the shower.

When she touches the side of the mirror over the sink, it opens. Inside are a few old-looking beige, circular paper-wrapped soaps. She undoes the packaging. The soap is so dry that one side crumbles in her hand. She gathers every piece, rescuing them, knowing she'll need soap for however long she's here. She turns around and opens the bathroom door. Sunlight streams through the square window fifteen feet in front of her. She wonders what time it is.

You put me here to read? Alone? For how long? Am I supposed to walk until I find people or food? Am I supposed to find my way back to Uncle?

In the back of the van, Jill never explained. She said there was no time. One deal was struck, and nothing concrete was said about what would be next.

Viola's stomach rumbles. She stumbles toward the old, off-yellow fridge and pulls on the latch. She breathes in the empty yet stale smell of bacteria and unseen mold.

Viola has always been sensitive to odors. She thinks of Zack, who is bothered by body odor. She shudders, remembering him naked in his black animal mask in the cottage. She sniffs.

What is that... fireworks?

The sleeping drug Jill injected into her must have caused her sense of smell to be off. The day after her neighbor Landon died, she thought it was odd how her senses defied her. This new smell is the same one she inhaled after her father shot everyone in Uncle's yard.

Stop it. Stop wasting time. Eat something, then get reading before it's dark.

She checks the three cupboards below the kitchen sink. There are two cans of black beans, a roll of toilet paper, a mini liquid green dish soap, a hammer, nails, and a wooden box half-filled with matches. Viola jimmies open the drawer next to the sink with the hammer's claw.

"Yes!"

A can opener and some plastic-wrapped, take-out utensils sit in an otherwise empty drawer. Using the stick end of the plastic spoon to crank the lid of the can of black beans, she sits on the floor with her legs crossed, scarfing the beans into her mouth like a starving orphan. She stops, realizing that she might need to save it for the next day or the one after that.

Viola sets the can on the countertop beside the sink. Her eyes move to a closet. She pulls herself up and goes to the door. Inside is an old mop, a bucket, and a well-used broom. Unaware of the time, she walks toward the front door. Her finger flicks the light switch on and off. She's thankful that it works.

She opens the front door to look again at the steel box with dried mud.

The book was buried. Where was it buried and why?

She goes to the fridge, plugs it in, and plugs her nose as she sets her open can of beans inside.

"I'll clean you out later."

She flops back on the bed and opens the front cover of the book to the first page. A folded paper is taped inside. She can tell it was removed and reattached to this page.

Did Jill dig up the book and leave it for me to read?

Viola opens the paper to see a topographic map marked with a blue X. She catches a pressed blue flower petal before it falls from the crease of the map. Her eyes blink at four words on one of two square sticky notes attached to the first page of the book.

"You have three days."

"Crap!"

She sits up. Viola scans the room again. She peeks under the bed and hits her head on the corner of the nightstand. There's a small drawer she didn't notice earlier. She yanks its round knob and finds inside two items: a key and a calculator-looking device, a GPS—a Magellan NAV 1000 to be exact. It's one of the first ever made. Mom made her use one to find hidden treasures in Uncle's woods. It was a game they used to play.

"Why didn't I look in here first?"

If Sandy were here, she'd add this to her list of the many things I'm unaware of.

Viola shoves the key into her pocket. She leaves the device in the drawer and lifts the book to read the next page. In light pencil are the words, *"Trust no one."*

Viola lies back on the bed, reading with a renewed purpose. As each corner in the room fills with shadows, she rises to stretch and wiggle her body from her toes up to her stretched fingertips, reminding her of her life before she knew the truth. She loved watching Jes practice ballet before they would cross the creek from Jes's families property, to Viola's townhouse in Telega.

In a one, two, three rhythm, on demi-pointe, Viola does "Tchaikovsky's," *Waltz of the Flowers*, across the floor. The music in her head starts right after the harp completes her solo.

"Down, up, up, oom, pah, pah, down, up, up, oom pah, pah."

Her finger reaches to flip the light switch on.

-..Chapter 3-. .-

Wednesday, July 8, 1992

Viola crosses a knee-deep river with the GPS in one hand and the hammer from the cottage in the other. She has another mile to go before she reaches the coordinates of her destination. Her soaking-wet running shoes squish, making her smile at the memory of her and Jes's attempt to jump the rocks in the creek behind Jes's house. One of them usually got a soaker foot from slipping off the smallest rock.

Sunshine warms her skin and trips Viola's happy thoughts. She remembers the second week when she and Jes were lifeguards at the Telega community center pool.

The floating pollen was impossible to clean. Viola worked hard to scoop it out from the middle with a net before Jes locked arms with her. Viola was about to tumble in.

"V, leave it. In thirty minutes, so many kids will be in this pool, no one will notice."

It was a Tuesday, and behind what Sandy called Viola's triple Cs—her cheapy, cheap convenience store-bought plastic sunglasses—it was the first time Viola had noticed Derek. She watched him walk toward the gate of the pool. It would be another year before they'd speak at his house party. He had numerous poolside admirers like her, watching the way his biceps contracted as he tossed his flip-flops, how his forearms strained when he placed his gray towel over the fence. She vividly recalls how the muscles on his thighs flexed as he bent his knees to dive.

She reprimanded him for diving in the pool—it was against the rules. He apologized to Viola without looking at her in her unflattering one-piece navy tank swimsuit. His objective was Karen, wearing a yellow bikini and slathering suntan lotion on her slim waist. Viola could tell she was deliberately slipping her fingers under her bikini bottom strings. Every boy eleven years old and up was eyeing Karen. Viola felt invisible.

She spotted movement in the park to her right of the pool area. It was a Native American girl, around eight years old, hula-hooping. Several elementary school boys jumped out of the water and started laughing at her, their faces and fingers wrapped around the chain-link fence to the right of the pool. She watched as one of their guardians sat in a deck chair, ignoring their harassment while reading a book. Viola strolled over to them.

"Did you know an American inventor discovered Native Aboriginals in Australia who were doing tricks with bamboo hoops? So, he copied them, made them into plastic toys, and now we buy them."

The boys ignored her. She moved closer to them.

"If you boys don't remove yourself from this fence and swim, I'll have to ask you to leave the pool."

The bratty kids gave her a dirty look, but they released the fence and cannonballed into the pool's shallow end—also against the rules. Consequently, Jes made them sit out for five minutes on the other side of the pool.

What Viola wouldn't give to remain invisible for the rest of her life with her and Zee. She misses her friend, Jes. She wishes she could call and tell her about everything that's happened. She does tell Jes in her own way, she wrote her letters, burned them in a stainless-steel bowl, then flushed the debris in the toilet at Zack's penthouse.

Viola walks on a path under the shade of a balsam fir tree next to white pines and black spruce, following the coordinates where X marks the spot on the map. Viola rubs her forearms. She left her long-sleeve shirt back under a thick sycamore tree with the Green Book wrapped in it. When she saw the river in the distance, she didn't dare chance getting the book wet while she crossed it. She's glad she layered for the trip and wore comfortable sneakers. Even if they are now wet.

A squirrel races up a tree. It hops across two branches, jumping to another tree.

"Hello, Squirrel. I saw a fox not far from here, and a hawk. You'd better watch out! They know you won't leave this area. You'll stay within an acre, always afraid of the unknown, circling, never running too far from home to find food. You trap yourself. You're supposed to follow your inner wind. Your tiny, conditioned brain won't let you."

Viola envisions the wilderness like in one of the last chapters she read earlier in the old Green Book. There have always been stories of tents and the chief who rules inside them.

Mom told Viola that all living creatures live under the tent. Mom had used an analogy of a circus ringmaster's ability to hold the audience's attention, forcing stronger, bigger animals like elephants and lions to perform the tricks he wanted them to perform.

When Viola was younger, Mom pulled out a children's book at the Blár Lief, the antiquarian bookstore where mom worked. The book of *Gaea Tales*. With few words, the children's book was filled with drawings of a circus. Mom told Viola the story as it had been told to her.

Mom pointed to a clown on a Penny Farthing bike, with its old-fashioned high wheel painted red, in the middle of a circus ring. The clown was looking at a boy in the crowd—not at the lion about to jump through a big flaming ring of fire.

"If you look closely, the clown isn't smiling," said Mom. "It's a painted-on smile. Pierrot the clown was known for his frown. This man was forced to be a clown. In this period, men who spoke against animal cruelty were arrested, and many were forced to be clowns in the circus. The clown was the outsider who never fit in on this stage of spectacle and illusion. See everyone's wide eyes taking in the show?"

Viola nodded as she looked at the audience.

"The big top is a microcosm of society," Mom said. "The clown is no different than a king's jester throughout history. Both represent the only permitted rebellion with their jokes. Poking fun at the ringmaster or the king was their way to speak the uncomfortable truth. Sometimes they were rewarded when they made the crowds laugh. Often, they were beaten or killed for saying to much."

When Mom turned the page, Viola pointed out a king wearing a crown in the audience. He looked like the ringmaster but in different clothes. They were the only two people in the crowd with anything on their heads. Her mother smiled.

Viola attempted to count the terrified faces among the crowd as they watched the ringmaster's whip strike the elephant in the middle of the arena.

"Viola, these people knew the elephant shouldn't be there nor beaten into submission." said Priscilla.

"I would stop that man, mamma."

"Would you?"

"Yes.

"How would you stop him?" Mom asked.

"I would steal his whip."

"But he has more than one whip, my little sprinkle!"

"How can we stop him?"

"What if the circus was like this life… a show. To stop the ring-leader, what would everyone in the crowd have to do?"

"Put the man in jail." Viola said.

"That can be hard to do when the king has final say, and the ringleader works for him. It's a much simpler answer, Viola."

The room was silent aside from the electricity from the light humming in the basement.

"All the people in the crowd had to do… was stop clapping." said Priscilla.

In old Latin, Viola's mother had written on the last page of the children's book.

"Semper idem." (Always the same.)

Viola spins around, captivated by the forest's natural beauty. She finds herself beside a berry bush, remembering Mom showing her a nonpoisonous berry in the woods behind Uncle's. She recognizes the berries. Her tummy growls. She's famished. Viola eats a few handfuls.

Strolling farther down the path, she sees a clearing ahead of her through the trees. Once there, she nervously looks around before stepping into the open.

She notes the scorched trees to her right and a stone founda-tion—a house or a barn once stood there—where long grass and dandelions now grow.

Was there a fire?

Viola walks to the spot indicated by the X on the map, glances at the GPS coordinates (42° 58' 12", -78° 44' 54.5") and smiles, realizing the significance of recently turned dirt from a dig and the shovel next to it.

This is where the Green Book was buried.

She takes the shovel, filling the hole in with dirt per the instructions left for her on one of the post it notes.

She retraces her path back, forging across the low river to sit under the sycamore tree to dry off. On the bark of the tree, she notices what appears to be a small carving. There are two letters carved into it.

A coyote's howl echoes in the distance. A vision of the Big Bad Wolf enters her thoughts. Her father's face. With blood in his mouth, he snarls at her. She shuts her eyes.

Face your fears.

-..Chapter 4-. .-

Friday, July 10, 1992

Viola leans against the large trunk, focused on the wind rustling through the leaves. The trees sway in circles, mimicking the sound of the ocean.

I remember the ocean. I remember the girl in the water. Mary was the girl who was ankle deep in the water. The shark bit her outreached hand.

In flashes, Viola's memories become clear.

Viola's standing at the water's edge. Her tiny toes dig into the sand. The water was suddenly above Mary's knees when Viola was refilling her pail with sand.

"Komm schon!" (Come on!) said Mary.

The water was up to Mary's waist when she motioned for Viola, to come in.

Viola waved back before slapping her hands together, shaking sand from her fingers. Hearing giggles, Viola glanced over at four other girls about her age, adding to her already massive sandcastle. There was a movement in the ocean several feet from Mary. A man ran into the water toward Mary, the exact moment Viola screamed!

"Hai!" (Shark!)

The other girls dropped their shovels, staring in shock.

Viola's eyes shoot open. She picks up the Green Book, cradling her arms around it like a baby.

"Oh, Zee, I know you're awake. I wish I was holding you. I can smell you."

Tears spill down her cheeks.

"Mom told me that after I went away, she didn't see me again until I turned four. I don't know if I can stand to wait that long. She said the answers I seek are in this book. I hope so. And Jill promised, as soon as I'm pregnant. She promised."

Zee is top of the bloodline, if that's even true. They'll take care of him. Jill swore an oath.

The wind dries Viola's tears like paint on a canvas. Should she have stayed with Zack's brother Jason, willingly having another baby, accepting the family she was born into?

No. Instead, she listened to her dead mother, rebelled, and ran. Only now, Viola can't be sure what will happen next. They want a female heir. For the time being, they still need her. Will Viola be disposed of later like her mother had been—once she delivers their desired heirs, or if she refuses to remain under the ringmaster's control?

Most of the stories in the Green Book tell the same tale. The women who wanted change, died young or after having their heirs. She hopes Uncle won't allow Zack to raise Zee if she dies. She hoped what Zack said was a vacant threat.

"Zack doesn't want a baby. He wants his nesting doll back in his king bed. He'll take whatever version of the doll he can get."

Viola sniffles.

"I'm the clown with the painted-on smile."

Viola can only assume so many of the women in this family live the same way: cooking, cleaning, staying fit, and spreading their legs whenever the man of the house tells them to. Her mother was raised with these beliefs until Priscilla grew up and decided for herself.

"That's why you wanted me to be independent, young, so I'd change faster than you did. You did it, Mom. I freed Zee from an animal. I'll live on berries and bugs if I have to. I'm taking responsibility for my baby."

Uncle's words enter her thoughts: "*Jeg er ansvarlig for meg selv!*" (I am responsible for myself!)

With her back against the tree, Viola turns to the page where she left off in the Green Book and starts to read the words in latin.

"*Anno 1818... filia maris, libera nos.*" (*Year 1818... a daughter of the sea, set us free.*)

When the sun moves, in the sky, Viola gets to her feet. She realizes she's been reading for many hours. Her body's stiff.

"The woman of the sea drowned. How many have drowned? How many have burned? How many have died to protect our children?"

Viola takes the hammer in one hand, the Green Book in the other. She heads back to the camp.

In its central fire pit, Viola dumps her used toilet paper, from the bathroom garbage, Zee's binky, the two sticky notes, and the folded letter she had written to Jes. She places the blue flower petal on top of it. She lights them with a match from the pack of matches in her purse and watches them burn.

One sticky note was from Jill, the other was in her mother's handwriting.

"Find your 'domus', your 'genus.' Look for the Orchid."

Domus in Latin means family, and genus, birth-kind.

What does Jason know?

The fire crackles. Viola stares at the dual-tone aesthetic orange flames and the swirling blue flames in the center.

Jill wants me to find the five girls I was grouped with from the picture. I already met one of them. Mary.

———

In the cottage, Viola smiles folds the Green Book book back into its waterproof sack. She takes the GPS from the nightstand drawer, grabs the box from the porch, and the shovel sitting against the wall on the porch, she heads down the steps of the cottage.

———

Back inside the cottage, Viola rinses her muddy sneakers off in the bathroom tub and leaves them outside to dry in the sun's heat. Viola cleans every visible trace of dirt in the place. From her pant pocket, she removes a few leaves of mint she had found in the woods earlier that day and rubs them on her teeth.

I can't stand my bean breath.

She showers and hand-washes her clothes, hanging them on the shower rod which is minus a curtain. In her damp bra and underwear, Viola makes a final check of her surroundings. She goes into the closet to get the broom to sweep the dried mud from the porch. She notices a bump on the wall and touches it: a round half-inch circle.

A key would go in if paint wasn't poured into it. What's inside?

She grabs the key they left her, holding it up to the spot. She can tell it's not the right key.

Viola retrieves a nail from under the sink cabinet. She starts scraping at the bump. It doesn't do a whole heck of a lot. She considers using the nail and the hammer to get it open. If it breaks, she's screwed. After Viola once lost her keys to the townhouse where they'd lived in Telega, she and her friend Jes broke a nail off in the front door lock when trying to get it. Mom was so mad.

Viola's earlier excitement about what she'd read had given her a momentary thrill. Viola lies down on the bed. She daydreams about a life where she doesn't have to run, where she no longer has to lie.

Nighty night, Zee.

-..Chapter 5-. .-

Viola jerks awake, catches her breath, seeing the light on.

Her husband, Jason Stanton, is sitting on the chair directly across from the bed.

I know I locked the door.

Looking into his eyes, there is no emotion whatsoever.

Her eyes fill, threatening a downpour. He's hurt, whether he shows it or not. He was under her tent and she was the ringmaster who lit the match that burned the ring Jason's lion jumped through. Her first instinct is to run into his flaming arms, leading him to believe the fire's out. But that's not fair to him. Not after the stunt she pulled. She lied so he'd jump.

I'm not sure what my running means for us now. Will he have to lock me up like a prisoner?

Her mom wasn't locked up. Instead, Viola was kept in an area with cameras and no travel allowed other than to Blár Leif Bookstore or Uncle's.

Jason glances at her in her bra and underwear on the bed.

Viola looks around the room. Her eyes pause at a blue orchid on top of the fridge, then at every inch of the ceiling. Her eyes lock on a camera above the bathroom door, and back to Jason. He blinks twice without taking his eyes off her, telling her that he sees the camera too. She wonders where he learned one blink for no, two for yes.

"What now?" she asks.

"You tell me, Viola."

"Will I see Zee again?"

"You left. I have no idea where he is."

I can't look at him.

"Do you know who—who took him?"

"Do you?" Jason asks.

"Jason, please. You're disappointed. I knew you would be. I had to get Zee out. I had to. I don't want him stuck in this life."

"What's wrong with this life, Viola? I thought you were happy."

"Happy with you, yes. I'm not happy about how I was brought into the fold. Pretty disgusting, if you want the truth."

"Are you capable of the truth, Viola?"

"We both know you're not," she says, glimpsing pain in his eyes. "Jason, I'm sorry. You didn't deserve that. You love me. I love you. I do. I didn't think things through. I overreacted. It happened so fast."

"What happened so fast? Why don't you start at the beginning? Explain to me why you did what you did."

"At Uncle's house, I found a note when I opened my suitcase. It said, 'When you're ready.' At first, I couldn't figure it out. Then it hit me. It was a message to save the baby before he's brought up to believe what you believe."

"When exactly at Uncle's did you find this note?"

"When we brought Mom's book back from England to Uncle's."

"Could it have been placed in the suitcase before we left England?"

Viola thinks of Aunt Lara in England, and her cousins Catherine and Mary, who came to the airport to see them off.

"No. I don't think so. No one touched my bag. Well, maybe the man who loaded the bags on the private plane. Come to think of it, I found the note in a zippered part that I didn't open until I was at Uncle's in Telega. It could have been placed there during any of our travels—Paris or Ireland."

"Okay," he says. "What do you mean by 'being brought up to believe what I believe'?"

"This way of living between siblings, having children."

"What part do you have a problem with, Viola?"

"Marrying a sibling is against the law, for one thing."

"Who's law? Who made it a law, Viola?"

"People, the government, the church, I guess."

"Which church? There are thousands of them. If you were born somewhere else in another country, you'd live by different laws. Most families interbred before laws were created to break up the power a family unit possessed. Laws were invented by people who wished to control society. So, who is living right? What people?"

"You sound like Uncle."

He doesn't move.

"Who lives the right way, Viola? Please explain to me what is right and what is wrong. Is it what they teach you—what they condition you to believe from infancy, or is this what your conscience tells you?"

Did he read the Green Book?

"Think about my life for a moment," she says. "Mom told me nothing. I was taken, raped, and impregnated by your brother. I think it's understandable for me to be confused about the right way to live, don't you?"

His face is like a blank sheet of paper. She can only guess what it would say if any words were inscribed.

"I have no clue what's next," she says. "That's not true. I need to have another heir. We do."

His eyes lower.

"You will have your next baby with Zack. I'm no longer an option for you."

"NO!" Her stomach drops.

"Viola, your actions have changed the course of your life—our possible life together. I wish you had spoken to me first. I wish for so many things..."

Her tears spill. It hurts. Her mind hurts. Even though Jason is her brother, and she doesn't believe it's right to be with him because they're related, she likes him a hundred times more than Zack.

I don't want to be with Zack again. I can't. I'd rather be with Jason if he's my only other choice. It's so unfair. Does he know Uncle faked their deaths for the sole purpose of pushing us together?

"Uncle told me you didn't want me, Jason. He said you agreed to have heirs with me, then you planned to leave me."

Jason doesn't give himself away. He's watching her mannerisms.

"You and I are pawns in a game of chess that someone else is playing, Jason. That may be hard for your ego to take. Uncle told me they wanted you with me, not with Zack. We were both played."

"Not played. The uncles make plans to better our family situation. Your mom was, and has always been, working against their plans. It's why you're so confused and make poor life-altering decisions. You've made your own life harder, and for what?"

"I don't want to argue, Jason. I don't want to have sharp words. You admitted that I'm conditioned. I made a mistake. Can you not forgive me?"

Viola concentrates on his face, waiting for his eyes to meet hers.

"No. There is no way I will ever again believe you love me. If you loved me, you could not have done what you did. I can never trust you."

"That's one way to view it."

"There's no other way."

"Jason, my love for you is separate from my love for my baby. Yet, I love you both. You're conditioned. I'm conditioned. I had to get Zee out. I had to. I don't want him controlled or forced to be with his future sister. I want him to go to school, meet a girl he's attracted to, and fall in love."

"Fall in love, Viola? Statistically, arranged marriages last the longest because they fall in love for the right reasons, not a lustful attraction that fades in time. Shall I go over the divorce rates in this country with you?"

"Okay, point taken. I would also bet money there have been many arranged marriages where it's been pure hell for the woman."

"Must you contradict everything I say?"

"Tell me why we're only allowed to be with our siblings. It seems like a sick cult if you ask me. I grew up in a different culture than you... It's wrong to me. We are forced to produce children—heirs, as you call them—to control them."

"All people have children and control them by teaching them their beliefs—"

"Can you stop trying to convince me?" She says.

"This is why I'll not have an heir with you. You're disrespectful, Viola. You would take my child away from me. Can you even hear yourself?"

Her stuttering breaths are fueled with anxiety. She's caught, lost, torn, unsure of her next move.

"Viola, there are many things you don't know," he says. "I wanted to tell you privileged information before you fled with Zee, but family secrets are meant for family members who are trustworthy. You have shown Uncle and me that you're not."

"Wh—What did Uncle say?"

"Does it matter?"

"Maybe? Yes," She whispers.

"Uncle told the immediate family that you and I have gone on a honeymoon, and Auntie is watching Zee. He's hoping to spare you from being locked in a room for the next however-many years by allowing me to find you and talk sense into you. If my superiors find out about this... And I must tell them, soon." He glances toward the entrance of the cottage. "You and I may be damaged."

"What do you mean, damaged?"

"We may never see each other again."

"No," she says without even needing to think.

I can't be with Zack, not again.

She gets up off the bed to rush to him. He stands, holding her away from him by the shoulders so she can't embrace him.

"I'm sorry, Jason. I am so, so sorry."

"You're not making wise choices. You should have told me how you felt. We could have worked on things together as a husband and wife or a brother and sister, whichever you prefer. I would never touch you if you did not touch me first. I am not that man. You no longer deserve me as your mate. That's hard for me to admit, but I must."

"Fine," she says bluntly, moving back so he releases her.

I know he's not an animal like my father. He's not a bad person.

Jason was brought up to believe he had to be with her. It isn't his fault—nor is it hers, for being determined to follow the Western beliefs she was raised with. She's not wrong. Just like Jes isn't wrong about her god, and Shannon, her Buddhist friend, isn't wrong. Their belief systems are different, but Viola could see either as a plausible way to live a good life.

Jessica's religion says being with a family member is a sin. Shannon's family believes that it is wrong to be with anyone outside of an arranged marriage. Both are controlled, like her family, telling them to believe what they're told. Each is convinced that their way is the only right way.

Jason leans down, unzips a bag, and pulls out a t-shirt. He hands it to her.

She looks down at herself in the plunging white Wonderbra bra Zack bought her and her light pink, white lace trim, days-of-the-week monogram panties. Jes and Viola each bought seven pairs, Monday through Sunday, to match from afar when Viola went to live in Buffalo. Zack rarely allowed her to wear them. He chose all of her undergarments for her.

"What day is it, Jason?"

"Friday."

His eyes drop to the white stitching on her Monday bikini briefs as she pulls the t-shirt over her head.

-..Chapter 6-. .-

Jason clears his throat, unzips a cooler bag, and hands her a wax-paper-covered Reuben sandwich.

"Did Auntie make this?"

"She was excited for you, Zee, and me to have time away from everyone. I told her we were going camping. She packed a lot of food."

"How did you know where to find me?"

His face is blank.

I almost think he's better than Mom with his no-tell face.

"The fridge works, Jason. You can put the food in there."

Viola unwraps the sandwich. She takes a bite too big to fit in her mouth. She covers the bread part, sticking out until she can chew it.

"Beans and berries don't satisfy for long." She mumbles.

"Please don't talk. Just chew. I don't want you choking," he says, concerned.

She chews and chews, and swallows. Jason takes out her domino set before handing her a stainless-steel water bottle, with what looks to be a water filter. She smiles at him and takes the game.

I meant to bring my dominoes. I must have forgotten them on our bed.

She watches him move about the room. He pulls out a burgundy book, two folded towels, and sets them on the chair.

"What's that?" she asks.

"It's a book Uncle Benjamin would like you to read."

"Is it his bible?"

"Yes, it's the *Family Bible*," Jason confirms. He opens it to the table of contents, his finger underlining chapter three. *DUTIFUL*.

When she doesn't respond, he adds, "It's a book we all read in our family."

"Okay. Um. There's a locked compartment in there, Jason." She points to the closet. "I'm determined to open it. Something important is in there."

"I'll take a gander in a bit. I'm anchored to the floor, Viola. I've not slept for several days, searching for you. I thought you were taken." He stares at her silently—longer than his usual pause. She's not sure what his expression means. "I need to lie down," he says. "Are you planning to run again?"

"Not today," she says, put off by his unfamiliar body language.

He sets the book down on the end table and falls onto the bed, with a long exhale.

"I'm going to sleep. I'm asking you not to touch me. Can you do that?"

"Yes, fine." She says, peeking at the book, surprised to see her name—Viola Ted, is inscribed.

————————

Viola grabs one of the towels Jason brought and heads outside for a walk. Her thoughts are scattered. Watching him sleep made her feel worse. She wishes he could accept being her brother, a friend, who might... set her free.

I need to clear my head.

A few small deer linger at the edge of the woods, chewing on nature's bounty. Viola heard Jes's boyfriend, Trevor, talk about hunting deer with his father during hunting season. She was sad about it. Jes patted Viola's shoulder and told her she was tender-hearted to worry about the deer. Viola feared for the deer family in front of her. A bullet would tear their father or mother away from them, possibly a brother if he were big enough.

I understand the deer population control issue, but don't humans also have a population problem? Instead, we tear up nature to make new concrete towns, pushing the animals out to seek new homes. They have nowhere to live. It's been this way since humans walked the earth. Our human defect. Our ego. We think we own everything. We don't. Nature holds so many medicinal cures for all of us, yet we've put our claim on the land, paving it over, destroying it.

She goes farther into the woods, stopping at the large sycamore she sat by to read the day before. She drops the towel. Viola's unsure about her next move with Jason or the family. She wants to run again. She doesn't want to be with Zack.

I can't. I won't. I'll get back into Jason's good graces, then Uncle's.

She thinks about her conversation with Jill.

Jill knows I won't take off without Zee. That's why they wanted him. They must have known I'd run far away if I had him right now. I'd never look back. I can't sway Jason to agree with my point of view. He takes it personally. Can he understand my need as a mother to protect my child? Our mother agreed to move him when he was a child, protecting him from our psycho father.

An ant crawls up her leg. She swats it off.

Great. Here I am wearing underwear, a bra, Jason's T-shirt, and damp running shoes. The mosquitoes will eat me alive.

She forgot to put on the clothes she had hanging in the bathroom. Viola fixes the towel on the ground. She sits cross-legged on it with her back against the tree trunk. She closes her eyes to meditate, finding herself wishing Jes were here. She instead attempts to pray like Jes did.

Dear, Jes's Good, what should I do? I'm so lost. I miss Zee. Please guide me in my steps so I can be with him again. I hope to keep him far away from this conditioning.

A twig snaps.

Coyote!

Her eyes open, her hand reaches for the hammer. She forgot it.

"Jason!"

Jason stands not two feet from her.

"I thought you were tired," she says.

"I'm completely knackered. I thought you legged it again. I heard the door."

"Where would I leg it to?"

"You ran already. I assume you will again."

"I ran to people who will care for Zee. How could I know I'd be put here, wherever *here* is?" Jason surveys the area. "Even so, it's nice here, isn't it, Jason? I love being surrounded by nature. It feels like home."

"It's home to all living creatures. You should feel connected."

"I've been coming out here by this tree for several days now, to sit and reflect."

"How's that working for you?"

She watches the veins in his neck flex as he tries not to yawn.

"I'm filled with a sense of peace. I'm—I miss my baby. I'm not sure what I'm doing, Jason."

"Why did you run?"

"Mother told me too."

He looks at her in disbelief.

"How did she do that... from the grave?"

"It was in the book that she wrote to me."

"I read it, Viola. There wasn't one word that said to run."

"She left me a message."

"You lied to me?"

"Yes, I did. She told me that when the time came, I'd understand. Mom never filled in the blanks. I had no idea about Dad, you, Zack, or that Uncle was my grandfather. She said that I would understand when the time came."

"You know about the family history?"

"Some, yes."

"Why lie to me about that?"

"I wasn't sure what I should tell you, Jason. Mom was so secretive. I was afraid to say too much about her to anyone."

"You don't trust me?"

"No, I never have." His shocked expression makes her feel guilty for saying it. "Mom told me to trust no one, Jason. I'm sorry. You're taking all of this personally."

"It is personal. I'm your husband. We have been quite intimate, yet you don't—Quite frankly, I'm devastated."

"Before I met you, Zack told me you were better at deception than Dad. I—I wasn't sure how real you were with me."

"You can't tell the difference?"

Why are his eyes so sad? Is he pretending?

"Since Mom died, my life hasn't been mine," she says. "I don't know what to believe. I want to believe you. That time you came into the nursery, and we made love, I hoped it was real—that we were real, us. I trust you more, knowing you didn't let Dad kill Zack, Auntie, and Uncle, but I find it hard to completely trust you. I'm not like you. I wasn't raised like you. I can't allow my baby to be changed into something I'm not. We don't believe in the same things."

"You're wrong, Viola. You believe a lot of the same things I do. It's just that growing up outside our way of life, the family line is hard for you to accept. You're stuck in a traditionally Western mindset."

Jason's tormented expression is too much for Viola.

"You play the injured bird very well, Jason, when you decide to put it on."

"I could say the same for you. You fooled Zack, you seduced me. How many more are you planning to seduce? What do you want, aside from freedom for yourself and your child?"

"Is that a question, seeing as I have neither? I don't play the injured bird well enough if you ask me. If that was even what I was doing."

"You're not going to convince me otherwise. You tricked me once, Viola."

"I can tell what you're trying to do, Jason. You want to make me out to be the bad guy for lying, hoping I'll tell you all that you want to hear so you can tell your superiors."

He shakes his head. "Viola?"

"The only difference between us is that you have been trained for years, trying to become the clever sex. A mother's genetic contribution is more important for intelligence than a father's genes. You do know that genes on the X chromosome may be deactivated if they come from the father, do you not?"

"I have no idea what you're talking about, Viola."

"It doesn't matter, Jason. The only absolute certainty to me is that we die. I can't give you my statistics but in my studies unlike nuclear DNA being a fifty-fifty split, I've read that the mitochondria DNA does appear to be almost exclusively inherited from the mother's side."

He looks away.

"You've read the old stories, Jason. We both came from the womb. Could women perhaps be born with a higher emotional intelligence? Could it be a reason why we've been oppressed by the men seeking power to feel superior? The same men who lifetime after lifetime are the ones scheming to control women, to instill fear, and start a war with other men to gain fabricated power? A war is a war is a war. So many good men and women go to war and are murdered, while the opposition considers the enemy their excuse to rape women, and murder people—all in the name of war. The women and men who happened to be born a little less blind... less *mine, mine, mine,* have had to figure out how to survive and keep our children alive, which has always been a natural instinct for a female, whether a child is ours or not."

"Do you really believe that? You're naive to say such things."

"We validate through testing, Jason! Like you're testing me now. Nothing I say matters. But don't you think it's these types of reports that start invisible competitive lines in the sand? I know there's no smarter sex, Jason. Only the smarter choice to be kind, or not be kind."

"Where did I read how books can confuse a curious mind?" says Jason.

They both smile.

"I think that's accurate. I've felt confused for as long as I can remember. I never questioned why I was taught what I was, for what specific purpose. When I pressed my mother for answers, she always answered 'for the greater good.'"

-..Chapter 7-. .-

Sitting under the tree, Viola recalls what Jill said to her before she stuck Viola with a sleep needle. Jill promised Viola would get Zee back once she was pregnant.

I'm not having another baby with Zack!

She stands and walks toward Jason. He doesn't move. She takes Jason's hand and places it on her chest bone. Viola reaches her hand out to place it on his chest.

"I know I'm generalizing, and you're not a man who fits into that power hungry category. I know that. Can we both, for one minute, remember what's between us? I love you, Jason. That's not a lie. I don't want to live without you. I felt I had to try to save my baby. I want him to have a normal life. A Western-world life."

"Who says that's a better life than our family can provide? I'm not the bad guy, I promise you."

Her finger covers his lips. "I know you're not. Can you feel my heartbeat, Jason?"

She forces Jason to move against the large tree. Viola's hands push down on his broad shoulders until he is sitting, like she was when he found her. She maneuvers on top of him, with her legs over his thighs, their sex touching through their clothes.

"Be with me," she whispers. Her hands rest on Jason's temples. She starts to hum a tune that her mother used to hum, rubbing his temples in circles like her mother did to her. After a full minute, she says, "Let go of your thoughts, Jason. Focus on my voice. Focus on my breath." Her fingers trail down his neck and shoulders. She places the palm of his hand over her heart.

"Feel my heartbeat, memorize it, connect mine with yours, allow them to beat together."

Viola pulses her hand over his heart in rhythm. "I love you. I love you. I love you."

Jason's eyes close. Her lips open as she presses them onto his. They kiss, softly at first. She slips her tongue into his mouth, finding his. He's with her in this meditative loop, this moment. Her lips never leave his as she undoes his cargo pants, pulling down his boxers enough for him to be free. With her other hand, she holds his hard length, mimicking her heartbeat, stroking and pressing into the head, rolling her thumb under the tip, exactly where he told her once before, is the most sensitive. A slick bead sits at his tip. She circles the top. Viola's other hand pulls her underwear aside, she lifts her hips. His tip meets her wet need. She inches down with the rhythm of their beating hearts. She takes his hand, making him circle her breast through the t-shirt and bra she's wearing, staying with the rhythm.

His moan reminds her to fake a smile. Their heartbeats speed up. Their mouths are urgent. With each movement, her lower region tingles, causing a shudder through the crown of her head. Viola's orgasm lifts off, taking him with her and joining them in song.

She whispers in between panting breaths, "I love you, Jason."

Jason whispers, "I love you."

They are one: one heartbeat, one breath. Their lips, their tongues, speak in a love language. When she tilts back, Jason's eyes are different, freed of his thoughts. She knows he is with her.

"Remember us," she says, sealing her words with a kiss. Eye to eye, Viola pushes herself up, taking his hand to stand.

They strip clothes off one another, letting them fall on the forest floor. Their lips, their sweaty skin, touch. She thinks of Derek, shutting off her feelings, lightheaded, as Jason lays her down on the towel, caressing her with his hands and mouth. She clears her thoughts, knowing that regardless of her true feelings, she must have an heir with Jason or Zack.

Viola once read about an ancient meditation that connects love energies in the book titled *Treowth*, kept by Mom in the basement at The *Blár Leif Bookstore*. The title is an Old English word that meant truth. The hidden room in the basement was dark and kept at 69 degrees Fahrenheit with 45 percent humidity. It had a slightly metallic smell, mixed with an old fabric book material scent. Mom used an incandescent light and a mirror's reflection to keep the heat off the pages. Viola felt like she was walking back through history every time she slowly turned a page, like a passage of time, with items that no longer existed, except in a museum.

People, however, Mom said, never change. Their nature and core beliefs remain consistent regardless of life's constant flux of time and circumstances. There were only a few written lines on each page, but the vivid pictures that were drawn on parchment read like a story. Mom called this story, *malum et anguis choros.* (The apple and the snake dance.) They're two forms, separate, with one similar need to create new life. It's not all that different from the Adam and Eve story. The apple waits on the branch, basking in the light. It's beautiful to look at. While the snake admires the apple, it travels the tree, protecting it from any harm from worldly elements. They share a love they don't understand. Mother's voice echoes in her thoughts.

Good knew their desire for each other in Gan Eden. So, when the red apple was ripe, the green snake would bite it, spilling its seeds. A birth and healing would take place, allowing more apples to grow—a magical moment between them. The still and shiny apple tames the ever-moving snake in harmony in their tree of life. The key to remaining in Gan Eden for the snake was to stay with his apple in his tree. When storms would blow from time to time, he would wrap himself around her, protecting her, his Cwene or Queen. He was never to leave her unprotected from unseen elements. But one day, his curiosity won. His good shadow jumped to another tree, knowing it was forbidden.

As he moved closer. What he thought was another apple, was a ripe purple fig. The fig's yellow snake appeared. It wrapped itself around the fig to protect her. The green snake slithered around in an attempt to see this unusual ripe fruit. The yellow snake hissed, hoping to warn the other snake to leave its tree. Frustrated, the green snake's mouth opened, sinking his fangs into the yellow flesh of his bropor—his brother snake—and with the first drop of blood, the yellow snake's good shadow fell from his tree to his death.

Meanwhile, the abandoned, unprotected apple in its tree swung by its stem. A gush of wind broke it off, and it fell from the branch, damaged beyond repair. Her green snake protector absentmindedly forgot he had left her alone in his tree. The apple was never meant to fall from the branch, and there was no coming back for the green snake.

In Gan Eden, the yellow snake's shadow falling from the tree started the transition from day to night. That moment started the war—the erratic heartbeat of battle: good versus evil. Two snakes fought and one died, the good one.

The green snake knew he was no longer good for what he had done. He stopped protecting the fig in the other snake's tree, feeling deep sorrow for his actions. Without his care, the fig fell, too. The green snake's desire, his temptation to leave his tree, was his undoing. His choice came with a mortal life sentence as a punishment.

Good gave eternal light to the fallen yellow snake, for he did nothing to warrant a war in his tree. Still, both trees fell. Good left the greedy snake to fall with the second fruit tree. The green snake caught fire, scorched by the yellow sun on its way down. It became ashes, hitting the earth.

As time passed, the first tree that fell produced a seed and began to grow. As it grew, the new tree flourished. In all of Good's light, Good offered the second tree a chance to grow next to her tree, giving him a chance to make things right. Both trees grew—setting up the scale, a balancing act between the rise of good and the rise of evil. Both would face the light and dark no longer as fruit, no longer as snakes. They were marked with their shadow under the sun and the moon's light.

The snake became part of the human, the flesh. The snake became the male sex, as he was now part of a mortal man. He was no longer in a blessed state of happiness in Gan Eden, striving to do good. He could only unearth his joy if he remained true to himself and faced his shadow.

The apple became a part of the human, the flesh. The apple became the female sex as she was now part of a mortal woman. They found one another again. They knew they would be tested. They must remain true to their trees.

As the story goes, the woman no longer trusts the man. He must earn her trust. While her undying love for him still existed, she remembered why their immortal tree had died.

He knew he had until the end of his human form to change his wrong choices. If he succeeded, he would return to Gan Eden as dust with good to live eternally or back to ashes beneath his tree, to be born again and again, living out the same history over and over until his temptation, his shadow stopped jumping trees and taking what wasn't his to take.

"Only eat from your tree, Viola, or you too will be ashes. The test is for both females and males." Mother said.

The few times Mom recapped the ancient story, she emphasized, "You must protect your seeds with your life. It takes time to understand this bond of love for your offspring. You have until your last breath. Let love be your guide back to good. Otherwise, it will be a life of chaos, turmoil, and hiding from good. And there is no hiding. Since the fall of the two trees, know that you cannot save man, and he can no longer save woman. The responsibility lies with each of you, individually. Your journey is alone, together. You must each save yourselves. Be true to yourself. True to your children, teaching them. This is the only way."

-..Chapter 8-. .-

Jason and Viola lay naked, satiated, in each other's arms under the giant tree, warmed by the sun.

"I'm in love with you, Viola. I can't turn it off. I've loved you since I was a boy. I was taught to. Now you're in all my thoughts. In England, Uncle Mark showed me our ways. Our traditions. He knew my cousins all spoke of their sisters. He didn't want me to be confused. I kept a picture of you. Each year my mum Cindy sent me a new one. I have them all in a box at our house in England."

"What about Zack?"

"I'm not sure. We never spoke about you. You were to be kept hidden. He stayed with our mum. They often visited. Those are some of my favorite memories, although Zack always got us into trouble."

"I can only imagine," she says.

"I felt guilty when he was left behind. He protected me from Dad."

"He did?"

"Yes. Dad would strike me when I didn't want to do the things he wanted me to with women, but I knew I had to keep myself for you. That meant everything to me. Zack didn't know that. He saw how much it bothered me. He would jump in to take Dad's mind off hitting me by doing those ghastly things with women. The few times Dad forced me, Zack took over, so I could stop. He knew I hated it. He was older. He'd pretended to want to be with them."

"I'm sorry, Jason. Dad was beyond a sick animal. I'm glad you feel you can tell me these things."

"I figured I may have given you reasons not to trust me. I've always been private. I'm used to keeping secrets, Viola."

"I'm terrible at keeping them," she says.

"Yes, I am aware, luv."

She swats his hard stomach. He takes her hand, kissing the back of it, moving in to kiss her lips.

"Viola, I allowed you to seduce me because I want you. I need you. I don't like to admit it, but you hurt me. I am not okay right now."

She kisses him again. Tears trickle down her cheeks, knowing he's good and that she betrayed him.

"I'm sorry, Jason. I don't know what else to say. I love you. I have a strong feeling inside that I'm not supposed to. None of my friends would consider being with any family member. It feels... wrong. When I think about what other people, my friends, would think of me if they knew—"

He touches her lips with his finger.

"We all worry about what our clan, our social circle, might think, Viola. This is why we are not true to ourselves. We've been taught throughout centuries to follow a leader's rules, even when they don't follow them themselves. Too many preach harshly about exactly what they secretly fear, hiding a truth within, afraid someone else will discover it. They'll kill before they look inferior to others. History shows us how truth-tellers die because of these people in power and their fear. Out of respect for myself, I live by my moral laws. I have a strong sense of duty. I fulfill it, staying true to my choices to remain what I consider to be a good human being."

She kisses his finger. "You are," she says, caressing his face. "Mom told me once that she left me so often so that when the time came, I'd be prepared to make my own decisions. Mom told me to keep it private because no one in my friend group would understand, or I could be taken away from her. If all truth-tellers are murdered, how can anyone be sure what's true?"

"I don't have that answer, Viola. We've forgotten how to think for ourselves. We fear our shadow."

"Facing our shadow is the only way, Jason."

His eyebrows furrow.

"I've read a lot of books," she says. "Our light shines brightly within. We only need to let it shine, to listen to it. Man can overcome his ego, but first he must be conscious of it. We are born individuals. We die individuals."

"So why do you care what others think?" he asks.

Viola blushes. She's on what Sandy called her "soapbox." Her ego is feeding her false need to be right. She's standing at the pulpit, preaching to Jason, judging him about something she's read, pretending she's right and he's wrong when she should only judge herself.

Mom warned me that thinking I'm morally superior severs any connection to Good.

"I apologize, Jason. I think the way I do because of the community I was raised in."

He blinks twice.

"We are separate, Luv, but connected by our choices."

"Mom said that about the two trees. They are separate yet connected under the earth by their roots, always touching, binding them to each other."

"Yes, a metaphor," he adds. "Like in so many of the old stories. If you're willing to research our history, Viola, you'll uncover that deep in the quiet of our soul is where truth lives. Your mum knew this. After all her hardships, she stayed true to herself. Her soul, her tree of life."

"What did Mom mean in her book about you and I being similar?"

He brushes his forefinger down her arm. "Her message was for me," he says. "There is more to tell you, but it has to wait. You will meet other family members who are committed to our way of life. There is no bending. You will listen and go along with your training, or be sent away. I'm not to interfere. A deal has been made. You're going somewhere to work in a lab. While you're there, it would be best to remain silent, especially when you want to speak out. Remember my words, please."

"Will I be forced to sleep with other family members?"

"I don't think so." He pauses. "I won't like it."

No fricken way, holy hell.

"I won't have a say, luv, not since you ran," Jason adds. "Uncle Benjamin can't hide your running away for long, or he'll face serious punishment."

"What kind of punishment?"

"Prison."

"Oh no. Prison for what? What have I done?"

"I have a plan. It will only work if you don't fight the family. For now, you must let go of seeing Zee. We won't get him back."

"You know who has him?"

"Yes. Uncle Benjamin received a message from a rogue group who call themselves *The Rise.* Uncle was told to come to this area. It's where your mother grew up."

Viola's eyes fill.

The fire. The foundation. Mom's childhood home. These were the woods she and my dad...

"Can you get Zee back for me?"

"Not right now, and it won't do any good for you or me to try. They won't hurt him, I know that much. We must tread this path carefully. I might not be as loving to you in front of others. I'm not yet at liberty to tell you everything, but I promise I will someday. I can't say when that will be."

"Are we in danger?"

Jason leans in to kiss her. "Forgive me if anything should happen to me. This will get complicated. It's been a long time coming. Don't blame yourself. It would happen regardless."

I'm going to be alone—again.

"Why is it happening now, Jason?"

"Two sides of the family are in conflict. They have slightly different beliefs."

"Welcome to Earth, where conflicts happen everywhere all the time," she spits out.

"We can't talk in the cottage. I can't make love to you there."

"I thought as much... The camera."

He lies back down on the ground, looking up at the leaves above. She follows his gaze, watching the leaves swaying in the breeze, the sun twinkles through. Viola's body is tucked next to him. His scent is mixed with the nearby wildflowers. She feels safe and loved by him, yet she's worried about what's to come. She regrets being selfish, for putting her family in direct conflict because of what she wants.

It's so hard to fake this with him. I can never allow myself to love him, not like he loves me. Doc was right when he said that I'm preconditioned. This is wrong. One day I will be free.

Her right hand plays with the earth under her fingers. She draws the mark she was taught, an 'я,' with two dots above it, one on the right of the letter and another on the left of it.

I swear this oath to myself.

She conceals it by messing with the dirt—covering her tracks, as she was instructed to do. Viola's mother, Priscilla, didn't want her to live this life. She tried to get her out, Jill told Viola in the back of the black van, that Viola getting into her neighbor, David's, car ruined Priscilla's exit plan for her. Jill was there to help get her out, but Viola had no clue.

I wonder who the man was who drove me to Doctor Strober after my accident. Jill said she didn't know. He wasn't family.

Viola watches the shimmer of sunshine through the blowing tree leaves. An emptiness hits her stomach—a longing to hold her baby.

Good, stay with Zee. Stay with Jason.

"Viola, I thought of something important!" Jason says.

-..Chapter 9-. .-

Back at the cottage, Viola and Jason sleep next to each other without touching. She turns over. Jason's boxers are tented, his fit torso on display. Slowly, she shifts on the bed. She sits up to stare at Jason's sleeping face. After what he told her, Viola has so many conflicting feelings. What would Jes or Abby do if they were in her shoes? But they're not. They weren't born into this fucked up family. Viola lowers the band of his boxers, moves her washed, damp Monday panties to the side. She lifts herself into position over his manhood. She grips the base of it, tapping her moist vulva onto his firm helmet.

Jason stirs. His eyes open. His lower region shoots up, he grips her waist, forcing her down on him, helping her cause.

"Viola!"

"*Shhh*, Jason."

They share a knowing look, a shared understanding—a staged intimacy. She thinks of the time she went to see her high school friend Abby at a horse show jumping competition. Viola presses Jason's chest back to the bed with her hand to continue the show for the camera. She envisions show-jumping his thoroughbred stallion—over a combination, a triple bar, and finally an oxer, with her perfect two-point form—into the winner's circle. Jason's hands drop to her thighs. Short of breath, she moves, fixing his boxers, leaving Jason to stare at the ceiling before his heavy eyelids close again.

Avoiding the camera watching, Viola feels sick to her stomach. She's torn about her predicament—wanting her baby back in her arms so she can gallop out of this in-gate holding area where her family is keeping an eye on her.

She pleads to Jes's Good to help her.

————

In the bathroom, Viola's thankful Auntie packed her shampoo and conditioner in the package Jason brought. At least she has one familiar scent to keep her grounded. She brushes her wet hair with the brush from Jason's bag. She folds the t-shirt Jason gave her, places it in his bag, then grabs another of his. She smells it before gathering her clothes.

Citrus, musk.

She glances at the blue orchid sitting on top of the fridge. Jason said it was a wedding gift.

What does he know?

A blue orchid is the rarest color to be found. Store-bought ones have a blue dye injected into the base of the plant to make their petals blue. This one is a fake.

————

Over the next few days, Jason and Viola spend little time in the room. Knowing the orchid will be left behind when they leave, she decides to plant it outside the cottage, not wanting it to die.

As she replants it, Jason watches her from the doorway, smiling. When she reenters the cottage, he's studying the lock in the closet.

"This requires a special key," he says.

"Do you think Uncle might know where it is?"

Jason pulls from his pocket the key Viola gave him, the one she found in the end table, but she already knows it won't fit the closet's lock.

"I wondered if it opens a box," she says.

"Have you tried the other cottages?"

"No."

She follows him out of the room, out the door, to the closest cottage. He unlocks the door with the key.

In the cottage, Viola scans the walls. There are four wooden bed frames without mattresses, and writing on the wall beside a dirty window. The drawing of a familiar herb is next to its name, Rosemary. Underneath it are three names: Lily, Camee, and Tae.

"Did our family run a camp here for kids a long time ago?"

"It would seem so," he says, "but I imagine it was only for family."

"Oh." Viola walks out of the cabin before Jason can read her face.

Shoot! I was supposed to see this without Jason. That's why they left me the key...I've heard these names before. There were six of us, including me. Who's missing?

Outside, they stroll together, shuffling through the other cottages. Aside from cobwebs in every corner, the rest of the cottages are empty.

"Did you ever stay here, Jason?"

"No." Jason pauses before they walk through a bug-infested, spider-webbed six-stall wooden outdoor shower area behind the farthest cottage. The hardware for the plumbing is old and rusted.

"What is it, Jason?"

"Nothing," he says, walking around the shower stalls, not through the middle of them as she is.

"Where are the bathrooms?"

"I assume they had outhouses here that have long been removed or destroyed since this site now has hydro and water."

Viola's sure that whoever has Zee also saw her mother's message in the Green Book. She will keep tight-lipped about it. After she read the book, she buried it as instructed.

———

They've been here for three sunrises. Jason has made mobile phone calls out of earshot. Yesterday in the forest, he mentioned that they'd be leaving soon. Viola wakes to a soft rap on the door. Jason is lying on top of the covers next to her, fully dressed.

Was he watching me sleep?

Jason gets up from the bed. He cracks open the door. He whispers to whoever is on the other side.

"It's time to go, Viola."

"Where are we going?"

"It's best if I don't tell you." Jason takes out a collapsed duffel bag and hands it to her. "Put your things in here, and this is for you."

Viola stares at a unfolded envelope. A letter. She recognizes Uncle Benjamin's handwriting.

"I don't want it." she says, just as a petite, pretty woman enters the cottage. She reminds Viola of a blond actress on the TV show "Melrose Place," which she used to watch with Sandy.

Jason stuffs the envelope in his pocket and hands the woman Viola's passport, the same one Viola gave to him the morning she left with Zee to run away from Telega.

"Let's get a move on." Jason says.

Viola feels a creeping panic.

"I'll see you soon, right?" she says when she realizes she will be leaving without him, unsure if she's pregnant yet.

Their eyes meet for a moment. His face is vacant of emotion.

Viola grabs the back of Jason's head, forcing him to kiss her lips. He kisses her back to make it quick, then shakes his head as she pats his bottom, a behavior she learned from Zack.

The woman looks away, her face flush. She turns to leave, giving Viola privacy.

"Do you promise me, Jason, that you'll come?" asks Viola.

He doesn't say another word and follows the woman out the door.

Viola quickly shoves the family book and her dominoes into the bag that Jason brought for her. As she slips her pants and shoes on, she doesn't change out of his t-shirt. She notices the closet door is open a crack. When she opens it, the compartment has a hole in it where the paint used to be. She reaches and pulls it open. It's empty, except for a nail and the hammer.

She shakes her head.

"I was supposed to use the nail and hammer to open this."

Jason pops his head in the door.

"Y'alright?"

She turns to face him.

"What was inside, Jason?"

"We're out of time." He says.

Viola lifts her bag and heads outside. Her eyes flit toward two men, then at the blue orchid she replanted in front of the cabin.

The woman takes her by the elbow and guides her to a car with Diplomat license plates.

-..Chapter 10-. .-

A male driver is in the front as the woman follows Viola into the back seat. Viola turns to watch Jason instructing both men. He's pointing to the main cottage. He doesn't look back at her. She stares at him until he disappears, as the car makes a sharp left onto an old single-lane gravel road.

"Viola, I'm Carly, a cousin of yours from England. It's nice to finally meet you. My father, Mark, has spoken of you."

"Oh no. Did he mention how rude I was?"

"No, he did not. He did say that you were madly in love with Jason."

"I love Jason very much. Will he and I be together soon?"

"I'm sure you will. But first, my brother has a training plan lined out for you at a private lab. You will meet him soon."

"What private lab, and who is your brother? Is he near the top of this bloodline?"

Carly laughs. "He likes to believe he's at the top, doesn't he, Brant?"

The driver smiles in the rear-view mirror at them.

"Viola, this is one of my brothers, Brant. You'll be meeting with Patrick, who is my mate."

"Are you in love with him?"

"Yes, of course."

"Do you have children?"

"Yes, I have four. They're in England with my mum and sisters."

"How many siblings do you have?"

"There are seven of us. Four boys, three girls."

"Wow, do all four get their sisters pregnant?"

Carly smiles. "You are truly amusing, as Jason said. I'm only with Patrick. We are the oldest. My four children are all his. My two sisters are to have heirs with the remaining brothers."

"I briefly met two of your sisters at an airport in London. Mary and Catherine, and Catherine is very sweet."

"She is. She will have Brant's child next. Brant is the youngest of us. He is learning under Patrick's supervision."

"Brant, do you love Catherine?" asks Viola.

He glances in the rearview mirror at Carly, who nods.

"Yes, I love Catherine, but I love Mary, too. She and I have two children together."

"Is it hard to be with both?" asks Viola. "Do you love one of them more and wish you could always be with her?" She watches his eyes search Carly's for several moments in the mirror.

"Viola," Carly interjects, "there is a hierarchy, a way relationships work. I can't imagine what goes through your mind after being thrown into the fold as you've been."

"It's darmy!" Viola says, making both cousins laugh. "Jason says that. I've been trying to learn the British language."

Carly scowls. "I assure you that is not a proper British term. It's slang, but—"

"Jason said you're a Doris."

Carly laughs. "Oh, Viola, you will keep me rolling in the tuffs. Doris means a female in the army. I could never be a Doris."

"I had my first baby with Zack," says Viola. "I hope to have my next with Jason—all my next babies with Jason."

Viola hears a tapping as Carly's fingers hit tiny buttons on a phone.

"So, you're not in love with Zack, only Jason?" asks Carly. There's a shift in her eyes.

"Yes. Completely, with Jason," Viola says with a sad face.

I hope Zack isn't killing more people with me gone.

"Why are you sad, Viola?"

Be a blue orchid and stop feeling sorry for yourself.

"I've upset Jason," Viola says. "I regret it. I'm a mess, honestly. I met with people. They took my baby. I was stupid. I—I didn't tell Jason where I was going."

Carly's eyes meet Brant's in the rearview mirror.

"Viola, I'm confused. Is your baby not with your Auntie?

"No."

Viola can see the effect her words have on Carly.

"I don't think you should repeat this at the Complex, Viola. You may never be with Jason again if you do."

What is the Complex? A school for our kind?

"Please help me. I don't understand all the rules. I want Jason, only Jason, but I—I wanted to protect my baby."

"Protect him. Do you mean by allowing strangers to take him?"

I can't tell them about the note left on Jes's doorstep. I don't want to involve her in any of this.

"There was a message in my suitcase with a number. It said, 'When you're ready.' I thought it meant getting my baby out before he was forced to be with his future sisters. When I called the number, a woman told me to meet her at a particular area the next day, so I did. They put a cover over my head. I felt a pinch on my arm. I woke up in the room you just picked me up from."

Carly stares at Viola, pondering her words.

"Carly, I'm lost right now. I miss my son. My heart is fractured that I've hurt Jason. I want to fix it. I do. Is there no room for forgiveness in our family?"

"Not when trust is broken, Viola. Trust is the top rule. You're not dutiful. You broke Jason's trust. He is aware of the consequences."

"He told me that he couldn't have my next baby," says Viola. "He wouldn't sleep with me. He said that I'll have to be with Zack again. I refuse, Carly. They'll have to strap me down. I'll only have my next baby with Jason."

Carly's hand goes to her mouth.

"Viola, to say such things is forbidden. You will be punished. I've never heard a female in our family speak like this. Did your mother talk like this?"

"Never. Doc told me that I'm conditioned from being brought up outside of the family. It's a problem."

"Heed my warning. Don't ever talk like that in front of Patrick. He will put you in a locked room, only seen to impregnate. That will be your life."

Viola whimpers. "Carly, I'm a terrible liar. I have a hard time holding my tongue—well, that's what Zack told me."

"How is Zack?"

"I'm not sure." says Viola. "I haven't seen him since our trip to Ireland and Paris to meet the family. When I met your sister Catherine in England, she told me a few things. I liked her."

"She is the best of us, to be sure, Viola. I am fond of my sisters, you—"

"She's in love with Garrett," Viola interrupts.

Brant's eyes shoot to Carly's again. He pulls the car over and puts it in park. He turns around to face both women. It hits Viola that Brant also looks a lot like a male character from the TV show, "Melrose Place. His lean physique, blue eyes, and dark wavy short hair."

"Viola, did Catherine tell you this about Garrett?" Carly asks in a severe tone.

"She didn't have to. It was apparent how she spoke of him, that's all. I can tell from how Brant said Mary's name that he's in love with her—Catherine, not as much."

"Oh my," says Carly. "Brant, I don't think we can take Viola to the Complex yet."

"I agree," he says, his face serious.

"Viola, our family lives and breathes these rules. Patrick upholds every law to the highest court. I'm going to take you to England first. You will spend time with my father. You need to understand things before facing Patrick. Only my father has authority over him. I genuinely fear for your future. You mustn't talk as you do. You—you have no filter, no wits about you. I'm surprised by your lack of knowledge, being at the top of the bloodline. Why would your mother keep our laws from you?"

"I don't know. Jason thinks my mother put the note in my suitcase before she died."

"Did you meet anyone during your travels in Europe who may have tampered with your bag?" asks Carly.

"No. Zack carried our baby. Jason carried our bags. He only put them in rooms. So, unless someone came into one of the rooms in Ireland or in Paris while we visited..."

Carly's eyes meet Brant's. "I'll explain this to Father. Viola, I'll say this once. It must never be repeated. We can trust Brant. Jason is the sharpest soldier in the entire line, the most respected, honest, good. Pure blood. He will be ruined because he's adamant that he will only be with you. He has sworn to it. He will not falter. If we take you to the Complex—well, Patrick shouldn't rule on this matter. I fear for Jason, who is innocent. He will remain alone if he's not allowed to be with you, Viola. Let me be clear that I'm not doing any of this for you. I'm doing this for Jason. He is a true leader because he doesn't wish to be a leader—do you understand?"

"Yes, I think so," Viola whispers.

"Why would Jason agree to have you go to Patrick?" Carly asks. "He's not daft."

"He follows our laws," says Viola, "or that's what Doc said once."

"It's true, it is," Carly says, staring out the window.

"I did sleep with him. I could be pregnant." Viola sputters.

Carly turns to give her a wry smile.

"When did this happen?"

"At the cottage. He told me I couldn't touch him again, not if I might give up our child, so I made him have sex with me. I knew he meant what he said."

"How did you make him?"

"He was asleep but dreaming of something. I got on top of him. He woke up. It was too late for him to change his mind."

Carly laughs for the second time.

"Oh, Viola, you're a naughty girl. Do you think you could be pregnant?"

"I hope so, especially if I'm never allowed to be with him again. I love Zack, it's true, but not a smidge of how much I love Jason. I only want Jason."

In the parked car, Carly's eyes flash sadly. Brant looks away. Viola believes it's because he feels the same for his sister, Mary. He doesn't need to say it. It's written on his face.

"The only chance you have, Viola, is for my father to grant you and Jason permission. Tell no one that you left to run away with your baby. Never breathe a word of this to Patrick. I can't use my mobile phone. Brant, drive to the next petrol station. I need a payphone to place a private call."

"Yes, ma'am." says Brant.

-..Chapter 11-..-

After Carly's call, Brant drives them to a private airstrip. When Viola reaches for the door handle, Carly places her hand on Viola's arm.

"Wait, Viola."

An old brown Ford truck with a cream-colored truck bed topper comes into view—Carly motions for Viola to go.

"And Viola—"

Viola glances back at Carly.

"This may be the last time you see him. I can promise you nothing."

After Viola gets out, she spots Jason in the brown Ford truck, and she sprints down the runway toward it. He angles his head for her to climb in. She does, but with a sinking feeling. She wishes Jason would take her and Zee away, rather than her getting on a plane and going even farther away from Zee.

Viola frantically kisses Jason with all she is. He remains stoic. A wave of emotion floods her veins.

Will this be the last time I see him?

"Jason, can we talk openly in here?"

"Yes."

"Carly's going to speak to her father. She's going to help you. I don't think she likes me, but she thinks you're a great man."

"Viola, remember what we spoke about in the forest. We must tread carefully."

She doesn't move a muscle, knowing Carly and Brant are most likely watching them.

I must get pregnant. I won't go back to Zack or anyone else!

Viola crawls onto Jason's lap, whether he was ready for her or not, she undoes his pants.

"Viola, what are you doing?"

"What does it look like? I might not be with you again for who knows how long. I told Carly we could be pregnant from a one-off, as you so graciously called it. I think we should make it a two-off."

He coughs, "You're talking tripe, luv."

Her schoolfriend Sandy crosses Viola's mind. She's the one who mentioned this go-to tactic. She grips Jason's semi hard length, in her hand and begins stroking it.

"Butter crumpets!" he mumbles, as he grips the seat he's on.

"Release your thoughts, Jason."

"There's no such thing as a two off, lu—luv." Jason gives in with a sigh.

"Who says, Jason?"

Viola flicks one of her shoes to the floorboard, lifts her bum to take one of her pant legs off, along with her panties. Jason uses his hands to cover her bottom, facing the windshield.

"Everything is made up," she says. "Every word, every story to some degree, so who cares what phrase I use?" She lines herself up.

"Viola, you're not wet enough—no need to spank my willy unnecessarily. Carly will give us more than a moment after seeing your arse in this windshield. You will make me the laughingstock of this family yet."

"Maybe envied Jason, not a laughingstock."

He moans, closing his eyes as she sinks onto him.

"We're making voyeurs out of my cousins, luv."

"Do you think we can trust them? Don't answer yet, Jason."

He helps her hips move faster, panting through his teeth. It doesn't take long. His release is louder than expected. He leans his head on her chest bone.

"I am a—What did you call me before, luv? Ah, yes, a mush pie. I'm a mush pie when it comes to you. You might get me killed. Remember... I shan't be soft in front of others," he reminds her.

"I heard you, Jason. I'll try my best. Carly said she thinks my loose lips are a ticking time bomb." She leans back to glimpse his eyes. "She's taking me to England, not the Complex, since I spilled the beans about the baby."

"She is?" Jason asks, his eyes wide.

"Is that not a good thing?"

"She will be punished, Viola. She was told to bring you to Patrick. He might take it out on her. She's making a decision based on what you've told her. It's unwise for her to do so."

"Why?" she asks.

"Patrick is aware I am respected, Viola. I was meant to rule his tower at the Complex. I'm pureblood like you. I declined my crown out of respect for him, for my uncle, his father, who raised me for most of my life. Patrick might throw a wobbler if his father overrules his jurisdiction."

"This Patrick, he's power hungry, isn't he?"

"No, luv. He doesn't wish to be. But over time, being in charge can and does change a man. The family has been docile for years. The Uncles realize what unfolds within a certain amount of time—which is always man's desire for something more. Men can't help but seek power, which leads to war. Unless we stay conscious of such things, history repeats."

"You think the family is headed for a war?"

"It's already started. Your mum was involved. She was on the opposing side. I assume she put that note in your suitcase a long time ago. I can't be sure. We'll try to find out."

"The people having Zee—? Is that the piece that will set this off?"

"Yes."

"So, it's my fault?"

"Well—" he hesitates, "You had no idea, Viola. Uncle Mark will see that once you meet with him. I'm sure he's wondered if you knew your mother's plans. But Patrick will not care. You broke the law, that's all he will think. You should leave now, Viola. Here," he says, handing her a key. "Remember what I've told you."

"What's this key for?"

"It's to our home in England. I meant to give it to you before we left for America."

"Oh!"

She looks through the back window of the truck.

"Why is there a bed back there?"

"I've the camper shell with the mattress in case I'm in the middle of nowhere and need a kip."

"What's a kip? A nap?"

"Aye, luv."

They stare at each other for a long moment.

"Will you tell me what you found in that compartment at the cabin?"

His eyes are blank.

"I love you, Jason."

"My Chatty Cathy, I'll miss you."

Viola glimpses a sadness in his gaze.

She kisses him. "Remember us."

-..Chapter 12-..-

In the private airplane, Brant and Carly are quiet. Jason warned Viola that there would be cameras and recorders everywhere along the journey.

The decor is light beige and cream with tan leather seating. It's decadent and not all that different from the plane she'd originally flown on to England. Her friend Abby would call this lush.

"Darn it, I forgot to grab my toiletries from the bathroom," says Viola.

"No worries. I've got extra in a cupboard at the back of the plane." Carly says.

"Thank you, Carly, and can I ask you a few questions about the family?"

"I'm not at liberty to answer your questions, Viola. It would be best if my father spoke with you first. Why did your Uncle Benjamin not explain everything to you?"

"My mom made a deal with him to wait until I was seventeen. My mom felt it was important for me to go to regular school. Even though I had no idea, she knew my life would change at seventeen."

"That's unheard of... Do you know who murdered your mum?"

Jason was stern in the forest when they planned. Viola is not to divulge information about his brother, Zack. Especially not about the lethal injection of drugs he administered to Viola's mother.

"My dad killed her."

"Are you certain?" asks Carly.

"Yes. Dad wanted to be the king of the family."

Brant shakes his head.

"What do you think of Uncle Benjamin?

"He's a good man, Carly—like Jason."

"What about Zack?"

"Have you met Zack, Carly?"

"Oh yes, I find him intriguing. He has a good sense of humor. Quite different than Jason, who is so serious most of the time."

"That's accurate, Carly. Zack made me laugh a lot."

"So why choose Jason over Zack?"

"I fell hard for Jason. He's so good. He's put me in my place more than once. I respect that. He spanked me once."

"What? Please do tell Viola." Carly says. Brant leans in from his seat by the plane window, eager to hear.

"I was mouthy one morning. I was jealous when Jason said something. I had no clue he hadn't been with anyone else but me. I thought his comment included another female, so I was saucy. He spanked me quite hard. Then we showered. He rubbed my bum. We kissed. I understood. He told me that if my father had raised me, I would never speak as I do. He would not raise baby Zee or our children to talk like I did. He was right. I apologized. At that moment, I knew I loved him."

"How... how did you know?" asks Carly.

"I wanted to change for him. My inner child told me to stop. That he was worth everything." Viola surprises herself at her words, noting an oddity in Carly's expression.

Carly's head dips. "And now, if you're pregnant?"

"No one will have my child, Carly. My biggest regret is meeting with the people who took Zee. I thought Mom wanted this. I wasn't sure who to trust. I trust Jason, but I fear it's too late. I hope not."

"Viola, I'm no chief or jury. I believe you. You have my vote if it comes down to that. Patrick is—I've no sway over him."

"If he loves you, does he not respect your words and thoughts?"

"The men are brought up not to be seduced by our bosoms, Viola. Did your mother tell you the ancient story of the apple and the snake?"

"Yes, she did. I thought it was a funny story."

"Why funny?" asks Brant.

"I read that we're the stronger sex," says Viola. "A woman's capacity to perceive one's emotions has been scientifically proven. I don't think that's a secret."

Brant crows. "Patrick will eat you alive, Viola. Carly, we can never allow the two of them alone in a room."

"Yes, I daresay you're correct, Brant," says Carly as she peers down the intricate cabin of the plane. Viola sees a small tray with multi-colored mini bottles.

"What are you thinking, Carly?" asks Viola.

"I'd like a drink, and I think I'm jealous for the first time in my life. Patrick will like your strength. I can see that Jason does. He cannot hide his feelings as well as he thinks he can."

"I agree. We women know these things. It's born into us. I think that's what got the Salem witches burned at the stake."

"Why do you say such a thing, Viola?"

"Come on, Carly. You do know there were never that many witches in history and there's no such thing."

"There's certainly enough books about them?"

"We know since the beginning, nature cures disease. Women and men relied on their intimate connection to the environment, gathering plants, animals and minerals to treat illnesses. We made tinctures. It's historically documented that nature is the Physician. Think about it, fifty thousand women who were considered 'witches' were burned at the stake over several hundred years. All that tells me is that, out of fear, men wanted to destroy our intelligence. And then there's the religious leaders and their weakness for the flesh—they made up the witch theory to be rid of us. Only the women who remained silent were allowed to live and push out babies."

Brant scoffs.

"When Uncle Benjamin told me the hierarchy of our family, where we are on the family tree, us ladies—it took everything in me not to laugh. We have so much more to offer. We can use our brains for the greater good. We are not daft, as you Brits say. Our sole purpose is not to push out offspring and die if we dare to speak intelligently."

"Oh, my Viola. Let us keep you locked at my father's place in England for your safety. I take back my no-wits comment about you. You have studied far too much."

"It's okay, Carly. Once I produce the necessary heirs or be passed around to the power-hungry males vying for my top-of-the-blood-line babies, I assume I'll be assassinated as my mother was."

Carly's expression is pained. Brant sits back, deep in thought. Viola has given these two cousins much to ponder. She is sure they've never heard about what happened to women throughout history, let alone in their own family.

-..Chapter 13-. .-

In England, Viola enters a four-story brick office building with Carly. They greet her father, Uncle Mark, whose dark brown hair is slicked back. Viola thinks he looks Greek or Italian. In a luxurious office conference room, his hands rest on one of the ten black leather chairs around a gorgeous oval table. He adjusts his wedding band enough to see the white of his tan line. An out-of-place five-arm antique milky white glass chandelier hangs above—something you'd see in a wedding hall, not a boardroom.

Viola can sense Uncle Mark's love for his eldest daughter, Carly. It reminds Viola of how Uncle Benjamin used to look at her mother, Priscilla. Not the same way. Viola thought he was her mom's caring older brother.

"Father, you met Viola in America, did you not?"

"Yes, please do sit, Viola."

A woman enters the room wearing pale blue hospital scrubs with a yellow pin on her lapel. Viola could swear that she's seen it before. The woman lifts Viola's arm, shimmies up her sleeve, takes a needle from her chest pocket.

"Whoa, what are you doing?"

"Don't worry. We want to check your HCG levels. It will show if you're pregnant," says Carly.

"Okay."

Do they want my blood for another reason?

"I've listened to your conversations on the airplane ride here," says Uncle Mark. "I believe your feelings to be true for Jason. He told me he believes they are. However, you have broken his trust. Do you understand this must have a punishment attached?"

"I do, Uncle Mark. Jason told me so."

"Were you unaware of this at the time of your deception?"

"If I could go back, I would have told—I would have shown Jason the paper and the number."

"Where is that paper?"

The nurse places a cotton ball, then a band-aid on Viola's arm. Viola glances at the light outline of a birthmark on the nurse's left wrist, then directly into the nurse's green eyes.

"I burned it after I made the call, Uncle."

Uncle refrains from speaking until the nurse leaves the room.

"Are you being truthful?" he asks.

"Yes, sir, I swear on my life that I burned it."

"I don't wish to cause Jason any additional pain. Since you were supposed to be at Patrick's station for additional training in our lab, Jason wishes for Patrick to decide your fate. He feels strongly that he should respect Patrick's authority. I disagree. I'll rule today. In the future, you will realize how Patrick does not bend any rules."

"That's scary," Viola says.

"Scary, how?" asks Uncle Mark.

"Scary to put someone in control who obviously has control issues."

Uncle's eyes almost bust out of their sockets, and Carly gets to her feet.

"Viola, you may not say such things about Patrick. He is—"

"Silence," says Uncle Mark."Viola, you're very wise, perhaps more than your mother," he says before turning to his daughter. "Carly, dearest, Viola is not entirely incorrect. All too often, men who hold authoritative positions feel an overwhelming, sometimes destructive need to maintain it. There is energy attached to leadership. It's one of the lessons we teach our boys—the importance to remain humble once we've tasted power. Viola, your mother knew this, and she purposely kept you away so you would grow up and demand change. You are at the top of the line, as was she. Therefore, you and Jason have the authority to rule regardless of what Patrick or I say. That is the law."

"Would Patrick agree, sir?"

"Patrick will be spoken to."

"What about Zack? Wasn't he firstborn, my dad's son?"

"Yes, but he is only half. He is below Jason in the hierarchy of the family line."

Viola nods in understanding. "If I am pregnant, Jason and my child will be next in line."

"Yes. If it's a boy, that's how it works."

"Must I meet Patrick? I can already tell it will cause more harm than good. He's not going to like me. Jason adores him, and I don't want to cause a rift between them. Can I please stay here with you, Uncle? Maybe Mary or Catherine can keep me company once she and Brant are pregnant. We can be friends. We spoke of it before I left for North America."

"Viola, that was before you met with strangers who took your child. Why would I allow your indecisive, unwarranted nature to jade my clan? You're to be punished first. Regardless of not knowing you're wrong."

"Fine. Can you lock me in an ivory tower for a certain amount of time so I can ponder my wrongs and learn from my idiocy?"

He stares at her face. "I can tell you've got some growing up to do. You don't seem regretful."

"But I am, Uncle. If I could go back and change what I've done—However, I can only move forward. I don't need a year to think about it. I was wrong, and I hurt..." Her eyesight blurs. She opens her eyes wider, refusing to cry. "I hurt Jason. I have to live with that. For me, that will always be my real punishment."

Will I ever get out of here?

Viola doesn't move. There's a knock on the door.

"Enter," says Uncle Mark.

The woman in pale blue scrubs opens the door. She bobs her head, then closes it.

A smile creeps on Carly's face.

Uncle turns to Viola.

"You're in luck today, Viola. You're pregnant."

Viola blinks, tears spill down her face. She's both relieved and tormented at the thought of how long she will be kept here, away from everyone, during her pregnancy.

I can't be far along. At least I won't have to be with Zack. I will get Zee back. I'll get out of this. I will!

Uncle stands.

"Carly, please leave us."

Uncle waits until she exits.

"Viola, I'll share one vital piece of information with you, especially now that you will have Jason's child. Your Uncle Benjamin and Jason have asked me to share it with you. I believe now is the time."

-..Chapter 14-. .-

Uncle Mark walks to another table, pours himself a glass of water, drinks it, then picks up another glass, pouring one for her. He set the glass in front of her.

"Thank you." She says.

"Viola, I believe you never would've met with these strangers had your mother or Uncle, told you the truth in the first place."

What is he talking about? What truth?

"Years ago, our family noticed something unique about our bloodline. Have you heard of golden blood?" asks Uncle Mark.

"No, sir."

"It's considered the rarest blood type in the world. Less than fifty people worldwide have this blood type. It's considered Rh-null. A lab in Australia has recently discovered the SARA antigen, which has never been seen before. Only two families have this blood type. We don't have golden blood or SARA, but our blood is also unique. However, you may want to research those to understand what I'm referring to."

"Why can't I learn about ours?"

"One day, possibly. We keep this information private. Our scientists are working diligently on a cure before we change how we live our lives."

"A cure for what?"

"You could say that we've kept our bloodline secret for centuries in fear of chemists and doctors or the government wanting to use us as lab rats. We are the only family with our blood type. We learned that we could not have children with other blood types long ago. If we tried, we would die."

Shocked, Viola stands without realizing it.

"Is this true or another lie, Uncle Mark, to scare me into staying in this cult?"

"When pregnant with a child not from our line, our women die. We cannot mix our blood, Viola. This is the reason we mate only with each other. It is not to offend others with a different belief. We have no desire to be a cult, as you've called it, although we are, as is every formed group or religion globally is if you want to use that descriptive word for it."

Viola is stunned. She clears her throat and takes a sip of water.

What the hell, Mom? You should have told me... He's lying, isn't he?

"We are merely trying to survive and thrive," says Uncle Mark. "Otherwise, we would have been wiped out centuries ago."

"Why didn't Mother tell me this? I wouldn't have said half of what I've said. It—it changes everything."

I can't breathe. Don't pass out.

"You needed to mature before she revealed our greatest secret. We needed to ensure you were vested in the family. This can never be spoken of. The majority of the family is only aware of part of the truth. And our line is extensive. If we teach you our ways from birth, then you're vested, and we maintain the secret about our bloodline to protect us as a unit without needing you to understand the greater importance of why we only mate with our line. Most never need to know, as they're happy with their unions regardless of this vital fact. The more people we tell, the more opportunity for our secret to become known."

This is why Viola's mother told her that she would die if she conceived. She meant to get Viola away from this family, but she knew Viola would never have children if she had been successful in getting her out. Priscilla did tell Viola about their blood. She never put two and two together until now.

She told me we were working on a cure for a rare disease.

Her fingers grip her stomach as she slides back into the leather high-back chair.

"If I were to get pregnant with an unrelated man, I—I'll die?"

"Yes, and if our men impregnate a woman not of our bloodline, then that female, along with the unborn fetus, dies. This is why we instruct the men as boys that it's their death sentence should they falter. No exceptions. We can't have an innocent female out there dying with a child, or an autopsy performed showing our DNA. Our family scientists have worked on this issue for centuries, Viola. It's why so many of us are in the sciences, and doctors. We're strategic where we place our doctor's at hospitals for any potential emergency procedures, as a safety, so no one uncovers the truth of our unique blood. Keeping this secret is the number one rule in the family."

"We kill people who find out?"

"If they pose a threat to us, yes. We don't wish to kill, but, as with any army, we sometimes must do so in order to protect our family. We protect our line at all costs."

"How many people are like us?"

"The family is large. We're immersed in many fields, yet clustered in areas so we have access in case of any emergency that may require our blood."

"Oh," she says, bewildered.

"The family has split in recent years. A small group of chemists have created special immunizations and tried tests on certain family members. Since we disagree with these efforts, they have gone underground."

"What kind of tests?"

The same mom had me working on?

"That's private information. The less you know, the better for you."

"Why does everyone say that? Well, Jason says that."

"It's safer for us not to burden you with extraneous information."

"So, Jason knows all of this?"

"Yes, he is top of the bloodline. He has total access, as does your Uncle Benjamin, Doc, and a few of our other Uncles."

"Does Patrick?"

"His access is limited as a station leader. He's trying to locate the family members who took your son, as is Jason."

"Are you saying they took Zee to do tests on him?"

Uncle Mark doesn't answer. Goosebumps rise all over her skin. She bends over to get her balance on the table. She can't believe her ignorance and foolishness, giving her child away to scientists.

What are they doing to my baby?

"It's for the best if you remain calm, dearest. Think of yourself and Jason's child, who grows inside you. Jason is very good at what he does. If anyone can find your missing baby, he will."

"I don't want anyone to kill Jason because of my stupidity."

"How your mind works. Why so negative, Viola?"

"We're born negative, Uncle. We must strive for the light all the time."

"Your mother taught you more than a few things, I see... No more lies, Viola, not to me. You're not as silly as you try to appear to be."

Viola's mind scatters as it makes a mental check list of all of mom's rules, including rule number three: No DNA.

"Never leave any DNA behind," her mother, Priscilla, said. "Don't use a hairbrush at a friend's place. If you drink from a cup outside our home, wash the cup. Any tissue you use is to be flushed, burned, or brought home. No blood is to be left on anything. If you cut yourself, stop the bleeding right away, wipe any surface clean, and you're to call me immediately."

"Why, Mamma?"

"It doesn't matter why. What matters is for you to understand the importance of these rules. I need you to promise."

"There's so much she didn't tell me, Uncle Mark," says Viola. "I had no clue that Uncle Benjamin was my grandfather. Until recently, I didn't know Jason or Zack were my brothers. Mom never told me who my father was. I only met him after she died. She kept so much from me. She only told me stories about the apple and the snake."

She glances his way to gauge his facial expression.

"You were told of the power of females?"

"Yes. Jason was surprised, too."

"You told him that you had read this ancient story?"

"Yes, I had to. He said he couldn't be with me or trust me because I ran. I want him. I'm in love with him."

Uncle Mark sits tall in his seat at the head of the boardroom table without looking at anything in particular.

"Viola, tell me everything your mother taught you—or you'll never see Jason again."

The back of her neck prickles. This Uncle is different than Doc and Uncle Benjamin. She must tread carefully, as Jason likes to say, or it will be her doom—and possibly Uncle Benjamin's and Jason's.

"What sorts of things do you want me to tell you, Uncle Mark?"

"When did your mother start telling you ancient stories? I want to know which stories she told you."

They're eyes meet.

Careful Viola!

-..Chapter 15-. .-

An hour passes before there's a knock on the door. A man brings in a platter of food. Viola and Uncle Mark eat while continuing to talk. Viola shuffles through her mental rolodex to share the basic things her mother read to her over the years.

"Is that everything?" he asks.

"I think so, Uncle. I'll tell you if I remember anything else. That's all I remember. Mom wasn't home very often. I'm not sure where she went—I presume to be with my dad. She went out a lot. I learned to be independent."

"And did you see her dead body? Are you confident she was dead?"

"Yes," she says as the blur hits her eyes. "She was most definitely dead. She had no heartbeat, no breath, her lips...were blue. I asked her lifeless body why she left me. I scattered her ashes where she instructed me to in her will."

"Can you tell me where her ashes were scattered?"

"Yes. Why does that matter, Uncle? It's so long ago. I'm sure they've blown in the wind and water, where she requested them to be thrown back to nature."

"I want a specific location."

"Okay, Uncle. I can tell you or show you the area on a map."

"Good," he says, smiling.

It's a fake smile. My father smiled like that when he was lying.

After another quick knock, Carly re-enters the room.

"Patrick is on the red phone for you, in your office, Father. I'll stay with Viola."

"Thank you, Carly." Uncle Mark stands. "I think we've both heard quite enough for today, Viola. Thank you for being honest. I'll speak with Patrick. You will stay here. You will have your baby in England."

From the open doorway, Carly smiles at the news.

"Thank you, Uncle. Um, do you mean I'll live in this boardroom?"

"Yes—until I can make a proper arrangement."

Viola looks around the room, at the long couch and a TV across from it. There's a lengthy hallway with a few closed doors and a floor-to-ceiling window at the end of it.

"Uncle? Patrick won't hurt Carly for bringing me here, will he? I don't want her hurt because of me."

"Hush, child," he says. Carly gawks in surprise. Uncle steps toward Viola. "Why do you think he will hurt her? Have you met Patrick?"

"No. I've heard enough to believe that he might punish her. I'm worried for my cousin and my husband. I don't want Patrick to take it out on them because of my ignorance, my mistakes."

"You're very caring, Viola," says Uncle Mark. "Would you die for Jason?"

"Yes," she answers without hesitation.

Uncle moves closer to peer into her eyes.

"Would you die for Zack?"

"Zack, my baby? Of course."

"What about Zack, the father of your firstborn?"

"I'm not sure, Uncle. Zack is selfish at times. Jason isn't. Jason would die for you, he told me so. I think he'd die for Patrick as well. He holds him in high regard."

Uncle grins, as if she passed a test, then asks, "Would Jason die for your uncle?"

Why is he asking me this?

"You'd have to ask him that question," says Viola. "He did say that he wished he could have saved Doc's daughter, Cindy. He said she was lovely."

"She was. I knew her well. Jason favors her, her heart."

"Did you love her?" Viola asks.

"Of course. I knew her mother. She was my sister. She—I loved her very much."

"Is your sister's eldest son yours, not Doc's?"

At that question, Carly, who is standing at the door, peers into the hallway before stepping in and closing the door.

"Why do you ask?" says Uncle Mark.

"Your eyes tell me much," Viola says.

"Do they? Did your mother tell you this?"

"No one told me. I bet my mother had no idea. I know you share sisters. I sense things, Uncle."

"What types of things, Viola?" he asks, clearly taking an interest.

"I sense when people love someone, and if I'm being lied to—like you seem to think you can tell if I've lied to you."

"Have you lied to me?"

"Not that I'm aware of."

He sighs. "Jason will have to watch out for you."

"He's the only one I can't figure out, Uncle, which I admit I find attractive. He's set on upholding the traditions, the laws."

"When did Jason find out who his birth mother was?" asks Uncle Mark.

"I can ask him, Uncle. I expect he must've been quite shocked to find out."

"I told him," says Uncle Mark.

Is he playing games to question mine or Jason's loyalty?

Viola's not sure where this conversation is going.

I need to stop talking. Both of our egos are in full shadow mode.

"I'm grateful for your honesty with me, Uncle. I'm so happy I didn't run away and marry a normal man."

"Define normal, Viola."

"People I went to school with. They have different beliefs. They date people they're attracted to, live in a house, have a job, a car, have babies, and those babies grow up to go through the same motions. That's what I consider normal. It sounds not so exciting when saying it out loud."

"Do you think it sounds boring?" he asks.

Viola recalls Zack asking her a similar question long ago in the cabin.

"No," she says, meeting his eyes. "If I had not met Jason, and if I wouldn't—" She glances at Carly. "I would have to say I'd prefer that so-called normal life to this captive one."

"Excellent. Perhaps the first true thing you've said today." he says.

"Not the first, Uncle. Remember, we're born to think negative-ly. Don't judge me too harshly. On the contrary, I care about peo-ple who care about me. My jury is out when it comes to you—but not Carly. She's good. You don't trust me because you fear my knowledge. I know who I am and who I'm not. My Uncle doesn't fear me, neither does Doc. They know my true heart. Ask them about me. I wish no one any harm. I can tell you need to tap into your good more often, Uncle."

Carly stares at Viola, aghast. Uncle starts to laugh. He lets loose a full-belly laugh as her own uncle used to whenever Viola said whatever silly thing popped into her head and came out of her mouth.

"My goodness." He chuckles before he's suddenly serious again. "Remember, Viola, Patrick can never learn that on your own ac-cord, you met with the people who took your baby. Benjamin, Doc, Jason, and I are all in agreement about this. Carly and I will tell Patrick that the baby was taken from you when you went into town that morning. You can't tell Patrick the truth, or I can't save you, and you'll never be with Jason again. Am I clear?"

"Crystal."

"Who is Crystal?" he asks.

"No one, Uncle. It means your statement is crystal clear, as in, I understand you as clear as crystal."

"Ah," he says, sharing a befuddled smile with Carly as he leaves the boardroom with Carly.

-..Chapter 16-. .-

The first night Viola sleeps in the boardroom, she opens both doors down its hallway to see another smaller boardroom and a bathroom with a shower.

The same man brings her food in the morning and locks her in when he leaves.

Viola doesn't keep track of the days that follow. It would be pointless since Uncle Mark made it clear that she'd be in England for her entire pregnancy.

Zoned out from watching uninspiring television programs, Viola's thoughts glance toward a painting on the wall.

Is this how Camille Claudel felt when she met the great artist Auguste Rodin? She was his apprentice, a teenager. Naïve and curious. Until the terrible day she was committed to a lunatic asylum and never again allowed to create?

Mom had told Viola that their family had commissioned Claudel to sculpt several female statues of Viola's ancestors. Viola thinks of Luci's statue from the 1800s. Luci was murdered during the Spanish Inquisition.

I wonder if it was true that it was Claudel's nude sculptures that inspired Rodin's most sensual works?

Viola loves her *Waltz with Veils*. Camille Claudel's sculpture titled *Implorer* was Viola's favorite.

Viola thinks of Zack, a man who wants his muse until he doesn't. Zack's make-believe devotion destroyed her daily. How long would he have trapped his hamster in the house until deciding that he'd finished with her?

I did free myself from him, for now.

For a moment, Viola wishes she could have gone to the private lab they were sending her to for training. She feels helpless sitting in the conference room under the chandelier, day after day, watching meaningless television.

She eats breakfast at the boardroom table. She falls asleep on the couch with a blanket and a pillow. When she wakes, she walks to the large window at the end of the hallway, reaching her hand to touch the glass. It's cool. It's still morning. The sun hasn't heated it yet. How many times at Zack's penthouse apartment throughout the day did she look out the floor-to-ceiling window and touch the glass... to feel... something? At least at his apartment, she could waste an hour watching the people below—rushing, smoking, pushing babies in strollers—with the binoculars he bought her when she refused to touch the telescope. There's not much to see here other than a row of tall trees and a highway of cars beyond them in the distance. The room is soundproof. She hears nothing from outside.

Why is Uncle Mark keeping me in the boardroom of his office building? Is my being here a secret to Jason? He hasn't called, has he?

She's glad to be carrying Jason's child, not Zack's. She hopes Carly tells Jason.

She likes Carly. Viola is sure Carly is loyal to Patrick, yet she can tell Carly also questions some of her mate's decisions.

There's another reason she feared taking me to this Complex, wherever that is.

When Viola hears a key turning in the door, she looks up at the camera she spotted yesterday, hidden inside the can light directly above the door. To Viola's surprise, her cousin Catherine walks in, looking like a fresh-faced supermodel arriving for hair and make-up and not needing any. She's a natural beauty with her shoulder-length dark flowing locks pulled into a loose knot.

"Viola, how are you? My mum told me about your good news. Congratulations. I'm so happy for you and Jason."

"Thank you, Catherine. How are you?"

"Wonderful. I'm also trying to conceive. I'm so sorry that baby Zack is missing. Mum told me that Jason will track him down."

"Yes, well, I'm worried about Jason."

"Oh, Viola, he'll be fine," Catherine says. "Mother said that the side of the family that took your baby is not evil. I'm not sure why the family is suddenly divided. Your Uncle will make a deal for the baby once Jason figures out where they've taken him."

"I hope no one dies."

"They will not. Our family doesn't work that way. Taking a life is against what we believe in."

Catherine's kept from the truth.

"How is Carly? I was hoping she would come by."

"She went to the Complex where Patrick's stationed. He doesn't like to be without her for long. They love each other so much."

"I like her," says Viola.

"She likes you, too. I had already told her how pretty you are."

"You're the one who's pretty. You're beautiful, Catherine. Inside and out. That's rare."

"Thank you, Viola. That's kind of you to say."

Viola points toward the playing cards she took from her purse and set on the boardroom table.

"Do you want to play cards, Catherine? I'm bored with solitaire and watching TV."

"I'd love to."

Viola goes to the table.

"Do you think I can have my duffel bag back, Catherine?"

"I can ask. I'm not sure why not."

Catherine picks up the receiver, presses a button, and tells whoever is on the other end to bring Viola her duffel bag.

In a few minutes, there's a tap at the door. The same man Viola has seen for days brings in her bag. Viola thanks him, then opens it.

Viola calls out to him. "Excuse me! Where is the book I had in here? I want it back."

Without a word, he leaves and shuts the door.

"What book, Viola?" asks Catherine.

"Jason brought me a book from my Uncle Benjamin. I want to read it since I'm stuck here."

"You're not stuck, Viola. Father has you here for protection. Whoever took your baby may want you next."

"Hmmm," Viola says, looking at the camera, wearing her stoic glare.

"I've got dominoes, too, Catherine. Jason told me you beat the snickers off him the last time he played you in cards." Viola says, pulling red ones out of her duffle bag.

"It's knickers, not snickers, Viola. I've had years of practice. All my brother's cheat. I've had to learn to be savvy, is all."

"Men can't help but be competitive at every turn, Catherine."

"I guess. I haven't thought about it. I've not played dominoes."

-..Chapter 17-..-

The Next Day

Viola wakes to find a tray of fruit and yogurt already on the coffee table. She hadn't heard the man come in or leave. She notices that he brought her book. Uncle Benjamin's *Family Bible* is on the table. She opens it to the first page and glimpses the titles, comparing them to Jes's bible.

In the beginning
"Genesis"
The Journey Out
"Exodus"
Dutiful
"Proverbs"
"When was this written or updated?"

Viola's mother was adamant Viola was not to be given Uncle's book. Priscilla handed it back to Uncle Benjamin once, explaining to him that every sane human on the planet knows the rules and how to live as a civilized human being.

Rule Number One: Don't kill another human.

Rule Number Two: Don't steal from anyone.

Rule Number Three: Don't lie to yourself.

According to Viola's studies, she read that the revisions of the text in Bibles began as far back as the first century BCE and continue today with each new religious denomination.

Uncle tried to give Viola this bible for a second time, years ago. Mom quickly grabbed it, sticking it back into Uncle's hands.

I don't know what this chapter Dutiful, will tell me that the first chapter doesn't already say, if it's similar to Jes's bible.

Viola thought about it last night. She'll keep her mouth shut when she sees Uncle Mark next, unless he asks a specific question. She could tell he was upset at her bluntness. Uncle Benjamin told her that it's not appropriate for women in this family to be outspoken. Jason warned her to be good—or it could be hard for her. She will leave the book for now, not wanting to come off too eager to read it. She wonders if there might be a message for her in it.

I need to read it and not share my unwanted opinions.

Viola reaches for a strawberry. Her tummy is queasy. She rushes to a nearby garbage can to vomit.

Great, morning sickness again.

She sits on the floor, awaiting the next round of nausea. She counts in her head.

I must have gotten pregnant the first time I came to see Jason in England with Zee—no wonder my emotions are all over the place.

Viola lies on the couch with her eyes shut. She could cry. She wonders what Uncle Benjamin or Doc may know. What did this uncle tell them? She hopes she's not a disappointment to them all—especially not Jason.

The door creaks. It's Auntie Lara.

Like Catherine and Mary, Viola met Auntie on her first trip to England at the private airport. She looked like she could be Viola's mom's sister. Mary and Aunt Lara share a remarkable resemblance. Their tiny frame and dark brown, almost black hair color. Catherine has her father's height. She could nearly pass as a relative of the multicultural supermodel Viola read about in a magazine, who is known for her distinct "walk of life."

"Viola, my darling, are you all right?" asks Auntie Lara.

"I'm pregnant and sick."

"Let's move you to the washroom. You've been sick on yourself, sweet girl."

"Thank you for your help. Is Catherine coming to visit me today?"

"Not today. She's busy."

Viola notes Auntie Lara's glance toward the bible with an eyebrow raised.

"Is she trying to conceive, Auntie?"

"Yes. She told you?"

"Yes. It would be nice to share our pregnancy."

"I used to enjoy when my sisters and I were pregnant at the same time," Auntie says.

"Were you sick as well?" asks Viola.

"No, I didn't have morning sickness. I did have many air biscuits."

Viola laughs.

"I like the British language. You have so many colorful terms."

"We think the same about our North American family, Viola."

All of a sudden, Viola's tears start again, and Auntie embraces her.

"Viola, why so weepy?"

"I've lost everything, Auntie," she says, pulling away, catching something in Auntie Lara's eyes.

"I'm sorry about your mum, Viola. It's not natural to lose a mum, especially when pregnant."

"Thank you. Could my Auntie visit? I'd do almost anything for one of her Reuben sandwiches right now, maybe after my nausea. I'd hate to waste good food."

"I'm sorry, Viola. She's tied up in the Americas. Something is happening with Zack. Have you not heard about it?"

"No. What's going on?"

"Zack is missing."

"What?"

"Yes, no one can find him. Jason is in America, searching for him. We think the disappearance has to do with your child missing.

Auntie called me. She said Zack was a mess. Uncle will send our son Garrett to help with the search."

"Will you thank Uncle Mark for me? I am grateful."

"Of course."

Viola looks to Auntie with questioning eyes. She has no idea what this woman is thinking.

"Patrick will be coming for a visit with Carly," says Auntie. "Carly's worried about you. She asked to come, to keep you company."

"I'd love that," Viola says. "I like your daughters. They are..."
Programmed

"So kind." says Viola.

"I've been immensely blessed, Viola. However, the body takes a beating, pushing out so many children."

"Carly told me you had seven. That's a lot of pregnancies."

"Yes, it is. I wanted ten. My eighth was a stillbirth. I fear my body has had enough. Uncle said no more."

"I'm sorry, Auntie."

"Thank you, Viola. I appreciate you're caring. Would you like to go out for a walk? Would that help your nausea?"

"Am I allowed? Should I— we? Auntie, Catherine said I had to stay here for my protection."

"Oh, really, well, I've heard no such thing. Mark said nothing of the sort to me. You come with me. I don't approve of you sleeping on a sofa. I'm moving you to our home. First, let's change your shirt. Maybe we should go shopping and buy you new clothes."

"We could go to Jason's house. The drawers are full of my clothes."

"That sounds like an even better idea." Aunt Lara says.

———

Viola takes out the extra house key from her purse that Jason gave her at the cottage. The air outside of his house feels empty, being back here without the noise of baby Zee and Jason. When

Viola opens the door, an alarm goes off. It deafening, loud. Viola and Auntie plug their ears. Viola quickly yanks the key out, shutting the door. The alarm stops.

"Oh, my goodness, Viola. Did Jason not tell you the security code?"

"No. I only lived here for several days before we went back to North America."

Auntie tries the door. It's locked.

"Jason pulls no punches regarding security," she says.

"Will the police come? Should we wait, Auntie?"

"No. I suspect the alarm is to alert Jason. He has cameras everywhere. You can tell him you stopped by for your things."

They get back in Auntie's Mercedes.

"Let's go to my place, Viola. I'll make us tea."

"Sounds great!"

Within less than a minute into their drive, Viola's face pales.

"Are you going to be sick, my dear? I can pull over."

"No, Auntie, I'm not used to driving on this side of the road. I'm closing my eyes whenever I think we might crash."

"I must admit, I'm a bit nervy. I'm not the best driver."

"You don't say." Viola replies in a playful tone. "It's fantastic to be out of that room."

Auntie Lara smiles and turns on the car radio. When they arrive at their destination, Viola is surprised.

"I expected a big house since you have many children and grandchildren."

"This is my private getaway, Viola. It's where I come to meet all my lovers."

Viola laughs at her joke as they walk inside. Auntie closes the door, locking them in, not laughing, no longer smiling.

"Viola, I'm sorry. I wasn't candid with you."

"What do you mean?"

Auntie shoves a needle in Viola's arm. It all goes dark.

-..Chapter 18-. .-

When Viola wakes, one of her wrists is handcuffed to a bed. The room looks like a painting from the Victorian era. There's a fireplace on one wall and an exquisite tea table in a corner.

I smell pot potpourri, herbs: marjoram, thyme, rosemary, and cloves.

"Auntie! Auntie, are you here?"

Auntie Lara pushes the door open to walk into the bedroom.

"I'm sorry to take you, Viola. Honestly, I am."

"What's going on? Why am I handcuffed to this bed?"

"I have four boys."

"Yes, Carly told me."

"My firstborn, my favorite, has had some trouble."

"Patrick?"

"No. Jeffrey."

"What kind of trouble is he in?"

"The same kind Zack has."

Oh no.

Viola can't live through another situation like her last and asks, "Are you keeping me here for Jeffrey?"

"No, silly girl. He's with Zack. They've been friends for years. Jason stayed in the Americas to handle them. Patrick told me so."

"What do you mean by 'handle' them?"

"In the past, Jeffrey disappointed Uncle, and he had one more chance. He's back at this foolishness again. Patrick felt I should know about Jeffrey."

"How do you—Jason is there—"

"Jason takes care of all these problems for the family, Viola."

"What?"

"Yes, I hope that doesn't change how you feel. He is respectful, after all. I don't want my boy's life to end. I must keep you here since you're pregnant with Jason's baby. As long as I have you, Jason won't kill Jeffrey. I let Jason know about the baby. My husband wanted to keep your pregnancy a secret for a while longer. I can't imagine Mark defying my wishes to keep my son alive."

"Does Uncle Mark know you're holding me prisoner?"

"Not yet. No one does but Jason. I'll make a deal with my husband. He won't do anything to me. I'm his mate. No one will do away with my son while I'm still breathing."

"Where are he and Zack? I thought Zack was looking for our son."

"No. They left the day after Mark arrived in America. Zack and Jeffrey are both higher than kites in some God-forsaken place, doing what they do. They have been more of a team since your dad's death. They used to hang out here when Zack visited Jason. When you were here the first time with the baby, Zack met up with Jeffrey. They went out to do what they do."

No wonder Zack was so accommodating about me staying here with Jason. I bet he was looking forward to traveling back and forth. And here I thought they'd be looking for the baby.

"The baby is fine, Viola. He is safe. We cannot touch him. Your Uncle made a deal."

"Are we royalty? Who are we, Auntie?"

Auntie's face falls.

"We are your loyal bloodline, my darling girl. Fan-bloody-tastic, isn't it?"

"That doesn't answer my question, and aren't you going to be in trouble for this, Auntie?"

"Yes, but I don't give two petunias, Viola. I want my boy back alive. Being a mother, you understand. I will have my way, or you will have to die. In the *Family Bible,* the second chapter states in

The Journey Out in 21:24, 'Eye for eye, tooth for tooth, hand for hand, foot for foot.' Or, in your case, a life for a life."

"You're talking crazy, Auntie."

"Yes, I admit I am. I am crazy to keep my crazy son alive."

"Auntie, you can't fix Jeffrey even if he returns."

"I don't care. I want him alive."

"How long have you had this place?"

"A while, Viola."

"Does Patrick know what you're doing?"

"He will, but only after Jeffrey is safe. Then I'll make a deal with Patrick for you since you're the new shiny toy. After that, I'll deal with my punishment from Mark. I told him I would not, under any circumstances, allow Jeffrey to be taken out. Mark should not cross me. I'm done with his controlling ways. He should have listened to me after what they did to Jeffrey."

"What did they do?"

"They injected him like they injected Zack. They wanted to try out a new serum to make our boys warriors. Instead, it made both those boys a tad off. I heard that Zack suffered more side effects than Jeffrey. Mark told me they've been working on a fix for years."

"How do you know this?"

"Jeffrey is friends with Zack. Your mum, Viola, was injected too at birth, or so I've heard. We don't have proof. We assume your dad was, too. Your mum turned out fine. From what I've heard, you're too wise. It affects a female's DNA differently, so they've been working on a new serum. They're constantly working on improvements. Zack and my boy Jeffrey did not fare so well. They tried to tweak whatever it was that was causing their misbehavior: an ability to shut off and do destructive things. Mark thinks it involves an animal in the serum, since they can sometimes be vicious. I'm no chemist. Jason is quite brilliant. Even as a young boy, Mark said Jason was the perfect soldier. They decided to try a more substantial variation on my unborn son. He was my last chance. My poor eighth child died minutes after the injection."

Is that why Uncle Benjamin studies the behavior of the sea lampreys? They're the biggest predator in the Great Lakes.

"I'm so sorry, Auntie, this is terrible. Why, why do this to us? Why do they inject us?"

Viola thinks of Doc injecting her while she was pregnant with Zee.

"They seek perfection, my dear girl. We have the world's top scientists right here, hidden within our bloodline. They are more intelligent than anyone who has won these so-called awards. They can't stop themselves from advancing the species. You're aware of our special blood, aren't you?"

"Uncle Mark explained how we could only have babies with each other."

"He is correct." Says Aunt Lara. "How do you think we figure out who strays?"

Viola shrugs her shoulders. "Cameras?"

"The woman and the fetus die every time. We have our warrior children take care of those who stray—those children who only want to be loved. We created murderers. We refuse to tell them what happens when you stray because we must keep the secrets of our blood. Our exceptional, sacred, one-of-a-kind blood."

"I can tell that you feel passionately about this, Auntie."

"That is a vast understatement, Viola. I'm mad about Jeffrey and my unborn child's death. They stole their lives. Why couldn't they let us live, love, and continue? No, they have to experiment. I told Mark they should conduct these experiments on animals, not our children. These men won't listen to reason. They never have. And they never will unless we enforce it. I'm sorry you're caught up in this. You, my dear, are critical. I will have Jeffrey back."

"Was I injected?"

"I would expect so. Your birth was kept secret. I can attest that none of my daughters were injected. I made sure of that."

"Who gives the shots? Is it Doc?"

"You'll have to ask Doc. My mate, Mark, was given the serum. He injected both our children. I'm not sure who gave it to him. He'll not say."

"I'm glad you took me. I hope you get Jeffrey back, and they don't take out Zack, too. They did warn him before Jason and me—"

"Did they offer him one last chance?"

"Yes."

"Do you love Zack?"

"Yes, but not the same way I love Jason."

"Jason is a professional hitman. You're aware of this, are you not, Viola? He's born to end the life of anyone the family tells him to. He is the black death they never see coming."

"I don't believe you."

"Yes, you do, Viola. You do, even if you don't want to—because then Jason would be a monster, and you're pregnant with a monster's baby."

Viola plugs her ears.

"Please stop. Please don't tell me anymore."

"You're looking for the truth. I'm filling in the blanks for you. No one will, otherwise. We love our secrets. We all want to be seen as upstanding people in the eyes of others, do we not? Do you think our men will tell you what they do to maintain secrecy? They break their own laws, the laws they've created, just like the rest of man. We're not any better than anyone else. Maybe we are worse—what do you think? Injecting our babies, killing our blood when they cannot be controlled?"

Viola hears a buzzing. Auntie Lara pulls a flip phone out of her jacket pocket.

-..Chapter 19-. .-

Aunt Lara reads a message, then slips the phone back in her pocket.

"Welcome to the family, Viola, and good luck. I've been wearing a smiling face for too many years, crying inside about my choices. At least I wore blinders until later. You. You're so young and already aware of so much. Now they're trying to throw you into this—their game. I understand why your mum did what she did. She was smart. You're at the top. You understand the outside world more than our world, and that makes you dangerous."

"I don't think dangerous is the right word, Auntie. It seems I'm in a heap of trouble."

"With the best people to get you out of it or die trying," Aunt Lara says.

"I don't want anyone dying for me. My mom died. How can I stop this?"

"I can't answer anything else for you, Viola. You and only you can decide right from wrong. We all do, individually. Yet we can't keep ourselves away from the darkness. It calls to us. It's a daily battle within, the raging roar of the mind. It's plain to see, in the beginning, the fall of the two trees!"

"What can I do, Auntie?"

"Stay true to yourself. That is all you will ever have, Viola. You're a reflection of self. I hated myself for not being enough for him—my despicable mate. I acted out of spite. I hurt others. I did that! I see it now. I'll die with regrets."

"You can change this. Auntie, let me go."

"This is me staying true to myself. I don't care about the consequences, not anymore. I don't want to hurt you. I will if I must. Do forgive me, will you?"

Viola watches Auntie hit play on a camera device. She smiles as she aims it at Viola before turning it on herself.

"Hello, Jason—the Grim Reaper himself. I wanted to show you, Viola, here, alive and well... for now. You have twenty-four hours to bring Jeffrey home alive, or Viola and your unborn child will meet their maker. I'll not reach out again. You must send me a video of Jeffrey alive. I want him back in England." Auntie places the camera on a dresser and pulls out a needle with liquid in it, flicking it. "A bubble," she says. "That's never a good sign. What do you say, Viola? Care to try this, maybe the baby? I wonder if he or she will like it. My last baby didn't."

Auntie moves toward Viola. Viola scrunches up at one end of the bed, ready to defend herself. Her hand covers her stomach. She yanks on the handcuff. It's no use. She isn't strong enough to break it.

"Please, Auntie, don't do this. This is not who you are. I've done nothing wrong to you. Nothing."

"Yes, that's true, but Jason has—or he will if he takes my Jeffrey away from me."

Auntie turns toward the camera, smiling.

"See you in a tad."

She presses a button, turns it off, puts the cap back on the needle, and sets it down on a dresser across the room, next to the camera.

"What's in that, Auntie?"

"Poison, Viola. It's the same toxin they gave my baby, only a bigger dose. They destroyed my baby boy, hoping to create the next Jason—but better. My husband didn't have the decency to tell me at the time. I was stuck with a needle. When I woke, my baby was purple, wrapped in a blanket."

Viola shivers. Viola is sure that Aunt Lara wasn't like this in the beginning.

"You have been through many terrible things," says Viola. "My mother, too. She lost her last child."

"Did they inject it?"

"I don't know. Mom made a deal to have a baby with Doc's oldest son—or should I say your husband's oldest son. He introduced himself to me as Dr. Strober. Is he the boy Uncle Mark had with your sister?"

"Did your mum tell you this?"

"Did you know?" asks Viola.

"Yes, I found out the truth. I never told my beloved husband I knew Dean was his son. I heard Mark talking with Doc on the phone. It was not a pleasant conversation. That's how I found out. Bloody brilliant, right? We're schooled that our men shall only stay faithful in tradition with their mates. What happened there? When we were younger, I knew Mark was in love with my sister. Doc was already her mate. I wasn't of age yet. I questioned him once. He professed his love for me. I never imagined my husband would lie to me. Mark met with her in secret. So much for words."

"Why can't people remain true?" Asks Viola.

"You can. It's called free will, Viola."

There's no free will in this family.

"I'm no expert, but I do think when the brain feels threatened by a lack of freedom, when it realizes its choices are limited, the ego can decide that it wants what it can't have. I used to live by our laws. Lately, I agree with your mother. I've been thinking that we shouldn't make up any rules or laws in this family. We might be better off if we didn't. Maybe then we'd make better decisions."

Viola lifts her chained wrist. Aunt Lara ignores the clank on the hollow steel headboard.

"Better decisions, Aunt Lara?"

"I know that my taking you was wrong, Viola. My snake jumped from it's tree by choice. Did you know the opposite of permitted is forbidden. The word forbidden was added to our bible in the 14th

Century. I blame the word forbidden for making the curious child inside defy what we know is right. Do you know of what I speak?"

Is she on something? She's not making sense.

Viola blinks twice as she tries to decipher Aunt Lara's speech, like she tried to interpret her mother Priscilla's riddles.

"Does everyone in our family read the story about The Fall of the Two Trees, Auntie?"

"They've stopped allowing it," Auntie says. "Surprising, isn't it? If all women realized the power they have over men, it wouldn't be good for men, now, would it? Have you noticed how many women are whores in the Bible?"

"Is that in our family bible?" Viola asks.

"The male interpreters of the gospels diminished women at every turn that they could. Even Mary Magdalene. Bloody men." Auntie spews.

"We're not so different, Auntie. I think we all want what we want. We manipulate each other, even the same sex, for what we want. Mom said we blame others for our mistakes by pointing fingers at everyone else. She said it would never change because no one likes to be wrong or told what to do. Our bad behaviors start as toddlers."

"And they follow us until our last breath." Auntie pauses, shaking her head. "Priscilla was a modest toff. I enjoyed our brief conversations, even if at the time I thought she was a fool. Now I don't. She was a force."

"She died anyway, Auntie."

"Your mum died free. She died with good. She will rise. My ashes will remain for all the harm I've caused innocent people. I've done it to myself. My bad choices have ruined my children's lives."

Aunt Lara looks away.

"Aunt Lara, your children are old enough to choose for themselves."

"True. However, a parent's sole responsibility is to teach them how to love, not how to hate. I poisoned my son's mind. His children will pay for it. How the past repeats."

-..Chapter 20-. .-

Auntie walks toward the door. She opens it wide.

"Are you talking about intergenerational transmission, Aunt Lara?

Aunt Lara swings around to face Viola.

"You've shown your cards, my dear."

My mother used to say that.

"I don't know what you mean, Auntie."

"I wasn't one of them. My sister's child was. My sister was murdered. I know that you've met her."

"I have no idea what you're talking about."

"Yes, you do, Viola. They group you together at birth."

Viola thinks of the photo that Jill showed her. The six girls in a circle. She scans the room for a hidden camera.

"Who is she, Auntie? Who was your sister, who was her child?"

"Fear not, my dearest. No one can hear us or see us. I've been a terrible mother, but I will never break my oath to my mater."

Viola's eyes fill. She yanks on the handcuff, rubbing the inside of it with her other fingers, wondering where Aunt Lara might have the key to unlock it.

"Did you know, Viola, that John Wesley was adopted into the Wesley family in the 1700s? He grew up like you did—with commoners. When he was told about our line, he vowed to never mate. He was raised in a religious home. He said that he'd not be stained by such wickedness with a sister. He was an heir. He was meant to change things, as were other male heirs. I'm sure you've read about them. You Viola, are that child two hundred years later. My sister's child spoke of John Wesley. His story's in a Green Book. That's how I knew who she was. She's a prodigy, like you are. At seven years old, Mary, or you may know her as Rosemary… she said, 'What one generation tolerates, the next generation will embrace.' John Wesley wrote that to warn others about the importance of preserving our moral and ethical self-worth. Radical or not, in this family, his words ring true." Aunt Lara sighs.

"Mary isn't your biological child?" Viola whispers.

"Are you your mother's biological child?" Aunt Lara asks.

The air is sucked from Viola's body.

"What these family scientist don't realize is when they mess with the natural order of childbirth, it will only lead to our extinction."

"Because it's unnatural to do so." says Viola.

"We're a part of this natural world, I'm sure you're mother spoke of this?"

"She did. She told me that trying to make a perfect human would come with unpredictable mental and health risks. She was talking about our family. I didn't know it at the time."

"What do you want in this short life, my dear?"

"I—I wanted freedom from this family, Auntie. Now, I want to find the cure to fix this blood that has sealed our fate to each other. I think it's best to fall in love with whom we fall in love with, even if it doesn't last. At least it's real. It's the natural pull of this universe. The force of attraction is a gift. I want that for my children."

"You're a dreamer."

"Maybe I am, Auntie."

"Hold onto it," Aunt Lara says, looking toward the window. "My children, my grandchildren, are left with a dog's dinner. God knows there's nothing else. Life after life, we fill it with more secrets, more lies. They pile up, Viola."

"The same is true for everyone, Auntie, not only our bloodline."

"You would know that better than I do. I've only interacted with our kind. My children are lost."

"Are you talking about Catherine and Garrett or Brant and Mary?"

"All of them, Viola."

Auntie's phone buzzes. She takes it out of her pocket and glares at it, pausing, before she glances toward the needle on the dresser, then back to her phone.

"Patrick and Carly are the worst. They've both cheated on each other. Carly has tried to catch Jason's eye to sleep with him, but he will have nothing to do with her. You're quite fortunate in that regard."

"Why wasn't Carly with Jeffrey if they're the oldest?"

"For the same reason, you're now with Jason and not Zack. Jeffrey and Zack are damaged. I'm surprised your uncle allowed Zack near you."

"Uncle Benjamin said they planned to send me to Jason. My dad had Zack take me to mess with the uncle's plans."

"I heard that your dad's life was in shambles. The injections ruined his life and his love."

"I never knew anything about these injections, Auntie. It's the first I've heard about them."

"It's a secret, Viola. Do with this information as you will. Help my Carly if you can. I didn't mean to demean Jason. He does seem hellbent on staying true to the *Family Bible's* way of life. It's in the chapter, *"He who weeps."*"

Viola recalls browsing past the title. She knows that in Jes's Bible, the word Job has the same meaning as he who weeps.

-..Chapter 21-..-

Aunt Lara walks to a round table, she pours a cup of tea. Takes a sip, with proper etiquette, sets the hand painted flower cup on it's saucer. Her eyes locked on the needle across the room.

"If Jason brings Jeffrey back, Viola, you must run away from here with him and your child—or Patrick will destroy him. Patrick is the jealous snake. He has to take what's not his. It won't end well for you or Jason. Jason wants to believe Patrick is true and that they are brothers. But they are not. Patrick has told me so himself. He doesn't want to, but he hates that Jason has seniority over him because of his blood. And he will hate you, too. Carly said he would try to seduce you to start a fight with Jason. Jason is by far the better man. That's why Carly brought you to England, but you will leave with Patrick. In fact, he's here to take you back. You will have the baby there."

"Where is there? Where is the Complex located?"

"My dear, I am sorry. I do hope you survive. You seem solid and smart as a whip."

She can't seem to focus.

"Please make another video, Aunt Lara. I don't want anything to happen to you. It'll bother me. You're not as crazy as you made yourself out to be."

Aunt Lara checks her mobile again.

"I would inject you and not blink an eye, my dearest. I only warn you about Patrick to save my Carly. She is good. He made her stray because he strayed. He broke her heart. She's in love with him, and he doesn't deserve her love. If I die, I want you to help her. You can help me by doing the right thing. Have Jason kill Patrick before he silences everyone aware of what he's been doing."

"You're asking me to have Jason end Patrick's life?"

"Yes. Patrick is far more evil than Jeffrey. It's ironic. Patrick is the great pretender. That might be hard to believe, but it's true. Jeffrey hurts himself. Patrick hurts everyone else. He pretends to be the upstanding child when nothing could be further from the truth. Uncle knows this. He chose to turn the other cheek because otherwise he would look bad to the other Uncles. He made the mistake of putting Patrick in the big chair. My husband is weak and pathetic."

"I'm sorry you think this way, Auntie."

"Patrick, my darling girl, told me to take you. There—I've said it. He told me he'd meet me here. Don't be surprised if he shows up and rapes you."

"Please tell me this isn't true. I thought I was going for training in a secure lab. Has he been told that I'm pregnant?"

Is everyone fricken nuts in this family?

"Of course. Don't you think that would make Jason even angrier? Having Patrick's seed mixed with his child-to-be? Or better yet, Patrick will keep you hidden until you have this baby, and then he'll impregnate you. He is determined to have a superior heir."

"You... you're not yourself, Auntie. I'm sorry for all you've lost, but you can make things right. You can release me. I'll ask Jason to protect Jeffrey. You don't have to do this."

"I knew your father," Aunt Lara says, checking her flip phone, pacing the floor.

"You did? I thought he never traveled—"

"I went to visit your father. We did. Patrick and I helped with the plans—Dean, the oh-so-perfect son, not like my Jeffrey, far from it. Patrick is my true embarrassment. Glory be to my wonderful life."

"How many uncles... How many cousins are there? Why are you telling me all of this?"

"Because I will die. Jason is the best. Patrick has lied to me. He's agreed to my death. See for yourself."

Aunt Lara steps toward Viola for her to read the message on her flip phone.

"Carly sent me a warning to take you, and for 'us' to hide—right now! Patrick is Judas. He's a backstabber. He's ratted out his own mother, so he stays clear of the hot seat. It would be nice if Jason could live and rule. At least he wouldn't let these men—my children—get away with breaking every rule, yet they enforce them for the rest of us."

Aunt Lara stops in the middle of the room. She smiles at a cross on the wall opposite her.

"Shakespeare was brilliant when he wrote, 'To thine own self be true.' Did you know Viola, in the play *Hamlet*, Polonius tells his son Laertes how to behave—yet Polonius was a hypocrite. Sounds familiar when it comes to our bloodline." She glances at her phone message again. "It's always the same, my dear girl. I failed as a mother. Does anyone stop to ask themselves what it means to be true?"

Viola watches Auntie's head strain to look at the poison sitting on the dresser. Viola swallows, unsure of what to say or not say, in fear of Aunt Lara injecting her. She remains silent.

"At the core of every sane human mind… we know, dearest. I lost myself a long time ago," Aunt Lara twirls to face Viola. "What do you think it means to be sane?"

"Were you ever with my Uncle Benjamin?"

Auntie scowls.

"No, but he was handsome."

"What about my dad? Was he with anyone after Cindy?"

"He only ever wanted your mother. He was obsessed with Priscilla. Zack's mother, Cindy, was the oldest girl of Doc's. It's why they agreed for your dad and her to have a child. She was a Sarah until your father, and she had Zack."

"Do you mean the SARA blood?"

"No, Sarah from the Family Bible. Sarah was barren. Cindy was, too. I think it's because of what they gave her at birth, though I'm not sure. But then she miraculously had Zack. I'm sure they helped her with a new technology. Look what they did to him. Trust no one, Viola. Especially those who act the most loving toward you."

"Do you mean Jason?"

"No, not Jason. I'm confident he loves you beyond anything else. Carly told me. It's why I took you. You're his weakness."

"Why are there no pictures of the family?"

"Families are kept private. We hide some of the top children in each line, as you were hidden."

Like you're hiding, Mary.

"Was Cindy Doc's real daughter, Auntie?"

"Yes. My cheating husband, Mark only had Dean, his oldest son, with my sister behind my back. She lost Mark's baby girl. She was a stillbirth. We all have heirs with our brothers, except the oldest male and female. They only mate with each other. That's the law."

"Won't Patrick want Jeffrey and Zack dead, too, since they're the oldest in their bloodline?"

"Zack and Jeffrey are not a threat. With their condition, they will never be successors. Patrick wants everyone in the line *before him* wiped out. It's ridiculous. We had quite an argument recently about it. Patrick forgets that we rise from the dirt or return to ashes. What will be his legacy? How many family members he murdered to be king? How will his children feel if they ever find out their father is a plotting murderer of his bloodline? And he was never injected—fancy that. I was the one who put it in my mate's ear to have his oldest son, Dean, be with your mom to have a superior heir. I started this—and look what happened! Your father killed her for it. I was hoping Russell would—kill my mate's oldest son. I only wanted Dean gone. Patrick, too, wanted his father's oldest son to die. The story repeats and repeats. Cain and Abel, Viola. The jealous brother."

More like the jealous mother.

"I told my son, Patrick about Dean. I've caused so much harm. Your mother didn't deserve to die. Neither does my Jeffrey." Aunt Lara says.

"How can I be sure you're not lying about all this?" asks Viola.

"You'll see, my pretty bird."

Aunt Lara turns off her phone. She glances about the room, then stuffs her phone between the mattresses below Viola.

"When Patrick lies you down, with or without your consent, you will remember every word I've said. He will do it, despite Jason."

A door opens. Viola locks eyes with Auntie.

"Patrick, we're in here, son."

-..Chapter 22-. .-

At the open doorway to the bedroom, a man has a gun pointed at Aunt Lara.

"Hi, Mum."

Auntie Lara holds her head high.

"Son, you seem worried? Lower your gun, or do you intend to play the royal guard instead of Jason? He's still in America—I assume. Who is taking the heat for you? I bet Viola would love to hear this story."

The gun goes off. Viola screams as Auntie's body hits the floor. A bullet hole is visible between her eyes.

Am I going crazy? This can't be real.

Viola shakes uncontrollably. The man—she assumes is Patrick—nonchalantly walks over, standing above his mother's dead body. He digs in her pockets, grabs the key to the handcuffs. He sets his gun down and moves toward Viola with his arms raised.

"I won't harm you. I'll unlock the cuff."

Patrick's hand trembles as he unlocks the restraint.

Viola rubs her raw wrist. Her teeth chatter.

One, two, three—focus, focus.

"Where's Jason?"

"He's still in America."

"I want to—please, I need him."

"Carly is outside. You can go. I'll take care of this."

"Why did you shoot your mother? She was not bad. She only wanted Jeffrey back."

"You didn't know her. She's caused a lot of unnecessary deaths. What did she tell you?"

"That she loves Jeffrey."

Patrick looks over at Auntie's bloody face.

"Jeffrey won't change. He's an embarrassment."

"Who isn't? Who throws the first stone, right?"

"Carly said you were a saint of sorts."

"Carly's the saint. Maybe tarnished from the company she's forced to keep."

This angers Patrick, and he grabs Viola's face.

"Patrick!" Carly calls to him from outside the doorway. "Viola, come with me."

Carly doesn't enter the room. Viola can tell she is in shock, seeing her mother's dead body in her peripheral vision, lying not two feet from her.

When Patrick releases Viola, she gets up and wobbles past the dresser, picking up the needle that Aunt Lara had set down earlier. Carly takes her arm at the door to guide her out of the house. Outside the house, Viola looks at the black van in the driveway.

"Carly, can I call Jason? It's important."

"It doesn't work that way, Viola. I must have approval from Patrick."

"Do you trust me?"

"A bit, yes"

"Take out your phone and dial Jason's number, please."

Carly's eyes remain locked on the house as she moves Viola to the other side of the black van. She hits a button and hands her phone to Viola.

"Yes," answers Jason.

"Jason."

"Oh, heaven's breath, Viola, are you all right?"

"No, no, I'm not."

Viola steps away from Carly, out of earshot.

"It's Patrick. He planned all of this. He—Aunt lara told me. Carly saved me just now. Patrick does not like me. He hates you, Auntie said so. We're not safe, and I'm worried about our baby, Jason. She injected me. I need Doc to check to make sure we're okay. Please help me, Jason."

"Viola, calm down. Breathe, luv. Stop!" She stops. "There's nowhere to run, Viola. Go back to Carly. I'll be there as soon as I can. Patrick won't hurt you."

"He will. He'll hurt me to hurt you, Jason."

"Viola, you must stop. If he was going to, he would've already."

She turns back and sees Carly by the vehicle watching her, though giving Viola space to speak with Jason. Walking back toward Carly, Viola says, "Jason, please stay alive. Please take me far away from this. Please. I can't do this anymore. I want to go back to Uncle. Please, Jason."

"Viola. Uncle Benjamin's dead."

"What! How?"

"When I got to his house, I found him dead, shot. And Auntie's missing."

"Shit. They're going to kill us. You know that, Jason? Patrick is tying up all his loose ends. That's what his mother told me. He wants the power of the bloodline. Five minutes ago he put a bullet through Aunt Lara's head before she could tell me more."

"He killed her?"

"Yes, Jason, I watched her body fall. He's pure evil."

When the line drops, she hands the phone to Carly.

"What did he say?"

Viola can't feel her legs. She's numb.

"My Uncle's dead, someone shot him."

"Oh my God, Viola!"

"Carly, how well did you know your mother?"

"Why?"

"I think your brother killed her to keep her from telling me all the bad things he's done." Carly stares at Viola. "Your mom asked me to protect you, Carly. She knew Patrick was coming. He told her to bring me here. Your mom said that he would rape me to have a superior heir. How true do you think that might be?"

"I hate to admit it: I think it's true, Viola. I'll help you. Please shut your mush until Jason gets here. My father called me earlier today. He's found out things about Patrick—who arrived today from America. I picked him up from the airstrip. From what you've told me, Patrick might have gone there to merk your uncle."

"What does merk mean?"

"Kill..."

Viola and Carly's faces are flush, their breathing irregular.

"My father said that Jason had a meeting set. I think Patrick knew Jason would find his body. Patrick wants a war."

"Can we run and hide?"

"No, if you run, he'll shoot you. Don't run."

"That's what Jason said?"

Carly hugs her.

"You're going far away, Viola. I'll go with you. Patrick won't want me to, but I'll demand it since you're pregnant and ill. Even so, I can't protect you, Viola, not from him, not for long."

Viola looks at the van's six-digit license plate and memorizes it, noting the X in the middle of it.

"Today, I wish I had never been born, Carly," says Viola.

Carly holds her as she cries.

Moments later, Patrick emerges from the modest house, carrying what looks like a body wrapped in a black tarp. He motions for Carly to open the back door. When she does, he sets the tarp inside, then goes back into the house. Minutes later, he barrels outside. He lights a match and tosses it inside, shuts the front door. He lights another match and drops it next to the house.

Viola stares at the house on fire as flames dance and grow ever higher. Carly slips her phone into Viola's pocket as Patrick motions them into the truck. Viola slides in the back, watches as he taps on his flip phone. Carly gets in the front passenger seat.

I'm glad I don't have Zee with me. At least he is safe from this maniac.

Viola can only hope that they—whoever *The Rise* are who have Zee—are the good guys, if any such people like that exist in this family.

The entire drive, Viola doesn't speak. She doesn't lift her head. When the van finally stops, Carly tells her it's time to go. Viola opens the door and sees she's back at the private airstrip. Three planes are on the runway. Patrick stomps to the back of the van, hoists the tarp out, and carries it onto a larger plane.

Viola quickly takes out the phone and looks at the time. Forty-five minutes have passed.

"Carly, how do I call Jason?"

Viola watches her hit the *Menu* button. Carly scrolls and clicks on the name *Jay*. She hands the phone back to Viola.

"Yes, hello."

"Jason, he's taking me on a large plane with Aunt Lara's dead body. We're leaving England, I think, to go to a Complex. I love you, Jason."

"Turn off the phone, Viola, leave it in the truck."

"How do I do that?"

"Press and hold the end button. I know where you're going. Be good. Don't say too much."

The line goes dead. Viola presses the end button and tosses the device under the backseat. Carly nods, lifting a duffel bag over her shoulder, she takes Viola by the arm.

Crossing the tarmac toward the plane, Viola stops. She vomits.

Patrick pops his head out of the plane. He swears under his breath.

"Bring her on board to the toilet, Carly."

"Yes, sir. Come, Viola."

-..Chapter 23-. .-

In the small bathroom inside of the plane, neither Carly nor Viola speaks. Viola places her hand over Carly's heart to show her it's all right. Viola doesn't want to do anything to jeopardize Carly's life.

In the sink, she rinses her mouth, and the two cousins return to the plane's cabin. Viola sits several seats away from Patrick. Carly sits next to him during take-off.

Once the plane is airborne, Patrick goes to the bathroom. Carly takes crackers out of her bag and hands them to Viola.

"Here, I'll get you ginger ale for your tummy."

"Thank you, Carly. This plane is bigger than the others."

"It's a longer flight. We need more fuel to avoid stopping at another airport along the way."

"That's a beautiful necklace you're wearing."

"It's a Brinks Mat gift," Carly replies with a smirk.

"Do you mean the Brink's bank that's been in the news?"

Carly's face goes white. "You read the news?"

"Of course, doesn't everyone?"

"Not the women in our family—it's a rule not to fill our heads or our children with negative chinwag."

"What's chinwag?"

"Gossip."

"I don't think the Brinks Mat bank robbery was gossip," says Viola. "It happened."

"It's best you don't mention this around my father, never to Patrick."

"Why? Did they help those men?"

"No. My father wouldn't do that."

"But your brother?"

Carly's pupils dilate. She shakes her head.

"Can I get you a champagne, Viola?"

"I'm pregnant."

"Oh, right. Sorry, let me get you that ginger ale."

"I would like a can if you have it."

"I do."

"Unopened, if you don't mind."

"Got it."

When Patrick comes back, Carly excuses herself to go to the lavatory.

Patrick strides over to stand in front of Viola.

"Why did you say Carly was tarnished from the company she's forced to keep?"

"I was talking about your mother, who seemed to have gone insane. Why did you grip my face?"

"I thought you were talking about me."

"Why would you assume that? I've never met you before."

"Right. Sorry. I'm not myself." He says.

"Who could be themselves when they shot their mother?"

"What did she tell you?"

"When she heard someone at the front door, she told me you would rape me."

He looks at her, shocked.

"She said that?"

"Yes."

"Viola, my mother was more crackers than the crackers you're eating. Why on earth would I need to rape anyone?"

"I'm not sure."

"I'm Jason's best friend. Do you think I would rape his mate?"

"Your mother seemed crazy. She did tell me she would kill me. She was mostly sad."

"Sad, how?"

"She said that no men follow the rules they force on others in the family. They pretend to be good, and they're not. Did your dad have an affair?"

"Did she say that?"

"No, she didn't. She said he was pathetic, so I wondered, since that's a strong word. Thank you for saving me. I'm sorry that I made you angry."

Mom said, "For men who are not mentally sound, look your best. Skip the compliments. Show them you're a prize."

Viola looks at him with Zack's fawn eyes. If Patrick wasn't a psychopath, she might think he was attractive. He favors his father's looks, although he has appealing dimples. Viola thinks about the last time she saw Jes and what she said about Zack.

"Some monsters look like ordinary people."

Patrick stares at her face, reaches out to touch her cheek.

"You're quite stunning," he says. Hearing Carly's footsteps, he quickly pulls back his hand. Carly sits in her seat with a tall glass of champagne.

"I'm sorry you had to deal with my mother, Viola," says Patrick. "She was completely off her trolley. I assure you that we're not all bad."

"I've heard that a lot, Patrick. My mom's dead, my dad's dead, my child is gone, Jason's not here, and I'm pregnant and ill. I watched a bullet go through a woman's head, who also told me she would kill me. Not much good in all of that, I'd say. There's always tomorrow, though."

He huffs. "You have a sense of humor." Viola remains silent. "Carly will help you. However, she must go home soon to care for our children since my mother can no longer help." he says.

Viola watches his eyes trail over her figure while Carly peers out the plane's window.

"Catherine is there, and so is Mary," Carly says. "They will help us, Patrick. Viola needs me, at least for this first trimester. After that, I'll go."

Carly turns to face him. Viola sees sadness in Carly's pretty eyes.

He nods. "Very well. Sleep, Viola, it's a long flight."

Viola's eyes shut, though she knows she won't sleep right away. She rubs her belly, where a peanut grows. Her tears drip onto her arm. Uncle Benjamin's gone, and the man who killed him is a few seats away from her. Her eyes remain shut. She senses Patrick watching her. She refuses to open them.

I'm not flirting with him, no effing way... Watch your mouth Viola Ted.

-..Chapter 24-. .-

JASON

Jason had to hang up on Viola. She was about to blow. He fears there's no way he can get to Viola fast enough, and it will be catastrophic if Patrick catches one whiff of Carly's deceit. Would Patrick kill her? Jason sits at Uncle Benjamin's kitchen table in Telega, trying to process that Patrick killed Uncle Benjamin and Aunt Lara, his own mother.

Patrick set this up.

He told Jason not to travel with Viola, that Uncle Mark wanted Jason to stay in America to track down Zack and Jeffrey. That was a ploy so Patrick could show up at Uncle Benjamin's without Jason suspecting anything, then fly back to London before there was even any news of Uncle's death.

Uncle Mark's name is on the flight registry. Why is Patrick trying to set up Uncle Mark? Patrick shot Uncle Benjamin in the back... feigen! (the coward!)

In Uncle's hidden room, Jason watches the tape that Patrick is on, as he checked the house for Auntie. The gun is in Patrick's hand. Jason found Auntie hiding in the bunker. She said that she saw Patrick pull up and check his gun as he got out of the car. When she tried to call Uncle, she realized that he had left his phone in the kitchen, where she was. Auntie heard it ringing. She heard Uncle Benjamin yell from the backyard to answer his phone in the kitchen. She quickly hid. Auntie took her purse with her. She shut off her ringer.

Smart.

After, she watched on the camera as Patrick left. She waited in the bunker for an hour. She came out long enough to text Jason, then locked herself back in. Jason made Auntie swear to contact no one at all. He put her on a bus. He kept her phone. He gave her a different one. He knew Patrick would want no loose ends.

After moving Uncle's body inside, Jason releases a haggard breath as he leans on the granite countertop. The back door closes. Jason eyes his gun he set on the table before him. Jeffrey and Zack enter the kitchen.

"Who did this, Jason?" asks Zack. Hatred is in his eyes as he stares at Uncle's body, now on a tarp in the kitchen. Jeffrey stands beside him with his arms crossed and a scowl on his face.

"Patrick," answers Jason.

Jeffrey grinds his teeth. "He fancies what Bobby wanted, the fokken stupid Plank."

"Jeffrey," says Jason, "Carly has been helping Viola."

"He'll wring Carly's neck."

"That's why I'm going." Jason releases a breath. "Zack, you need to take care of everything here. Can you stay focused? I need you. Viola needs you. She's pregnant."

The brothers share a look. Zack acts indifferent, not giving away his feelings.

"He'll kill her," says Zack, "or he'll keep her for himself. You and I both know her, Jay. She won't be willing,"

Jason's eyes move to the floor.

"That would be what I would do if I were a Prat Prick throne—cocksucker like my brother," says Jeffrey. "Jason, whether you like it or not, buddy, Patrick must go. My father's next, then you—or vice versa. That will be his play. You're the king whether you like it or not."

Jason taps the pads of his fingertips together. "What about Carly's kids? I don't want them to grow up knowing their father—my childhood best friend—was killed by my hand."

"So be it," Jeffrey replies, "but he'll nix your arse. You won't even meet your child."

"You stay, Jason," says Zack. "You clean the house. I'll deal with Patrick. I've wanted to shove his skinny dick in his mouth for years."

Jeffrey chortles, popping his knuckles.

Jason doesn't respond.

"We both love her, Jay," says Zack. "She's good. Carly's good, too. Neither deserves to be held captive by that dipshit big-brain wanna-be. It will be hard for you to do it. He'll arrange it so that either you die or she does. There's no easy exit."

Jeff stretches his post-college wrestling arms above his head.

"What's the plan, Jason? You're the crown Uncle now, like it or not. We might not have had this mess had you taken the lead when it was yours."

"Jeff, leave it." Zack slaps Jeffrey on the back. "Jay never wanted it. We've all faced a lot of bullshit. It's time to stop."

Zack stares at Jason.

"Dad's gone, Jay. We've still got a few more bad trees that need to fall."

-..Chapter 25-..-

VIOLA

Viola wakes. Carly and Patrick are not in their seats, but she can hear them. They're having sex beyond the curtain at the back of the plane. Viola feels for Carly. Her brother is not a good person, yet she loves him. No doubt she feels torn. Viola felt empty with Zack, forced to pretend to enjoy his one-sided, vacant behavioral addictions, which Uncle said spiraled him into his substance use. She closes her eyes and pretends to sleep, not wanting Patrick to think for a moment that she has any interest in their personal lives.

———————

Carly taps Viola's arm.

"Viola, we're about to land in ten minutes. Would you like to use the lavatory? We have a bit of a trek ahead of us, so maybe you should."

"Yes, thanks. Uh, why do you call the bathroom a lavatory, Carly?" Viola reaches her arms in the air, then stands, doing a dance, tapping her toes to wake them up.

Carly laughs at her.

"A bathroom must have a bath to call it such. Viola, what are you doing?"

"Waking up my bones. I've sat for too long. Uncle and I used to do this when I was a child. I think he mostly did it so I'd laugh."

"Did you two spend much time together?"

"Yes. He was like my father in a way. When I was little, he'd sit in this huge reclining chair and let me sleep on top of him. When I'd wake up, he'd make us do these stretches. He'd have me stretch my nose like this."

Both girls laugh as Patrick slips out from the curtain with a drink.

"What's so funny?" he asks.

"Viola showed me what her uncle used to do after they fell asleep for a long while in a recliner. It's quite funny."

"Was he a good Uncle, Viola?"

"He is. He has always been my constant. He taught me how to cook, fish, tie my shoes."

"Didn't your mother teach you that?" he asks.

"I spent most of my time with Uncle or my friends. My mom was gone most of the time. I spent a lot of my childhood alone. It was fine. I kept busy."

"When did you find out you had brothers?"

"Not until after my mom died."

"You found her body, right?"

Viola peers down. "Yes, unfortunately. I hate thinking of it."

"How did you and Jason get together?" Patrick asks.

"It was my doing," says Viola.

"Really?" asks Carly.

"At the start, he and I were not getting along," says Viola. "I guess that we're both stubborn. He did everything for me. I was seven months pregnant. I needed him. He was amazing. He delivered our baby."

"Don't you mean Zack's baby?" says Patrick.

"Yes, but—Jason is a good man. My true love. The same as the two of you. It's in your eyes. You're a match."

"I think so," Carly says, smiling.

"When did Jason say he would arrive to meet us?" Viola asks Patrick.

"When he finishes with his duties, he'll come," he answers.

———————

After the plane lands and comes to a complete stop, Patrick's phone rings. He picks it up.

Viola remains seated while Carly stands to organize her bags.

Patrick hangs up the phone. He covers his eyes. His blissful demeanor changes.

"Who was that?" Carly asks.

"Father."

"Is everything okay?"

"Stop asking questions, will you, Carly?"

"Sorry."

"Why the sad look, Viola?" he asks.

"I was thinking about your mom. She was so excited when I first met her. She helped me with baby Zee. Being the mother of seven and grandmother of many, that's a loss for everyone in your immediate clan who loved her."

Patrick steps in front of Viola and slaps her face.

"You will stop talking about her like she was a wonderful mum. I told you she's done bad things."

"I'm sorry," Viola replies, cupping her face. "We all do bad things sometimes, Patrick. You asked me why I was sad. I told you what I was thinking."

"Don't bring her up again."

"Yes, okay."

"Yes, what?"

"Yes, uh, Patrick."

"You will direct me, as sir, from here on out."

"Are you serious?"

"Yes, I am. Where we are going, I lead. I demand respect!"

"My—"

"I would watch the sarcasm if I were you, Viola. My punishments won't leave you looking pretty."

Viola glances over at Carly. A stream of tears rolls down her cousin's cheeks.

"Why are you suddenly different?" asks Viola. "I thought I was coming here for training. You said you were Jason's best friend."

"That's none of your business. You will not speak to me again unless spoken to. I would recommend that you remain mindful when choosing your words."

"Yes, sir."

"Let's go." says Patrick to his brother, Brant .

-..Chapter 26-. .-

JASON

"I 'll go," says Jason.

I can't handle the thought of Zack dying because of me.

"Promise me, Zack, to care for Viola and our children if I don't make it." Jason says, with a stern look.

"I will, Jay."

"Call Doc. You clean all the houses and close them up for now—until we can regroup."

Jason glances toward Jeffrey.

"Jeff, I need you to contact Dean, and warn him about what's happening."

Jason motions toward the door.

"Both of you, go."

———

Jason calls the Complex to give a heads-up to the men there who are loyal to him. He tells a few of them to leave immediately, worried that when Patrick arrives, he might have them shot. If Patrick's plan is a takeover, he will shoot men on the spot should any of them blink wrong. Jason can't save them all.

Jason doesn't want to kill Patrick. He hopes to subdue him and bring him in for trial. Jason has seen the notes from the family master files, the sequence and process.

Patrick can be rehabilitated...Good Lord, help me release my guilt. Help me do the right thing. Amen.

The ancient Hebrew word, *Amen,* in the Eastmann Family Bible, means "certain truth." Jason's mind drifts to a conversation he had with Viola's mom, Priscilla, six months before she died. When Priscilla caught Jason watching Viola in Uncle's hidden room.

"What are you doing in here, Jason?" She asked.

"I'm permitted."

"You like her?" said Priscilla.

"She's beautiful."

"She is."

"Does she know there are cameras in the house?" Jason asked.

"No."

"She's very independent," he said.

"She needs to be ready for what's to come," said Priscilla. "You're worried about her, aren't you, Jason?"

"She's so innocent. I almost wish she could live her life without us interfering."

"That's not an option, son. She can never have children otherwise. How would she feel about her life? Viola told me she'd like children one day. Only you can give her that. Why are you so stubborn about all of this? You have enough money and resources, Jason. You can take her away from here. Then live your life free from what they have you doing. You were meant for so much more."

"I don't know how to be with her."

"You'll learn. So will she. You'll learn together."

"I've got to go. I'm meeting Dad."

"Okay. Be safe."

"Yes, ma'am."

Doc was right. I should have taken Dad out sooner. There was no changing his behavior. Science can't fix a born killer. Priscilla would still be alive and in Viola's life. I should have married Viola when Priscilla told me to. Her blood is on my hands. This is my fault. I must fix it for the sake of our children.

-..**Chapter 27**-. .-

VIOLA

An army camouflage truck awaits them below the jetway. On the driver's door is the letter Z painted in white, with a white square painted around its perimeter.

Brant steps out of the driver's seat. He takes Carly's bags from her, and the siblings share a quick glance as they head toward the truck. Wherever they are, it's warm—though not as hot as it was in England. The land looks unhappy with its lack of greenery and mounds of dirty, mossy, grey-green shrubs. There's nothing to be seen in the distance as she spins around.

"Is this your private airport?" asks Viola.

"No speaking, Viola, unless spoken to. I won't remind you again." says Patrick.

Brant gives Carly a concerned look before wiping his expression clear. He hops in the driver's seat of the truck, starts it, and their bodies jet forward as his foot hits the gas pedal.

"How are the men, Brant?" asks Patrick, holding the side of the door.

"Good, sir, ready for a lengthy visit. We're stocked. Do you want to stop for anything before we head to the Complex?"

"Go to the petrol station. Give me your phone."

"Yes, sir." Brant reaches into his pocket, handing his brother his mobile.

"Viola, I was curious. How was it... being with Zack?" asks Patrick, looking at her, then Carly through the rear-view mirror.

Both women sit in the extended cab, cargo area of the military vehicle as it bumps along the uneven road.

"I didn't always enjoy the experience, if that's what you're asking. He was much better to me the longer we were together. He has good qualities, too."

"Interesting that you lie for him."

"I lived with him for almost a year. Zack has different needs. I couldn't support those needs long-term. We were honest with each other about it. Do you know Zack?"

"I do," he says. "I hung around him and Jeffrey a few times when I was younger. They're both beastly. Very unconventional."

"Did you join them or just watch?" she asks.

Viola sees a flicker in his eyes. She caught Patrick off guard. Brant coughs. Auntie told Viola that Patrick cheated on Carly, and knowing Zack's explicit sexual addiction, Viola would wager he and Jeffrey might have had a hand in the opportunity for such unconventional things.

"My mother always preached that we must forgive to move forward," says Viola. "To push love at hate. It's the only way someone hateful can change. The more they hate their choices, the more they hate themselves. If they're shown love, they can turn it around. That's what I tried with Zack. It is our purpose, after all, before the death of the flesh."

"What have you read about that?"

"I read the apple and the snake story, Patrick. They're not my mistakes. Each human is responsible for self. Two trees stand alone. I can't fix another. Only self-love can."

"Do you feel separate from Jason?"

"We are separate. We're separate beings. His choices are not my choices and vice versa."

"If you knew Zack or Jason cheated on you, would you cheat on them?" His eyes lift to see Carly in the rearview mirror, then back to Viola.

"I find that an odd question. Are you asking to validate something about yourself?" He gives her a warning look. "The answer to your question, Patrick, is no. I'm not responsible for my mate's actions. I will live my life as I see fit. I don't need to copycat. I don't judge it, either. I'm responsible for my own actions. We commit to ourselves, our inner good, or allow our ego to rule. It's that simple, yet hard for others."

"You're extremely opinionated for a woman."

"You asked me. I spoke. I don't have to talk. I can remain silent if you prefer."

"You're different. How well did you know your father?" says Patrick.

"Not very well. For a while, we had lunch once a week. That was nice. He was secretive. He didn't answer my questions. How well do you know your father?"

"Very well."

"Did he approve of your mother's death for my kidnapping?"

"His Uncle approved... for Jason to... I took the lead, is all."

Brant shifts in the driver's seat.

Brant didn't know?

"It's hard to admit we're not good," Viola says. "We all want people to think we're better than others when we're not. That's what drives hatred. The dark, the lies, the deceit."

"You talk like you know more than you say," Patrick says calmly.

"My dad was not a good person, but you already knew that before you felt the need to ask."

"I thought you were directing your comments at me."

"Patrick, I don't know you. Maybe you should look within and ask yourself why you think I'm addressing you. Besides, what I've been told is that you're with Carly and have four children together."

"*Hmm,*" he says. "I have guilt for killing my mum. I can't believe she's gone. Although I pulled the trigger, it was Uncle's orders, not mine."

"Have you asked yourself why you did it? Was she bad or did she know too much?" When Brant speeds up, Viola fastens her seatbelt, not saying another word.

Patrick glances at Carly, who is staring at him in the mirror.

They drive for almost an hour in silence, pulling up to a gas pump at a petrol station.

When Patrick is out of the vehicle, Brant doesn't turn around in his seat. He sputters in an attempt not to move his lips as he speaks.

"Viola, stop. Please don't speak again. Patrick took the safety off his gun. I fear your next words will be your last. He rules here, and you... Your mouth is unbelievable."

"Thank you for the warning. I wish I cared, Brant. I don't fear him. Every story in history shows how bad leaders lie to make themselves look good. They make people fear, so we'll follow. They know that if they keep repeating the same lie, eventually people will believe it. I didn't fear my dad, but I had Uncle Benjamin to protect me—or I'd already be dead."

"Viola." Carly touches her arm.

"It's okay, Carly. My baby, Zack, is somewhere out there, and he needs me. I'll shut up, but this extremist won't bully me. Going through what I have with my dad has changed me. I don't know. I'm angry inside for putting up with bad men and not being brave. Patrick is weak and insecure, which is why he's doing what he's doing. He might kill me. Patrick's a dead man either way. He's not a good person anymore, if he ever was one."

Brant steps out to fill the truck with petrol after Patrick gives his thumbs up through the petrol station's window.

-..Chapter 28-..-

JASON

Uncle Mark's car picks Jason up at their private airport in England. Neither of them speaks in the backseat as they drive a few miles in Uncle's Mercedes.

The chauffeured vehicle makes a sharp turn down a grassy patch of land. It stops. The driver shuts off the vehicle, and the two men get out.

"What's the latest, Uncle Mark?"

"Patrick's plane has landed with Carly and Viola. Brant is headed from the Complex to pick them up. I won't hear from Brant again. I told him no communication. He used another guards phone to update me. I pray that he tossed it. No doubt Patrick will check everyone's phones."

"Brant has multiple phones, Uncle. He's not daft. Most likely he destroyed it."

"You won't be undetected. Are you planning to walk right in, grab Viola and Carly, and walk right out?"

"Something like that," says Jason. Both men smile. "I've got a few plans in place, Uncle. I still hope Patrick will realize he's lost and come in—first Bobby, now Patrick. I was bowled over when Viola told me he shot Aunt Lara. I never saw it coming, nor him killing Uncle Benjamin."

"You and me both. That was a massive misstep on his part. Both sides have heard about it."

"How?"

"I'm not sure. There's an inside informant. The Plant found out what Patrick did. They, too, are coming after him because of Uncle Benjamin. Why don't you wait in the wings at The Complex and grab the girls once the army arrives for him?"

"I can't wait," says Jason. "If Patrick orders our forces at the Complex to fight back, they will. Why have that many family members be eradicated? It's best if I go it alone. There are a few bad seeds on each side. If we cook them before any further damage, the rest will come back into the fold, Uncle. We need peace in this bloodline. Fighting internally is not the way."

"Patrick will have his men shoot you on sight. What if we send in Garrett first?"

"Too risky, Uncle."

"Garrett has always been faithful to me," Uncle says.

"Garrett is loyal to himself. Plus, Garrett is aware that Patrick killed their mum. He's too angry, and that will get him killed. Does Brant—?"

"No. I didn't tell him." Uncle says. "He was closer to my wife than the other children."

"Brant's not skilled enough to attack Patrick."

"But Carly is," Uncle says, with a worried brow.

"Maybe, Uncle. I was hoping she might make a move before anyone else tried."

"Do you think Viola will try anything?"

"I'm sure she has something up her sleeve. I can't think of what that may be. She's clever. If Patrick keeps her locked away, then nothing will happen. She's a wee bit of a rabblerouser. Patrick will be finished if she can talk to his soldiers."

Uncle chuckles. "She is clever."

"None of this makes sense, Uncle. Patrick must be out of his head. Killing two people on two continents in one day is a lot for a man who has never physically hurt someone as a kid."

"He's trying to prove he can lead, that he can do what's necessary." Uncle says.

"Killing doesn't prove a thing, Uncle. I know that better than anyone."

"I'm sure you do, Jason. My son has done wrong, and he knows it. Guilt is devouring him from the inside out. He won't ask for forgiveness. If only he would open his eyes..."

"His eyes are open, Uncle. They're closed on the inside."

"Do what you must, Jason. I pray that Patrick doesn't shoot Brant. I'll kill him myself if he does. Please bring the girls home alive."

"I'm not worried about Carly. I can't imagine Patrick killing her. But Viola, I—she doesn't back down. I watched her stand up to Dad in a video. She didn't care if he snapped her neck. Viola doesn't have the fear that most everyone else does."

"That is worrisome." Uncle says.

"She's tough as nails." Jason smiles.

"She's everything to you, Jason. Be careful. I assume you are for her, too. However, she's reckless, and you're not. She could get you killed."

"She's more likely to get herself killed, Uncle."

"No. I don't think so. I would bet Patrick desires an heir with her."

Jason's jaw tenses.

"There, I saw that. You're better than that, Jason. You're too far gone for her."

"She is my mate."

She's my life purpose. She owns my soul. I gave it to her long ago. I will die for her. I already die each day I'm parted from her. My life grows inside of her. I'll protect her at all costs.

"Time is not on her side, Uncle."

"How's Jeffrey?" Uncle asks.

"Livid about Carly's involvement. He was raging about Auntie. He said you're next. Your signature was forged on flight records. Patrick was setting you up for Uncle Benjamin's death. Jeffrey wants to safeguard you."

"Did he say that?"

"In so many words, yes," says Jason. "Even with his destructive needs, Jeffrey is our best soldier. He's sharp-minded. He cares about the family, Uncle."

"Lara always thought so."

"Cut him some slack, Uncle. He didn't ask to be like this."

"Push the knife deeper, please, Jason."

"I apologize, Uncle. Allow Jeffrey to come back into the fold. We need him."

"If you say so."

"I do."

-..Chapter 29-. .-

VIOLA

The Complex is like an underground prison, only it's built into the side of a massive rock mountain. Everything inside is made of what looks to be stainless steel and concrete grey—sitting in a cell-like room on a twin bed, with one door that leads to a bathroom in a corner, Viola's happy to be out of Patrick's presence. She shuts Uncle's *Family Bible*. She's happy that she's pregnant.

Jason is on his way. Jill promised that I can see Zee after I'm pregnant. I want to be with Zee. I don't want to be here. Can I trust Jason completely?

Her thoughts drift back to her conversation with Jason in the forest.

"Jason, I want to have your baby. I can't be with Zack again. Please... I can't."

"When we're in the cottage, Luv, surprise me once. I'll let on that I'm asleep."

"Why only once, Jason?"

"Let's hope that you're pregnant. You must know when you are, they'll check your timeline. They'll assume we're not being honest when they do. We need to play it this way, at least with a one-off. I can't give in to you otherwise. You broke my trust. I cannot appear weak."

"You're not weak. You're the strongest man I've ever met."

"It's considered weak to love you more than my brothers, Viola."

"I'll try to remember not to punch you in the room when you're a cocky bugger."

Jason laughed. "It's unwise to punch your husband in front of anyone."

"Noted," she said, saluting him like an officer would in the army.

Jason kissed her. He pulled back to catch her eyes.

"Viola, you're about to learn more than I ever planned to tell you. I wanted to shield you from this. The more you uncover, my luv, the more of a threat you are to key people in the family. I can only protect you so much. You're running away... It will be known soon. Both sides will know what your mum taught you."

"I don't understand, Jason."

"You will."

Viola turns over on the hard cot, not wanting to show her face to the camera. The family, who Jason called "The Rise," has her baby. Zee's safe. That's what Auntie Lara told her. But of course, Viola has no clue where he is. That was the agreement. She would have agreed to almost anything to hide Zee away from Zack. They blindfolded her. They put her where they wanted her to be found—only giving her the needle before she had to be taken from the van, nothing too complicated. They knew Jason would demand to find her, whether the hierarchy said yes or no. They made sure Uncle got a note with her coordinates.

"We hope it doesn't hurt Jason's relationships," the blue square sticky note said from Jill in the Green Book.

Why did they do that? What is their next play?

Viola can only guess that a family lineage as old as hers would require a lot of secret planning to survive and thrive through the ages. There's truly no turning back. Nothing is real—only her youth til seventeen. At least she had that. Or was even that real? Was it a pretend life? A life of make-believe as she and her friends focused on little things.

"Better lock the car. Did you hear about the break-ins?"

It was all minor stuff they thought was a big deal in Telega. If they only knew. What would happen if they flipped a coin and entered her world? Had she not been brought into this, she wonders if she would have enjoyed living a simple life where her biggest problems were talking about other people, like everyone else.

"Did you hear about Katie's mom cheating? Now she's trying to kick their dad out and take him for all his money... even his pension!"

When her class friend Tammy's grandma died, her whole family was fighting over her grandma's money and the house. She had more than one Prada purse. Viola didn't know why a purse had a name. Priscilla told her, "People create names for things or stamp a high dollar amount on things to assign them an imaginary value. It's our ego that believes they're worth more."

Tammy told Viola that she had taken several pieces of her grandma's jewelry right off of her dead Grannie's fingers before her cousins could. Viola remembers thinking that was stealing. She's never understood why family members who've never worked for that money, house, or eight-carat diamond ring somehow felt they were owed it. Tammy told her at school that her mom was taking the sister to court, and they were never speaking to her aunt's family again. They fought over stuff like vultures sneaking onto the highway, trying to rip one more piece of meat off the dead carcass before another car came, before they could be seen. The weakest got the least—or were they the strongest?

There's a light rap on the door before it opens. Brant enters, wearing a half smile.

"Viola, come with me. It's time to eat. Oh, I'm to remind you, no talking to anyone."

Brant pushes on the control panel for the lights, moving them from a dim setting to the brightest. Viola squints as she walks into the hallway. She marches in formation behind Brant. Looking around, she sees cameras everywhere.

Brant pushes on two swinging doors, leading them into a huge vacant lunchroom that resembles a school cafeteria. He turns through another door into an empty, sizable kitchen. He offers her three options. She chooses a salad with breaded chicken and a glass of milk. He warns her that the milk is reindeer milk, and the chicken is reindeer meat.

"Can I ask where we are? Does it have to remain secret forever? I don't think I'm getting out of this Complex anytime soon."

"We are in an exclusive area within Siberia."

"Siberia, as in Russia?"

"Asia Russia is what I call it."

"I find this building chilly, but isn't it supposed to be freezing here? You know, you throw water in the air and it freezes instantly."

"That it does," says Brant. "But you've arrived in the short summer months when it's nice. Trust me. It turns the opposite of warm."

"Why reindeer meat and milk?"

"There are hundreds of thousands of them around here. It's easy to buy—healthy too."

"Can I read a book about this area? I love reading."

"I'll ask Patrick. I can't see that being a problem. I've been told that aside from meals, you will stay in your room."

"Fan fucking tastic!" she says with a cocky smile.

He glances from side to side.

"Why do you talk like that? It's not proper."

Reading Uncle's book has my blood boiling.

"I'm being held captive by a crazy person. A killer of our bloodline. It feels good to swear. I'm letting my frustrations out in words, so I hopefully don't start smashing shit. I'm hormonal, Brant. Did Mary ever go through mood swings?"

"Oh yes. I didn't mind."

"Is Catherine pregnant?"

"Yes. Thank goodness that it didn't take long for both of us."

"So, you admit I was right about what I said?"

He nods. "We follow the laws. We abide by them. I'm with Mary and our kids each time I'm home."

"Is Garrett with her now?"

"He already was—when I was with Catherine. We have an arrangement. We're close."

"Your mom mentioned the whole baby-making process. Is it weird to—"

"I pretend it's Mary. I wish I didn't have to be with anyone but her. People die, children die, and the only way to continue is to populate the line."

"How many babies do women have to have?"

"As many as they can safely. The minimum is two per brother."

"What happens if you have all boys or all girls?"

"Then we keep trying, or we mate with a female cousin next in our line. That's how it's been done for centuries. Only the top of the line has never had to do so. Not yet, anyway. That's what Carly told me."

"Will I see Carly while I'm here?"

"I don't think so. I can't ask my brother. He's warned me to keep my mouth shut!"

"Will you hold a burial ceremony for Auntie Lara?"

"No. It's the law that everyone is burned, broken to bone dust, and thrown back to the earth. There are no graves, no history, no mistakes. If we do have a grave, it's for show. There's nothing in it."

"Why do you call it bone dust? Why not ashes?" says Viola.

"I thought with your knowledge that you've studied science."

"I have. After the body is cremated, the bones remain intact, and then they're crushed until they're a heap of bone dust. But most people don't know that. They all call it ashes in North America. It was a question, Brant."

"Why do you think people call them ashes?" he asks with a snicker.

"I would guess they'd prefer the idea of receiving ashes than being told their loved ones' skeleton is put through a grinder 'til it's bone dust." She glances toward what appears to be a small window in the ceiling.

"Is there an area here, like in most prisons, where the inmates can walk and exercise without running away?"

"You're hilarious, Viola. Yes, I believe we have a fenced-in area for exercise. Let me ask Patrick, although you won't be able to walk outside for too much longer. The cold is on the way."

"Thank you, Brant."

-..Chapter 30-. .-

It's another day before Viola is permitted to walk outside. The air is different, clean here. It's like rain in her nostrils, yet dry. If she were born and raised around here, she might believe this was the only area on earth. Nothing is visible for miles around except dirt, rocks, and patches of lime green grass mounds.

Viola assumes her training in whatever lab she was supposed to go to has been halted as she peers through the clear wire fence. A road runs along the fence line to one side, and she quickly looks around so Patrick won't suspect her of fishing for a way out. And where would she run to? From the sky, she assumes no plane would know what this mountainside-looking building is at the edge of its muted green scrubland. Trees line the top of the mountain.

Viola does a couple of cartwheels in a row away from the fence.

When she was younger, she asked Mom to put her in gymnastics, but five nights a week was too much commitment. Viola finds rocks no bigger than one inch in size. She crosses her legs to sit on the ground to play make-believe, to let go of her current predicament in the middle of this no man's land.

She talks to the rocks as she'd talk to her Teddy bear and Elie, the elephant footrest in her bedroom. Wishing now that she had kept her mother's nesting doll, not only the baby one. How many days she'd play independently, inventing stories for them. She smiles, thinking of one time with her mom. The dolls would sit on a boat, crossing to a magical island. Her mom described it in detail. There was a hidden town, under the sea. Viola could envision it. Mom was an excellent storyteller.

"What are you doing, Viola?"

Brant calls out as the mountainside stone door slides shut, and he walks toward her.

"Playing," she answers without looking up.

"With rocks?"

"Yes, Brant. I can play pretend with almost anything. That's what you do when you're an only child."

"All I ever did was get picked on by my brothers." he says.

"Is my time up?"

"It's been over two hours. Are you hungry?"

"Yes, I am. Can I come back out after I eat?"

"I'll ask. You know, things might be easier for you if you were nicer to my brother."

"I know that, Brant. But I'm not willing to lead Patrick on because he's married, and so am I." she says.

His eyebrow lifts.

"Come again!"

"If—How do I say this? When I'm with one brother, I commit myself. I believe in the union of a marriage. That's why I left Zack and chose Jason. Zack's a cheater. Cheating is a choice. A marriage without commitment is chaos. Carly loves Patrick. He's her mate. It's my choice to respect her marriage, but more important, I respect myself. Why would I raise my son with a man who is an emotionally vacant cheater? My son would either become a cheater, or he'll hate his father. Neither is good."

The corners of Brant's mouth twitch upward.

"I agree with you."

"What is this place? Is this where the family will gather if there's a nuclear war?"

"Possibly," he says. "It's pretty high-tech. We have a high-voltage energy substation nearby. We mainly train soldiers."

Viola saw the shift in his stance. His guard's down. He trusts her. She doesn't want to change who he is by stating too many of her opinions. The chapter in the Family Bible was clear that women must have the necessary heirs to continue the line, striving for a minimum of ten. She doesn't agree with it, being raised as she was. Still, she understands from reading about other societies in East and South Asia that they, too, practiced fraternal polyandry when they were faced with scarce environmental resources. Polyandry in the family journals has been happening since the beginning of time and was embraced to populate a community.

Millions of women died giving birth since the beginning of the world. They still do.

In the *Family Bible,* every female born is considered a sacrifice for humankind. In latin they're the *Mater,* the mother of earth, as every male or female born is given life through the mother's womb. *In utero.* Within the womb. *Ex utero.* From the womb.

The scale remain in balance. We can't make a baby without a male's sperm. Why can't men and women work together. Why does the ego have to create false power struggles. We were meant to remain equals. There's no winner if one gender is obliterated.

Viola thinks of what she read about the New World. She read that only fifty of the original one hundred and two passengers on the Mayflower survived the first winter in Massachusetts when they arrived in November 1620. Twenty-five of the fifty were children, siblings, and only five mothers of those children survived through the next year, and one of the women died after the winter, leaving four women. To avoid extinction, sixteen of the twenty-seven marriages from the Mayflower produced children, contributing to the population of the New World community that is now known as the United States. It's been estimated that thirty-five million people are directly related to these Mayflower survivors. Viola cried when she read that it's also believed that those four surviving mothers from the Mayflower denied themselves food portions to ensure the twenty-five children survived.

They, too, were Luci.

Viola drops her rocks, rubbing her hands together.

"What month is it, may I ask?"

"September," Brant says. "It's going to rain tomorrow. After that, the weather will change, getting colder and colder."

"Have you spoken with your father?"

"No. I haven't talked to anyone since you arrived. Patrick took away all the phones."

"Wow. He likes phones."

Brant laughs.

"You're something else."

"So, I've heard. I miss Jason."

She looks toward the fence.

"I know you do. I'm sorry, Viola. It's been quiet. I suspect it won't last for long."

I need to see Carly. We need to make a plan to get out of here.

"Do you think Patrick would let us play cards? Maybe with Carly? He could play, too. It's dull being by myself all the time."

"What about me? What am I—chopped liver?" asks Brant.

"That's a good comeback from a blimey Brit."

"That's the wrong word use again, but nice try."

"I'm glad Patrick lets you talk to me. It's probably best I don't talk to him. I'm bound to get a gun shoved in my mouth."

"Yes, that's best. I'm sure of it."

"Is there a doctor here, Brant? I'd like to have an ultrasound."

"There is a doctor. He arrived from another post when I did. But I'm not sure we have that type of equipment here. Carly's been the only other female at the Complex aside from you, and in the past, I believe she went home for such things."

"So, am I here having my baby old school, hoping for the best?"

"I can't answer that, Viola. Patrick's waiting to hear what decisions will be made before you stay or move. He's had a few phone calls and clobbered the sh—ip out of some stuff."

"What do you mean?"

"He destroyed a room."

Viola's eyes are wide.

"I'm the errand runner, trying to pacify the situation as best I can. I don't have access to many details, Viola."

"Do you train?"

"What do you mean?"

"Zack mentioned that all of the boys train from a young age."

"Yes. I do. It's private, for men only."

"Carly said she could fight."

"She can. Jason was her instructor. He taught her defensive fighting moves a few years ago. Patrick approved it."

"Why her?"

"Back home, Carly was attacked one night, after picking up munch at the supermarket."

Viola's eyebrows rise in question.

"Munch?"

"Munch means grub, food and lucky for Carly, she got away. It scared the bejesus out of Patrick. He's been over the top since that night. He's protective of her."

"Normal. She is his mate."

Brant looks up. Viola's eyes follow his gaze. She can't see anything but a mountain top.

"What are you looking at?"

"I saw...look, there on the roof."

He points to a ridge, below what appears to Viola to be a mountain, on the side of the Complex, not a roof.

"Do you see that, Viola? Right there."

Viola gets to her feet. She steps in front of Brant to see what he sees.

A shot rips through a part of her arm.

A scream escapes her.

-..Chapter 31-. .-

Brant grabs Viola. He covers her body with his as they both hit the ground hard. He yanks off a walkie-talkie attached to his belt and pushes a button.

"Ее подстрелили. Кто-то на крыше. Скорее!" ("She's been shot. Someone's on the roof. Hurry!")

Mere seconds pass before soldiers swarm around them, their guns aimed at the roof. Other soldiers can be seen scaling the wall as Viola's body is turned over.

A big man comes running toward Viola, the shaved-head guard who opened the sliding stone door to let her outside. He gathers her in his arms to carry her inside.

"My baby! I'm pregnant. Do you know Jason? Please call him. You have to help me, please." She says.

He gawks at her with his green eyes.

"Jason, as in Jason?" he asks.

"I'm his mate, his sister, Viola. Patrick's holding me hostage. I'm pregnant. He's trying to take over the family. He killed his mom and took me."

The bald brute of a man is rushing her through the halls.

"I'm Janic—a cousin. I'm friends with Jason," he says before stopping before a heavily fortified door.

"ЛАЗАРЕТ." (INFIRMARY.)

A soldier opens it for them. Viola sees a man in a medical lab coat, with his back to them.

Janic yells, "Arm wound."

The man stops what he's doing. He turns around wearing a large loupe, which he focuses on the bullet wound in front of him.

"It's a clean shot."

I would bet it was Patrick who shot me. Why would anyone else?

The doctor instructs Janic to lie her down while he moves supplies to the corner of the room.

"Lucky for you, it missed your humerus bone," the doctor says, sounding bored. "We need proper training here. One of the soldiers yesterday shot his own foot. It must be painful, Carly. I can give you a shot before I stitch you up."

Viola ignores the fact that he called her by the wrong name.

"I don't want anything. Clean me and stitch me."

"This will hurt," he says as he strolls over to finish whatever he was doing.

Her head tilts to see the sun shining through a panel of windows on the other side of the room and potted plants hanging down in planters from the ceiling. Something you'd see in a greenhouse, not a lab. She notices the positioning of the ventilation system.

"I'm pregnant. Drugs aren't good for the baby. I don't want any."

She watches the doctor counting a few items before placing them into a cabinet. He slips on latex gloves.

"If you're pregnant, why are you here?"

Janic answers, "This isn't Carly. It's Jason's sister from America. His mate."

The young doctor turns around and flips up the loupe to examine her face. His eyes bulge out of his head.

"Who—What are you doing here and pregnant? This is no place for a woman. I thought you were Carly."

"Patrick's doing bad things," says Viola. "Aw," she squeezes her arm below the wound. "He's killing family to be king. He killed my uncle and his mother days ago. I was there. Now he's holding me hostage. He's going to kill Jason."

"What?" the doctor says, giving her a strange look. "Let's keep this between us, Miss—Hold on, what's your name?"

"Viola."

"I'm Henry," he says. "Viola, listen to me. You mustn't say things like that here in the open. You'll be shot between the eyes if there's any truth to this or if it's a lie."

"Why would I lie?"

"Where's Patrick?"

"I think he was on a ridge near the mountain top, shooting at me!" she says.

Janic and the doctor exchange serious looks.

"I'll find out," says Janic.

"Janic, this stays here, and you," he says, pointing to Viola, "say no more. I need you to swear it. Patrick has us locked down. Ready for war. He thinks a traitor is trying to kill him. None of us have phones. He believes it's someone amongst us. Everyone's on alert."

"You're all being lied to. Patrick is the traitor—if you know Jason, you know I'm telling the truth. Janic, if you can't find the shooter from the roof, check Patrick's gun. Check his room—Henry, is it? Dust Patrick's hands for gunpowder residue."

"Are you carrying Jason's child?" asks Henry.

"I am. And he will come for me or die trying."

Henry nods to Janic as he prepares to sew Viola up without pain medication. He uses a disinfectant on Viola's wound.

"Ouch!" She grabs his shirt.

He steps back out of her reach. He slides his hand down his dress shirt, over her smudged fingerprint of blood on his crisp white button-down. With a heavy sigh, he sets the disinfectant on a stainless-steel surgical instrument table to do up the buttons on his lab coat.

"Janic, send in two men. We'll need to hold her down for this."

"Will she not lose the baby if she's put through this much pain?" says Janic.

She shakes her head.

"No, do it. I don't want to lose too much blood."

"She's right," Henry says. "Go, Janic. And Miss, stop talking. Say nothing to anyone else who comes into this room. We all report to Patrick. How can you not know this?"

Viola moans in pain.

"Open up," he says, placing a plastic stick in her mouth. "Bite down on this when I tell you. I need you to breathe through your nose for me, all right? Deep breaths. Please show me."

She does it.

"Great job."

When two men rush in, Henry instructs them to hold her down.

The doctor starts to stitch her up.

-..Chapter 32-. .-

V iola's eyes blink open.

I must have passed out from the pain.

Carly and Brant are hovering over her. Henry has a heart monitor set up. There's a drip with a needle taped to her arm.

Viola winces at the pain in her arm.

"Is my baby okay?"

"We don't have an ultrasound scan here. I have this fetal doppler that I've used in my lab on pregnant animals. Take a listen for yourself," says Henry, the doctor. He places a handheld machine on her belly, adds gel, and turns it on. They all hear the fast heartbeat.

Viola bursts into tears, happy that her baby is still alive.

"Carly, what's the plan for this pregnant woman?" asks Henry. "I mean, she's been shot. She needs to go to a bigger city. She needs a proper ultrasound. Who is she?"

"She's a cousin," Carly says.

"Where's Patrick?" Henry asks.

"He's trying to figure out who shot at her and Brant from the roof."

"Do you think the shooter was aiming for me?" asks Brant.

Henry grabs a piece of paper and hands it to Brant.

"Where were you standing?"

Brant makes a quick drawing. Henry takes a ruler and adds lines to it. He looks at Carly, then at Brant.

"I could be wrong, but I think they were aiming at Viola. As she told us, her movement in front of Brant most likely saved her life."

Carly's feet stumble. Brant reaches for her with a worried brow.

"Carly, what is it?" Brant asks.

"I saw Patrick go out the roof door. He must have had a gun hidden up there. He knew Viola was outside. Why is he doing this? What can we do? We have to sneak her out before he kills her."

"And Jason's baby," Janic adds.

They're all startled, looking at Janic, not realizing before he spoke that he was back.

"Are you the traitor?" Carly asks Janic.

"Try Patrick," Viola says. Carly gasps.

"Hey! She told me herself when I carried her in, shot and hysterical. She said who the father was. I believe her." Janic says.

"Believe her—Who? About what?" says Patrick, walking through the infirmary doors.

"This woman is pregnant!" Henry says.

Patrick pretends to be surprised.

"What? Are you sure, Viola?"

She won't look at him.

"I've secured the roof," says Patrick. "I believe someone among us tried to kill Brant and then got back into the building before the alarm sounded. The cameras were all off. Winston, was the guard in charge of that area of the building's security. He's being held in the Box."

"What's the Box?" Viola asks, focused on her bandaged arm.

"It's where we put people who need punishment," says Patrick. "It's a small room. We call it the Box. I want to find out how the cameras were offline while a shooter was on my roof."

Viola turns to watch the doctor clean up. Henry moves the papers he was drawing on. It's only now that she notices everyone is wearing the same light beige army uniform except for the doctor, Henry, who wears a suit and a white lab coat over his pressed white, now blood-stained button-down.

How many men are in this army?

"What's the verdict, Henry?" says Patrick.

"She should be fine. The baby, too. But I think she needs to be moved, Patrick. We need to update this facility if women are now allowed to be here and pregnant. That much I can tell you after this incident."

"Make a list," Patrick says dismissively.

"Yes, sir," Henry replies.

"Carly, why are you crying?" asks Patrick.

"I want Viola moved today. I'll go with her. We shouldn't be here, Patrick."

"You will go to my quarters. Stay there until I return, Carly."

"Yes, sir." Carly walks toward the door.

"Janic, you can go, Brant, you too. I want to speak with Viola alone."

Neither of the men moves.

"What about me?" asks Henry.

"Are you about done?"

Viola glances over to see Patrick give the doctor a stern look.

"Give me a moment." The doctor shuffles around.

Patrick stares at Viola's bandaged wound.

"Why did you move in front of Brant?" he says with a sly smile. "Who'd have thought a girl protecting a man?"

You liar!

"How would you know that, Patrick, unless you were watching me through the scope of your gun."

Patrick lunges for Viola. Brant and Janic rush to hold him back. Janic puts Patrick in a sleeper hold while Brant has his arms. Brant takes a few knees to his stomach from Patrick in his attempt to fight back.

"Holy hell, move aside," says Henry. They all watch as he injects Patrick with a syringe.

Viola locks eyes with him.

"What's in that?"

"It'll put him out for at least a couple of hours. Are we sure Patrick's the traitor?"

No one answers.

"Are we sure he shot at Viola? If we're not, Viola is still in danger. And if she's right and it was Patrick, she's in danger once he wakes up." The doctor says.

"I'll check the main phone line in the command room and I'll check Patrick's mobile phone," says Brant. "Keep him here, Janic. You watch him. I'll tell his nits that Patrick instructed me to the command room. I'll check and see if we can clarify the gun used during this shooting. Carly saw him, but that doesn't mean he did it. We need more proof, or they'll lock all of us in the Box."

"Viola, you have more balls than most men." Janic laughs. "She's a definite match for Jason."

"Yeah," Brant says. He moves to Viola. His eyes on where hers are focused.

Henry is kneeling over Patrick's body, feeling his pulse.

"This is a day for the history books," Henry says.

-..Chapter 33-. .-

Within fifteen minutes, Carly is back, texting on a flip phone. She tells Henry to cover the infirmary windows and lock the door from the inside.

"Brant is checking Patrick's room. He has soldiers back on the roof looking. Unfortunately, with the cameras turned off, we can't prove where Patrick was or where he may have stashed a gun unless someone saw him. I saw him go in the door. That's it." Says Carly.

"What's really going on, Carly?" asks Henry.

"Can we trust him, Carly?" asks Viola, gesturing towards Henry.

"You don't hold anything back, do you? I just saved you and your baby's life." Henry reminds her.

"I'm grateful, Doctor. I truly am. We need to be sure whose side you're on before we tell you things."

"It's OK, Viola. He's one of Doc's son's kids."

"The oldest?"

"No. Dean is the oldest. Henry's Ryan's son."

"Are you near the top? Do you want to be the top dog like Bobby did?" Viola stares him dead in the eyes.

"Does it look like I want any more responsibility than I already have?"

Viola glances at his lab coat, down to his fancy leather loafers.

Who wears a suit under a lab coat and leather loafers in the middle of nowhere?

"Let's wait to speak, Carly," says Viola.

"You don't trust me?" he says, amazed.

"Listen, Henry. I thank you for stitching me up and allowing me to hear my baby's heartbeat, but I only trust Carly and Brant. If you knew all the bullshit I've been through over the past few years, you wouldn't be offended."

"It's true," Carly tells him. "Her mum, her dad, and now her uncle have all been murdered. Patrick killed her...Uncle...he killed my mum."

"What the hell is going on in this family?" Henry scoffs.

"Power trips, big ones," Viola replies.

"All right, once Patrick wakes up, what do we want to do, Carly?" asks Henry. "I can keep him under, but not forever. The guards will come looking for him."

"I can move him to the Box," Janic says.

"His men will let him out," Carly says, tapping a message on her phone. "Brant will call my father. We'll let him decide. Henry, promise me you will tell no one. Can I have your word?"

"But shouldn't Doc hear about this? I can't believe Uncle Benjamin's dead. They've been close their entire lives."

"Doc is aware that something unusual is happening," Carly says. "Jason doesn't think we should tell anyone—no uncles, at the moment. We're keeping this between a select few cousins until this murderous run takes its course. Viola and Jason's baby were almost the next victims. Patrick has been doing terrible things behind the scenes. He wants everyone above him wiped out. He told my mum that, before he—he killed her." Carly sucks in a breath.

"My God," Henry says as he steps toward Janic.

"Watch out!" Viola yells, watching Henry heading for Janic.

Janic turns, he grabs Henry's hand, and jabs the needle meant for him into Henry's stomach.

Within moments, the doctor's out.

"Fuck," Viola says. "I've got to go today, Carly. I'm not safe, and neither are you and not Janic anymore. Henry must be in on this with Patrick if he tried to stick Janic. Either way, it's not good. How many others here do you suppose are with Patrick?"

"That's hard to say, Viola," Janic replies. "It depends on what Patrick promised them. A lot are loyal to him. Although some, like me, feel Jason is our true leader. We need to move now."

"Where can we go?"

"I can take you somewhere. Jason must be on his way. He called me before you arrived, asking me to keep an eye on you."

"So, you're the one?"

"What do you mean?"

"He told me he had a brother inside."

"That would be me," Janic says, smiling.

"Can I borrow your phone, Janic, to call Jason?"

"Patrick took our phones."

"Viola," says Carly, tearing her eyes from Patrick lying on the floor. "You can use mine once I hear from Brant, to see what my father says."

There are three bangs at the door. Carly hurries to open it and let Brant in. She shuts it behind him and locks it.

"What's going on?" Brant says, looking at Henry's body on the floor.

"Henry tried to stab Janic with a sleep needle," says Viola. "He's in on this."

"This is bigger than we thought, Carly," says Brant. "We need to sneak Viola out of here."

"Did you speak with Father?"

"Yes. He's safe. They have Doc locked down in America, too. We're not sure who is telling the truth or what this power struggle is about. In any case, Jason is unable to come here yet. That's all Father said. For the moment, we're on our own."

"Janic has an idea of where to hide us," Carly says.

"It's short-term," says Janic. "Once the cold hits, with Viola being pregnant, it's a death sentence in winter. Any idea when Jason can pick us up?"

"No, and my father said not to fly out. The planes are being watched," says Brant. "This thing, whatever it is, has blown up fast. Uncle Benjamin's death has caused an enormous problem. We need to leave—and I mean now. Father said a war's headed our way. I want to go sooner rather than later."

"I can't leave Patrick here," says Carly.

Brant hugs his sister and steps back.

"Car—You must make your choice. I'm sorry. Patrick won't make it out of this, no matter what. He's not the man you'll want to raise the kids with. He's going to prison. He's murdered family members. Viola needs you. If, for any reason, we're stuck out here for God knows how many months, there is no way I am delivering a baby in this barren frontier. We need to gather supplies, food, and water, and get out. We'll run for it and hope Jason and the others get here before the cold hits heavy. We'll stop at the main house first. We'll load up, and go wherever Janic says."

-..Chapter 34-. .-

"I want to go home," says Carly. "Mum's gone. I can't abandon my kids, Brant."

"Brant, let her go," Viola says. "I'll be okay. Jason will find us."

"What if he doesn't, Viola?" asks Carly. "My father hasn't heard from him in days. He said that's not like him."

"It's okay. Jason would kick my ass if I gave up now. We're not giving into these heathens trying to off everyone we love for power. There's no honor in life, living that way. I'll die being true. Janic. What about you?"

"I'm in. You sold me," Janic says. "Plus, I'm a dead man if I stay now."

"Car—" Brant says. "I can't let our family line be destroyed because Patrick decided to be a greedy snake. If you want to go home, go. I'll tell the gate that Patrick wants you on a plane right away. Watch my kids for me. Tell Mary I love her."

"I will. I'm so sorry, Viola," Carly says, with tears in her eyes. "But I can't leave my kids. With Mum gone, my sisters will need me. I'm the oldest."

"I understand, Carly. Thank you so much for doing all of this. It's more than enough. My mother was an admirer of Mother Teresa. She used to quote her, 'Not all of us can do great things. But we can do small things with great love.' You've done so much for me, Carly. Go. If Jason and I don't make it, will you promise to find my baby and be a good Auntie for Zee?"

"You will make it, Viola. Once this is all sorted, we'll raise our kids together. I should go before these two wake up. I'll cover for you. I'll leave a note so Patrick will think we're on that plane together. Hopefully, that will give you more time. Brant, are you sure? Janic can stay and help Viola?"

"Car, I can't go home with this happening here," says Brant. "Uncle said they, whoever they were, are here to eliminate Viola. She has a hit on her. You don't. I can't run away from this. Patrick is a lamb. This time, I'm a lion."

Viola looks between Carly and Brant, confused.

Carly laughs with tears streaming down her face.

"You're a cute lion." Carly says through tears. "I love you, Brant. Thank you for being a good man. Mother would be so proud."

He nods. "Go, but first help us get Viola out of here. Car, go be in charge since you're so good at it."

Carly sticks her tongue out at her brother before she unlocks the door and heads out of the infirmary.

Viola remembers her friend Jes sticking her tongue out at her younger brothers.

I wish I had a normal family.

———

Brant gives Viola a soldier's uniform to put on. She smiles, seeing her round tummy poking out. Janic, Brant, and Viola mix in with other soldiers walking inside and out of the building.

When Janic jumps behind the driver's seat in a large army truck, Viola slips in the back. Brant sits in the passenger seat, then Carly hops in with them. Carly tells the guard at the gate that she's going to the airport per Patrick's orders. They let the truck pass through without question.

Janic drives toward the private airport, dropping Carly off a mile away from it, per Carly's instruction, so the guard at the airport won't check the back of the truck where Viola is. Viola hops in the front. The truck turns around to head the other direction, toward the main house.

Brant shoots off a text. When his phone rings, Brant picks up, saying a few things in a code Viola's not heard before.

He hands the phone to Viola.

"It's for you."

"Jason?" she says.

"I'm here, luv."

"Here, here?"

"Not yet, luv. It's complicated, but I'll come. I'll find you. Carly called and filled me in."

"I'm headed out with Brant and your brother Janic," she adds.

"Somewhere safer." Janic calls out.

"Find us when you can, Jason, when it's safe," says Viola. "The baby's fine. Henry and Patrick are both bad news, though Henry did patch me up before he tried to stick Janic."

"What do you mean, patch you up?"

"Patrick shot me, the bullet went through my arm, then he tried to convince everyone that Brant was the target."

"Bloody hell, Viola! I'm stuck for the moment."

"Don't do anything stupid, Jason. I'm fine."

"Stay with Brant and Janic. Might I have a word with Janic?"

She hands the phone to Janic.

"Sir, we're headed to the R. You might have to dig. I'll leave a trail. Please, before we freeze our *osly* (ass) off. Will do. You bet. Absolutely. It's my honor. I can't imagine you with anyone else. This one might have bigger balls than you." Janic laughs.

"I second that." Brant calls out before the call ends.

-..Chapter 35-. .-

JASON

"Zack."

"Where are you, Jay?"

"I'm trapped in a double L W."

"Like a real L!"

"Yes, Zack. I'll call you back when I can move."

"Should I come help? I'm through here."

"No. We need Y wheels down."

"Got it. Already done. What's happened?"

Jason hears another mobile phone going off.

"Where are you, Zack?"

"I'm in Buffalo, cleaning one of dad's guns in his kitchen. Someone's calling my other phone."

"Do you need to get that?" asks Jason.

"Jay, you know I run a business, it'll wait. Can you talk?"

"I've got a minute. Carly is flying to England. Viola's with Janic and Brant. They're headed out to the wild. There's a hit on Viola. Henry is N for the moment with Patrick."

"That fucker. I told you we couldn't trust him."

"Zack, Patrick shot Viola. She told me she's fine. Arm wound. It's patched. Carly told me Patrick wants her dead. She can't stop him."

"I'm going!"

"Zack, I need you to stay put. If I'm too long, you head to D—only after."

"If she dies, Jay. I'll fucking kill—"

"Calm down, I've got it. If I don't make it, Zack, take care of our family."

"You'll make it. Let me—I wanna pick her up."

"No, only I can, you know that. It's crucial you stay in North America and protect Doc."

There's a moment of silence. Jason hears Zack exhale.

The line goes dead.

-..Chapter 36-. .-

VIOLA

They arrive at the main house. Brant enters a security code. The gate opens. An intimidating, ten-foot-tall fence surrounds the property. Once on the property grounds, Viola sees what looks like a storage building with a slanted roof.

At a large front door, Brant pulls a key from his pants pocket and unlocks it. Inside, it looks like a home—almost, but with a lot of closets with padlocks around a large main room. The kitchen is small, and the bathroom is a barrel-looking tub and toilet, above which is a high circular ring and an attached curtain to pull around it for privacy. The bed looks out of place, set in the middle of the room. Viola's eyes lift to see the sky through a small solid window.

"Is the roof slanted because of the snow here?"

"Transparent solar panels," says Brant. "They're on the entire roof. Take anything, we might need to birth a baby, Viola, just in case. I'm not sure how long it'll take Jason to get here. Gather the warmest clothes from this closet," Brant says, opening it with another key. "Carly has a bunch of stuff."

"I've a way to go before the baby arrives. Has Carly spent a lot of time here?" asks Viola, eying a polar bear skin throw blanket on a king-size bed.

"During her last pregnancy, she stayed nights here with Patrick while he worked at the Complex during the day. They store stuff here for winter or the power outages. We'll need to stay warm. Janie, get extra petrol out back—the gray barrels. Bring a few of the green too. We're dead men if we run out of petrol. Grab spare tires, too."

"Ten-four," Janic says, unlocking and exiting through a back door.

"What does Patrick keep in all of these closets, Brant?"

"I'm not sure, clothes, I assume, although he said most of them are filled with gold." Brant titters. "I have no interest in finding out what my brother's extracurricular activities might be."

He walks over to Viola, taking her hands in his.

"Viola. If anything happens to me—"

"Stop talking, Brant. We're going to make it. Patrick won't find us before Jason does and until then, we have each other. I hope to hell Janic doesn't get us lost in the middle of nowhere. How messed up would that be after all of this?"

Brant drops her hands to peek out the window, ensuring Janic is still outside and not within earshot.

————

They drive for a few hours, passing homes in a tiny village. She loves the detail around their front windows, with carved designs and bright colors. One house's door is aqua blue; another's window trims are vibrant green. Metal buckets sit over wooden fence tops, not far from barn sheds—Spruce and pines are vibrant and thriving in the chilly autumn air. Viola sees a few horses behind a fence and a wooden contraption.

"That's the harness for the horse," says Brant. "It goes over the horse to pull a sled."

"Where are all of the cars?" she asks.

"Sleds are the main transportation out here, Viola. A car takes a beating in the winters here."

In the distance, Viola spots what appears to be a mountain ridge, as Janic pulls in behind a sizable logwood house.

"Let's go, kids," says Janic.

Viola examines the octagonal wooden structure before her.

"What is this place?"

"A bit of a *Banya* or a *Venik Platza*—ahhh bathhouse," says Janic. "It improves your health. My girl will be here. She's one of the healers and can help us. I left her a message telling her we're coming."

Brant makes a gruff sound.

"It's a brothel, Viola."

Viola laughs. "Wow, I've read about those."

When they enter, it's hot inside. Six women greet them, all wearing floor-length gowns. On one side is a wood stove, and a steaming bath on the other. It looks like a large cooking pot with a wood-burning fire and shrubs beneath it. Thick chains hang from wood ceiling beams. The pot is big enough to fit several people in it. A few other wooden barrels are in another corner. On one wall is a ceiling-to-floor curtain.

The women speak a language Viola's never heard before, and Brant converses with them. His eyebrows raise more than once. He laughs, looking at Janic.

"I'm told that Janic here has a nice white cock."

Janic starts to cough, making Viola laugh.

"Who are they?" asks Viola.

"Daughters of nomads," says Brant. "They were born and raised here or brought here from other villages. Most nomads raise reindeer. They live off the land. Their families gather their herds, and in the winter, they're always on the move so the reindeer can dig for the plants under the snow for food. These people work hard. They get paid for reindeer meat, every part of the reindeer. They were here long before the Russians."

Viola turns her eyes toward Janic.

"Do their families care what they do with your white cock for a living?"

"It's not a big deal, not in here. Money is money, Viola. I'm not the only one who visits."

"What's that smell?" she asks.

"A *venik*," Brant says. "It's a leafy bundle of birch, oak, juniper, eucalyptus, tree twigs. It cleans the skin, accelerates healing," he says with a wide smile.

"We'll need to pick a nomadic family and move with them if you're going to be safe," Janic adds. "When Patrick realizes you're not on that plane with Carly, he'll come here looking."

"Why would he look for us here?"

"I'm not as impressive as I want you to think, Viola. I can get us out of this area, but I need Jason to find us before Patrick does. Patrick knows that many of us come here from time to time. He has the luxury of a mate with him. We only see ours when we go home, which is not near enough if you ask me. Don't worry, Viola. I told Jason in so many words during that phone call how to find us. But once winter sets in, we're screwed. And I don't mean by one of these fine women. It's a cold like you've never experienced. Your nose can freeze in seconds. We must keep everything covered."

One woman saunters up to Janic. She undoes his pants and pulls them down far enough to clean his penis with a steaming cloth. Viola and Brant sit on a wooden bench, covering their smiles. Another woman places a pillow before Janic's feet, taking the cloth from the woman who cleaned him so that she can drop to her knees. She sucks his nice white cock in front of them.

Janic tries to play it off comically. Using his hands, he attempts to cover what he can until he cums, and like any man, release is release.

Viola crosses her legs uncomfortably, turned on. She turns her head, not wanting to stare at Janic's hard manhood less than two feet from her face.

A different woman approaches and speaks with Brant.

Smiling, he shakes his head and says something to her that makes her laugh. She says something that makes all the women laugh.

"What did she say, Brant?" asks Viola.

"She asked me if I wanted the same as him or a private room."

Brant points toward the curtain.

"I told her I was happy with you. Then she asked if she could make you happy. I told her you were happy with me. She said she highly doubts that, but if I say so."

Viola laughs, as does Janic, with his pants securely back in order.

"Brant, ask her for me where Lady B is," says Janic.

Brant speaks to one of the women. He nods as they all start chiming in.

"Uh, Lady B died. A pregnancy complication," Brant says.

"Oh no," Viola gasps—her hand to her mouth, understanding why she probably died.

Our blood.

"Janic, did you have sex with Lady B without protection?" she asks.

Janic glances at Brant, and back to Viola.

"I'll be sent to the Box for this. I abide by our laws. I understand that we're never to be with other women without protection. She was my special girl. I had her as a девственник. (virgin) We were together. I paid to keep her for me. Do you hear what I'm saying?"

"She was paid for. I get it. Did you love her? Don't answer, Janic. I can tell that you do."

"Viola, in my family, there are four boys, two girls. I'm the youngest—the buffest, though," Janic says, pumping his chest out. "I have been with one of my sisters. We have two kids, a boy and a girl. She's had most of her children with two of my brothers. It's also why my uncle sent me to the Complex."

"That makes sense," Brant answers. "I'm the youngest. I've had two kids with Mary, both girls, and a baby on the way with Catherine. We're not sure what sex is yet. I was told I'd be here in Siberia for a while to train."

"I was told the same thing, Brant," Janic says. "This is year three for me."

"Three years!" Viola says. "When were you home last, Janic, and what kind of training—military?"

"We're not at liberty to say, Viola," says Brant.

"I was last home three years ago," adds Janic.

"Well, no wonder you come here," she says, looking around the room.

The women start speaking with Brant.

"What is it, Brant?" asks Viola.

"They said men in white suits came after Lady B's death. They took her body away. They also said that she was not the only one. Others who died were pregnant. The same men came and took them away."

"What did they look like? These men." Asks Viola.

"That one there that sucked the dew off Janic's willy said they look like Janic," says Brant.

"Holy shit," Viola whispers. "Ask them if they've seen where they take the women."

Brant speaks to the women, and they motion for him to go outside.

-..Chapter 37-..-

When they walk out, the nomad women points toward a distant peak.

"Everything out here is flat, so how did that peak grow over there?" asks Viola. "I think it's manufactured."

Brant glares at Viola.

"How could you know that?"

"I don't, but look at it, Brant. It's out of place, yet it looks like it belongs. I'd bet our family built it years ago. Maybe for our scientists. It might be a lab?"

It's probably where Iwas meant to go for training.

"Janic, this stays between us three." says Brant. "I fear Janic will learn too much with you around, Viola."

"He might." she agrees.

"What are you two talking about, Brant?" asks Janic.

"Viola is very communicative, no secrets in her life book. She's also near the top of the line and has access to information it seems no one else does."

"He doesn't know what he's talking about, Janic." she says.

"Why are we kept in the dark?" asks Janic .

Viola can't meet Janic's eyes.

"Look at what's happening right now, Janic. You and Brant are hiding me so i won't be killed. All because some green snake is power-hungry, and he's jumped into another snakes tree."

"I take it you mean Patrick jumped into Jason's tree?"

"Tell me you didn't ask me that question out loud, Janic?"

"Sorry Tiny One. I'm uh, trying to piece things together."

"Brant, can I tell Janic about Laby B? I mean, I'm not supposed too."

"Up to you, Viola. I've no bloody idea what you've found out about his Lady B, unless you've been up to that peak over there that you seem to know so much about."

Shoot. They don't have a clue about our blood. It's not fair. They don't realize they are murdering women by having unprotected sex with them.

"No, and I have no proof of any station over there." says Viola. "Anyway, don't worry about it, Janic. It's not important. I'm sorry about your Lady B. Please wear protection with everyone you have sex with unless it's with family."

Viola follows the nomad women back into the bathhouse. She wonders if the family doesn't teach these soldiers at the Complex about proper sex education. They need to be told the truth, or they need to have a container shipment of condoms arrive in Siberia for the unimaginable number of men who most likely visit this healing massage shack.

"Viola, does the family shoot anyone we have sex with that's not family?" asks Janic.

Viola decides she will not say another word about it and let Janic believe what he thinks. Could he face the truth... that he inadvertently killed the girl he loved by having unprotected sex with her. Would it completely demolish him?

"Only non-family sex partners you didn't wear a condom with are disposed of. So, wear one. You should be okay."

He nods at her with a strained expression.

"Okay, both of you don't look." she says. "Keep your eyes on me. There's a camera in here."

Brant's head moves. "How can you know that?"

"I've had them watch me my entire life, Brant. I know what they all look like. Please don't look around unless you want to be in more trouble. We are a private family without privacy in our day-to-day affairs. There are valid reasons for this. I'm not at liberty to say or its my death. So, there you go. I expect that camera is how they can tell who you're getting pregnant."

"Shit." says Janic. "Viola, some wild stuff happens in this room."

"I'm sure whoever's been watching has been having a grand ole time."

Brant starts laughing.

"I've never heard a female talk as you do."

The women in long gowns of animal skin skirts, with a hand sewn lace blouse attached at the waist, smile, staring at the three of them as they speak in english.

-..Chapter 38-..-

J anic jumps into the old army truck with one of the women—his new lady. His foot presses on the emergency break. They drive for six hours before they pitch tents to sleep in.

The next day, the lady and Brant converse. She directs their course, taking them quite far until they happen upon some large cone structures.

"Where are we?" asks Viola.

"This is where her family lives," Janic answers.

"What are those... Teepees?" asks Viola.

"They call them lodges," says Brant. "What you're seeing is a bunch of thick lodgepole pine wood, which holds up deerskins that they've sewn together. They're easy to put up and take down. Throughout the winter, the Nomads keep moving across the tundra with their reindeer. The reindeer eat the lichens and fungi they dig out from under the snow in the winter, and in the short summers, the reindeer eat lemmings, bird eggs, and arctic fish if the families set up near the water."

"What do the Nomads eat?"

"They eat their reindeer."

"Really?"

"Don't give me that look, Viola. They consider the reindeer a part of their family. They thank them before they eat their meat, and they use every piece of their bodies, from their skin to their bones, for utensils."

"This is fascinating," she says.

"It's not an easy life," says Brant. "In the winter, the only water they have is ice put into a pot to boil. There are no bathrooms. I can't imagine that being fun for these women. You're lucky you won't have a menstrual cycle while we're out here being pregnant."

"What do these women use during that?" asks Viola.

"I read that they use moss for most things," says Brant. "They collect loads of it during the summer for their winter travels."

"So, they put it there, then toss it outside?"

He shrugs his shoulders. "I've no idea. Do you want me to ask her?"

"No, not now, but maybe later. So interesting."

"To be sure." Brant smiles ear to ear at Viola while he rolls his eyes.

"I know you're mocking me, Brant."

"You do realize you've got a habit of rolling your own baby blues?" he says.

"I don't—or not that much."

Janic grins as he parks the big truck beside the furthest lodge. Brant and Janic start unloading big barrels. Viola assumes they're petrol being lifted off to get to the water barrels at the back of the truck bed.

They bring out a large black trough.

"Are we supplying a new water trough for their reindeer before we go to a safehouse?"

"No, Viola," Brant answers. "I brought this so you can bathe."

Her brows almost reach up to her hairline.

"This is a luxury, trust me, Viola. These people don't have the means to carry a bathtub wherever they go. I figured you, being pregnant and with our upbringing, you would demand to clean yourself."

"Thank you, Brant. Are most men like you and Jason so thoughtful?"

"Um, hello, how about adding me to the list?" Janic says. "You do realize you keep leaving me out, Viola?"

"Oh, I'm sorry, Janic. I didn't realize. Would you have brought a bathtub, too?"

"Well, no. Probably not, so I guess I'm a heathen like the rest of them."

They all laugh. Viola senses something off in Janic. She didn't mean to offend him. She's pretty sure he's pissed off, maybe thinking the family shot his pregnant Lady B. Maybe she'll tell him the truth when Brant is out of earshot.

They set up their simple lodge with a circle of deer skins to sleep on and a fire pit in the center for warmth and cooking reindeer meat. Brant hands an old man money for the deer skins.

Viola thanks an old, white-haired woman for giving her herbs. The woman somehow knew Viola was pregnant. She touched her stomach when Viola helped gather pots and utensils from the truck for cooking as the men split wood for the fire. Viola loves the lodge, which, out here in the middle of nowhere, is another name for a sleep teepee. When she lies down on the deerskin, she can't feel the cold ground below her at all. Brant sets up a fire. The smoke rises up and out of the hole in the top of the teepee, and the pot of boiling water smells delicious. Viola mentioned her love of mint to Brant in the Complex, and now he's making her mint tea.

When she pokes her head out to see where the guys went, Brant waves to her to come and see the bathing teepee. She stares out at the endless flat lands filled with various plants, pockets of moss, layers of lichens. There's nothing across the wide-open panoramic view over twenty centimeters tall but for scattered small fir trees. To her left, at least a hundred deer graze, nodding their heads, resting on the dirt, at one with the land. She watches their graceful movements. There's a gentleness in their eyes coupled with a fierce power in the buck's antlers.

If I lived thousands of years ago, out here, I would believe the Earth was flat. It's endless, like nothing else exists. I'd believe a lot of made-up stories if this was the only life I knew.

Her arm flips the animal skin door open to enter the bathing teepee. She touches her tender wound. A fire in the middle of the structure heats one end of the big trough. Smoke rises and is sucked out of the opening. She watches Janic stir the water with a stick. Another large pot of water is boiling, and against one side of the teepee is a green barrel that contains water for the bath.

"This is incredible," says Viola. "Um, are you planning to cook me?"

"No, you great numpty, " Brant says, "this bath is controlled. Janic started the fire. It won't go beyond forty-two degrees. This tub, my lady, is made from a special material."

"Wow!"

"Once the water boils, Viola, we'll pour it in the tub to warm it up for you," Brant adds, pointing. "Then you can clean. Soap and a few towels are in that bag next to the tub. I put a hook over there—well, a stick if you want—for your towel. Janic and I can use the other one we brought," says Brant.

"This numpty loves it, Brant—and Janic. Thank you both. Uh, how long will we stay?" she asks.

"Janic's lady told me the nomads intend to stay here for seventeen days before we move again. I hope Jason gets here before then, 'cause it will be cold soon. We're talking forty below and heavy snow. Then this family travels every four days to feed their reindeer. We won't take the truck or the tub. We'll take what we can fit on sleds," says Brant.

"It sounds like an adventure if we weren't certain that someone was trying to kill me because of my birth parents," says Viola.

Janic's face drops.

"Janic, what is it?"

"I have many questions about what is happening in this family at the Complex. I don't understand why we're at war within our bloodline."

"You and me both," she says.

-..Chapter 39-. .-

In their sleeping Teepee, Brant sits motionless next to her on his sleep mat, made of deer skin. Viola is grateful for the kindness of her cousins, as she stands and carries a change of clothes from their sleeping tent to the bath teepee.

Once inside, she undresses and steps into the tub to bathe. As she soaps her breasts, which have started to fill with pregnancy, the image of the woman on her knees in front of Janic at the bathhouse enters her thoughts. Her hands slide down. She touches herself, flicks her nub, slides her finger along her slippery slit, dips her pinkie in, forgetting where she is, she allows her mind to fantasize. She massages her right soapy breast. Derek's mouth is on her. She watches him behind her closed eyes. Violent tingles build inside. Janic's mouth is on her, then one of the women from the brothel. Brant's mouth. She forces her fantasy back to Derek, only to see that it's Jason. Her orgasm takes off slightly louder than she'd like it to.

Who— What?

A male's heavy breathing fills the teepee. Viola's eyes open. She looks toward the entrance. Brant has his penis out. He's gotten himself off.

"Viola, I apologize," he says panting as he turns away. "I found—Your sock fell outside. I saw it. I brought it. You were touching yourself, your breast—I, uh, I'm sorry."

"It's okay, Brant," she says, covering both breasts with her good arm. "My arm hurts when I carry too much on that side. I must have dropped it. I—I was thinking about the lady with Janic."

"Me too," he admits.

"Yeah. It wasn't easy to watch someone that closely and not be affected by it."

"I swear I had no intention of walking in. I heard you. For a second, I thought maybe you were with Janic."

"No. Janic's not my type. He's very caveman. He might look better if he had hair."

Brant laughs. "He looks like most Russian men, and it's hard to tell them apart when they shave their heads."

"I don't want anyone, Brant, only Jason. I do this, though, when we're apart."

"I think we all do if we're being honest, Viola. I'll leave you to it... to do whatever you'd like," he says, as he departs.

A moment later, his arm pokes back in through the teepee opening. He makes a waving motion, he drops her sock. His arm disappears.

Viola laughs, embarrassed. She sinks below the water line.

––––––––––

After dinner and introductions to the lady's family, they all stand outside in a circle around a bonfire. The old woman chants as three men and two other nomadic women sway. Viola laughs at Janic singing. She asks Brant to inquire about the Nomad's children.

"They said they've grown and moved away for school and work. They come to visit on the first day of summer. They said they'd be dancing if they were here. They'd party with us."

Viola smiles as she watches the orange, yellow, and blue colors of fires flames dance along with the old woman's song. It reminds her of something... someone.

Viola remembers little girls in a circle. They're singing *Ring Around the Rosie* in German, holding each other's hands. She's swinging so fast.

Janic breaks up her memory as he sways toward Viola, pretending to join the nomads' dance. She smiles at him, waving her arms in the air like he is. He steps on the toes of her shoes, taking her hands, he lifts her up.

Viola recalls that she had tripped and fell. She was dizzy. One of the girls reached for Viola's hands. From the ground, Viola looked out at a field filled with red roses. She can smell them. There were thousands of them. The girl stepped on the toes of Viola's shoes. She took her hands and pulled Viola up off the ground.

Viola remembers saying, *"Danke, Polina."*

Viola heads toward the sleep teepee.

The girl who helped me up had a birthmark on the inside of her left wrist. I remember thinking that it looked like a lamb or a puppy.

Viola's hand goes to her chest. Polina is the missing girl in the photo Jill showed her. Polina was under the table when the man, Alexander, shot the woman wearing the white wig. She bit his ankle. Polina was the nurse in England in Uncle Mark's boardroom who took Viola's blood—she had the same birthmark on the inside of her wrist.

The nurse's pin was a yellow flag and a black lion on all four paws with a red tongue and red claws.

Aunt Lara knew about the group of six. She mentioned her oath the day she took Viola.

Belgium. We were in Flanders, Belgium. I said your name. Polina, you're a cousin.

Brant enters the sleep teepee.

"What did Janic say to you?"

Viola turns. "Oh, um, he asked if I was through with my bath for today and if he and the lady could have a go at it! I, of course, granted him my blessings in the trough."

Brant chuckles.

"Did you tell Janic you caught me today?" she asks.

"No, Viola, I wouldn't do that," says Brant, peeking out the entrance toward the bathing teepee. "At least one of us is pulling a proper tidy."

"I like the lady's family." She adds.

"Viola, I told Janic when we arrived that we're staying here with his lady's family, but these nomads are not her family."

"Who are they?"

"They're related to one of the other women from the bath house. She mentioned that she recently come back from a visit. I asked her what her family tribe name was so I could tell them that she sent us. I saw Janic on his phone when he was outside to get petrol at the main house. I checked the number when he went for a shite. He called the Complex."

"Oh no! He's not with us?" A chill runs through her core.

"I don't think so." Brant peers out again toward the bath teepee. "Stay as you are, but watch what you say. I think he's sided with Patrick, not Jason. Please keep it in the back of your mind as days go by. Patrick will eventually check and see the passcode I used at the main house. He'll know that I didn't go to England with Carly. We're far from the Lady's family. We should be fine. I assume that when Patrick sees the footage from the bathhouse, he will find them first. I hope it'll take him a while to locate us. It helps that Janic doesn't speak their language. I've been giving him the wrong coordinates." He glances her way, then continues, "He'll speak with Patrick when Patrick can't find us. Janic will know I've been lying. Oh, and the lady must sleep in here with us since she's not their family. I'm sure that'll be a treat for us."

"Can we give her a name, Brant. Something more than Lady?"

"It's what we call prostitutes here."

"My mother said that all *men* and women who weren't born in the King's seat are wage slaves, Brant."

"Huh, that's a befitting term, don't you think, for women who do jobs for money."

"My mom also said a man's ego can't admit that most men are prostitutes at their jobs for money. They're verbally taking it in the you know where, yet you don't hear me calling them whores."

"I'm surprised your mum spoke that way."

"I'm sure it had a lot to do with where we lived. The community I grew up in. This lady, Brant, is doing a job for money, for survival."

"Alright, Viola, my apologies. Let's call her Natasha."

She sighs. "Thank you, and do you think Janic will figure out that you're lying, Brant?"

"I was able to snag a signal earlier. The man in charge of this family told me where to stand to make a call. I spoke with Zack. Jason is unreachable."

"What?"

"Zack told me he's fine. He's not able to talk wherever he is right now. I told Zack our coordinates and the family we're with. He'll only have to say their name to uncover the directions when Jason comes. If anything happens to me—if Patrick finds you, go with him to the Complex. Jason has a contingency plan in place. That's what Zack told me."

"What kind of plan? Will this ever end? Will I ever have my life back, my child?"

"Let's hope for the best. Try and get some kip." says Brant.

"Ha, I know kip means a nap!"

"*Ta-daaaaah!*" he sings, waving his palms in the air. "Ya know, I was about to start charging ye for these proper english lessons, lass.

"Put a sock on it, Mate." she snickers.

"Oi! Is this how it's gonna be. I'll never live down that sock!"

"You dropped it like it's hot."

"Hail, to my sock drop!" he says, sneaking another peek out of of the sleep teepee entrance.

-..Chapter 40-. .-

Viola can't sleep. She doesn't want to believe that Janic could help someone like Patrick.

She turns over. Brant's still at his post, keeping watch at the teepee opening.

"Brant. Why would Janic choose Patrick over Jason? I thought Janic was Jason's brother."

"Title? Money? You heard Janic. He's the youngest. He was sent away. If this was your life in the middle of nowhere, would you make a deal if you could change it for something better?"

"I guess. Well, no, not if it involved harming others, I wouldn't."

"And that, my dear cousin, is why you're with Jason. Hey, Janic likes you. It'll be hard for him to kill you, I can tell. I think he'll make sure Patrick gets you. Then it's out of his hands."

"What about you?"

"I'm sure Patrick's already decided. He'll keep me alive since I'm his brother, or he'll consider me a traitor."

"It's crazy how different you are from Patrick, yet you were raised in the same house."

"It's called self-reflection, Viola. You either desire it or avoid it. Our core values, our beliefs help form our identity. I believe in God. I'm a better man when I pray for his guidance. Patrick chose to form different beliefs. He wanted to win at everything when we were kids. He's always been jealous and a cheater. He doesn't like it when Carly speaks highly of me. Most of my positions under him have been rubbish. He wants me to be his servant. He's read our

Family Bible like I did. I don't understand how he can't see that he's choosing to be the brother Judah."

"It's a classic Osiris, Isis, Horus story," Viola adds.

"I've never heard of it."

"You've never read the Egyptian myths? She asks.

"No!"

"I read that Egyptian myths are where all of the origin stories come from. Who knows anything for sure, Brant. My mom said that many of their stories influenced the Western and non-Western religions. She told me that's where the Virgin Mary story came from, and the resurrection story was also in their papyrus, on their temple walls. It was carved into their coffins. The Egyptian stories were written around the twenty-fourth century before Christ. Mom said their stories most likely gave the Romans the idea for nailing Jesus up on a cross. Why do you think the men in our family are brought up only reading the Family Bible, Brant?"

"You tell me!" he says.

"How would I know?"

"You act like you do."

"I apologize, Brant. I've studied for as long as I can remember. I don't speak for anyone. I only know what I feel and think. I wish people didn't fight or hate over a difference of opinion when it comes to religion. My friend Jes believes Jesus thought the same way, and that love is the only answer. Jesus was killed for telling people we're all the same. The men in charge didn't want commoners to think they possessed their own power."

"Simmer down, Viola. I'm taking the mickey out of you, you know. I appreciate your intellect. You remind me of Mary. She speaks her mind when we're alone. And no worries, I like my beliefs. They make me a better person."

"Jason said the same thing! My mom didn't want me to be taught one bible. She didn't want me to judge myself or other people based on one belief system since there are thousands of religious narratives. Most have either made me feel bad about myself or made me feel like I'm better than most people. Both are negative narratives."

"I agree!" He says. "Religion does foster mostly positive feelings. My faith gives my life meaning." Brant adds.

"Have you ever thought, Brant, that if we're ninety-nine-point-nine percent the same DNA on this planet as science says we are, that means there's only a point-one-percent difference between any two individuals? I can't understand why we're not considered one story."

She stands. On one side of her deerskin sleeping mat she drags her heel across the dirt and then another line on the side closest to Brant's sleeping mat.

"There. I've created my lines. Now you try it."

Brant smiles, pausing before he drags his foot to one side of the teepee opening, where he's standing, then the other.

"Two lines, Viola. Woohoo!"

"Suppose everyone draws their lines, Brant. If we're left alone long enough in this space to create something without interference, and then we join our lines together, it would be beyond what one mind can imagine. We could find ourselves out of any maze instead of hitting the same dead ends that force us to turn around and go back the same way, lifetime after lifetime."

Brant gives her a quizzical look.

"When I think about how many centuries we've allowed a point-one-percent difference to separate us, the point-one-percent that we see: our skin, eye, and hair color and texture. Other environmental factors play a role in shaping human traits, but because someone created lines on a map, we've separated the human race from itself on one planet. Every evil I've witnessed and felt has been because of what the I through an eye can see."

"How did you come up with that?"

"Close your eyes, Brant."

He does.

"It feels good, doesn't it?" she asks. "That's where good lives. I don't have to judge myself against anything else or anyone. My soul, my life force, is good. The moment I open them... my mind is tempted to cross the line into chaos. For me, every religion begins and ends with shutting my eyes. That's my conclusion."

She lifts her arms out to her sides.

"Like the tent in your bible, Brant, this space is my tent. At the end of my fingertips, I draw my invisible lines. An invisible force keeps my center strong. Inside my lines is good, one step out, I face evil, and all day long, I'm faced with choices. I have to choose to recenter myself, so I'll continue to like myself as I walk in this life. I'm sure most people at some point have asked themselves these same questions."

He glances at her.

"I've never thought about it."

"Well, anyone who reads about history or studies science must have questioned whether what they were told to believe rubs raw against what feels to be true for them."

"I don't think so, Viola." He giggles, licking his upper lip. "What made your mum teach you this?"

"She was a force for good, but I made this up. It's my personal belief system. I've known some bad people, but I think most people are good, they are for the most part trying to do the right thing. It's only when an individual doesn't stand inside their lines long enough to determine their own moral code, they'll take on someone like Patrick's right and wrongs as their own. Sometimes, out of fear, you run under another tent. It can take a long time to stake your own tent. If someone showed you the wrong way and you sat under their crooked big top tent your whole life—you're tent center will be weak—it'll fall when you choose to step over other people's lines, when we invade their space. We as parents wreck our children's tents if we refuse to stake our own tent first—like Patrick, who refuses to listen to anyone."

"I want to kill Patrick," says Brant. "I know he killed your uncle and my Mum. Carly told me."

"It's those kinds of thoughts that cause your next generation's tents to fall. Your children look up to you, Brant. They're in your tent until they're old enough to stake their own."

"I won't kill him even if I want to. Honestly, I'm amazed at how similar you and Jason are."

"Really?"

He peeks out of the teepee.

"Viola, not to change the subject, but once Janic finds out I've lied about where we are, it'll hit the fan."

"Maybe I can help," she says.

"Oh, for crying out loud, Viola. What are you thinking?"

-..Chapter 41-. .-

Brant and Viola are seated on a deerskin sleeping mat, playing cards, when Janic and his lady, Natasha, enter the tent. Janic tosses his dirty clothes on his side of the teepee, drying his bald head with a hand towel.

"Look at you, all scrubbed up," says Brant.

"What's this?" Janic points to a deerskin next to his.

"Brant told Natasha's family I would be more comfortable if another woman was in our teepee," says Viola. "I don't want to look like a hoe sleeping with two men."

Janic laughs. "Whose Natasha, and haven't you already done that: sleep with two men?"

Viola scoffs. "She deserves a name."

Viola knows Janic means both of her brothers. She jumps up, grabs, and throws an empty pot at him with her good arm.

The pot hits Janic on his elbow. He lunges at her and effortlessly lifts her, tickling her sides.

"Watch my arm. I'm going to pee my pants, please, please stop—JANIC!"

"Not until you say, Uncle, Tiny One."

"UNCLE UNCLE UNCLE!" she yells.

He sets her down, then side-swats her ass with his hand towel. They all laugh.

"Now I have to pee," says Viola.

"Take Lady V to pee, will you, Janic?" Brant says with a broad smile.

Viola huffs. "Call me that again, and I'll throw more than a pot at you, Jacko." Viola bites her bottom lip, so she doesn't laugh out loud at the shocked expression on Brant's face.

"Outside, Tiny One," Janic says, pointing. "You have miles of land to choose from. Pick a direction, and away you go."

"Fine, give me your phone. I need a light so I can see." Janic pulls his mobile phone out of his pants pocket. He is about to hand it to her, then jerks his body around and examines the space. He grabs a flashlight and hands it to her instead.

"Why would I need a flashlight this big?"

He shrugs.

She whispers under her breath, "Disrespecting the beaver."

"My phone screen isn't bright enough for this type of dark. Uh, what's a beaver?"

"Oh, um." She looks at Brant.

"It's her fanny," says Brant.

"What's a fanny?" asks Janic.

"Fanny sounds like someone's backside, not a birdie," Viola says.

"What's a birdie?" asks Janic.

"Can we stick a pin in it? I have to go to the bathroom," Viola says. "Earlier, I heard you two talking about wolves, so one of you needs to come with me."

"Seriously, Viola," says Brant, "you openly pick a fight with Patrick, who will kill you, yet you're afraid to tinkle in the dark?"

Viola saw the change in Janic's face when Brant said "kill."

"Fine, Brant, be a Prat. Janic will protect me and help by carrying the flashlight." She tosses it back to Janic. "I can't use this arm one hundred percent yet, and he's a gentleman—not in the bathhouse, mind you, but outside of it, most definitely."

"Duly noted," Brant says sarcastically. "I'm not teaching you any more British slang if you continue to use it against me."

Janic stands. He twirls the flashlight with his big fingers. He grabs tissues and hands them to Viola.

Viola holds up the tissues.

"What did I say, Brant? A gentleman."

"Fine, Janic wins. He's the crowned King of the loo palace! He's top-drawer."

"Thanks, *priyatel* (mate)," Janic says. "I'm feeling good right now. Let's go, Tiny One."

-..Chapter 42-. .-

Janic dances around, singing a Russian song off-key and far too loud as he flashes the light on and off, then back to her, keeping her laughing.

On their way back to the teepee, she jumps up on his back, using her good arm to hold on. She sticks her other hand over his mouth to playfully shut him up. He sucks her fingers into his mouth, surprising and grossing her out.

"Have you always been a horrible singer and so open with bodily fluids, Janic?" she asks while sliding off his back.

"Yes." They both laugh. "How are you, Tiny One?"

"I'm pregnant." She giggles. "But I like being pregnant. It's a gift to carry a miracle, a life inside that will become a big boy someday—like you."

He slows, then stops. He lifts the flashlight to see their faces.

"Janic, I'm sorry I mentioned the baby. How clueless of me after your Lady B died."

"Please tell me, Viola, why they killed Lady B."

"They didn't, Janic. You were raised to only be with your sisters because we have unique blood."

"What do you mean?"

"I need you to swear that this does not leave this spot. I'm only telling you out of care for your hurt feelings about Lady B."

He raises his right hand. "Я присягнул" (I have sworn.)

She waits for his eyes to meet hers, then says, "I'm not sure when, but long ago our family realized we could only have children with our bloodline. If you impregnate someone or if I get pregnant with a man who does not have my blood, the woman and child die every time."

Janic drops the flashlight. "Ni v koyem sluchaye to pravda?" he says under his breath as he bends to pick it up.

Viola reaches for his hand to move the flashlight so he can view her face.

"What did you say, Janic?"

"I said, no way—Is that the truth? Why—why don't they tell us that?"

"I can't say, Janic. I wanted out after I met my brothers. I wanted to love freely. Thank goodness I didn't, or I'd already be dead."

"Do you love Jason?"

"Completely. Not my brother Zack as much. That was hard for me at first, being with him. I got used to it. I love him too."

"I felt the same with my sister. I love her, but, uh, not how I'd like to love someone."

"Like the way you loved Lady B?"

"How'd you know?"

"Your eyes," she says. "They were so sad when Brant told you that she had died. It's not your fault. You had no idea. Why don't you consider asking to be with another cousin? I've heard that it often happens when a spouse dies. Don't think you cannot love someone else in the family like you loved your Lady B. Time and care for each other will create that lasting love. Jason has shown me that by being himself."

"You're lucky."

"Am I?"

"Why don't you think so, Tiny One?"

"Because unhappy people hurt happy people. It's been that way since the beginning of time, Janic. Jealous, envious feelings make them hateful and vengeful. They live to wound happy people with slanderous words or actions."

"You're talking about Patrick, aren't you?"

"What do you think?"

"He wants to have it all at any cost," says Janic.

"Don't you think he's lucky? He has four children with Carly, but look at him! He wants more. What's more going to get him? He'll lose her. He already has. She knows he's bad. His actions have changed her heart. You win a heart, Janic, by being a good man. Otherwise, you are lost to yourself—your tree rots. Each leaf spreads disease to the branches, and soon one strong wind will split it in two. It dies—but don't forget that its roots are still connected to the tree next to it. Now that tree feels alone, all because you were greedy." She pauses.

I hope he's hearing me.

"We'd better head back," he says, "or Brant might think you're taking advantage of me."

"In your dreams, *ocharovatel'nyy prints*," she calls out in Russian and continues walking.

He's another Zack, almost.

Janic taps her shoulder. She turns. He lifts the flashlight to his face.

"You speak Russian, Tiny One?" he asks, his tone serious.

Shoot!

"I understand a few words, Janic. Zack, my brother, sometimes spoke Russian—mostly swear words. I call him my dark prince. He always corrects me, telling me he's my 'Prince Charming,' my 'ocharovatel'nyy prints.' That's how I know these two words."

"Thank you, Viola. Thank you for telling me the truth."

"We all deserve the truth, Janic."

-..Chapter 43-. .-

Brant wakes Viola the following morning.

"What is it?" she whispers.

"Trucks. In the distance. Get dressed."

"Oh, no!"

"Viola, it's important that you don't get philosophical. It won't work on these men. I know you've acquired your knowledge in many psychological and biotech fields, as have I. But know-hows are more important than knowledge. Are you with me?"

She nods. "Street smarts outweigh book smarts in this army."

"Aye. Spot on!" Brant says.

Viola hurries to get dressed. She shakes Janic awake. He rolls over.

"Good morning, Tiny One," he says.

"Janic, trucks are coming."

"What!"

"I know you're with Patrick." His shocked expression makes her sad. "It's okay. We all pick a side. Please don't let him kill Jason. It will ruin this family. Jason can make things right again."

"You could, too, Viola."

"I can't, not without Jason by my side. I need him." He nods. "Janic, I need you to do the right thing today."

She stands up. Brant hands her a sizable over-the-shoulder bag.

"What's all of this, Brant?" she asks.

"Water, snacks, things you'll need for the baby inside you. It's a long trek back to the Complex. That's where we're going. Don't run. Don't fight Viola."

Oh no! He's taking care of me. He thinks they're going to kill him!

"Where's your phone, Brant?"

"Hidden under some serious smelly doo doo," he whispers cross-eyed, jokingly. The curve of his shoulders reveals his true feelings inside.

———

Outside, they wait anxiously as three large army trucks pull up. Soldiers jump out of the first truck and line up in formation. The nomads stay in their teepees. Minutes before the trucks pulled up, Brant ran to warn them to stay inside. Natasha comes out of their teepee. She stands next to Janic. He tries to tell her to go, but she doesn't understand. Brant knows he's too late to ask her to hide in her native tongue.

The four of them wait, ready to be taken as prisoners, as men jump out of the other trucks. Janic raises his arms in the air. Three men have visible strips on their uniforms.

Brant leans over to Viola.

"The tall one is Leo, who is second in command. The redhead is Anton. He's an asshole. The fancy-looking, pretty one is Bogdan. He goes by BG. He's Patrick's bad ass MoFo chief cadet."

"Good to know," she says.

The soldiers raise their guns, aiming at the trio, not including Janic.

"Brant, I'm surprised you're a traitor," says Bogden. "Who knew—and your brother at that?"

"BG, you tosser, you, I wasn't raised to disrespect, let alone murder a pregnant woman simply because I was hungry for a title of power I didn't deserve to have."

"Nice. Your brother will love to hear those words from your mouth—if you have a tongue left to speak them."

"Janic, well, well, what do we have here?" says the redhead. "You brought us a present."

Janic chuckles. "Lady, meet the Ant—Anton meet Lady. I hope we can drop her back at the bathhouse on our way, as I promised."

"Patrick was wondering why you gave him the wrong coordinates," Anton says to Janic.

"It seems as though Brant found me out. He led you on a wild goose chase. No worries. You found us."

"Not without casualties," says Anton. "That's extra work for us. I didn't appreciate it, Janic."

"Everyone up against the truck—not you, Janic," says BG.

The three of them move to the back of the last truck. Janic follows. The tall soldier, Leo, pats Brant down, checking his bag before moving on to Lady.

BG kicks Viola's legs further apart than they already are. He stands close behind her, his breath on the back of her neck.

"God, you smell good. I can see why Jason loves to tap this ass. What I wouldn't give to shove my dick in there," he says.

Janic snorts. "Bogdan, she's pregnant. Chill."

"Fuck off, Janic. I'm the boss out here." He touches Viola's back between her shoulder blades. His fingers follow her bra straps; they graze the skin under her ribcage. His hands move up. They cover both of her breasts.

"No weapons in here. Wait. Maybe," he says.

Viola's eyes close as he continues his search down her stomach.

"I feel the bump. A baby Jay, I bet."

His hands move to her hips. Then he grips her bottom cheeks.

"My god, you're perfection, that lucky son of a bitch. Why can't my sister look like you?"

She hears a few chuckles from the group. He takes his right hand and moves it to the front of her pants. His right-hand moves to cover her vagina. His left-hand pops the button on her pants.

Janic takes a giant step forward and punches BG in the temple, knocking him out cold.

Anton strikes Janic in his back with his gun, and Janic turns to punch him.

Leo steps in, holding his weapon between their faces.

"J-Ant, STOP! This is wrong. This is not going to happen, not here. Anton, back the fuck up, or I'll shoot you. BG was way out of line. I was about to kick his teeth in myself. We don't do this stuff, not to family. Henrik and Lause, pick up BG and put him in the front truck."

"Janic, man, you've gone and fucked yourself," says Anton.

"I don't think so, Ant, this isn't who we are. I'd slit anyone's throat who touched my sister's ass, let alone her breast and *pizda* (cunt*)*. You're a fucking piece of *der'mo* (shit)."

"Enough," Leo says. "Let's get on the road. We need to get back to the Complex before it's too late. It's going to be cold tonight."

"Leo, have someone bring that truck." Janic throws him the keys without taking his green eyes off Anton's. "It has extra petrol and tires."

"Good, we might need them," says Leo. "Hanley, you drive the last truck."

"Yes, sir."

"Ant, you drive with Hanley and cool the fuck down."

"Yes, sir."

"Miss, I'm sorry for BG," says Leo. "Not every soldier here is that disrespectful. Please accept my apologies. Please hop in the front of the middle truck. Janic can drive."

"Yes, sir," Janic says.

Viola walks past Anton, staring straight ahead.

He grunts. Then, without warning, a gush from a gunshot blows past.

Viola reaches for her ear. She's shocked when Natasha's feet lift off the ground like she's at a track and field meet, going for the gold in the long jump.

Anton shot her in the back of the head. Anton's gun is now pointed at Janic's face.

Janic is visibly pissed. Brant's shaking his head.

"Janic, I'll assume she has your seed in her. We can't have that now, can we? Oi, that's breaking the law."

"*Ty chertov Mudak* (You're a fucking asshole), Ant," Janic says, fearless despite Anton's semi-automatic rifle shoved in his face.

Leo whistles. "Ant, pick that dead woman up, put her in the back with Brant, then get the fuck in the truck, or on my order, everyone here will shoot you. Understood?"

"YES, SIR!" the group shouts in unison.

Anton walks away with a sneer on his face. He bends down to pick up the dead lady, and the soldier next to him drops to the ground.

The old white-haired nomad woman who gave Viola herbs and showed her how they make medicines stands in the open, with a second bow and arrow aimed at Anton.

Viola memorized the benefits of a rare plant species, *Hedysarum Theinum*. She gave Viola a small dish with dirt and seeds.

Brant steps in front of Anton. He calls out to the woman with his arms out. She speaks in her native tongue.

"Soldiers, hold your fire," says Leo. Clicks are heard. "What did she say, Brant?"

"She said that the dead lady must stay."

The old woman drops to the ground. Everyone's safety's click off, their rifles are aimed to shoot. Viola is confused. No shots were heard.

"What happened to her...Sniper?" asks Brant.

"Klaus put Dyson's body in the truck. Henrik put the dead lady next to the old woman, now. We need to get out of here." Leo says, looking around at miles of flat, barren land.

Brant stands over the old woman on the ground.

"Leave her. They'll collect them once we go," says Leo, scanning every direction.

All the soldiers mimic Leo, looking around. Their rifles shifting side to side, ready to shoot at an invisible threat.

Brant kneels, shutting the old woman's eyelids with his fingers. When Anton starts to walk, the men do as they were told, all guns are pointed at Anton until he's in the last truck.

Henrik moves Natasha's dead body next to the old woman, then slowly backs away. Brant prays as everyone watches, then he stands and wipes a tear as he heads to the back of the last truck.

Janic helps Viola step up into the middle truck, then shuts her door. He gets in the driver's seat. The soldiers move to the various vehicles with caution, and each truck, in order, one by one, turns around and heads back in the direction they came from.

-..Chapter 44-. .-

No matter how hard she tries, Viola can't stop her tears. Witnessing the murders of two innocent women fills her with shame. Using her hands, she wipes the crotch of her pants in haste, wanting to erase BG's hands that violated her sacred space, which is meant for love, to birth new life.

Janic's face is beet red.

"Janic, thank you. I'm sorry about Natasha."

"Viola, my apologies. I should have stepped in sooner. I—I shouldn't have brought a prostitute with us. We could have stayed with any of these nomads without her. It wouldn't be the first time. Me and my dick got her killed."

"It's not your fault. It's the domino effect. They won't stop until something terrible happens.

"I don't understand."

"President Eisenhower tried to warn the world during the Cold War that if one nation fell to communism, neighboring nations would follow, and it's still happening. Weak leaders like Patrick use their army to do the dirty work because people who hate... who are hurt, they hurt other people," she says.

"Then I blame Patrick for her death." He says.

"It didn't start with him, Janic. It's generational. Someone or something poisoned his brain. It only stops when individuals choose love over evil. We're lucky that Leo is a decent person."

"He is. But like all of us, we do bad things, Viola. We know Patrick isn't a great leader. We get away with a lot. Everyone is on their best behavior when Jason's around. He demands it, which is why many guys hate him."

"Do you?"

"No. I don't. I go along with the chitty chat bred *sivoy kobyly* (bull shit.)."

"To fit in?" she asks.

"*Da*. (Yes)

Patrick's mom said he will rape me."

"Why would he do that?"

"He wants a war with Jason. He wants the respect some of these guys have for Jason. His mom told me he'll probably keep me here, and once I have the baby, he'll get me pregnant to have my heir."

"I can't imagine the men going along with that, Viola."

"You saw what happened today. Only you stood up for me. How can anyone know what will happen to me in the Complex? Patrick will keep me in a room. Everyone will turn a blind eye, like people everywhere already do. We watch terrible things happening in the news to other people, and we're thankful it's not us. I care about people. I care about people in our family, Janic. So does Jason. Hateful people like Patrick only care about themselves. Just think: You might not even live after today because you stopped BG from sexually assaulting me."

"He's part animal, that one. I don't know why everyone fears him."

"Fear changes us into people who pretend the real stuff isn't real," says Viola. "It's none of our business, right? But what happens when it's happening to you? You'd hope someone would be good enough to do the right thing, to do something. We all know how to do the right thing. It's something that doesn't need to be taught. Even the nomads understand. That old woman died trying to protect us. She knew who she was. What BG did was wrong. What Anton did was wrong. Patrick will probably give him a medal if he has any at the Complex."

Janic's face is flush. "Why did Brant protect Anton? He should've let her shoot her arrow."

"Brant was protecting her. A bullet's faster than an arrow."

Viola watches Janic's body tense.

"One day at a time, Janic. Please don't get yourself killed because of me. You can be smart and do the right thing when the time comes. You know enough of the good guys. People like Leo can make others listen. He has respect. One or two of them on your side could change what's going to happen next. I'm guessing I'll either be dead or locked in a room—probably Patrick's room."

Janic's hands grip the steering wheel. "*Ya by ubil yego.*" (I would kill him).

Viola hates that she's manipulating him.

Patrick will rape me. I know it as soon as I'm through the gate. I want my baby to live. I want Jason to live. He's good. He's better than me. He deserves to live.

Viola has never met a man like Jason before, with his integrity, his character, his morals. She heard him at night when he whispered his prayers like her best friend Jes did. Viola meditates to align her good so it can shine. She needs to be smart. She needs to take the advice she's giving Janic. She closes her eyes.

Patrick is no leader. When she thinks about it, neither are the uncles—the ones she's met, anyway. They all let things slide. She recalls reading a wise man's words about war. He said all war was madness, a disease. He said a man who leads other men into war, into mass suicide, is no different than a man who walks into a place and shoots bullets into strangers. They're the same. Neither serves any purpose aside from not facing what word or action broke their joy as a child.

Who stepped inside their lines?

Viola's mother told her how an injured boy or girl can grow to be vindictive, and it's not always a mental illness that drives someone to kill. The hurt child who grows up in violence sometimes doesn't realize they need to seek help to change their learned behavior.

What happened to Patrick as a boy?

Viola wishes she was in Brant's truck. He's thoughtful and an emotionally sound person. He's who the uncles should have put in charge of the Complex.

Brant is good through and through.

Her head turns away. She smiles for a split second, thinking of Brant shaking the dew off his willy while he watched her in the animal trough, having her wet dream bath. Then with a wave, dropping her white sock on the ground, like he was giving her his white flag of surrender.

Oh, life!

-..Chapter 45-. .-

It's pitch black when Janic wakes her. Goosebumps are visible on her arms. The loud sound of the heat vent blowing on high, rattles a stainless-steel water canister in the truck. Janic hops out as Viola sits up. Only the hue of rear taillights on a truck up ahead can be seen.

"Sorry to wake you, Tiny One. The last truck—the one Brant's in—blew a tire. Leo radioed. We've stopped to change it. I'm going to grab Brant to keep you company. Don't do anything stupid. We're in the middle of nowhere. Lock the doors, and I'll tell him to knock three times, *ladno*?"

"OK, "she says.

Viola wonders what level of crime has to be committed for someone in this family to go to prison. How many murders did her father get away with? What about 'the Box' at the Complex? How long do they keep someone in there?

Such a mindfuck!

Viola can't explain why, but she's not afraid even if she should be. Mom telling her to face her fears a gazillion times has finally hit home.

I refuse to hate. Good, stay with me.

Three knocks startle Viola. She leans over, unlocks the door, relieved to see Brant climbing in.

"Viola, are you alright?"

"Yes, are you, Brant? I can't believe Anton shot Natasha!"

"I'm surprised too. I wouldn't expect that from him, but like attracts like. The longer these soldiers stay at this post, the more they fold into the BS. Bogdan is a total yes man, brown noser, nutter, all up in my brother's arse. That's why he's Patrick's main guy."

"Aren't you his second in command?"

"No. I'm in training for his position when he moves on."

"Where does he go from here?"

"He becomes Uncle when Uncle dies," says Brant.

"Leo seems like a decent soldier."

"Leo is the best. Patrick worries that he's brighter than him, so he keeps him below the ranks but high enough to help them make smart decisions when they need to be made."

"It's crazy how these insecure men secure the top spots."

"Sadly, the people who put them there are too embarrassed to admit they were wrong in the first place."

"Why did Jason put Patrick in his seat?"

"Viola, I didn't mean Jason. I was thinking of my father."

"It's okay. Jason's not that old, Brant. I don't expect any of us to be able to see through every fake friend in our twenties."

"Certain people with a particular personality become incredible liars," he says.

Making Viola think of her dad when they first met. She believed every word he fed her. She *wanted* to believe him so badly.

"Jason is a General. He only declined to rule when he's here. The Uncles are who voted. Then Patrick got the spot," Brant says. "Jason didn't put him here."

"Who was the deciding vote?"

"That's a great question. I'm sure my father chose Patrick. I'm sure he regrets it."

"Why are some of the men in this family so cutthroat? I thought you were conditioned from birth to be good and do good."

"I'll loan you my books on personality types that will blow your mind if we get out of this alive."

"I'd love that." She smiles. "Do you think we'll make it?"

"Never can tell. No use crying over spilled milk."

"What milk are we talking about, Brant? If it's reindeer milk, I'm sorry, I might accidentally spill that yuck. It's worse than glue."

"Oh, and you've tasted glue?"

"I have."

"Of course you did. That's gross, Viola. For reals."

She smiles for a second, then she puts on a serious face.

"I'm sorry about your mom, Brant."

"Thank you. She was a great mum growing up. Dad never loved her like she needed him to. My mum took the low road. We all knew he cheated on her. It's true what you said before: Patrick follows my father's ways, and my father knows I've no respect for him."

"I'm sorry, Brant. Maybe your dad wouldn't have become the way he is if he could have been with his other sister. Our laws make for bitter hearts. Who determines who you end up with?"

"The hierarchy."

"Do you think your dad knows what Patrick's been up to?"

"I don't know, Carly said Patrick planned all of this with my mum."

"Your mom told me the same thing."

"Carly's been through a lot, Viola."

"I'd say a lot of us have."

"She, more than the rest of us in my line."

Viola can see the sadness in Brant's eyes.

"Jeffrey seems to be right up there with her," says Viola.

"My father acts like Jeffrey doesn't exist."

"Why? What is so terrible that he shuns his child?"

"It's private, Viola."

"Do you wish you were with Mary?"

"Only all the time. And you?"

"I wish I were with Jason, too, and my baby—I'm trying not to think about it. We can't change a whole heck of a lot at the moment, now, can we? Hey, lock your door, Brant. We don't need the two stooges finding us without Leo nearby."

Brant locks it, then turns to face her.

"In the back of the truck, I was thinking about how the family is split right now. We will be split again once we're back at the Complex, and I think it will keep splitting, Viola, until one side wins."

"It's like the fall of the two trees all over again."

"It seems to happen lifetime after lifetime." Says Brant.

"How can we make these guys listen? How come they forget when the bad snake won, we all lost?"

"Do you think your bosom is enough to fix this, Viola?"

"No. Man will have to figure it out himself or not."

"That's what I'm thinking, too. Here. Put this in your bag." Brant pulls something from his pocket and hands it to her.

"What is it?" She tucks it away.

"A poison dart, I assume," he says." I pulled it from the woman's chest. Did you see anyone move before she fell?"

"No."

"Me neither."

"So, it wasn't a sniper. What do you think this is, Brant?"

"It's curare from the Amazon," Brant says.

"Do we have family there?"

"Mum said we do: an Uncle Samuel, the oldest brother. He's lived there since he was a teenager. She said he has nothing to do with the family, so we're unsure why we keep finding these. This is the third curare dart used since you arrived."

"Are you serious?"

"Yes, ma'am. Did your mum ever mention the family over there?"

"Brant, I had no idea this family existed until after she died. I didn't know I had brothers. I thought I was an only child."

Two knocks sound on Brant's door.

-..Chapter 46-. .-

Brant squints out his window, trying to see through the pitch black.

"It's hard to tell who it is," he says.

"Janic said three knocks," she whispers.

There are five more knocks, harder this time. Brant tries to roll the window down—he forgot they don't roll down, not here.

Viola opens her door, pops her head out. "Who is it?"

"It's Leo. Open the door. That's an order!"

Viola closes her door, locking it.

"I'm not sure that it's Leo, Brant."

Brant looks over at her.

"It's BG."

"Do you think he'll leave us out in the cold?"

"Not you. We'll have to open it. I worry he'll have you before you return to the Complex."

"What if he killed Janic?"

"Eventually, I'll have to open this door. We can't stay here forever, can we?"

Five more hard knocks bring fear to Brant's face—a first, since she's met him.

"Must we open it?" Viola asks.

Brant looks around the truck cabin. "The windows are bullet-proof. He can't shoot us in the head unless we open the door. He can disable the truck. We'll be stuck here. I wonder if he killed Leo." He shakes his head, staring at the truck directly in front of them, blocking their way.

"Wouldn't the other men take him out for doing that?"

"No. Everyone's afraid of BG. He's an odd duck."

"How odd?"

"No need for detail, Viola. Trust me."

"Shit, shit, shit," she says under her breath.

They hear a high-pitched sound. Brant peers into the darkness, lifting himself out of his seat to gaze at the ground beside his door.

"I think he's been shot."

"Do you think he's faking so you'll open the door?"

"You're one smart Lady V." She gives him a dirty look for using that nickname. "I didn't think of that, Viola. I'm not sure he's smart enough to think of that."

"Let's wait, Brant."

They wait, with Brant continually glancing at his watch.

"It's quiet out there," he says. "I don't hear any voices."

"What do you think's going on, Brant?"

"I wish I knew Viola. It's nerve-wracking."

Tap Tap

Tap Tap Tap

Tap Tap

Recognizing the knock, she opens her door. A man with broad shoulders climbs up, sticking his head in the cab. His ice-blue eyes twinkle under his black balaclava knitted ski mask, which he pulls from his face.

"Hi," she says.

"Hi, Jason sent me. I'm Jeffrey. You must be Viola?" He looks past her. "Little brother, I see you're on this side of the dirt."

"Did you kill everyone?" asks Brant.

"No," says Jeffrey. "They're all taking a wee nappy-poo."

"Where's Patrick?" asks Viola.

"He's locked up for the moment. We're not sure who is on whose side. We'll uncover it soon enough. I've got to load a few of these men into the trucks so they don't freeze. Then I'll come back. We'll leave together. Jason asked how his peanut was doing in the shell."

"His peanut is happy you've arrived," says Viola.

"BG was about to rape her," Brant adds."Bogdan sexually assaulted her in front of everyone."

Jeffrey looks at Viola. "What did Bogdan do?"

"A pat down, that's all," Viola says, looking straight ahead.

"He was rubbing her bottom, bobbies, and... her fanny. He was talking filthy," Brant adds. "Anton was as bad. He killed an innocent. A Nomad. Two nomads were killed."

Jeffrey pauses. He searches Viola's face. He pops his knuckles.

"Leave the keys in here for Janic for after he wakes up. We'll leave in Leo's front truck and take him with us. I think he'll be on our side—hard to know. Give me twenty, lock the doors." Jeffrey pulls the ski mask over his face, he jumps out and shuts her door.

Viola locks it. She and Brant do a happy dance in their seats, then he peers out of his window.

"Ah, shoot. Poor bugger," he says sarcastically.

"What is it?" she asks.

"Jeffrey is finishing BG off, I'd say."

"What do you mean?"

"Stay in your seat, Viola. Jeffrey's demonstrating for the rest of the men to see what happens to anyone who inappropriately touches a woman."

"Oh no, did he shoot him?"

"That would be too easy for Jeff. From the looks of it—" he says, squinting. "Ah... BG no longer has hands. He's being nice, in any case. Jeff's shoving them back into BG's pockets for him. To keep them warm, I'd guess."

"I don't like this violence."

"Neither do I, but that's Jeff for you. He's doggy."

———

Twenty minutes later, Jeffrey stands in front of the truck lights, using his finger, he tells Viola and Brant to exit the vehicle. After Viola hops out, Jeffrey wraps a deerskin around her shoulders. He has Brant help him move a few tires from the back vehicle, along with one of the petrol bins, onto the front truck.

Viola glimpses Jeffrey carrying a knocked-out Leo, putting him in the back of their truck. Brant jumps in the back of the truck with Leo.

Jeffrey comes to her side, opening the door for Viola to get into the truck's front cabin, then he jumps into the driver's side, tapping the parking brake off with the heel of his boot.

"Do we have to go to the Complex? Can we go to the airport? Can we leave this place?"

"Not possible," says Jeffery. "We can't leave with the soldiers divided."

"Are we safe to talk in here?"

He lifts a device from under the seat.

"Yes, this Betsy finds such gadgets. I was in this truck the whole time."

Viola shifts to view the space under two jump seats. Jeffrey's army outfit is sweaty, no doubt from loading soldiers and the barrels back onto the trucks with Brant.

"What if you had to pee?"

"Does that matter right now, Lass?" Jeffrey asks with a smirk.

"No," she answers. "Sorry, pregnancy makes a woman think about such things and often. Can we kill Patrick and be done with this?"

"Jason hasn't approved his removal."

"Keeping him alive is like believing the *Titanic* can't possibly sink," she says.

He chuckles.

"Will BG die from his injuries?" she asks.

"Yes, and that will show the men what they can expect before arriving at the Complex. It'll give them time to decide whether they want to join BG's cause. I hope not, but one can never tell until the hammer drops."

"Shouldn't you have waited… to kill him? Aren't we taught only to kill if it's in self-defense?"

"I've watched BG kill many innocent people—and children," he says without looking at her. "No self-defense was involved. If things don't work in our favor, BG would have raped and killed you. He was explicit about the details when he woke up in the truck. My arse of a brother didn't want you brought back," he says, glancing at Viola. "BG ordered Leo to wait in the truck. I knew Leo wasn't going to wait. It was about to be a bloodbath—one I'd rather not clean up out here in no man's land. I'm fine with getting rid of a rotten apple before a swarm of fleas joins the feast to spread disease. Are you all right?"

"I am now."

"Your arm?" he asks, looking at her face for an extra beat.

Standing next to Jeffrey earlier outside the truck made Viola feel like a child. He's a foot taller than Brant. Viola thought Jason was built. Jeffrey's body looks like a carbon copy of a professional wrestler sitting next to her. His face does too.

"I'm fine," she says. "It's healing. Was it Patrick who shot me?"

"We found the weapon under a floorboard in his suite. Carly told us where we might look."

"Is she okay?"

"She is. She will do the right thing. Father raised her right. It was Mum who got Patrick's head all twisted."

"I'm not so sure. Your mom loved you so much. After all, she only kidnapped me to save you. Patrick lied. He killed her to hide his lies. I don't think your dad is as honest as he lets on."

"What makes you say that?"

"A gut feeling. Anyway, Patrick wants to be the top dog. Your mom wanted to stop him. She said he went too far."

"Yes, it's all coming out of the woodwork."

"Is Doc aware of everything?" she asks.

"I think so."

"Where's Zack?"

"In America, holding down the fort. Best if you catch a kip, Lass. It'll be a long night. You're safe."

Viola closes her eyes. Hearing Jeffrey say those last two words reminds her of when Derek once said them to her. She's grateful some good men are still alive in the world—more than she was beginning to think existed.

Jason, where are you?

———————

The truck stops. She yawns.

"I need to speak with Leo," says Jeffrey. "I'll be back."

"Are we getting close?" she asks.

"Yes, it's only a few miles away. For the moment, Patrick is in lockdown as a traitor, but he still has followers inside. I'll need you to stay by my side until we get things sorted, and I can safely take you to the airport."

-..Chapter 47-..-

In the Complex, Viola trembles as she floats down the hall beside Jeffrey. She's had a terrible guilty feeling in the pit of her stomach, a premonition that she would be killed here, or Jason would be killed in an attempt to save her.

Jeffrey does Viola's childhood signature knock, and the door to the command room opens. He ushers Viola in. He shuts it. She looks around the room. There's one person inside.

Her eyes meet Jason's. They stare at one another. She falls into his arms. His mouth is on hers. Both of their hands are touching each other everywhere as if they don't believe the other is real. Another knock on the door. She doesn't want to let go. Her hands cup his scruffy face.

Another rap at the door, louder this time, and Jason pulls back.

"I need to open it, luv, stay in here."

When he opens the door, Jeffrey, Leo, and ten other men march into the command room. Viola listens as they discuss their next steps to set up discussions with other Complex soldiers before the cavalry comes. They hope to imprison Patrick's followers and relax the situation by reinstating a new chief cadet. Jason asks Leo to take the lead.

Leo accepts as long as Jason stays at the Complex long enough for the transition to take place.

Garrett is flying to the Complex to take over for Patrick, with Brant by his side. In the morning, they'll transport Patrick on a plane to a jail cell.

Viola sits in a corner of the sweaty, testosterone-filled command room, amazed by Jason, watching and listening. She eyeballs each man present, trying to catch a vibe of who might *not* be on Jason's side—impossible to know. She notes one brut of a man's eyes squint, as he feigns interest in a map behind her.

When Viola lived with Zack, she read John Gray's book *Men Are from Mars, Women Are from Venus*. She disagreed with many parts of it. Who could agree with it when you're with Zack? She thinks back when Zack grabbed the book from her hands.

"You think I'm a fucking Martian... from Mars?"
"I was thinking more along the lines of Jupiter, Zack."
"I like youranus."
"Do you mean Uranus?"
Zack laughed louder than he ever had before.
"Your a vulgar, disgusting, pig, Zack."
"I love being your pig, Princess."
Zack tossed the book on the coffee table. Viola leaned over to pick it up. She didn't bother explaining why she said Jupiter. She was thinking of Jupiter's gravitational field being two point five times more intense than Earth's, attracting a lot of impacts, like Zack's big personality, having a strong pull on women who were unaware.

The men around Jason get to their feet and follow Leo out. When everyone is out of the room, Jason nonchalantly walks to the door, shuts it, and locks it.

"Are we safe?" she asks.

"For the moment. Come here."

She walks toward him. He lifts her arms and takes her top off in one movement.

"What are you doing? Aren't their cameras in here?"

"No."

He undoes her bra. She lets it fall to the ground. Smiling, she stands still, allowing him to seduce her.

"Can't you wait 'til we're in a room?" she asks with a grin on her face as he bends down to remove her shoes, then her pants and underwear.

"We're in a room," he says, looking up at her with a mischievous sneer.

"Maybe a room with a bed?" she adds, touching his curly hair. It's grown out quite a bit. She likes it.

He stands, to caresses the skin around her injured arm. He steps back to look into her eyes.

"I won't be able to leave this command room for another day. You will leave in the morning. It's now or nothing, my luv."

Her insides are a mess. He's waiting for her approval. How can she say no? Jeffrey telling her that BG was sent to rape and kill her. She keeps having visions of him doing it—her guilt of leaving Zee behind to fend for himself. She's grateful for Jason coming for her, risking his life. She wants to let it all go. She makes her decision. Leaning in, her lips brush against Jason's.

His fingers reach for her hair, he pulls her to him, owning her mouth, and like two kids behind the school, making out passionately, hoping no one will come around the corner. She senses that he's waiting for her to make the next move.

When she pulls his shirt over his head, his smile brings tears to her eyes. Her mouth lands on his warm skin. She kisses his neck, his shoulder, she sucks the crease of his armpit. She hears him moan. She wishes she was anywhere but in Siberia, in this complex, in this family.

His signature smell fills her senses. She breathes him in, her fingers drape down each of his stomach muscles to his pants. In two moves, they're around his ankles, and she grips him in her hand. A sharp tingle hits below. She wants her hero's love to be her cure, to show her how to let go of the madness of being hunted by evil poachers who've chosen to follow a lost ringleader's command—like she's a rare animal, close to extinction, that they can hang up in a rec room in a make-believe victory. Her head falls back. She gasps for air as Jason's body presses against hers, his hard length slides back and forth along her wet opening, taunting her. She digs her nails into his back. She needs to find release.

Jason backs her body into the wall behind her. She jumps up so he can move himself into her. In the same moment, his mouth covers her nipple, circling, sucking, blowing, licking, driving her insane. She shrills—inhales, closing her eyes, making her fantasies real, thinking about Derek's tongue first circling, watching Jason's mouth on her. Her eyes shoot open as she explodes, panting like a puppy after a short run.

Jason's arm wraps tightly around her waist. He lifts her higher, the veins in his neck straining almost as much as his manhood. She can't hear anything. She shuts herself off. Viola stares at the wall in front of her. Her legs lift to wrap higher around his hips. His breathing heavy. She can feel the sun shining on her face.

She's transported back to their time at the cottage, in the forest.

The dirt and rocks rub against her bare backside on the ground, in pain, and pleasure. The shake of his thumb back and forth on her nub, his hot mouth on her right breast, torturing her with orgasm after orgasm, filling her hard, fast, then slow, angles hitting nerves inside, making every tiny hair on her body zing to attention.

In the command room at the Complex, she looks into his eyes, wanting to be present for him. In this cold concrete space, far away from everyone she knows. She's never felt this conflicted.

"Jason—"

Viola pulls his hair as his body goes stiff, and the sound of his release fills the room. Their naked, slick bodies fitted against each other. With their eyes open, he kisses her lips, their words unspoken, their sweaty bodies swept away by animalistic needs and her relief that he's alive.

-..Chapter 48-. .-

Viola rearranges the last of her clothes. Jason moves in behind her and kisses the back of her neck, sending chill bumps up her arms through the top hairs on her head. She turns around, bringing her lips to his. She kisses him the same way he kissed her before she left him in his Ford truck to fly to London. Three soft lip-taps. She rubs her hands over his arms that are around her waist. She drags her fingers down the front of his concealed washboard stomach to his pants. She gives his semi-hard spent dick in his pants a sassy tug, and zips up his zipper, making him chuckle.

"Now, that, Jason Stanton, would have made you the laughing-stock of this family." He gives her bottom an unexpected pinch, making her jump and giggle.

"I have Uncle's ashes," he says. "We'll spread them together once this is over."

"Is he fake-dead?"

Please say yes.

"It's real. I'm sorry, luv. I had suspected something was off with Patrick, but not soon enough. I'm blown away. I would never have expected anything like this from him. We have Uncle Mark safe. We believe a hit was out on him. Zack hid Doc."

"What about you?"

"Oh, the hit on me has been on for a few years—old news."

"When will it stop?"

"When it stops. I don't have a better answer. I'm following the strings."

"What does that mean?"

"I put up a board with names, places, and dates. I tack up strings until I uncover the center."

"Did you figure out who's in the center?"

"Yes, for the most part."

"When you take them out, do we return to normal?"

"It's not that easy, luv. It's how I take it down. It went up, string by string. It needs to be taken down, string by string. I can't leave loose ends, do you understand?"

"Clear as mud," she says with a fake smile, hoping to pause the seriousness of their situation.

"I love you so much, Viola," he says, brushing a hair from her cheek.

"I love you, too."

His hand slides until it rests on her tummy. He searches her eyes.

"If something happens to me—"

"I don't want to hear that," she interrupts.

"Viola, if anyething happens to me, Zack will take care of you. Don't run away, promise me."

"Nothing is happening to you. It can't."

"It can. I can't take out an entire Complex full of men who want me dead or are unsure. I'll have you taken to the airport soon. You'll go to Doc until I clean up here."

"Come with me, Jason. Let's both leave this behind. It's not your responsibility, but this is," she says, placing her hand over his on her stomach. "This is our future."

He smiles. "I think it's a girl."

"No, it's a boy. I'm carrying low. That means it's a boy."

"Who told you that?"

"Carly."

"She thought each of her girls was a boy, and only one was. I wouldn't bank on her suspicions, Viola."

"I don't want to live without you, Jason."

"Nor I, you, luv. Focus on what we've shared. No one gets out alive. We're mortal. We're given life to live. My life is fulfilled to have known your love. This, for me, is enough. I've thought about it: Had Patrick been successful—had he killed you that day—I would be gutted but thankful to have had the experiences I've shared with you. After Aunt Lara took you—finding Uncle in the yard—I had to let you go."

"What do you mean, let me go?"

"At any moment, you could be gone, luv. When you called from Carly's phone, I thought she was calling to tell me you were dead. There was no way I could get to you in time. Patrick planned it that way. I'm not sure why he kept you alive."

"To have an heir?"

"No, he wants us wiped out," says Jason, dragging his fingertip along her collarbone.

"Kill Patrick before he kills you," she says. "The others will accept it. They'll follow you, Jason. These men, these boys, need a leader. Patrick isn't a good one. You are. The intelligent ones will see through him."

"And they're the first to die. An envious, ignorant man gets rid of his astute obstacles, Viola. I'm not that man. When I die, I'll die intact as who I've chosen to be. I respect myself. That is more important than fearing my cousin—or the power these soldiers are blinded by. Why are we fighting? No one in this building can tell me. They do what they're told, in fear of what others might think if they don't."

"Blow them up, blow the whole fricken place up. Let's leave today you and me, please."

He stops. "You're changing. Don't change. Violence is not the answer."

"Dumb people piss me off. Who knew there were so many?"

"No one's dumb, luv. We are all unknowing until we learn—if we choose to. I left a few things for you at our house."

"Don't. Please." Her bottom lip trembles. "I can't think of losing you when you're right here in front of me."

"You can't trust anyone, Viola—except Zack."

"Please tell me you don't believe that."

"I do. He and I made plans. We have no negatives. Let him help you with our children. Don't push him away. He's all I've had all these years. I'm the same for him, regardless of our differences."

"Can we keep the door locked? Can we pretend you don't have an entire building of men to deal with?"

"I want nothing more, my luv." He looks at his phone. "I've already missed three calls."

"I thought we were pretty quick." She says playfully.

His thumb brushes her top and bottom lip. He leans in to kiss them softly, as if they were made of delicate tissue paper.

"A lot is happening all at once. I need to stay focused. Seeing you alive and well is more than I could ask for. Thank you for loving me."

"You're very welcome, Jason Stanton."

After a loud knock, he leans in to give her one more quick kiss.

"Stay in your room. Lock the door. I'll collect you when it's time to go."

"Yes, sir." She salutes as he opens the door, and he ushers her out.

Leo walks in.

-..Chapter 49-. .-

I n her bunker, Viola's *Family Bible* is on the bed.

I didn't leave it there.

She picks it up, turning from the camera's view to open it. Inside is a piece of paper small enough to crumple in one hand. Someone in the Complex left her a message. Viola pretends to read a page of the bible before she sets it in her unzipped bag.

The note says, "Change of plans. Jason is key."

I'll need to get rid of it.

She wonders if Jeffrey wrote it. Viola is mentally exhausted. She goes to the bathroom, starts the shower. Taking out a match, she lights the tiny note, tossing it in the toilet before it burns her finger.

After her shower, she slips on the T-shirt she stole from Jason during their cottage time, she grabs a clean pair of silk panties Carly left her. She lies on the twin bed. She drifts off, dreaming of her two kids in the future, swimming in the ocean.

When she wakes, the lights in her room have been dimmed. The small bed dips as his body cuddles in behind hers. His hand moves to her stomach. It drifts up to her breast under the t-shirt, making her smile. She pushes her backside, wiggling into his growing hard-on as he kisses the back of her neck. She realizes he smells different—unlike Jason. He smells like Patrick when he grabbed her face—his cologne.

Slowly, Viola reaches under her pillow for the needle she took from Auntie's dresser in England. She pops the lid under the thickness. She can feel his bare, hard length against her legs. His breathing through his nostrils is heated and heavy. He lifts the back of her shirt. He pulls her underwear down. She turns, and jabs the needle into his thigh, pressing the liquid into it before he can grab her hand.

He twists her wrist hard.

Viola screams.

Patrick yells, "YOU STUPID FUCKING BITCH!"

She fights back as he rips off her underwear. His hand presses into her neck. He cuts off her oxygen as he gets on top of her, using one of his arms and his knee to spread her legs open.

Viola kicks her legs free, her arms flailing.

Then he's gone.

She moves on the bed, holding her throat, heaving, staring through the shadows in the room. She sees that another man is there.

Jeffrey.

Patrick is on the floor with his stiff, pistol dick on display. Blood pours from his neck. Jeffrey slit Patrick's throat.

"Are you okay, lass?" he asks.

"Y—yes?"

"I need you to get dressed, gather your things, and come with me."

He turns around to give her privacy. Tremors ripple through her body as Viola moves, grabbing her clothes and a new pair of underwear from the bag Carly left her. She shoves the book in a corner of her bag. She picks up the needle she stuck in Patrick's leg from the floor, along with her torn underwear, and stuffs them in her bag. She slings it around her shoulder.

"I'm ready."

"Stand over here." Jeffrey arranges Patrick's body. He dresses him like a mother would dress her sleeping three-year-old.

"Why are you doing that?"

"I need the men who find him in here to think he was killed before and not after he attempted to rape you. Nobody needs to have more chinwag than they already do around this mancave."

"Camera," she says, pointing to the ceiling.

"It's off. They're all off. We need you out of here, Jason's orders."

"Can I see him before we leave?"

"I'll take you to him. Fix your bed covers first to hide the rip in that sheet, and his blood from you stabbing him with your needle. We need to go."

———

As Viola walks behind Jeffrey, he carries a gun in one hand and a knife in the other—the one he used to kill Patrick. Viola watched him wipe the blood on Patrick's clothes, like a butcher cleans his knife, before he walked away from his body without any expression on his face. Jeffrey marches them down a corridor. He stops at the infirmary door, knocking three times. When it opens, Viola's surprised to see Janic. The door locks behind them.

"Janic, thank goodness you're alive!"

He doesn't respond. Viola's eyes move to Brant, who is hunched on the floor. She sees Jason on a bed. His face is pale. He looks like a corpse. A scream escapes her. She runs to Jason's side, feeling his chest for a heartbeat. She puts her ear to it.

"Janic, is he—?" Jeffrey asks.

"No, he's alive." Janic answers.

Jeffrey walks over to Viola. He wraps his arms around her. "Let go. Breathe," he says next to her ear.

Janic walks up to Jeffrey, dragging another body. It's Henry, the doctor, who patched Viola's arm. He's missing his shoes. His face is bloody from taking a severe beating. His suit jacket and his pant pocket are torn.

"The doctor injected something into Jason's back," says Janic. "I found this needle sticking out of him."

Jeffrey releases Viola. He pops his knuckles, as he eyes the bleeding doctor cowering below him. He speaks calmly, "Henry, your fearless scumbag leader Patrick is dead. I need you to tell me what you injected into Jason. If you don't tell me in sixty seconds, I'll cut each of your fingers off. I'm a sensitive man. Are you right-handed?"

Jeffrey steps towards him. "It's an easy question: Are you right-handed? Yes or no!"

"Yes." Henry stares at Viola. His eyes wide with fear.

"Alright," says Jeffrey. "I'll start with your left hand since you're a doctor. If you refuse to tell me, I'll kill every family member in your direct bloodline this week. Your treason will seal their collective fate. I'll kill your children. I have no problem wiping out an evil line. It seems like a sensible idea. If that's how you'd like this life of yours to end, so be it. It's your call. He taps his watch. "Starting now."

"You're fucking nuts?" Henry says, spitting blood.

"I am," Jeffery says with a laugh. "It's no secret. The entire family is aware. What did you inject into Jason?" He grabs Henry's left hand, his knife to his pinkie finger.

"Stop!" Henry says. "I gave him Jimsonweed extracted from the seeds. I didn't inject it all before Brant knocked me out."

Viola knows precisely what he gave him. Seeds from this poisonous plant can cause fatal health problems.

"Is there an antidote?" Jeff says.

"Physostigmine," Viola blurts out.

Henry stares at her with eyes of desperation. From her short time spent with Jeffrey, she knows that the doctor is already a dead man. She tears her eyes away from his to look at Jason.

"Where is it?" asks Jeff.

"In the third cupboard on the left," Henry says with a shaky voice.

"This stuff?" Janic holds a vile of liquid up.

Henry nods. "The needles are in that drawer, the second one down."

"How much do we need of it?" Jeffrey demands, nicking Henry's pinkie, making him wince.

"Twenty-five point five milligrams should do it. He'll live, maybe."

"You'd better hope you're right. If Jason dies, your line dies. Are you with me?"

"Not all of it entered his system. Can I look at the syringe you pulled from Jason?" Henry says.

Janic retrieves it, only allowing Henry to view what's left of the contents.

"He might make it," Henry says.

"That's not good enough, Henry." Jeffrey pulls Henry with him. He rips a piece of cloth from an infirmary blanket. He rolls it into a ball.

"WAIT!" Henry yells a moment before Jeffrey stuffs Henry's mouth with it.

He lifts Henry's left hand. He cuts off his pinkie in one movement. Henry's scream is muffled by the mouth covering. He starts hyperventilating. Henry stares at his missing finger.

"Tell me how much now that you've seen what's left. What do we need to save him? He lives—or it's your hand next. Last chance, you piece of shite."

Henry pulls the cloth from his mouth. He uses it to put pressure on the hole where his finger used to be. He picks up his finger from the floor, putting it on medic bed near him before he moves with Jeffrey directly beside him, nudging him. The doctor instructs Janic where to get a bag of saline to get Jason situated after his poisoning.

"Hook up this bag before it has time to set in his intestine," Henry says to Janic. The two men work fast to get the antidote into Jason.

Viola is still on the floor next to Jason's cot, unable to move or speak. Her lungs are heavy. Her breathing is shallow. And seeing the cloth fall and the blood drip on the floor from Henry's missing finger is disturbing.

"He's got a fever," Henry says, touching Jason's face with his right hand. "We'll need acetaminophen. It's in the third cupboard next to the sink." Janic rushes to find it. Jeffrey keeps one hand on Henry, the knife ready in his other hand. After Janic gives Henry the needle to administer the drug, Henry steps back. "That's all I can do for now."

Jeff must have got a message. He walks away from Henry to check his phone.

Viola's eyes follow Henry's movement as he quickly rushes, grabbing and wrapping gauze around the palm of his hand, covering his pinkie area. He pulls out a baggie from a drawer, goes to a small fridge, and takes out a chunk of ice. In another cupboard, he takes out a bowl, puts the ice in the bowl, and carefully picks up, placing his severed pinkie from the medic bed in to the baggie, then the baggie into the bowl.

"When should he wake up?" asks Jeffery.

"I'm not sure. He's in a coma. He's stable," Henry says as if it pains him to speak.

"Do you feel heroic, Henry?" Viola asks from the floor next to Jason. "What has Jason done to you?"

"He's top of the line," Henry answers without looking her way.

"Wow, that's all you got?" she says, a death stare on her face.

Jeffrey checks his phone again. Viola thinks he must have it on vibrate. He makes a call, saying nothing to whoever's on the other line. He taps off a message, glances at Viola, then back to Jason.

"Anything else we need to prepare if a fever hits or Jason starts convulsing?" Jeffrey asks.

"If his vitals don't remain stable through the night, I'll give him more Physostigmine," Henry says.

"Show me where your stash of this poison is," says Jeffrey.

Henry stares at him.

"I want to have it for the scientist arriving, ya muppet."

Henry tells Janic where it is. Janic moves to the fridge and brings out a few trays of concoctions.

"All right, brainiac, show us what's what."

Henry goes down the list, lifts a jar, and hands it to Jeffrey. Jeff's phone vibrates. He's typing on it. He slips the phone into his Army cargo pants pocket.

"What was the lethal dose? How much?" Jeffrey asks.

Henry pulls out another identical syringe, the same kind Janic lifted earlier. He fills it. He hands it to Jeffrey. Jeff tells Janic to write it down.

Jeffrey injects it into an unsuspecting Henry.

He picks up the bloody cloth Henry dropped earlier and violently stuffs it into Henry's mouth, shoving him to the floor as they all watch Henry convulse before he loses consciousness.

-..Chapter 50-. .-

Jeffrey's head tilts toward a clock on the wall.

"It won't be long now, Viola, no worries. We have a top doctor on his way here from the airport as we speak. He will tend to Jason."

"I'm not leaving his side, not until he wakes."

Jeffrey turns his body square to face her. "I'm to take you from here, lass. This war is far from over. It's not safe. We'll transport Jason and you as soon as we secure every section of the Complex, all right?"

"Where is Anton?" she says. "You need to find him."

Janic points behind them, toward a far corner of the room. Viola sees Anton's dead body.

"We're pretty sure Anton shut the cameras off to free Patrick," Janic says. "Henry pretended to be on our side. When Jason's back was turned, Henry made his move, going for Jason. But Brant saw him. He leaped on Henry, trying to push the needle away. Right then, Anton walked in the door and shot Brant. Anton was about to shoot Jason when I walked in. I jumped him, and we fought. I was able to turn his gun on him to shoot him, or we'd all be dead."

Viola catches Jeffrey's eyes on his brother's form on the floor.

"BRANT!" she screams. "Oh no, no, no. Brant." She runs over to him. She thought he had been knocked out. Now she can see the gaping hole in his chest... his blood.

"Oh no, not you! I need to tell Mary."

"That's fine, Viola," says Jeffrey. Her eyes are on Brant's face as Jeffrey picks him up to move his body to a bed.

There's a knock at the door.

Tap Tap

Tap, Tap, Tap

Tap Tap.

That knock…I did that knock when I first took baby Zee to see Jason in England. The same knock Jeffrey did on my window at the truck when I thought BG was about to…

"Jason told them to do that," she whispers, crying into her hands. A horrible feeling washes through her.

Jeffrey opens the door. He commands Janic to stand watch outside it.

A handsome, tall man enters, looks around the room. He stares at Viola like he's seen a ghost. "You must be Viola. I'm Dean. I was close to your mom. You could be her twin."

Viola runs to him. She hugs him. He holds her as she cries.

"You're the one she loved?" she asks.

"I believe so. I hope so. I loved her, too. I'm sorry for everything you've been through. We'll talk in a bit. Let me tend to Jason."

"Yes, thank you." Viola steps aside, letting Dr. Dean Strober check Jason's vitals. He is the same doctor who long ago stitched her arm after a car wreck in Telega.

Jeffrey goes over everything Henry told them. The doctor fingertips the syringes, counts them, and takes one. He walks toward Jason, injecting it into him. He goes into the fridge. He pulls out a bag of blood, along with another bag of liquid.

Her eyes move to Brant's lifeless form. She walks over to him, sits on the edge of the bed, holds his hand in hers. She remembers wishing her mom was sleeping like she wishes Brant is now. Her lips move closer to his ear.

"If you could wake up, I swear I'd allow you to call me Lady V for the rest of my life," she says through tears. "Mary was so lucky to have you for as long as she did. Catherine too. Poor Carly. I don't want her to find out. I don't think she can take it, not you, her little bro, Jacko... Carly told me about her secret name for you. She said you were an instigator, a ripe shite disturber, and I'd need ammo." She sniffles. "Thank you for being an incredible man, for making me laugh during a terrible—Thank you for helping me, Brant. If you had left with Carly that day, you would be... I wouldn't be alive. It's all too much." She lifts his hand to kiss it.

"If Jason and I have a boy," she tells him, "I'm naming him in your honor. If Jason makes it, it's because of you. Thank you for saving us. I'm glad we became friends. And the teepee, the trough... Yeah, I promise that stays between us."

She notices Jeffrey watching her with a blank stare. She gets up with tears streaming down her cheeks. She goes to see what the doctor has hooked up to him.

Dean has laid Henry down on a bed. He's reattaching Henry's pinkie finger.

"Why are you fixing him?" she asks.

"He's one of my brother's children, Viola. He is a talented doctor. Even if he goes to prison for his part in this scheme, they will still need his knowledge. He'll need his hands." He looks at her with a solemn face.

She brushes the curls of Jason's hair from his forehead, thinking how, less than twenty-four hours ago, they were frantically making love, with his fingers in her hair.

I don't want to lose you.

Jeffrey comes over and holds her as she cries. She's not afraid of Jeffrey, even after knowing his anesthetic ability to slit a throat and cut off hands. After living with Zack, she knows they both have an on-and-off switch. In their current situation, she's unsure if that's a good or bad thing.

"Jeff, is Zack...?"

"No need to worry about that bitsy hound," he says with a slight smile.

"At least, that's one of us. I'm sorry about Brant."

"I didn't grow up with him, Viola. I've been away from my family for many years. I've only had some interaction with my golloper of an ass brother, Patrick, and... Carly. We've stayed in touch."

"It would be best if you were with her when she's told about Brant. They were so close. She was the big sister he looked up to. He respected her. He was good."

"She told me that before. I thought Patrick was too—until he wasn't. He hurt Carly. My mum," he says, looking away. "I wanted to kill him. Thank you for the opportunity. I'm sorry about Jason. He's the best guy I've ever known. He ordered me to stand at your door. I got here the day you ran. Bloody Bellend. When the cameras went out earlier, I met him in the hall. He ordered me back to your door. If I had stayed with him, we wouldn't be here right now."

"I would be dead. Patrick would have killed me. I would never let him rape me alive."

Jeffrey looks down at her, "So it is true."

"What?"

"You're a Battling Doris."

"Not always," she says, looking at Jason.

"Chin up, lass. I have a good feeling Jason is going to pull through. Too much to live for, this one."

She touches her stomach without thinking. Then she pats Jeff's hand to tell him she is okay. Jeff pulls a chair closer to Jason so she can sit beside him.

He hands her an embroidered cotton handkerchief for her tears.

-..Chapter 51-..-

As time passes, Viola peers over at Dean. She's amazed at how calmly he moves around the room, reading medicine bottles. The names on most of the bottles, which most people can't even pronounce, are in German, Russian, and French. He is reorganizing as they wait.

Three knocks.

Janic walks back in as Jeffrey looks down the hallway with a semi-automatic gun and knife in hand, ready to kill.

"What's the latest?" Jeffrey asks, stepping back in the room, locking the door.

"Leo has it under control," says Janic. "He said to tell you that Garrett's plane had landed. Carly's with him."

Viola stands. Jeffrey's face goes pale.

"How did my father allow this?" Jeffrey says more to himself.

"Jeffrey, go and get them. I'm fine, we're fine," she says. "If Janic says that Leo has it under control, I trust Leo."

"You should never trust so easily, Viola," says Jeffrey.

"At this moment, we have to trust someone," she says. "Leo's shown me that he's a decent man. He respects the chain of command. If he doesn't, then we'll die, won't we? It's going to happen one way or another."

Jeffrey frowns. "You're different, lass."

"That's what I hear—a lot. I hope that we're all different. Otherwise, we'd be like robots."

"Oh, believe me, we have an entire complex of robots right here."

"You may be right, Jeff. The only good and bad thing about that is they've been taught not to think for themselves. They fear, so they follow whoever leads. So, let's lead."

Viola turns, sensing Dean's eyes on her. She has an odd feeling.

"Dean, why are you staring at me?"

"You forgot that I've met you before, Viola."

"I know," she says.

After Dean fixed her up in the basement following her car accident in Telega, her mother warned Viola when they got home to never speak of seeing Dean in that building. Viola's starting to understand. Dean may secretly be with *The Rise*—a potential problem for Jason.

"I remember meeting you," she says.

"We have many things to discuss—not here, not now. I'm happy to see you again," says Dean.

Viola watches Dean move swiftly, setting a vial inside of a cupboard. The symbol on the vial sparks something inside of her.

"Likewise, I hope," she says.

Dean gives her a puzzled look.

"I don't trust you, Dean. I'm sorry if that's blunt. I sense something off in you." she says.

Jeffrey moves two steps toward the doctor, his arms at his sides, his weapons angled for use.

"I have no idea whom to trust, either, Viola. Everyone here, except for Jason, has betrayed me. I have many scars, you could say."

"Me too," she says. "I won't harm you, Dean, even if you mean to harm me. If you're thinking about it, please make sure it's fatal. I'm not built for murder."

Dean, Janic, and Jeffrey gawk at her. Her upfront, in-your-face demeanor, her words leave no room for wonder. She means what she says.

"You don't fear this situation?" asks Dean.

"I fear losing Jason. That's it. I don't want to imagine or give one thought to living this life without him. So, if you can bring him back to me, I will forever be in your debt."

"I'll do everything that I can. If he's going to wake up, I assume it should be soon. I need to get whatever's left in this syringe to a lab. I think we're missing something. He should already be awake after what I've given him. Something's in this that Henry didn't tell you."

"Were you close to Henry?"

"Yes, when he was a tot." She watches Dean go to pick up the young doctor's shoes. He puts them back on his bare feet.

Where are his socks? He seems so proper wearing a suit.

"My brother sent Henry to me when he was young to learn the basics. Aside from that summer, he lived with my brother, my younger sister, and his siblings."

"So, you didn't converse much otherwise throughout his youth?"

"He was away training to be a doctor at the same time my youngest brother was."

"Can we move Jason?" Jeffrey asks.

"Not yet."

"A war is coming, Dean," says Jeffrey "We'll need to safety this room by locking us in or get him to another area before the Lancers' army comes."

"Who are the Lancers?" asks Viola.

"The other side of the family. They heard about what happened here. I'm sure there are spies everywhere, as usual. The Lancers are aware of the divide. They'll take advantage of it, hoping to grow their army."

"Why has it taken them so long to get here?" asks Viola.

"Because we're in Russia," says Jeffrey. "Protocols must be approved before a private army can enter another country."

"I'm interested to see what the Lancers stand for, Jeffrey," she says. All heads turn toward her. "What? Have you never asked that question before? It should be pretty obvious if people in this family could tell the fucking truth for once!"

Dean's brows angle with concern.

"Viola, there's no need to speak that way. It's not very becoming. I don't think your mom—"

"Dean, my mother swore a lot. I'm sorry if she was an angel while you two were knocking boots. She was proper in front of people, as she was taught. She was real with me."

Jeffrey goes into a full-on outburst, a fit of bellowing laughter.

"Oh, Viola," he says through laughter. "Where have you been all of my life?"

"That's what Zack says."

He laughs again. "Every man in this family needs to fear you the most," adds Jeffrey.

"I don't see what there is to fear. I hope the women fear. They need to fear being back warmers with their legs in the air, thinking their sole purpose is to produce babies. We have so much more to offer the human race, for crying out loud. That pisses me off."

Dean eyes her with a slight smile. "Now that reminds me of your mother."

"I got some of it from her. The rest is from *not* being raised by this bloodline. If I offend anyone, I don't care. I'm living my own life. I've cheated death too often to give a shite about anything else."

Jeffrey chuckles. "You picked that up from Jason. His favorite swear word."

"Please, Dean, please be good if you haven't been in the past. Today, your slate is wiped clean. Today, I need you to be Jason's hero. He's been everyone else's. He deserves to live. He doesn't want the top spot. Please don't prove to be another envious vying small-minded prick, thinking you need to kill him off for a fu—a title."

"All right, Viola. Enough said. I heard you. I'm only here to do everything I can to bring Jason back, to wake him up. I give you my solemn word."

"I need more than that. I need you not to stop until you do."

Jeffrey looks at a text message.

"Viola, with your permission, I ask you to go down to bring Garrett and Carly up. They're here."

"Why are you asking me?"

"I've sworn fealty to Jason not to allow you out of my sight until you're safe, away from here."

I'm fine. Janic can stay with me. We'll lock the door until you're back."

"Okay." Jeff opens the door. "I'll be back in under ten. Janic, watch the window, mate."

"Yes, sir."

Minutes later, Jeffrey knocks. Janic opens the door. Viola bypasses Garrett to hug Carly as Jeffrey ushers them in.

"Carly."

They both start crying.

"Is Jason going to make it?" Carly asks.

"I hope so. We're not sure. We have to wait and see if he'll come out of the coma."

"Oh, Viola, I'm so sorry."

Viola cannot contain her sobs. She stands before Carly, trying to hold off the inevitable.

"I'm only alive because of Br—Brant, Carly. Jason is alive because of him. I'm so very sorry, Car." Viola moves aside.

She watches Carly's eyes travel past Jason, when she realizes who is lying on the other bed.

NOOOOO!" Carly screams. She runs for Brant, Jeffrey catches her by the waist before she can. Carly hits and hits him. She pounds her fists into his chest, screaming until she exhausts herself, folding into his arms.

Viola turns to see Garrett standing next to his brother's body, tears roll down his cheeks.

"Where is Patrick?" Garrett asks Jeffrey.

"Dead. I killed him."

"Good," Garrett says. "That was my first objective coming here. How does one like Patrick change into this? After all of our education about the history of man, why would he stray? Why fold into the dark? For what? Death? There is no love in any of this. He has destroyed our family. His kids will find out someday. Disgraceful."

Jeffrey continues holding Carly as she weeps.

"He was always number two. He hated it when we were young." Jeffrey says. "Carly remembers. Dean could tell us stories, being the oldest."

"Yes. Too many egos and pretending." Says Dean. "Jealousy eats up a person—regardless of our upbringing and the solidarity within this bloodline. Evil can and does win, depending on the man."

Janic moves from the window. "I think the Lancers have arrived."

Jeffrey walks Carly to Viola. Carly folds into Viola's arms. Jeff moves to peek out the window.

"Boy, they're not messing about," Jeffrey says. His phone barely rings, and he picks it up. He doesn't say anything other than "Uh-uh," then hangs up. "Dean, I need to use blood. Can you put some in a syringe for me?" He watches as Dean fills the tube with blood for him. "Janic, I'm opening the door for a moment. I need you to cover for me. Ladies, please move to the far corner until I'm back in the room."

Viola stares down at Anton's dead body. She leans down to touch his gun. Her head turns to see what Jeff's doing. He's using the blood to make a mark on the door, then he's back in, locking it. He dials someone on his phone.

"Done," he says, hanging up. "We should be fine in here. I want everyone away from the windows, away from the door. There'll be a lot of shooting."

Viola stands. "Shouldn't we try to talk and see if we can't sway them now that Patrick's gone? Garrett, you're in command. You must get out there and stop the mass killing of our bloodline. I'm certain they've heard that you're here and in charge."

"Thank you, Viola. Are you always this outspoken?" Garrett asks.

"Yes."

"Impressive. I like it." he says with a slight grin.

She feels odd, knowing that if she has a girl, this man was set to be her next babymaker after Jason. Catherine is madly in love with him. Viola would never do that to her.

I wouldn't agree to it anyway.

But she does like him, his face. He's a physical match for Catherine. Viola likes that he appreciates her strength when speaking her mind—as Zack and Jason do. It's because of Carly. Somehow, she and Carly are on the same page, even though Carly was raised in this family. Carly's mom had this strength, too. She said what she felt was right, even though she did terrible things.

"I want to take Patrick home. Uncle wants a proper burial for the children." Garrett says, directing his words to Jeffrey.

"We'll do that later," Jeffrey answers. "Right now, Garrett, this is going down. You'll stay in here with us. Leo is your chief cadet. He knows what to do."

Carly gets up. She saunters toward Brant. Her hands shake as she touches him. Carly is having a private conversation with him, from her soul to his. Viola hopes that we still exist even after death, as her mother said we do, from the book of Treowth.

"Our ancestors live in the air, invincible but ever-present. When the body dies, their energy, their good, watches over us, in the elements, in nature, all connected, all the time, in the unseen, where we are born, where we will die. The fall of the two trees, so shall we."

Viola takes a seat next to Jason.

I know you're in there. I can't let you go—not today. I need you. We have a war to win—not one you started but one you hoped would end for the greater good.

-..Chapter 52-..-

Viola hears it start as they sit in the infirmary. Guns. Yelling. Running. Doors opening, slamming shut. In the coming hours, new patients will join them here.

She turns, catching a look between Jeffrey and Carly. It was so quick that you could almost have missed it. Viola caught it.

What are they not telling me?

More guns can be heard, even a few shots near their door. It feels like forever as they sit, idly waiting. Dean adds a new bag of liquid to Jason's drip. He smiles at her. She smiles back. Viola pictures her mother with him. They suited each other, she thinks. He's intelligent and kind. Patrick resembles Dean. They have the same cheek dimples—Dean's hair is lighter, almost blond.

Her dad was handsome, too. He was clever but devious. He fooled her at first. Bad energy emanated from him two feet in every direction when they'd meet for lunch in Buffalo. She felt it every time they were together. Her dad was always conniving or looking at a woman like she would be his next kill. Viola wondered how many other people were like that in the world: sick, demented, and needing to be permanently locked up to keep everyone else safe. Viola feels fortunate to have had love in her life and baby Zee.

I never stop thinking of you.

Even when Patrick almost killed her in her room, her last thought before her nearly last breath was Zee. Her hope for his future.

My beautiful boy.

He's her driving force to get through all this. Yes, she cares for Jason, but Zee is her whole heart, her responsibility until he can fend for himself. He's in her tree. Viola hopes that someday he, too, will create beautiful littles to carry on.

"Soldiers of Complex Y." A loud voice booms over the speaker system.

"It's Leo," Jeffrey says.

"This is your chief cadet. Put down your weapons. We have surrendered. I repeat: Put down your weapons. Soldiers of Complex Y have surrendered. If you do not comply, you will be shot. I repeat. Put down your weapons and stand where you are with your arms in the air—now. That is an order."

Everyone in the room eyeballs each other.

Janic moves to peer out the window. "They're doing it. They're putting down their weapons."

Jeffrey stays close to the door. Garrett moves to look out another window; his arms crossed over his chest.

Viola walks over to Carly, touches her shoulder, and hands her an embroidered cotton cloth Jeff had given her to wipe her tears. When Carly stands, they hold onto one another.

"I want this day... to stand still," Carly says. "I don't want it to be real that Brant and Patrick are gone. Brant deserved to live longer than this. Patrick was wrong. I hate that I couldn't get through to him for the sake of our children. He wouldn't give up. God, Viola, I love him so much. We've had so much together. I can't believe he wouldn't change for me. That's what hurts. He chose this! He never got it. You're lucky Jason did."

"Carly, Jason had it long before he and I got together. I have no idea how someone's mind works. I used to think the same about Zack as you do about Patrick. I had to let go of thinking I could make him change. I couldn't. I realized that he was who he was. I told him I loved him, but I loved myself more."

"I kept making excuses for Patrick. I focused on his good qualities."

"I get it," says Viola. "But there's a line, Carly. A point in time when you are no longer willing to cross that line with them. That's when it's over."

"I guess," Carly says. "I've no choice now, do I? He's—How will I tell the kids?

"Today is not the day to think about that. Think instead of saying goodbye here. Thank Brant and Patrick for the love they gave you. You can't fix your broken heart. Little by little, someday, flowers will bloom through the cracks, reminders of the good. My mom told me that when someone dies, the best memories will reach out to us to help us through. We need to remember them more than the bad. It helps to carry on."

"Thanks, Viola. I'm glad you're alive."

When there's another bang on the door, Jeffrey moves to open it. An older man walks in, three soldiers trailing him in pale yellow army fatigues. They're not from the Complex.

"You're Jeffrey?" asks the man.

"Yes, sir."

The man looks over at Jason. "Is he alive?"

"He is in a coma, sir. Dean is trying to reverse whatever the other doctor put in a poison cocktail to kill him."

"Do you have a sample?"

"Yes," Dean says, handing him a container of the liquid. "We need it thoroughly analyzed. Something's amiss. Something's been added that's responsible for his remaining in the coma. I've listed what I've administered here." Dean gathers his notes. "Jason is still not responding. His vitals have stabilized. The fever is at bay with the meds he's on. I've done a mini transfusion to protect her internal organs."

With one nod, the older man adds, "We'll secure the Complex. We will move out the bodies. It shouldn't take too long. Then we'll air-flight Jason out of here."

"I want to go with him," Viola says to the older man.

"And you are—?"

"His mate, Viola. Who are you?"

The man gives her an odd look.

"My name is Ardent. What may I ask is your birth name?"

Viola almost says Viola Stanton, realizing her actual birth name.

"Althea Eastman." She says.

Janic's eyes nearly pop out of his head.

"Let me speak with the Plant," says Ardent. "I don't think it's wise for you to come to where we are going."

"Why not?" Viola asks.

"There's no coming back. Once you've been inside the Plant, you stay."

"What about Jason? I'll never see him again, is that what you're telling me? I'm pregnant with his child. How will I ever see him again if I can't leave with him?"

Ardent's stare bends toward her stomach. On her tiny frame, her bump is noticeable. "We'll figure out something. We always do. The plan now is for you to return to England, where you can have your baby. Jason's Uncle Mark is taking you in. You will be his responsibility."

"I don't think so," she says.

Ardent approaches Viola, eye to eye. She doesn't budge.

"Do you want a thrashing right here before everyone, young miss? I'm about two seconds away from pulling down your pants and spanking your arse like a three-year-old over my knee. You will address me as sir and show respect, do you understand?"

Viola doesn't say a word. Invisible steam is pushing out her ears. She's so angry at this stranger, this man, telling her what she will do—wanting to force her to part ways with Jason.

"Sir, correct me if I'm wrong, but I am full-blood, which ranks me higher than everyone here, including you."

With a shocked expression on his face, Ardent asks, "Do you not want the best care or chance for Jason's survival?"

"Yes, I do," she says.

He cracks a smile. "My goodness, your Uncle Benjamin wasn't kidding when he said you're stronger than an Ox for a wee one." He exhales. "If you decide to come with us, with Jason, you will stay there for the remainder of your life, or you can stay in England with family and have your child. Once Jason wakes, you and he will be rejoined as a family. This is your only option."

Carly's hand touches her arm. "Viola, come home with me. We'll help you with the baby. It'll be better than being alone, locked in a room, waiting for who-knows-how-long until Jason wakes up. You don't want to be alone, do you?"

Hearing and feeling the word "alone," Viola breaks. She wants to stay strong in front of this stranger. The note in her room said Jason is key. The thought of being apart from Jason while having his child is too much. And what about Zee? How will she get him back? She wipes the wetness on her cheeks. Heartbroken.

"I'm torn," she says. "Jason is—I can never let him go. And not to see him... I don't want to be alone. I've lived my entire life alone. I can't stand it."

Ardent backs away from her, giving her space. He awaits her decision. Viola thinks about her mother's words.

Face your fears. Who am I? Eat from your own tree. You can't save the man. He can't save the woman.

"Fine. I dema—I humbly request to be updated daily, please. The moment he wakes, I want him on a plane, train, boat, whatever, back to me, to us." She holds her stomach. "I want whoever is above you to hear about my request, my plea, I ask, with the utmost respect... sir."

"Madam Eastman." He dips his head like he's bowing to a queen.

He's mocking me. I don't care. If my name, my blood, holds power, I'll gladly use it to help my cause, having Jason alive. Jason is key.

"I'll get everything ready, sir," says Dean.

"We leave at 0900 hours."

The moment the door closes behind him, they all look at Viola.

"What?" she says. "I don't care if he thinks I'm an immature twat of a girl. He was a supreme Tosser."

The family in the room burst out in laughter at her unexpected choice of words. All except Dean. He moves around the room, preparing for Jason's move.

-..Chapter 53-..-

Jeffrey's making the decisions. He tells Janic to have Patrick cleaned up and moved to the infirmary. Garrett is to go to the command room. Jeffrey takes Carly to the kitchen to get food and bring it back for Viola and Dean.

Viola sits beside Jason. She holds his hand and stares at his beautiful face.

"Viola," Dean says, standing not a foot away, "you've been through an awful lot for such a young person."

"You have no idea, Dean."

"Not the whole picture, no."

"I didn't want this life. I wanted to stay where I was with my friends, go to school, get married, have kids, and live and die a normal life. I didn't want this endless pit of drama, hiding, running, secrets, being raped. I've even been shot."

She can tell he's disturbed by her information as she assesses his body language.

"Zee and Jason are the only good in my life."

"It seems like Carly is good," he says.

"She is. I meant that Jason and Zee are my heart. Everybody in our bloodline lies, Dean. These secrets are lies. We hide them with more lies. We're destined to play the role of an actor our entire lives, to maintain secrecy in fear that the powerful want to take us down. Protect the bloodline at all costs. That's a high price to pay. In my short life, it's already astronomical. I can't imagine what will come if I live through my twenties. Someone is always going to try and kill me because I happen to have been born with Pureblood. Wonderful, right?"

"It won't always be like this. Right now, it's a war. There will always be crazy wannabes. A few here and there with their wires crossed." He adds.

"What is that number, Dean? I read that one in twenty-five people has a screw loose. That's a statistically significant number when you think about it. How many of us are there in this bloodline?"

"I'm not certain, a lot. More than one hundred thousand, I believe I heard Doc say one time."

"I'd like to know. But then, do I? Really? I promised my mom never to give up, and I won't. Everyone I love the most dies. It's hard to take, Dean."

"I lost my mom, my sister, a younger brother, and my son, Viola. I understand."

"I'm sorry if I'm not what you expected," she says. "I will stay to myself for as long as I can, like my mom did—or they can kill me, and onto the next in the bloodline."

"She was incredible—your mom."

"She was."

"I'm not happy with how things have happened either, Viola. I look to the future. I have other children and grandchildren. I'll do what I can to make things right and do the right thing. There are pluses in this family. We have the most brilliant scientists and doctors, probably in every critical field known to man. Live your life the way you see fit. I encourage you, too. That's what your mom would have wanted. Try to remember, you get nowhere being a hothead or being vulgar. I think you got some of that from your dad."

"Please—all of it, I'm sure." Viola frowns. "I like you, Dean." Too bad my dad didn't die sooner, and you and my mom could have had the baby. I would have loved a sister."

"I didn't think—Did you say your mom was pregnant?"

"Yes. My dad messed with your oldest son's head, Bobby, because you were with my mom. He made Bobby believe that he could be the top Uncle. Jason was sad about it all. I hope it's over now."

"What? Bobby? Your mom... was pregnant? When exactly?" Dean asks.

"Yes, um, she was with your baby. She told me in a journal she wrote for me. My mom was in love with you. She knew my dad was going to kill her. He beat her up. She had a miscarriage the summer I was going to start middle school. I had to stay with my friend while she recuperated at Doc's. I wish sisters and brothers would stop the jealousy and fighting over who is the better sibling. That's a false life. They should always have each other's backs. They were born to help each other, despite their flaws, but they don't." She thinks of the story in the book of Treowth (Truth). "When we blame others, we're lost."

Viola can see Dean's wheels turning. She hopes she hasn't opened a whole new can of worms. Maybe she should go to the Plant and stay stuck in a room where she can never be told anything and, in return, never reveal another flipping secret.

I hate secrets!

Dean hesitates, then asks her a question, "Did Zack kill my son or Doc?"

"Uh. I was told that Bobby was about to shoot Doc. Doc had Zack ready in the wings to shoot Bobby only if he raised a gun to shoot Doc first.

"Bobby was an incredible young man," Dean says, seemingly confused.

"I'm sorry I told you this, Dean. I didn't mean to upset you. You were with my mom, and in love, were you not?"

"Yes, Viola, I was. I was utterly in love with her." He says, staring into the distance.

Viola wipes her face clear of emotion. Dean's response confuses her.

-..Chapter 54-..-

The Next Day

Viola feels the dread she felt when she had to let the paramedics take away her mother's body. Holding Jason's hand on a medical helicopter while sitting beside him, when Ardent, the man who had words with her the day before, enters the aircraft.

"Madam Eastman, it's time. You must come with me or go with him. We must get the air ambulance back in the air."

"Okay," she says. "One more minute."

Ardent blinks twice. She leans close to Jason's ear.

You're the only person who loves me. How will I get out of this? Don't die.

"Fight the poison. Fight for us, for our baby. Remember us."

She turns and jumps down from the helicopter, then Ardent taps the side. The turboshaft engine revs up. A medic inside with Jason shuts the sliding door.

Ardent places his arm around Viola—not as a friendly gesture, she can tell, but to make sure she moves out of the way to avoid injury as the helicopter takes off.

Viola walks with him, turning every so many steps to watch as they fly Jason away to the Plant. She grabs Ardent, hugging him. She sobs into his chest. She needs someone.

She senses his hesitation. He gives in, holding her until she can calm herself enough to continue walking back into the Complex.

"Thank you," she says. "And I apologize for being so rude yesterday. I've had to face a lot of bad men. I just—I don't want to live without the only good one. I can't save him, I'm aware. I will continue to remain true to my tree. Even if he never returns to me."

As Ardent stares at her, Viola presses her hand to his chest momentarily, then walks away.

Two armies of men from both sides are lining up the bagged dead bodies as Viola enters the Complex.

———

With Patrick dead, Carly refuses to remain in her room, so she bunks with Viola in a new room. They console one another over their joint heartbreaks.

Hours pass before there's a light tap at the door. It opens. It's Jeffrey.

"Ladies. We okay in here? Can I bring you anything?"

"No, Jeff, thanks. When are we wheels up?" Carly asks.

"I've got a few details to help Garrett with. We are planning for Dean's other son to come. I need to wait for him. He'll be a second to Garrett, taking Brant's place."

Carly's head falls at the mention of Brant.

Jeffrey approaches, then kneels, placing her in his lap like she's a child. He kisses Carly's hair, whispering something in her ear. It hits Viola.

They're the oldest. They were supposed to be together.

Carly nods her head. He places a small kiss on her lips. Then he remembers that they have an audience. He peers over at Viola, who is pretending not to have noticed. He gets up. He leaves without looking back.

"It'll take time, Carly," Viola says as the door closes. "We carry on. We have to. They would want us to."

"It's so much all at once," says Carly. "Mary is a mess, which is to be expected. She and Brant were madly in love. Catherine is upset, too, because Garrett's here now at The Complex for who knows how long. Mums gone. My kids have no idea their dad is dead. It feels like there are no men left in our family."

"Hey, not true, there's Jeffrey, and he seems to really love you."
Carly's head lifts with pouty, pushed-out lips.

"You saw that kiss, didn't you?"

"Hard to miss," Viola says. "Very sweet."

"We were told we'd be together. We were in love at a young age, like most siblings. Then a boy in my high school class in England touched me. Jeffrey saw it. He came to drive me home."

"I didn't know you went to school."

"It's a school for our bloodline. We have a large number of family living in England."

"Oh," says Viola.

"That same night, Jeff killed my classmate."

"Holy shit. How is he not in jail?" Viola asks.

"He made it look like an accident. Father got a call. He sent Jeff to America the next day. Then Father told me I would be with Patrick instead."

"Had you already been with Jeffrey sexually?"

"We kissed, but no. I was waiting for seventeen. He was waiting for me. Then I was with Patrick."

"But you secretly loved Jeffrey?"

"Yes. It faded once I fell in love with Patrick. At first, it was amazing with Patrick. He changed over the years—after we had two girls. He was upset we didn't have a boy. We had arguments over silly things. I think he felt pressured to have a boy. I told him we would keep trying. I didn't care how many we had. We were bound to get a boy eventually. He went to America for a program that the family put the males through. It had been weeks. I asked my mum to let me visit. I missed him. I was ovulating. She agreed to watch the girls. I went to surprise him."

"What town?" asks Viola.

"I don't remember. I took the private plane, and a driver dropped me off at a two-story house. When I got there, a girl was walking out, so I walked in, and there was Patrick, naked, with four naked girls in a living room. Zack was there too. All of them passed out. It was early in the morning. I wanted to get out of there. Jeffrey arrived from a night job as I was running away. He told me to wait there, then went into the house. He saw what I saw. He took me to an apartment—I guess it was his. He said he didn't realize that Zack and Patrick had women over that night. He thought they'd gone to a bar to hang out. They must have brought them back to party. He was shocked that Patrick would join in. He was sad for me. I was angry. I felt so stupid. I kissed Jeffrey. I let things happen."

"How did you feel... after?"

"Bloody fantastic! He was the best lover. We stayed in the apartment together the whole time I was there. I didn't tell Patrick. We went out for breakfast one morning. I saw him, Patrick, with a girl. They were in a booth, kissing. Jeffrey got us out of there. My world changed after that. Later, I tracked Patrick's whereabouts in England. He cheated on me often."

"Did you tell Patrick that you saw him?"

"Not right away. No way was I giving up what I had with Jeff—and he didn't want to give me up. Mother only allowed me to visit America because I was ovulating. I got pregnant. I knew it was Jeff's. I got scared. I hadn't been with Patrick. We did have a huge fight because I wouldn't be with him for several weeks after he got home. That's when I told him that I had gone to America. I told him what I'd seen that morning. He thought I went straight back on a flight home. I let him assume what he wanted to. I left out the week with Jeff. I told my mom what had happened, that I was pregnant. She made me forgive Patrick and sleep with him so he would think the baby was his. She helped me."

"Do you think she told Patrick?"

"No, we both swore an oath not to and it wasn't worth it. It would embarrass the family."

"When she kidnapped me, your mom told me you both cheated," Viola says.

"Did she say with who?"

"No. Just that you both cheated, she told me you tried with Jason."

Carly's mouth drops open. "I'm sorry. I did try. He was training me. He's top drawer. I touched his face. He grabbed my hands, removed them. He told me eye to eye that he would only ever be with his sister, with you. That was the last time he would train me. That's why I said what I said to you in the car when we picked you up. Jason will bend his rules for no one."

-..Chapter 55-. .-

Viola fixes the bedding in the room, the way her mother taught her with mitered corners.

Mitered corners or military corners was the term used to describe forty-five degree angle folds.

"Carly! May I ask... Did Jeffrey ever find out about the baby?"

"Yes, Viola. He was so happy. So was I. We have a boy. A couple of years passed. Jeffrey would return to England when he could. We'd sneak away to spend time with our son. When Patrick was sent on assignment, Jeff and I got pregnant again. That's when I first came to the Complex, which is forbidden for women, but I had to sleep with Patrick to make him think it was his child. After that, Patrick wanted me to continue visiting him here."

"How did Jeffery feel about it?"

"He hated it, but he had to be okay with it. We had a girl. Ironically, we had both heirs anyway, even with Father splitting us apart. I haven't seen Jeffrey as much lately, not at all since I got pregnant with our daughter. He told me he's been unfaithful."

"Are you all right?"

"No, but at least he told me the truth. It's harder for him to be apart from me for such a long time. He said it tortured him, knowing I was still with Patrick. Jeff has some of Zack's tendencies with women. He told me he did much of what I saw with Zack and the girls that morning. He said he stopped caring once he was sent away. He knew I was to mate with Patrick. These past few years, Patrick has been stationed at this post. He wanted me here.

I know it's so he didn't have to screw the nomads. He said they're all bog-standard."

"What does that mean?" Viola asks.

"Not attractive. Plain. I think it's only because all the men had them first. Patrick was above sloppy seconds—he called it that. Since he became king of the Complex, I think I was—What do the magazines call it? A trophy wife."

Viola laughs. "I'm only laughing because I've seen the women. You're heads and tails above any girl here."

"I'm going to tell my dad the truth—all of it, Viola. Jeffrey's been punished enough for what happened too many years ago. I want him in my life and my children's. I refuse to keep my secret about him anymore."

"Good for you. Secrets destroy us, Carly. Lies suck the good out of us. Every secret, every lie, fills the soul. When we fill up with lies, we feel its weight. Heavy storm clouds shade our light within. Then one drop of rain is released. One lie falls because we've told so many, and we forget half of what we've said. That's when the storm arrives. It will either pour out, clearing up our soul, making room for the light again—or destroy everything in its path."

Carly gives Viola side eyes.

"So... you know that Dean's my father's son?" Carly says.

"Yes."

"I hope my father doesn't ask me to be with him next. I dread it. That's also why Dean's son is coming here, too. My father is the ruler of the Complex. Each Uncle rules territories."

"Why was Jason going to rule here? He said something about allowing Patrick."

"Wherever Jason is, he's the top General for however long he's there."

"Of everything?" asks Viola.

"That's what Jeff told me."

"Why wouldn't Jason tell me that?"

"They're not allowed—some sworn oaths. I wondered if you should have gone to the Plant with Jason. I'm sure he's been there before. I can't imagine you wouldn't have been allowed to leave. They must be testing you."

"What for? To see if I'm honorable enough. I'm sure my potty mouth has solidified that."

Carly laughs. "You're a born leader, no doubt about that, Viola. You don't fear. I'm sure Uncle Ardent will be talking about you."

"I don't give a rat's ass." Viola smiles, happy to make Carly smile.

Carly covers her mouth.

"You have dowdy language. Will you be okay if Jason—"

"Please don't ask me that question, Carly, not now. You, Missy, need to tell your father the truth about the kids being Jeffrey's before a new deal is made for you. It's important."

"I will. I love Jeff. I loved Patrick, too, Viola. I wouldn't have been with Jeff if Patrick had been true to me. I was so blind. Looking back, I tried too hard with Patrick. I wanted to keep him happy. It was hopeless. He always had to have more and be the best. He was so competitive."

"He was insecure, Carly, in more ways than one. That's all. I like Jeff. He's rugged and strong. Do I need to get my own room?"

Carly quips. "I think he has his own."

"If he doesn't, he can sleep in here. Do try to keep it down."

Carly grabs her pillow. She throws it at Viola.

"Take your shower, Viola."

"Can I borrow your shampoo, Car? Using the reindeer soap on my hair is ruining its pH balance."

"You and your pH rabble, science whiz. My stuff is all in that bag. Have at it, Lady V."

"Hey, I warned you, only Brant was allowed to call me that... Snaggletooth," Viola says with a sly grin.

"That bloody bugger—he told you?"

"He was mad that you told me about Jacko, so—"

"I still have that historic doll. I hid my new dolly from him after that," Carly says, pointing her finger in the air. Her finger drops.

"Brant was the best of us siblings, Viola. The absolute best."

————

That night, Viola wakes, hearing the room's door click. Jeffrey sneaks in, she can hear whispering, then kissing, then more kissing. Viola covers her ears with her pillow to give them privacy. There's no hiding the sounds of sex in close quarters.

I'm happy for them. Carly cried all day.

Viola peeks over as their bed creaks. Their bodies—concealed by a sheet—move in a rhythm. The sheet moves down with Jeffrey's broad, muscular back tensing as he lifts himself onto his elbows to increase his movement.

Viola shuts her eyes, remembering that last night at Uncle's place before she ran away with Zee. In the nursery room, Zee was sleeping in his crib. She lifted the pillow from her face to see Jason's head pop up from under the covers after giving her an epic orgasm. Viola can feel his lips kissing their way up her body. One last soft kiss on her neck as his love pushed into her.

She tried to clear her thoughts. She knew she would run the following day. She turned her head, to make sure Zee was still asleep after hearing him coo. The image of Jason's incredible upper body was in the mirror's reflection in the old vanity in the corner of the room. She watched as his muscles flexed. She was sad to leave him, to hurt him. She felt ashamed. She told herself it wasn't love. He was only pretending to love her. She was desperate to believe it, not to have to hurt him. But she had to get Zee out.

After Jason came inside her, he looked into her eyes. He told her that he loved her. She felt it. She kissed him. She couldn't stop crying. He asked her if she was all right. She said she was sad about her mom's life, her book. She hated lying to him. He kissed her so passionately. She knew in that moment that she would break his heart, and break her own, twelve hours later.

Viola pulls the pillow harder into her face, this time to hide the sobs coming from her open mouth, wanting to cry out for Brant and Mary and their children, who will never know how incredible their father was. Her cry for Uncle, her mother, Jason, and her unborn baby. Her tears of heartbreak, tears of love, seeing Zee's sleeping face before she walked to the van that day.

Forgive me, Zee.

-..Chapter 56-..-

It's early, and Viola's hungry. She tucks her shirt into the cargo pants Carly loaned her. She attempts to quietly close the door behind her. In the hallway, she marches toward the kitchen.

I'm 'Hank Marvin'—Will I ever get these British words right? I'm pretty sure Jason said that meant I'm starving when I asked.

Yesterday, after Jason's departure, she couldn't bring herself to eat. Not four steps out the door, Jeffrey is on her tail, tucking in his shirt.

"Jeffrey, you'll have the men talking about us. I don't need that right now."

"My apologies, Viola, I'm to follow you wherever you go. My orders."

"From Jason?"

"Yes."

"Who is this Ardent that's here?"

"He's an Uncle and the commander in the Big HQ. They call it the Plant."

"Have you ever been there?"

"No."

"This family has so many secrets, Jeff."

"Doesn't every government?"

"How would I know? I'm a simple girl."

"Oh, lass, you're far from simple."

She turns to stop him. "You need to tell your father about your feelings for Carly before other deals are made. You need to step back into your family and be the man you know you are." She turns and continues to walk. He trails behind her.

Inside the cafeteria, everyone stops when she enters, whispers erupt.

As her friend Abby used to say, *"Word travels fast."* Viola is aware that any of these men could attempt to assassinate her.

I don't care. I'm hungry. I'm hormonal. I'll die when I die!

Viola walks to the spread of food: eggs, potato wedges, bacon, and milk.

"Effing deer milk!"

She looks around the large room and sees his salt and pepper hair first, then the unique badge on the shoulder of his army garb, before his body turns. Uncle Ardent is glaring at her. She heads his way with Jeffrey in tow. She notices that Uncle Ardent has his gun out.

"Might I sit and eat here?" she asks.

He motions with his hand, unsmiling.

"It would be best to stay in your quarters for another day," he says. "Jefferey can bring you food."

"Okay. Thanks." She says as she places a napkin in her lap. She picks up her fork and knife like she was taught to eat her food.

"Do you have a death wish, Madame Eastman?"

"No, but I refuse to hide away like a scared mouse from any skinny cat who thinks it's phat."

"No need to make it easy for them."

She drops her cutlery purposely on the community table and stands.

I've had enough of all of this!

The room goes silent. Jeffrey has his gun raised. She notices the armed soldiers at the doors, ready and prepared to shoot anyone who moves.

"I can only assume you know who I am," says Viola. "I'm not your enemy. You're not mine. We are blood-related, all of us. This internal battle is a waste of lives lost. Think about it. Why do you want war? What will it do for *you* but get *you* killed? Patrick was not a leader. He was an insecure boy who was thinking with his head filled with greed—and to lead what exactly? To have you do things you wouldn't do on any normal day. Would you kill your brother, your sister, or your mate if he said so? I'm also someone's sister and their mate. Pretend for a moment I'm yours."

After chuckles erupt from other men, she continues.

"How many of your relatives are dead because of Patrick's quest for power? His power over *you*. Not *your* power. And you aren't weak, are you? Only if you follow a boy who tells you to do bad things. Then you choose to be weak with him. A strong man is a wise man who won't promote war. Why do that when we are good? We choose to be good. Your ego, the snake—don't let it take the lead. You're smarter than that. Kill me. Then what? You'll have to keep killing the next innocent me, your sister, your mate. I don't have a gun. I'm defenseless. If you want to kill me, my blood is on your hands."

"Sit down." Ardent says under his breath.

"Think of why you want a top spot with all the jealous men sitting next to you, who were once your friends but now will want you dead. For what, a title? An invented word. Stop. Think. You're nothing without honor. Killing your blood is not honorable. Be the man you were born to be. Be Good." She picks up her deer milk, drinks half the glass, sets it down, covering her mouth in an attempt not to gag. She walks out of the cafeteria doors with Jeffrey behind her.

Uncle Ardent follows them into the hallway.

He calls out, "STOP!"

She turns to face him.

"Need I remind you that you're not in command here? If you think your rant made a dent in this war, you're a power-driven, insecure misfit yourself."

"Some of them heard me, and that means something to me. I don't want to hear about Garrett being killed next. If no one says anything, that's the call his mate, children, and family will receive." She walks toward her uncle. "I don't care what you think about me. I only care what I think about myself. I don't want any titles. So, take that back to your secret Plant. And for the record—" she stands directly in front of him "—you will not spank me. No man will touch me or violate me ever again while I'm living and breathing, so be ready for a fight if you *dare* attempt to lay your hands on me. I will *not* go down willingly." She stares at him, and an angry tear slips down her cheek. She turns on her heel, to continue toward her room.

Jeffery stops before he unlocks the door for her.

"Viola, I've a ton of respect for you. Jason would be so proud. I'm sorry. I hope you both make it through this. I don't think there's another partner for you. It's almost unreal that you two are so alike, determined, and in sync. Yet you didn't even know him growing up."

"I want him back, Jeff. I don't want to have our baby without him. You understand how that feels." He nods. "I wish I had gone with him. I'm afraid of being alone."

And not getting Zee back.

"What if Jason never wakes up, and I'm stuck where they take me?"

Jason is key!

"I chose wrong," Viola tearfully tells Jeffrey. "I see that now. I must face my fear."

———

Viola paces back and forth.

I can't stay in this room for one more second. I should have gone with Jason. I made a mistake. I hate myself for it. I know that's why I'm being mean and rude to everyone. I'm leaving. I have to get Zee.

Viola can't relax. She opens her door to find Jeffrey still standing guard.

"Please take me to the command room."

He rolls his eyes, "Yes, ma'am." They walk side by side. He knocks three times. The door opens.

Inside the command room are Garrett, Uncle Ardent, and five other soldiers. She sees another man—a boy, really, he looks to be thirteen—standing around a table covered with maps.

"Hello," she says to Uncle Ardent. "Might I have a word with you, sir?"

"You can call me Uncle Ardent. I have a name."

"Uncle Ardent, may we have a word in private?"

"This is as private as it gets, Madame Eastman. What can I do for you?"

"I've changed my mind. I want to go to the Plant with you."

He glares at her. "You will remain there for the rest of your life. You do understand that."

"As long as I'm with Jason, I'm okay with that."

"If he doesn't make it, what will you do?"

"But he will make it. We have the best scientists in the world. I can't imagine you'd take him there if you felt there was not more you could do for him."

"We leave in one hour."

-..Chapter 57-. .-

Viola has her things packed. She hugs Carly and Jeffrey and asks him to fill Zack in about everything. She will also try to contact him as soon as she lands.

Jeffrey escorts her to the helicopter pad. When she gets there, Leo's waiting.

"Hi Leo, is Ardent on his way?"

"I'm sorry, ma'am. He left."

"When? I didn't hear the helicopter."

"He went by truck to the airport. He said to tell you that head-quarters has denied your request. You're to go to England as your Uncle Mark commanded."

Viola is crushed. What game are they playing? Ardent lied to her face. Carly was right. There is something more going on here. They don't want her to uncover any of it.

Are they afraid of me? They could kill me, and this could be over.

"Thank you, Leo, for all your help. I want to go to the airport. I want to leave right now."

Jeffrey and Leo's eyes connect. "I'll call the pilot. I'll see when he can take off."

"Thank you," she says.

Jeffrey falls in step behind her. He stops her once they're far enough away for privacy.

"What are you doing? It's not safe to travel. We should wait for my father until he can figure out what's going on. Viola, trust me when I tell you something strange is happening. I'm not privy to the information."

"I think there's a shift in control," she says. "I hope they want to help bring Jason back and not take him wherever to finish him off. Then there's me. Zack's already out of the succession."

"That's not true, Viola. Don't forget your baby, Zack."

She knows how true that statement is.

"I'm not waiting, Jeffrey. You gave Jason your word. Please respect that and take me away from here today."

————

Dean's son Kirk arrived. Viola didn't realize he was the young boy in the room when she went to speak with Uncle Ardent. Carly also wants to go home and return her dead brother's bodies to the family. Dean asks to go with them to England. He'll catch a connecting flight back to America.

Before heading to the airport, they say their farewells at the Complex. Viola hugs Janic for an extra-long beat. She thanks him and tells him to keep in touch. When he writes down his mobile number for her, Jeffrey looks at him with a WTF expression. Viola observes Dean speaking with his son.

He's too young to be here amongst all these beefy men.

This is precisely what she believes starts these internal riffs—having a young boy in command over capable, well-trained men. For a moment, she wishes she could have a say in their laws of hierarchy and change a few of them to stop the internal battles. They wouldn't exist, she believes, if the best, most qualified man sat in the big chair and did not just sit there because of politics or birthright.

In the back of the truck on an extended bench, with two bodies wrapped in tarps on the truck's floor in front of them, they drive to the airport in silence. Viola catches Dean peering over at Carly.

Jeffrey saw it, too. He moves across the long seat to sit next to Carly on the bench in the back of the truck. He takes her hand in his as Dean watches.

Jeff moves in, kisses her on the mouth. She blushes but kisses him back.

Jeffrey's finally making it real, taking charge, letting Dean see that Carly's off-limits.

Way to go, Jeffy.

Viola glances at Dean, smiling. He smiles back. Love can't be controlled. You can try to push it aside, not see the person for an extended period. You'll have moments where you're okay without them. But you still see their face behind your eyes when you lie down to sleep at night. You feel their hands touching your skin, a feeling you only have with that person. You try to push it away. But the heart wants what it wants.

-..Chapter 58-. .-

After the plane lands on the airstrip, Viola and Carly walk down the steps onto the tarmac. They hold onto each other, whispering in giggles. Jeffrey and Dean glance their way.

Viola walks up to Jeffrey, takes his hand in hers.

"Thank you. It doesn't seem like it's enough, Jeffy. Thank you so very much." She pulls him close to her. "Go get your woman."

"I can't let you leave without me, Viola."

"You have to. I'll be okay. I'll message you on the phone you gave me once we land."

"I don't like this," he says.

"Then hurry up, make a deal for Carly and your children," she says. "Then come find me."

"You're one of a kind, lass," says Jeffrey.

"In a grander scheme of things, aren't we all. Make the deal. I'll hang out til then."

"Don't forget what we spoke of, Viola."

"I won't. Please keep your end of the bargain. I'm determined to go to the Plant sooner rather than later."

"I'd expect nothing less from you, lass. Viola... stay alive so Jason doesn't wake up and kill me for leaving your side."

"He wouldn't do that, Jeffrey. And I promise, as much as I can promise."

They both smile. He takes out a handgun and tosses her his army bag. He stuffs his gun in the back of his pants. They both turn at the same time to see Mary standing next to a car, on the tarmac between their plane and a smaller private plane being refueled.

Viola bursts into tears as they run toward each other and embrace.

"Viola, I—I—"

"*Shhh,* Mary."

Viola pulls back to look into Mary's glassy eyes as her tears pour down her cheeks.

"I'm sorry, Rosemary, for your loss. I'm so sorry. Brant was like no other."

Mary nods her head, glancing over Viola's shoulder, seeing Jeffrey coming their way.

Mary whispers, "Achara made contact. She said to tell you Tae will meet you at your destination. You're no longer safe, Althea. Be careful."

Viola exhales, feeling the full weight of Mary's statement. Viola recalls what Jill told her when Zee and she got into the back of the black van.

Viola was eight years old when Jill showed Viola the picture before hypnotizing her. This was the same image that Jill left in an envelope on Viola's best friend, Jes's, doorstep in Telega. At that time, when Viola burned it in Jes's fire pit, she didn't remember too much of what had happened.

Later, on her first trip to England, the moment Viola saw her cousins, Mary and Catherine, with their mother, Aunt Lara, Viola knew that Mary was Rosemary, the girl in the ocean who'd been bitten by the shark in Germany. Viola remembered what happened to Mary's left hand.

Mary blinked twice, acknowledging that she remembered, too, and as soon as Viola read the names scratched into the wood at the cottage, Rosemary, Lily, Camee, and Tae. It was then that Viola realized she was part of their group, along with Polina, whom they called Polly for short, and Ali, short for Althea, completing the six in the group photo.

In the Van, Jill explained what happened years ago.

"Polina is my daughter. Our lives changed after Alexander, my mate, shot my mother. She gave you her ring. Alexander kidnapped Polina that day you got away. Your mother tried to help me find her. When your mother caught Stephen touching you in your room when you were five, she called me, and we made a pact not to stop until we got Polina and you out of the family. It was your mother who found out where Alexander had taken Polina, and although it took several years, it was your mother's plan that got her back for me. I was supposed to get you out. But when you got into that car accident in Telega, it changed the course of our lives."

"What do you mean by, 'our lives'?"

"Important people thought I was dead."

Viola's hand went to her mouth.

"I'm so sorry, Jill. I didn't know."

Viola sits on the smaller plane, watching Mary and Carly out her window, as Jeffrey and a few other men lift the body bags of Patrick and Brant from the other plane. Viola trembles as she hears the plane's engine. She buckles her seat belt for takeoff. She refuses to remain in England. She told Jeffrey her next destination is America.

Viola feels strange sitting across from Dean, who is also going to America, knowing that he and her mother were in love. As she moves around the area, she doesn't want to make him uncomfortable. She needs to get to Uncle's in Telega to send a private message to help Jason. Now that she's pregnant, she wants to contact Jill. According to Jill's one-sided conversation in the van, Viola will be allowed to have Zee back once her pregnancy is confirmed.

She wants to get her baby and go as far away from this family as possible.

"What are you doing, Viola?" Dean asks.

Using a rectangular box, a device from Jeffrey's bag that Jeffrey gave to Viola, she moves about the plane's cabin until a red light turns green. Viola pulls a metal nail file from her purse that Carly gave her. She stands on the arm of a chair and reaches into a can light, popping off something. It's a bug. She goes to the bathroom and flushes the toilet.

What device is that?" asks Dean.

"Sorry, Dean, I was using this Betsy that Jeff loaned me to check for listening ears. Is it all right if I ask you a few questions?"

"Sure." He says as she stuffs the device back in the bag.

"Did my mom ever say anything to you, Dean, about getting me out?"

"There's no way out, only in."

Viola swallows hard. That's what Mom told her when she was a girl. Jill also told her the same thing in the van. The only way out...is in.

-..Chapter 59-..-

When they land, Viola wakes to find Dean standing over her.

"We've landed." he says, stepping away from her.

Viola notices one of his arms is behind his back. Viola watches out the window to see they've landed at the private airfield near Buffalo. A diplomatic black car pulls up to a stop.

Dean gathers his bags and tells Viola to go in front of him while exiting the plane.

She pretends to have to use the restroom first. Once in that small compartment, she types a message to Jeffrey on the phone he gave her.

We've landed. Something is off with Dean. I'll call soon if I'm able.

She stuffs the phone into her purse, then opens her bag.

WHAT! Where is it? Someone took it.

The poison dart, the one Brant pulled from the Nomad woman, is missing.

It was in my bag, now it's gone. Did Dean take it? Jeffrey told Janic to watch my things so I could shower before we left the Complex. Did he go through my things?

Viola steps out of the bathroom. The landing stairs are down.

Why is he still here? Why is Dean waiting for me?

"Dean, I'm sorry. Why don't you walk down the stairs first?"

"Excuse me."

"I'd like you to walk down the stairs first," she says.

"Okay," he says.

Dean stands at the opening briefly before starting down them.

Who are they? Am I going to be kept in a house again? This is why Jeffrey didn't want to leave me alone. My determination to do good for my cousins and their love story may have ended my moment of freedom... Face your fears, Viola Ted.

She walks down the stairs after Dean, who waits at the bottom for her. She can't tell who is in the car. Its tinted windows are too dark. She rubs the goosebumps on her chilly bare arms.

The door opens; a man steps out. Then, another emerges from the passenger side.

"What the hell!" she says.

You were the paramedics who took my mother's body away in Telega.

There's nowhere for her to run. All Viola can do now is hope Dean isn't a fricken dickhead, handing her over to these men for whatever reason.

Without a sound, one man goes down, then the next.

Dean turns toward Viola—then he falls to the ground too.

Viola stares at all three men on the ground.

"What in the hell happening?"

A brown Ford truck with a cream camper shell is racing across the tarmac toward the plane. She recognizes it as the same truck that she and Jason had their two-off in before she left for England with Carly and Brant.

The truck comes to a screeching halt. Zack jumps out with an odd-looking gun slung around his shoulder.

"Princess, damn, you look *Mmmm* good. Let's go, get in."

Viola hurries into the truck, shuts the door.

Zack brought her winter jacket. It's on the passenger seat. She grins.

He's generally selfish, but thoughtful enough to remember this.

Zack drags the men's bodies back into their car. He moves Dean's body to the back of the truck. She shivers, thinking of how many bodies Zack has dragged away.

He hops into the driver's seat. He leans over to give her a quick peck on the lips. His mouth lingers to see—What? If she'll kiss him back?

"Hi to you, too, stranger," she says, smiling.

She gives him a quick kiss, hoping to make him happy.

"Thank you for bringing my jacket."

She slips it on because she's cold but mostly to avoid another kiss.

"God, I'm glad you're alive. I've missed your pretty face, Princess."

She shifts her head to look at the other car.

"Did you kill those men?"

"No. They're not dead. I shot them with tranquilizers."

"I take it Jeffrey asked you to pick me up?"

"No. He *told* me to pick you up, to be on time, or he'd kill me. I had very few options."

She laughs. When he looks at her puzzled, she says, "I never thought I'd see the day Zackary Eastmann would be afraid of anyone."

"Have you seen Jeffery?" he asks.

"Yes. I can see how he could be intimidating."

"If you saw him in battle—" he whistles through his teeth "—that's a whole different ballgame."

The mention of ballgame reminds Viola of her dad. He said that once. When she wanted a passport so she could run away across the world and be free, that didn't work out very well.

"What's this?" she asks, looking at several items Zack tosses on the solo bench seat between them.

"Whatever I pulled out of Dean's pockets."

Viola eyes the syringe in a baggie.

"Keep this, Zack. I think he brought a sample of whatever the young doctor injected into Jason. We need someone you trust to find out what is all in it."

"Why?"

"Jason should have woken up, but he hasn't. He's still in a coma. Dean thought the doctor, Henry, lied about the contents of the poison. We need to find an antidote."

Zack carefully hands the baggie to Viola.

"You hold it. I'm bound to break it or lose it, Princess. I have a guy," he says. "It's a drive. We can go tomorrow. Right now, I've got to get you out of sight, young lady."

Zack revs the truck and lays his foot heavy on the gas.

"YEE-HAW!" he hollers.

"You fool, don't kill us." Zack's wearing his signature Henley. "Have you been working out?" she asks.

"You could say it's part of my therapy. Every time I want to fuck the shit out of someone's mouth, I lift weights—heavy ones—until I'm spent. It's been helping."

"Good for you."

I'm glad he's trying to stop.

"And you... Shit. You look sexy as sin. I see a wee bump." He peers down at her stomach. His eyes linger on her legs. "I remember you looking as you do right now with Zee in the pouch."

"I love being pregnant."

"I love you, pregnant Princess."

"How are you, honestly, Zack?" She can see that his pants are tented.

"It's a new, improved kind of living. Harder than I thought to make decisions on my own without Dad telling me everything I have to do."

"Do you like it?"

"I miss some of it. I'm sorry... about Uncle. You were his favorite everything. His *Vee Bee*. I still can't believe he's gone. It doesn't seem real."

"You saw him... after?"

"Yeah, asshole shot him in the back. He was shot a few more times once he was down."

"I hope it wasn't because of me." She says.

"Why would you say that? Patrick had a plan in place, Princess. Uncle Mark was his next target. You had nothing to do with that."

Her eyes drop toward the floorboards. Zack lays his hand on top of hers and intertwines their fingers. He rubs the inside palm of her hand with his thumb. It was something she did to calm him when they were together.

-..Chapter 60-..-

Their drive takes over an hour. He stops the truck to open a gate, drives through, hops out to close it. They drive across grass. There's no road. Before too long, they pull up to a tiny white house.

Viola unzips Jeff's army bag to check her phone to see if Jeffrey messaged her back. Zack eyes it.

"I'm checking to see if Jeff replied. He gave me this phone. I messaged him before I got off the plane." She looks out her window. "This is a pretty house. I like it."

"It was one of Uncle's spots."

"One of his or one of yours?" she says with a raised eyebrow.

"No whor—women in here."

"What about me? I'm a woman. I'm here."

"You're family." He says.

Before they step out of the vehicle, she watches where he hides the key. Zack pushes the bottom of the door's armrest. A department pops open for the key. He reaches into his pocket, pulling out another set of keys.

"That's neat."

"Jason's quick getaway spot." He says.

She smiles. "For show?"

"Cameras everywhere. Gotta show them keys. We always put them in the foyer."

"We have a lot of customs and traditions, don't we, Zack?"

"I need to teach you more—Jason's orders. It will only be more complicated if we don't die first."

"Excellent," she says sarcastically. "Any food in this place? I'm starving."

He stares at her for an extra beat.

"I've been told I make a mean egg on toast," he says, his eyes never leaving hers.

"Zack, those early days at the cabin are not memories you need to refresh for me." His face changes. "You were my kidnapper—a rapist, in my mind. I know you never had a girlfriend experience until me. I wasn't mad. I was furious. I want to live my life forward, not backward. My good memories I have to hang onto. I have to."

"I'm sorry, Princess. Every moment with you was good for me—even your bad ones. I don't have those feelings, the ones you do. They don't exist in me. When I thought you had killed yourself, that time you ran—that was the first time I ever cried. I didn't even feel the tears on my face until you licked them. I felt your tongue."

"They injected you when you were born. Jeffrey too. That's why you feel certain urges and can't feel other feelings."

"Who told you that?"

"Patrick's mother."

"Jason told me. He's in."

"What do you mean, in?" she asks.

"All the way in."

"Do you think that they'll keep him in a coma? Can anyone save him?"

"They won't kill Jason. He's too valuable."

"Wouldn't that make people want him dead?"

"Only the insignificant."

"Not true, Zack."

"Princess, Uncle Benjamin's father, Isak, is the Top General at the Plant. Ardent is Doc's father. They came for Uncle's body when he was killed. Jason was there. I hid out in the shed. I saw them."

"Why wouldn't they want me there? Ardent said I wasn't allowed to go."

"Jason's been through crazy shit with them watching, never interfering—unless they have to."

"We're caged animals," she says.

"Princess? Jason will be groomed for Uncle's spot—make no mistake. He'll most likely be put back here to take Uncle Benjamin's position if he lives."

"We need to get this syringe to a lab—pronto, Zack. I don't want to wait for someone to find us and take it. We need to find out what's in this."

I know that look. He's not happy.

"Go to the bathroom. I'll grab food. We'll get back on the road."

"Thank you, Zack."

"Hey," he says, stopping her. "I'm glad you're alive. I wanted to come when I heard that Patrick shot you. I wanted to rip everyone's heads clean off them."

"Zack." She squeezes his hand. "I know you love our baby and me."

"Jason told me what you did, Princess. I was mad as hell at you for giving our boy up. You need to be punished."

I know that face. He wants mean sex.

"You're a good person, Zack." His eyes close. "Zack Eastmann, you're good. Look at us now. Yes, you have a bad side, a bad man who can do terrible things. The real you, the good still exists in there."

He sneers with his fists clenched.

"You're a mother father, Zack. You want to tape my mouth shut, don't you?"

He nods, opening his eyes.

"Don't you mean mother fucker, princess?"

"Why can't we have a normal conversation, Zack? Did you hear one word I said?"

"Maybe two. Can we go inside before this speech grows longer, Princess? There's a small, quaint graveyard nearby. I can take you there if you need to talk. Say everything that's on that big, beautiful heart of yours."

They both step out of the truck to head into the house.

"You're the definition of a shithead, Zack."

He laughs. He moves behind her to smack her ass. "I like this mother-father talk."

"Believe it or not, Dean told me there was no need for my vulgar language. I'm trying to find cleaner versions. You were a terrible influence on me, fyi."

"Dean! Shit. I forgot he's in the back of the truck."

"When will he wake up?"

Zack eyes his watch. "Not yet, Princess. I'll need to inject or tie him up soon."

He unlocks and opens the door for her. He flicks on the lights.

"Whose side is Dean on?" she asks, walking toward the bathroom straight ahead of her.

"He's not with the Uncles. He's got a tiny rogue group, that's what Jason told me. He's not bad. He wants to make things right again. Everyone close to him dying changed him."

"Does Jason trust him?"

She turns to shut the door. Zack's eyes are glued to her lower region.

"Yes and no," he says. "Jason thinks he'll get himself killed. Dean's trying to do good things. I'm protecting him by keeping him."

"Don't you think he will have questions when he wakes up? He knows you shot Bobby."

"Hurry up, Princess. We should get going."

"I love how you can blow me off so easily. This is serious—how he feels."

"You lost me at blow you. My mind went places. Good places."

"What's your problem, Zack? If you're intentionally trying to piss me off, it's working."

"Princess, I don't want to do that. I'm trying to be us without touching you. Without ripping your clothes off and fucking you right here like I want to. Everyone I fuck has your face. Is that what you want to hear? Cause that's what it's like for me. That's what happens. I like it. I can live that way. Having you in my face, right here—" he exhales "—this is not easy for me. You chose Jason. Yeah, he's the better man. I like him more than you, if you can believe it. I don't want to fuck him. I want to fuck you. That's my problem."

"Should I go somewhere else? I didn't—"

"If you apologize, I'm going to lose my shit. Stop talking. Let me get this out. We'll move forward, as you like to say. I'll deal with my feelings, or lack thereof, as best I can. I hear you, Princess. I care what you think, how you feel. If you're hurt, you've changed me. I can't change back into my completely disastrous self. It's for the best. It's not because I don't have you. I fucked that up. I have to leave you alone because I'll still fuck other women. You don't like that—our last conversation. I remember. That's where our crossroads meet, and we walk the other way, or you walk. I turn around."

"Why do you do that? Why do you turn?"

"Because the red in me has needs that won't stop, not with drugs, not for love. I like me more like this. I hate you sometimes."

"That's good," she says.

"How is that good, Princess?"

"Mom said that when you hate someone you used to love, it shows you that you still love them. Can you try to focus on loving me as your sister and our son we created together each time you want to hate me?"

"What do you think I do? There's no fucking magic healing that will happen with this conversation. It is what it is. I'll deal with it. Jason has been dealing with the same feelings."

"What are you talking about, Zack?"

"You fucking took off after swooning your love for Jason in everyone's faces at Uncle's. Then you jump in a car with Derek! It's Jason we're talking about. He followed your tracks, right down to Derek buying a new fucking base for an infant car seat. He asked me who this Derek was, so I told him about you and Derek."

Oh, no!

"The look on his face, Princess, almost made me fucking cry for the second time in my life. I saw a piece of my brother die right there in his eyes."

"I—I was going to tell him. I told Uncle the day before I left that I wanted no secrets between him and me, but—"

"Yeah, but."

"I have to go to him, Zack."

"Not right now, Princess. You can't. He's still unconscious or in a coma or whatever."

"He told me I hurt him. I saw that look, Zack. I thought he was acting. Shit! He was waiting for me to tell him! I didn't—didn't even cross my mind. I wasn't *with* Derek that day. I don't think about him anymore. Those first love feelings have changed. I don't want Derek."

"I hope to hell Jason wakes up so you can tell him. I know you. This is going to eat at you until you speak to him. Ah, fuck, Viola. You need to stop and think before you run off and do whatever the fuck you think you have to do. You have a good heart. You're smart—but not when you fly off the handle. You have this know-it-all, must do the right thing..." He pushes out a long breath, running his fingers through his hair. "You're not always right, Princess."

"Thank you for telling me, Zack. It's true. Patrick almost killed me a second time because of my compulsiveness. With everything happening as it has, I don't think I'd ever have remembered to tell Jason about Derek."

"I only told Jason that Derek was there for you when your mom died. You were sad. You wouldn't move. You wouldn't eat. You had no one. He stayed over for about seven days, then that night, he arrived late. He started kissing you. Things happened, as they do. I told him I knew because I saw it on the screen. I felt fucked up because he was so fucked up. He wanted details. How long were you with that guy? I told him you weren't with him. I thought it was only because your mom died. Derek started coming around, helping babysit you for Uncle. You were alone in the house. I told Jason I followed you before that, and that you were always alone. Derek was never in the picture."

"What did Jason say?"

"Not a lot. He said it was his fault. He smashed shit on a table, which is not like him. Then he said he was okay. He calmed down."

"How was me sleeping with Derek his fault?"

Zack shrugs his shoulders.

"I had no clue he was waiting for me," says Viola. "He slept with no one since Dad made him... He said it was me or no one when we were in England. I should have told him then. I thought about it. I didn't want to ruin our moment. Even Carly tried before with him. He wouldn't."

"Did he tell you that?"

"No, Aunt Lara did. Carly admitted to me that she hit on Jason. He told her no way, that he would only be with me. She told me I was lucky to have a man like Jason. Everyone else cheats. I feel like I cheated on him with Derek, even though at the time, I didn't know Jason existed."

"There you go. You didn't know shit, Princess. So let this go. Jason's had to. No one's cheating, though I'm cheating with you in my mind daily. Remember your own words, sis," he says with a smile. "There's no going back, only forward. It sounds like you and Jay had already moved forward before Henry got him."

"We did. We have. I just—I want to tell him everything the minute he wakes up. I want no secrets from him."

Zack slides his arm around her shoulders and holds her to him. He leans in to sniff her neck.

"Fuck, I love the way you smell...Use the bathroom and be quick about it, so we can get going, Princess, or I'm gonna strip you naked."

-..Chapter 61-. .-

In the truck, Viola pretends to be asleep. Derek slipped her mind. She didn't want to get him in any trouble. She tried to forget the ordeal with Zee and how she even got to the black truck. It was reckless of her to call Derek and involve him. Viola felt it the minute she saw him again, seeing the hope in his eyes. He didn't care that she had another man's baby. He was willing to drop his life for her. She had to stop him in his tracks. She was worried he might try to look for her or go to Uncle's. She hoped he would leave it alone as she asked him to.

I was selfish. I am selfish.

She will tell Jason absolutely everything the next time she sees him, when they can talk. She felt closer than ever to him when he told her about what he had gone through with their dad. That was information he never wanted her to find out, but he shared it with her. She now realizes, to build trust. And then he waited for her to tell him about Derek—but she didn't.

I have to set things right with him. I must get to the Plant. I'll stay there until he wakes. I'll have our baby in the same building where he is. He wasn't faking his feelings or his hurt.

The pain she saw on his face was real in the forest that day. What she said...

I was ridiculous. He deserves better than me. He wasn't wrong.

Viola doesn't think it's right to be with him, but she doesn't want him to be with anyone else.

I hate feeling this needy.

Sex connects her. She's insecure. She's jealous for no reason.

This is so messed up. Mom tried to warn me about this. Let it go, Viola.

She hears a loud banging from the back of the truck, and her eyes pop open.

Zack pulls over. "I think our cousin is awake," he says.

"Zack, let me talk to him."

"And what are you planning to tell him?"

"Please hang back. But rescue me if I get tongue-tied."

"I just got a hard-on. You can't talk about your tongue like that, Princess."

"Zack, can you behave for one minute, please?"

They both get out. As she climbs into the back, Dean seems surprised to see her. "Viola, what's going on?"

"Dean, Jason wants to protect you. They—whoever they are—seem to believe you've gone rogue. Jason sent Zack to pick you and me up. To take us to a safe place."

"Is Zack here?"

"Yes. If you try to hurt him, you'll have to stay tied up."

"Better keep me tied up. I will wring his neck if my hands are free."

"We're headed now to a lab to see what's in the poison Jason was injected with."

"You found the syringe?"

"Yes."

"What about my men?"

"They're fine. Zack said they're probably waking up right about now."

"Can I call them so they don't hunt for me?"

"Let me talk to Zack about it. I don't want them to trace our whereabouts. Maybe give me a number. I'll call from a pay phone."

"You're getting in the game. Are you sure you want this? Once you're in, you're in."

"I go where Jason goes."

"It's not wise to live like that. He will always have a target on his head."

"And I won't?"

"Where do you go if one day he disappears?"

"I take my kids. I live my life until it's my time to fly."

"Just like that?"

"What answer are you looking for, Dean? I'm not your responsibility."

"No, but your mom wanted you to have freedom. She was working on a solution. We worked together. Did she mention that to you?"

Viola is royally confused. She's not sure what information he's trying to pull from her.

"Yes, she did."

"That's really why they wanted her dead. Viola, it could be serious for you if they find out. I mean, it will be."

Zack comes into view behind the truck.

"Viola, what is Dean talking about? What are you not telling us?"

Dean stares at Zack.

Fuck, fruit... fuck, Zack! If you waited for thirty more seconds. Damn it.

Viola stares ahead. She reminds herself not to roll her eyes. Jason told her it was a bad habit. So did Brant and Jeffey.

"Dean, look, man," says Zack, "I'm sorry about Bobby. He had a gun raised at Doc. My orders were my orders."

"Did you even listen to their conversation?"

"I was ten feet away. Doc was giving him a chance to back down. I assume he didn't want to, with how it played out."

"How did it play out, Zack?"

"Is there another story I should hear? They all keep changing. I can't keep them straight anymore." Zack says with an I-don't-give-a-fuck look.

"I think Doc wants me dead," says Dean. "Doc wanted my heir dead. Doc wants his son—my brother Ryan—moved up since I'm not his. I analyzed my mother's blood when she died. She was poisoned. I did the analysis myself. Doc was angry that my mom cheated with Uncle Mark. He's not safe, either."

Viola is stunned at the news about Doc. She loves Doc.

Zack turns to Viola. "We're not sure. We can't rule out Doc might have been in on this with Patrick when Uncle was shot, Princess. Patrick mentioned it to someone. We've kept it a secret, trying to uncover if it's true."

"Doc had access to your Uncle's room," Dean says. "With all of the heart attacks, aneurysms, and strokes in the family in a short time, a few top Uncles wanted an inquiry. Doc created many serums that Jason found in a hidden lab."

"Are you sure it's his lab, Dean?" she asks.

"We believe so. Your mom uncovered it. She lived with Doc for four years before she reunited with your dad. She confirmed some of his equipment. When my mother died, she was healthy. It didn't add up."

Viola is stunned. *Doc?*

"Why would Doc kill my mom?" Her eyes meet Zack's. "Did he work with Dad? And Patrick and Auntie Lara? Henry too? It would make sense then that Doc would send Henry to get rid of Jason." Viola catches Zack shaking his head no to Dean.

No, to what? What else are they not telling me?

At Dean's request, Zack keeps him tied up in the back of the truck. They all agree it would be best to table the conversation and to first get the sample to the lab where Zack has connections.

Viola watches as Zack checks his mirrors every so many seconds, scanning vehicles on the road around them.

"Is this what you do? You watch your back every second of every day in case someone is following you."

"What choice do I have, Princess?"

"Thank you for picking me up and telling me about Derek."

He side-eyes her with a smile. "You're welcome. I didn't tell Jason how long you'd seen Derek for. I mean, Uncle did cut me off once he caught me peeping. I assume you were with the guy more than once."

She nods her head. "Not for long. You took me away soon after."

"I was ordered to wait a bit since your mom died."

"Dad's order?"

"I was pissed off that Uncle allowed you to be with that guy. I almost drove to that Derek guy's house. I wanted to put a bullet in him. Dad said it would change you—not in a good way, with your mom dying too."

You killed her. She didn't just die!

"Uncle only allowed it, Zack, so I could learn how to teach you and Jason how love should look. I would have been lost otherwise. That's why they were going to have me with Doc's youngest son, Archie. So, he could teach me. They gave me a shot so I couldn't get pregnant. It was always the plan to have heirs with you and Jason."

"Both of us—or just Jason?"

"Both. Uncle wanted me to have a baby with you, not Dad. Dad only wanted me with Jason because he thought you were half blood."

"Fuck. Uncle was on my side. He told me that we could try since you seemed to love me. I thought he felt like Dad did, that I wasn't good enough for you. Story of my life."

"I'm sorry, Zack. That's why Mom wrote what she did. We three need to stick together. I'm proud of you for working hard on yourself. I'm glad we have our son."

"Me too," he says. "Jason told me Zee was safe. We'll get him back once all this crazy is over. I want to try for a girl... after you and Jason have two heirs."

Viola says nothing. She's stunned that Zack would think she'd ever be with him again. She doesn't want to hurt him more than he's been hurt. She nods with a slight smile, which makes him smile from ear to ear.

I need to tell Jason if he wakes. There's no bloody way in hell I'll be with Zack ever again. I wouldn't even consider it if Jason died. I'd be with cousins, many of them before Zack. I can't go back to his ways.

The rest of the drive is silent.

-..Chapter 62-. .-

It's dark when they arrive. There aren't any streetlights, only vacant buildings on both sides of the street, and storefronts with bars on the windows.

Dean seems calmer. He allows Viola to untie him, not Zack.

Zack tells them to leave their jackets in the truck, and he walks over, knocking on a solid steel door. After a slat opens, he says a sequence of numbers. The slat closes. A huge buff man opens the door. He checks out Viola from head to toe. Zack gives him a fun slap on the face.

"She's off-limits, Zini."

"What about this guy?" he says, sizing Dean up and down. "He's pretty."

"He's off limits, too." The man reaches for Viola. "Zini, no pat down necessary." Zini gives him an odd look. "These are my special guests." Zini moves aside to let them pass. "Is Caleb here?"

"Yeah. He's in the lab. Wait, he might be in the pit."

Zack turns to Viola with a smile. "Get ready for an interesting night. You'll be entering my world for a bit." He takes an orange bracelet from Zini, puts it on Viola's wrist, then puts another on Dean's. "I need to get Caleb. Then we'll go to the lab."

Dean and Viola share a confused look as they follow Zack through a hallway. Viola hears electronic dance music. A DJ plays the same song that she heard at one of her high school dances.

"Stay close to me," Zack says as he uses his fingerprint to open a thick, solid steel door. "If you're approached, show the bracelet. You'll be fine."

The music is so loud that Viola covers her ears. She looks around, her face heats. Most of the people in this place are fully clothed. The rest are naked and having sex. Viola reaches for Zack's hand and squeezes it hard. He turns to smile at her.

A gorgeous nude woman walks up to Zack, stopping them in their tracks. Dean bangs into the back of Viola.

Dean must be blown away by the people in this place, as much as I am.

The woman kisses Zack's neck. She rubs the front of his pants. He grips her face in a friendly manner, then shakes his head. She eyes his hand holding Viola's. The woman moves to her, softly grazing her fingertips over the side of Viola's breast. Zack watches intently while Viola is glued to the spot. Dean lifts Viola's arm to show the orange bracelet to the woman with his eyebrows raised. She removes her hand from Viola. She grabs Dean's pants, rubs him several times, licking her lips before he calmly removes her hand from his private area.

Zack throws back his head and laughs. The music is so loud that Viola can't hear what he is saying. He guides them to a long bar, lifts two fingers at the male bartender. He sits Viola down, facing the crowd. He mouths that he'll be back. She nods. Dean moves next to Viola to protect her, if that's possible in this place. She attempts to move her barstool. She looks down. It's nailed to the floor. She's forced to watch the events in front of her.

People are clustered in different areas. Viola's eyes are drawn to three people inside of a glossy white Plexiglas-fronted boxed-in area. A bed with one woman and two men is moving higher, rising, so the room can watch. Snow-white sheets and a white wall behind them make their tanned, slick naked bodies pop.

A breeze above Viola blows a piece of Viola's hair into her face. She peers up and sees that the ceiling is black. There's a slight glare. *Camera.*

The air smells familiar. It's not an air freshener scent, more like a clean, warm vanilla cinnamon.

I know this smell all too well. He would come home smelling like this.

Her eyes travel back to the main event, to the handsome man standing behind a woman, his erection in hand. He strokes as he stares at the woman on all fours, her ass in the air, her knees on the edge of the bed, purposely giving him a bird's eye view. The man grips the woman's hips with one of his hands. He waits.

What's he waiting for? For his cue to start?

The woman leans over another man who is lying on his back under her. Her mouth moves up and down on him.

Viola swallows, unable to move. Uncomfortable, she shifts her gaze. A man in an unusual mask is behind a woman, his hips thrusting hard, the woman's buttocks and breasts moving like a pendulum swinging. His thigh and his stomach muscles flex with each propulsive plunge.

It's fake. It's a show. I can see it in their faces—phony.

Viola likes the man's curly, hairy, muscular legs. His neatly tapered hair trails down his belly button.

His body reminds her of Derek's. Viola can't seem to take her eyes off of him as he pulls out, only to pound right back in—Viola feels her lower region pulsing in the chair as if she's that woman, but it's Derek she's thinking of, not this stranger. She double-takes, and for a split second, she wonders if Jason has ever been here.

Jason would never do this with anyone, never behind a woman. My dad messed Jason up.

Viola flexes in her seat. She crosses her legs while observing the intimate act. Viola feels her heart beating in her moist folds. Though not wanting to, inside she aches. She feels dampness in her underwear.

Watching this, how could anyone not be—?

Her head turns. Jes's parents spoke of porn like it was pure evil. "Sex is meant to be for people in love, to have children," Jes's mom told Viola.

Two other people in another area are on a sofa having one-on-one sex. Both are in excellent physical shape. The pale woman is turned away from the muscular dark skin man, her breast facing the crowd as she rides him. A crowd of orange bracelets watch.

Why do her breasts look the way they do? They don't bounce. This is Zack's sex show. His and Dad's business. Now his! Why bring me here? Punishment! He wants to throw in my face what he's been doing behind my back all along. He's sick.

Another man under another spotlight near that couple has his face between a woman's thighs. A TV screen above on a stand shows his tongue. Viola forces her eyes away from the TV, instead looking at the blindfolded woman lying back on the sofa bed. Viola's surprised to see that the woman also has an orange bracelet on.

Is the man standing in front of her, her husband or boyfriend? Why would you—it's disgusting.

He's touching himself while watching the muscular man between her legs. Viola lifts in her seat as the woman's hips lift in orgasm.

I want out of here. I don't want to be a watcher.

She turns her head the other way. Two women under another spotlight are kissing each other, touching each other's breasts. Only then does Viola see a third woman kneeling.

Two men under another spot-lit area next to the woman look like male models straight out of a glossy magazine. They're on a lift. One man disappears. Too many people are in front of them. Viola peers up at a TV screen. She reaches for Dean's shirt, pushing her face into his chest.

He lifts his arms around her head, trying to push them by her ears, knowing this is loud and a lot to take in visually.

The song morphs into another. Viola has no idea what songs have played, and she's no longer interested in any of the naked bodies all over this room.

Zack returns. He touches Viola's arm, lifts her from the chair, forcefully releasing Dean's grip on her. Zack's pants are pushed out—no doubt turned on by this place—his place. He motions with his head for them to follow him to the other end of the room. He enters numbers on a keypad, a door opens, and they go in.

-..Chapter 63-. .-

It's quiet. The ebony walls are dimly illuminated by a hint of light coming from the highly placed frosted cones which line the long hallway. Viola and Dean follow Zack until he stops to enter another code on a push pad.

They walk into a room. It's a lab. What they create here, Viola can only imagine.

"Dean, set up," says Zack. "Caleb will be here shortly. He's finishing up in the pit. We'll be back. I'm taking Viola to the bathroom."

Viola hands Dean the syringe in the baggie before she follows Zack out the door. He walks to the end of the hall, entering a code, opening that door. It's a beautiful room with a massive double king-size bed and cameras on each side. It's familiar to her. She senses Zack's gaze.

"This is where you film the porn," she says.

He smiles, "You have an excellent memory, Princess."

"What's the pit?"

"It's an orgy arena. A theatre-in-the-round. Would you like to see it?" he says, with a gleam in his eye.

"I can picture it. I've watched your porn, remember?"

"Do you think about them?"

"No. We live in our own fantasies, and yours are different than mine, Zack. I can clearly see that now."

"I have a tank of sea lampreys—in memory of your obsession with them. Would you like to see them, Princess?"

"Where's the bathroom, Zack?"

He laughs as he points to a door, and she heads that way. She's had to pee for at least an hour. Pregnancy. Viola wonders if there's a hair dryer for her underwear. When she enters she sees a huge open shower with a camera on the ceiling. She shuts the door.

This room is as big as my bedroom growing up.

She finds it odd that Zack would mention sea lampreys. They're an incredibly destructive invasive species that have inflicted economic damage, harming the eco system and changing the way of life in the region around Telega, where she was raised.

If they can be controlled to improve the fishery, why can't we control monsters like Zack to improve our community? We can make it better... one villain at a time. Trap him before he traps me.

She flushes the toilet and washes her hands. She leans down to drink from the tap as Zack enters. He grips her hips, rubbing himself on her backside, waiting for her to finish. She stands, wipes her mouth with the back of her hand. Zack turns her around. He gently thumbs water from her chin.

"Why do you always drink from the faucet, Princess?"

"Habit," she says. "I used to get up in the middle of the night when I was little. Instead of going downstairs, I'd go to the bathroom for a drink. I like the feel of the cold hitting my dry lips. Try it!"

"You realize how many germs are on that thing?"

"Are you serious, Zack? You're worried about germs? You own a sex club. I don't even want to think about what germs are all over you. In you... try it."

"Fine," he says. "I vet everyone I'm with. They're all tested, which is why I have a lab. I don't want a disease. I don't like germs or certain smells. Oral is off limits, unless it you, Princess."

"That's one-sided."

"So what! It's my club. I can do whatever the fuck I want." He turns on the cold-water, leans down to take a drink, making sure his mouth doesn't touch any part of it. He stands up.

She laughs.

"Whatcha think? It's nice, huh?"

"It's cold. I'd still prefer a glass." He snickers. "God, I've missed you, Princess. I can't believe you're here. I thought Patrick was going to kill you. I can't tell you what that did to me. I went apeshit when you were there. Here I was, cleaning up Uncle's death mess. When Jason told me Patrick shot you—" His finger brushes her arm. "I've never wanted to kill someone that bad before. I wanted to chop him up like Dad used to do and feed him to my fish!"

Viola swallows hard at the visual from Mom's book. Her father had a dead female in his soundproof room and was eating a part of her if he had blood in his mouth. Her vision blurs to Zack's blood-filled tank of sea lampreys. She shivers.

"If I hadn't moved when I did, I'd be dead, Zack. Brant covered my body with his. I guess Patrick didn't want to kill his brother. He was good. Brant was so good."

Viola can't hold back the tears in her eyes as she talks about Brant.

Zack leans down to lick them, making them both laugh.

They both stop laughing face-to-face. Zack leans in, lightly kissing her mouth. He leans back for her reaction.

Viola is mortified.

What do I do?

-..Chapter 64-. .-

Viola's in his domain, a horny Zack, whom she's led to believe she will sleep with on some far-off day in his quest for yet another heir.

How should I play this? If I stop him now, he will be angry and force me.

His lips move in again. Viola allows his kiss. He presses his body into hers, kissing her with all he has.

She starts to cry harder and harder. He pulls back when he realizes that she's stopped kissing him back.

"I'm sorry that you're sad about Brant. I only met him as a kid."

Viola pushes her face into his chest. She sobs into his shirt, smelling that all too familiar smell of cinnamon sex that filled her nostrils in the bar area.

I can't do this. I don't want him, but I don't want to hurt him.

"Zack. I—I can't do this with you right now. I'm sorry. I can't."

"All right. *Shhh.* I'm cool, Princess. Relax. I wanted to be with you at Uncle's place, not here."

"That's why we were there?"

"Yeah."

"We should get back to Dean. I want to be there when he uncovers—" She looks up at him. "I don't want to have sex with you tonight, Zack. I'm with Jason right now. I hope that's okay."

The expression on his face changes.

"Well, you fucked him pregnant with my baby. I don't see what the problem is."

"I thought you were dead. Jason would never have touched me at Uncle's house after you died. He ignored me. I made him be with me. I was so alone. I had no one at all. I needed to be touched, to be loved, to feel something. I was so mad after you didn't—Why couldn't you tell me the truth? Your plan with Uncle and Auntie? I would never have slept with Jason had I known you were alive. I'm not built that way, Zack. I can't be with two people. I don't want to. It's not me. I'm committed. Yes, Jason is in a coma. I can't let go. Not now, not yet. Even if he dies, I need time, Zack. I would need to be with you, talk, to spend time with you, so we fall in love again. I can't do this, one brother, then the other, the next week. I'll hate myself. I will lose myself. Please don't be mad."

He looks away. She grips his arms.

"I'm not like those people out there. Please don't force me to be. I've never asked you to stop being you, even though I hated it! I hated going out to dinner—to buy groceries. You always looked at other women. I felt like I didn't matter." A deep sob escapes her throat. "I felt in—insignificant. Like I was... nothing. I HATED that I wa—was—I WAS NEVER ENOUGH FOR YOU!"

Zack stares at her, shocked by her outburst, her truth. He places both hands on her face. Her lips quiver.

"Princess. I didn't know. I—I should've told you about the plans. I didn't give it a thought. Shit, I couldn't stop fucking people. You—you were miserable. I don't know why I expected you to stay celibate. I guess because you're you. It's not fair to you how I am. But I still want you. I'd be happy to share you with Jason. He told me that you couldn't do that. I couldn't believe it when he left."

"He left because he knew it was wrong, Zack. I asked him to stay. He wouldn't because of you. He put you first."

"Fuck. I wish I was good like him... for you."

He turns away from her. Viola thinks of Uncle Benjamin and what he said his daddy told him.

"Don't fall for lie because it's easier to believe. Oliver Wendell Homes wrote in 1881, "Even a dog distinguishes between being stumbled over and being kicked."

"Zack, you and Jason are different men with different needs. You can't be what I want, just like I can't be what you want. Why do the men have a ponytail holder around their penis?"

Zack spins around to face her.

"You mean in the lounge?" he asks.

"The man on the bed behind the woman... and the other guys."

"It's a cock ring, Princess. It makes them stay harder, longer. Fuck, you're so innocent. God, you're adorable. I miss your out-of-the-blue questions."

"Do they all wear that? It looks like it would hurt."

"Some take a double h. A hammerhead to last longer. It's a magic pill to stay hard."

"Do you take that stuff?"

"Sometimes, yeah."

"Did you take a double h at the cabin?"

"Does it matter, Princess?"

"No, I'm just asking."

"Yes, I did. I wasn't sure how long I'd be allowed to be with you before Dad... I wanted you so bad."

"I bet you'd love me out in that bed with the two men."

"No, I'd want a lot more all over you. Men, women, and me," he says with a sly smile.

She shakes her head.

"Do you do... stuff with men too?"

"That's not my jam. I like all kinds of kink, Princess. Many men here—their wives , don't give head through to the finish, so they visit for a private massage. In the Pit, some are okay with another guy sucking them off. They won't fuck them. We've had some fights. Men cannot touch other men wearing orange bracelets unless they touch them first. They know the rules. They stand in a particular line, then move on in the Pit once that scene ends."

"Why do you call it a scene?"

"It's a show. Entertainment. Late date night fantasy. Whatever you want. We offer an adventure in this underground palace of pleasure."

I have to tell him the truth. I can't be with him. I can't.

Her body's stiff. Viola flexes her fingers.

"I used to cry every time at the apartment, on the balcony, so no camera could watch when you'd go out. I knew you were with people. I had no idea to what extent. I do now."

She stares past him at the wall, seeing herself, surprised there's a mirror in here. There's another behind her, making the room look larger than it is.

"I'd wash my face. I'd tell myself, I'm okay. I could smell them on you. That smell."

She points to his shirt.

"You'd always try to sneak in, act normal, you needed another shower."

She takes a step back from him.

"Zack, if Jason dies, I won't be with you again unless you can only be with me. Otherwise, I can't do us. I want to love someone so much and for him to love me. That doesn't include anything to do with this place. Can you still love me and our son and move on, knowing I'm still here if you need me? Just... I can't do that out there. I wont. There is no love out there, Zack."

"Did you ever love me?"

"Yes, Zack. Yes."

"I wondered."

"Zack, how could I not love you?"

I need to get out of here. You're lost. Everyone out there has left their tree.

"You're an amazing man who happens to have been injected at birth. You have an addiction, a compulsion that you can't control. I want to find out who did that to you, to us, and never let that happen to any of our children. Can you be with me on that?"

"It doesn't matter who or how many I fuck out there Princess."

He steps closer to her, taking her hand in his.

"You'll always be the love of my life, Princess."

Tears trickle down her face.

You have no idea what love is.

"What happened to your girlfriend?"

"Somehow...she got pregnant. She died. We're still trying to figure out how it could have happened. Doc thinks that Patrick was trying to have Jeff and me put in prison."

"So you think Patrick set you up?"

"Let's see if good ole Dean has figured that shit out. Jeff's on his way to retrieve you."

"Is Jeffrey allowed to be with Carly?" asks Viola.

"He told me he's signing his share of the Pit over to me. He's moving back to England to be with *his* kids. I would take that as a hard yes."

"When this is over, Zack, I want the three of us, you , me, and Jason, to live near each other with our kids."

She forces him to look at her.

"That's my wish."

"That's alot, Princess. It might be too much for me. I'm happy to see our boy. I don't want him to know who I am... here."

"I'll never lie to our son, Zack. He can never step foot in here, or I'll kill you."

He stares at her mouth.

It's better to be honest, Zack, than to lie. Hey, there's alot of people out there who seem OK with their hidden lifestyle. Who am I to judge what makes someone else fulfilled? It's none of my business. I only have to judge myself."

"Fuck, I'll miss you, Princess. But I won't miss that."

His forefinger circles, then he takes it to her lips, zipping it. He chuckles.

"Come here, Princess. Let me hold you one more time before you're gone again."

Viola walks into his arms, proud of herself for telling the truth without it getting ugly.

Zack's life has sadly brought him to this place. He's the ringmaster of this repulsive, vacant, loveless circus show.

In her attempt to figure him out while she was with Zack, Viola read psychological journals about sexual fantasies. No one can stop them from entering their thoughts. They're a natural byproduct of the human imagination. We're born, made to procreate. Viola can't orgasm without a fantasy or two. With Zack, she worried about how long it would take her. Zack's frustration—his needs if she took too long, made her anxious. He wants to get to it. To fuck.

A man who can't love can only care about what he wants. Viola wants one man, one love. She wants to leave and never return to this Pit. This dark cavity in the ground, Zack calls a pleasure palace. How happy can empty feel?

Viola pulls back. Zack leans in to place a soft kiss on her lips. He tries to deepen it.

Viola bites his bottom lip hard. He moans. She pulls away, she smacks his ass like he's always slapped hers.

"Let's go Dark Prince."

-..Chapter 65-. .-

Jeffrey arrives at Zack's lab within the hour with a raging hard-on pushing out of his pants—no doubt from walking through the Pit, his and Zack's secret sex place.

Jeffrey side-hugs Viola, squishing her to him.

"I've to thank this tiny tot here," Jeffrey says, indicating Viola. "If she hadn't kicked me in the arse, I'd be in the pit and not with the woman I luv."

Zack smiles, but it doesn't reach his eyes.

Zack didn't get what he hoped for tonight... me.

Dean looks up from a table in the lab.

"What is this Zack?"

"Ah, I see you've been busy in here, Dean. Where'd Caleb go?"

"Caleb seemed preoccupied. He told me he'd be back soon. Where did you get this?"

Viola studies the sealed tray of vials of what appears to be a black goo.

"Someone we know is testing it. I have no idea what it is, it's not my wheel house Dean. I'm charging him a storage fee."

Dean moves to a counter top with a computer on it. He hits a button and notions to Viola.

"Henry shot Jason with a heavy tranquilizer. It's not poison." says Dean, stupefied.

"That can't be. The doctor, Henry, told us it was poison." Viola says.

"Absolute bollocks. Why would Henry lie? I cut his fokken finger off!" says Jeffrey.

"Henry's with me," Zack says, calmly.

"With you…all along? Are you sure?" asks Viola.

Zack stands motionless.

"I don't think so, Zack. He tried to stick Janic with a needle, too." says Viola.

"That's because Janic was with Patrick, Princess," Zack says.

"On the phone, Jason said he had a brother on the inside. Who was that?" asks Viola.

Jeffrey huffs. "Leo. When Jason called me, he said he knew it was bad news when you mentioned that his bro Janic was with you."

"Well, Janic's on our side now—I think." she says.

"Did Janic tell you who his father is? Not that you'd know of him, but we do." says Jeffrey.

No one says a word.

"I'm waiting," she says, looking between Jeffrey and Zack.

"About four years ago, Janic's father, Alexander, went to prison for treason," Jeffrey says.

"He's in prison?" Zack questions.

"Where is this prison?" asks Viola.

They all ignore her question.

"His family has no uncle at the moment, Viola." says Dean.

"Can someone, please, tell me what this has to do with Jason being shot with a tranquilizer?" Viola demands.

Jeffrey shrugs his shoulders.

"I'd take a punt at saying Henry was ordered to protect Jason, to get him out of there. There's are a lot of what-ifs and whodunits at the moment. I was ordered to keep my mouth shut." says Jeffrey.

"Ordered by who?" asks Viola.

She refuses to look at Zack. A pain hits her chest.

I can't take this. They're all liars.

Viola turns. She walks out the door and down the hall. A woman exits a nearby room. Viola catches that door before it closes. She goes inside. She lets the door shut behind her.

There's a large fire place behind a wall of tempered glass, on the other side of the room. Viola's eyes search for a bathroom. In the middle of the room, a man is naked and blindfolded.

Viola's hand grips her stomach.

I think I'm going to be sick.

A woman dressed in black leather from head to toe has the man's arms tied above his head. There's a black leather whip in her hand. The woman glances at Viola's orange wristband and holds out the whip for Viola to take.

When Viola doesn't move the woman walks to her, taking her by the hand, she leads Viola behind the man.

The woman wraps Viola's hand around the whip. She motions for Viola to whip him.

Viola's numb. but she does it. She pulls the whip back and strikes his bare ass.

The woman takes the whip from Viola's hand, pulls back, and violently swings the whip, hitting the man's ass, causing him to moan.

To enjoy this pain, you must be in pain mentally.

Viola hears the door shut behind her. She takes the whip from the woman's hand. She pulls the whip back, swings it, and whips the mans arse as hard as she can—the man moans.

Zack whistles through his teeth.

"Get out. Take him to my room." Zack says to the masked woman.

The woman takes the whip from Viola, unlocks two hooks attached to the mans wrists. She carries the ropes, guiding the man out.

Viola doesn't turn around. She stands there desensitized, waiting for the door to close.

"It's my fault, Zack, that Jason doesn't trust me. He doesn't want me."

Zack pulls her around, forcing her to face him.

"He only wants you, Princess. I know that for a fact."

"Then why let me think he might die? Why tranquilize him? Why can't I see him? Why hasn't he called me? I'm so sick of all of this, Zack. First, it's your fake death, then his fake death—all while I'm pregnant with your children. My heart is shattered. Do you understand? These uncles are grown men playing silly games with real lives. Promise me you'll help me get out. If you truly love me like you say you do, please help me. I'll take Zee and this baby."

Her finger tips touch the bump on her lower abdomen.

"I'll give them the best life. I—I can't do this anymore, Zack. I can't be tossed around like a baseball game, around and around, the bases. I never reach home plate. It doesn't exist. I'll never win their game."

Her hands lift. They shake in front of her face.

"I HATE THIS FAMILY!"

Zack takes her hands in his.

"Calm down, Princess. Jason isn't doing this to you."

"How do you know?"

"Because I know. Do you trust me?"

"No. I don't. I don't trust any of you. I do think you're the lucky one—right now. You can live the way you want and not give a shit about anything. I truly think you've got it all."

Zack grips her forearms.

"Shut the fuck up, Princess, or I'll have to smack some sense into you. Ever since I was with you, every day I wish I wasn't like this. I would take you away myself. Live our life away from all of this with Zee. I wish I was that man—but I'm not that man. You have that with Jason."

"Would you let me go, Zack?"

He releases her.

"I don't want to. But I will. I will." he says with glassy eyes.

"You do see how fucked up all of this is, don't you, Zack? My life. Not yours."

"I know of no other life, Princess. Only you do. That's why your mom did what she did. She was smart. She knew how to change this. She's fucking done it, even in death. Whether we can get you out or not, you've already won. Did you see the family we visited overseas? How obedient thou art!"

"They're like programmed human robots," she says, "Doing what they've been told and taught. How do you get away with all of this, Zack? This place... how do keeping our family secrets hidden."

"Because the men in our family visit my place, not all of them. It's their getaway. Their beach vacation. Their business trip."

"It could be better if they would change even a few of the rules, the old laws." she says.

"Better for who, Princess?"

Viola understands. It could be better for the women—the men, not so much. They have their cake and eat it, too.

"You need to go, Princess. Dean and Jeff are getting you out of here. Please do as I say. Go with them."

Zack pulls her to him, kissing the top of her head like Uncle used to.

"I love you, Princess."

He bends down on one knee.

"Hi, little one. You're gonna have the best mommy on the planet!"

Viola fakes a smile as Zack lifts her top to kiss her baby bump.

He touches her stomach, glancing up at her with a child like innocence.

She ruffles Zack's hair. This gentle side of him comes like a wave and crashes as it hits the shore, flatlining on the sand—his internal battle between his not-so-bad and evil side.

A sinking feeling hits Viola as she watches the intense bursts of reflection, from the wall of flames, flicker in a wavy dance in Zack's eyes.

-..Chapter 66-. .-

Viola's back on the private plane with Dean and Jeffrey. Destination: Who the hell knows? She certainly doesn't. She's nervous to see Jason at this so-called Plant. She's unsure if she even wants to know why she was lied to. Was it Jason's wish? She doesn't trust anything Zack has to say. He covers one lie with another, like her father did.

Jeffrey has worn an odd expression since the aircraft took off.

"Viola, Carly doesn't.... ah... about the Pit."

"I recommend that you tell her, Jeffrey. Take it from me: Lying now only makes everything worse when the truth comes out, and the truth always comes out, Jeffy."

Dean remains quiet.

"She won't care—well, she might," says Viola, "but she won't. Carly knows you've had women. She doesn't blame you because she's been with Patrick. She knew how much you hated it. You need to ask yourself honestly if you're done with that world. If you're not sure, then you don't deserve her."

Viola eyes Dean ever so slightly.

Jeffrey exhales heavily with understanding.

"I only want her. She's the one for me, Viola. I was ripped away from her when we were to be married. It's a breath of fresh air for me to be allowed back into the fold."

"Funny," she says. "Here I am, holding my breath, hoping I can get out of it." Dean shuffles in his seat. Viola stares at him. "You're quiet. What are you thinking, may I ask?"

"Truthfully, I was thinking about your mom when Jeff said what he said. I was going to ask Doc if I could marry her when she turned of age. Then she reunited with your dad—and that was that."

"Did you ever tell Doc how you felt?"

"No. At the time, Priscilla didn't feel the same way about me. She would always bring up your dad, which drove us all nuts. I wanted to kill your dad when she came home with Doc, broken and beaten up. But I knew I couldn't; I didn't have it in me. When your mom was pregnant with you, I did her ultrasounds. Doc was training me. Priscilla was so beautiful, so happy to be pregnant with you. When we told her she was having a girl, she told us your life would be different. She never elaborated. That's all she said."

"When did you—when were you with her?"

He stares at Viola for a long moment.

"Uh, we got together a lot the year before you went to high school. She told me your dad and she were over with. It was over for her, anyway. It was never over for him. I was never told about her later pregnancy or miscarriage. I wonder why she didn't tell me."

"You still love her, don't you?"

"Always have, like Jeff has Carly."

Jeffrey gives him a thumbs-up.

"Now we need to get you to Jason," says Dean. "But first we need to go over a few things."

———

When they land in England to refuel, Uncle Mark boards the plane. Viola feels uneasy seeing him. He hugs Dean, then Jeffrey. He turns to Viola, half-smiling.

"Jason is awake. I hear that he's been asking for you."

The heat hits her face.

What does that mean?

"Did Ardent approve it?" She asks.

"Ardent is not in charge, Viola. Isak Eastman is. He's the Top General at the Plant."

"Is he my great-grandfather?"

"Yes," Uncle Mark says. "You're to call him Uncle."

She nods. "Does he know I'm coming?"

"No, but he will soon," says Uncle Mark. "We have much to discuss in a short amount of time. We all need to be on the same page. Each page must turn precisely at the right time for this to work, or Jason is dead—possibly you as well," he adds.

"I'm listening," says Viola.

"It's about Ardent, Uncle Mark says."

When an older man comes out of a truck waiting on the tarmac. As they deplane, the man hugs Uncle Mark, Dean and Jeffrey.

Jeffrey turns to Viola.

"This is where we part ways," he says. "You can do this. Watch your back."

"Thanks, Jeffrey, for being loyal to Jason and for saving me."

"Anytime. Now... go get your man!"

She attempts to smile, and he gives her a quick squeeze before Viola walks over to the uncles.

"Althea, this is John—my father," says Uncle Mark. "This is Althea Eastman, although she goes by Viola Ted."

"I'm amazed how much you resemble your mother," says Uncle John. "Your Uncle Isak will see on the video feed that you're here." They glance toward a camera in the hangar. "Do you understand the importance of everything you've been told?"

"I do," she says. "I'll question Uncle Ardent in front of everyone when the time is right."

"And you must introduce yourself as Althea Eastmann. You're only known here by that name."

"Yes, sir."

Uncle John's gaze is focused on her baby tummy poking out, then at her face.

"What a beauty Althea is," he says to Dean and Uncle Mark.

"That she is, like her mother." Dean smiles.

They drive past a beautiful blue-green stretch of ocean along a long, lush forest-filled hillside. Viola rolls her window down two inches and hears a goat calling out. She watches its eerie stare as they pass by.

The truck pulls up to a tall gate. She notes two almost identical flags on the passenger door. The Australian and New Zealand flags.

The guards nod, and they drive through the open gate. Viola's surprised, having expected a massive fortress semi-hidden on the side of a mountain like the Complex. But this is a gray stone Gothic mansion with a darker gray shingled roof. Its beautiful grounds feature manicured roses and trees. Perfection. She's in the Southern hemisphere, on the other side of the world. It's November and springtime.

Dean and his Uncle John head toward the house while Uncle Mark waits with her. Not five minutes later, a man who resembles her Uncle Benjamin comes outside. He stops to smile at Viola.

"Uncle Isak, this is your great-granddaughter, Althea," says Uncle Mark.

"Hello, Uncle," she says.

"You may leave us," Uncle Isak tells Mark, as he turns to face her. "Hello, Althea. Why don't we take a walk. You don't remember me, but you spent your first summers of life right here with me."

"I remember you. I couldn't pronounce Uncle, so I called you Papa."

"Yes, you did!" Uncle Isak holds his arm out for her to take as they stroll to the gate.

The men open it, they follow behind with their guns raised, far enough away for them to have a private conversation.

"I read your mom's book before you did. Most of it was true. She wrote parts of it to protect family members that she knew would read it or talk about it."

"I'm confused, Uncle."

"We have much to discuss in a short amount of time. Jason will want to see you once he finds out you're here. He's been a hard one to contain since he woke up."

After a thirty-minute talk, they head back through the gate. The guards trail them back to the truck, where Jason stands, waiting, with Uncle Mark. Viola kisses Uncle Isak's cheek before running to Jason.

He picks her up, holding her so tight, almost squeezing the breath out of her.

"Hello, luv," he whispers as he sets her down.

"Hi!" She can't stop touching his face, so happy that he's alive. She kisses him.

He pulls back slightly, knowing they have an audience.

"I see you've met more of the family."

"Finally," she says. "No offense, Uncles. This is the man I wanted to see. Thank you for allowing me to come."

"We expected you'd find your way with or without us," says Uncle Mark.

"Yes, you're right about that," she says, smiling.

Isak motions, his hand moving in front of his face in the same way a king waves, as if he were replacing a light bulb. Viola remembers him doing the same wave on the beach when she was a toddler.

She spots more guards on the house's rooftop and around the grounds as Jason takes her hand and they start down the long roadway that Uncle Isak and she had come from. Once outside the gates, again the armed guards follow.

Jason stops and turns to hold her flush against his body.

"I can't tell you how badly I need you to hold me right now, Jason," she says.

He leans back far enough to kiss her.

"I love you so much, Viola," he says into her mouth, kissing her in between words.

She holds his face still.

"I thought I lost you. When Jeffrey said you were okay and Dean told me it was a tranquilizer, not poison, I thought you didn't trust me. I thought you chose it to get away from me. I thought you didn't want me."

"Never." He says, searching her eyes. "I love you more than I ever thought possible."

"Zack took us to the Pit. Have you been there?"

"Once, when he and I needed a private chat," he says. "It was closed. The cleaners were there... That must have been quite the experience."

"Terrible, but totally Zack. Dean protected me." Their facial expressions mimic each other. "Zack wanted to be with me. He kissed me. I stopped him. I told him I was with you. He was angry when I explained my feelings. That world is not mine. I told him I only wanted you. Carly told me she tried with you."

His eyebrows move. "I didn't—"

"I know. She told me what you said. I mean, she is attractive. It must have been hard to say no to her."

"I'm a man. Of course, I look. I don't want anyone else. I never have. No second thoughts."

"Derek used to say that about looking at other girls."

"Who's Derek?"

"Zack told me he told you about him."

"He did?" His eyes soften.

"I'm glad he told me because I haven't given Derek a thought in a long time. I'm sorry I didn't tell you about him at the cottage. I told Uncle the day before I left that I was telling you everything. I wanted no secrets between us, but I forgot about it. It was my mistake to call Derek to get Zee and me out. The minute I saw him, I knew it was wrong. I was using him, hurting him by asking for his help."

"Do you love him?"

"No. I thought I did. It was more like a first crush. He's not who I would spend my life with."

"Are you sure?"

"Yes. I can't see myself with anyone but you. I don't want anyone else. You have my heart."

"You have mine." He smiles.

"Do you have any questions for me? I'll answer whatever you want about me or the Derek situation."

"No. I don't need any more details, luv. That's in the past," he says, pausing momentarily. "You were supposed to move to England. After your mum was beaten. I said no. I was afraid. Uncle and your mum pushed hard. They said I was making a mistake... waiting for you. I didn't know what to say to you or how to have a relationship. It's my fault that she was murdered and that you were with Derek and with Zack. None of that would have happened if I had faced my fear of being with you when I had the chance."

"It's not your fault, Jason. Please don't blame yourself. I chose to be with Derek. He didn't force me. I didn't choose Zack, but believe it or not, after being with him, I'm very solid about who I am and who I'm not. I prefer to think of it all as experiences I needed to go through to be standing right here with you, feeling certain."

"Would you still feel the same if our blood wasn't a factor... for children?"

"There's no way to answer that now because our blood is a factor. I love you. We are having a child together. There's no going back, only forward. I no longer want to live where people who once knew me are. I wouldn't feel comfortable lying to them. Let's live our lives with our family the way we choose. Everyone else in the world can choose their way."

-..Chapter 67-. .-

Jason peers at the ground. Viola lifts his chin with her finger.

"Please tell me what you're thinking, Jason. I came here to tell you everything. I want no more secrets between us. I'm here to give myself to you completely. I'll tell you the truth about Mom."

"You will?" he says, staring at her mouth.

"Yes, and if I tell you, you must promise me with all your heart that you'll also tell me the truth. If you lie to me, Jason, or leave things out, it will be over between us. I'm done with hiding. I'm giving you all of me, everything, in return for your trust. I've sworn an oath to secrecy. I only trusted Mom. She said not to trust anyone. She made me swear on my life and hers. Mom said I would die if I told anyone. Can I trust you with my life?"

"No," he says.

Her throat closes.

"Are you saying that your feelings are not—?"

"No, of course not! I love you too much—or so I've been told by every top uncle in that house. I've been monitored. I demanded to go to you the moment I woke up. Viola, it would be best if you didn't tell me her secrets, not today."

"Okay."

"What I want to—What I need to know, Viola... is who put the note in your suitcase."

"Auntie."

"Aunt Lara?" He asks.

"No. Uncle Benjamin's... Ruth. Auntie Ruth used to write me notes all the time on my square Reuben sandwich napkins. No one paid attention. I got rid of them. I made sure she and I never spoke much. Her first message to me said: 'We will keep each other's secrets.' She was in on things with Mom. They would meet in front of our townhouse. I'd see them through the window. They'd talk. Auntie would hand her a bag of groceries. They were regular visits—never too long. Mom would come back in, make me something to eat, and leave for wherever she'd go. One time she told me not to be afraid and not to call Uncle—she was gone for three days."

He nods. "What did Aunt Ruth's last note say?"

"It wasn't a note. I lied to you at the cottage. I knew Zee was safe. I had to be pregnant before they would let me have him back. That was the deal. She had the woman in the truck tell me an address I'm to go to once I can safely get away from you and the family."

His expression is blank. He leans in to kiss her, kissing her cheek, to move close to her ear. He whispers, "Don't say anything else. Tell me what the note said from the suitcase when we are inside. That's all." He kisses her cheek, again and her mouth.

It's a relief for her to trust him. Their next steps would be difficult for both of them. Dean told her before she got off the plane.

"There is no privacy within the Plant, not one corner, no room for error," Dean warned her.

"Zack called me," says Jason. "He told me you want out. He'll help us."

"Jason, I don't trust Zack. You're missing something. Think. I don't trust anyone but you—not even Jeffrey. We're both next on the list—wherever that list is. I think the plan is for you to die. I'll have your baby. I'll be given to Zack. He doesn't care if I like it or not. Men from here go to the Pit. Zack has their private information. He can blackmail them. He has power. He'll force me into a relationship like he did before, until I pretend, like before. He can't stop himself. He doesn't know any other way. He cannot be fixed. He's hit me. He'll hit me again without Uncle to protect me. My life will never be my own. Jason, we're both in danger. Uncle John told me that when I got off the plane. He said I should leave soon, today."

Jason kisses her again, he lifts her, keeping the smiling act going. Happy to be reunited. "Say none of this inside, no matter what you're asked. We need to go in. We can't leave now. I'll try to speed things up."

She smiles. She kisses him as they walk hand in hand toward the gate to the Plant. She stops him before they enter the house.

"If we die, I'm happy we fell in love. I'm glad I'm having your baby."

She takes his hand, places it on her stomach.

"I love you, Viola."

She leans her forehead against his. He kisses her lips. He takes her hand to walk in through a ten-foot-tall, four-foot-wide front door. She takes a mental picture of what appears to be a stone family crest above the door's archway.

In the center are the two bones in the shape of an X that were in the Green Book. The same crest Mom drew in her book for Viola.

———————

Viola steps into a beautiful foyer. A massive crystal chandelier hangs from a high ceiling. Fragrant fresh-cut flowers sit in massive vases on either side of a statue of a beautiful woman. Viola wonders who she was.

Jason takes her by the hand, leading her up a winding staircase and down a hallway. Using a pin pad, he enters numbers, and a door opens. It's a nice-sized room: beautiful light blue-sky walls, chandelier lighting, crisp white bedding.

"We don't have much time, luv. Uncle Isak has called a meeting for all the uncles since they were already here over the incident at the Complex."

"Can I take a shower? I hate this smell on me."

He glances at his watch.

"You have fifteen minutes."

"Oh, that's enough time," Viola says, copying Carly's pouty lips. She drops her purse and sprints to the bathroom. He chases her. He closes the door behind him, locking them in the massive bathroom. Both strip off their clothes at a winning speed. He starts the shower to the left. She lays a large bath towel down on the floor, to the far right, lying back on it. She grabs his calf, making him drop to the floor with her. He's in a plank position over her. His mouth is on hers. Viola reaches for him. She places him right where she wants. Her hips lift to meet his need for her. Their breath catches.

Jason stops, pulls away from her.

He grabs the gun that he had set on the bathmat next to the large tub. He motions to her—*shhh* —with his finger. He hands her shirt to her.

Slowly, he picks up a bar of soap from the soap dish on the tub's edge. He tosses it. It lands in the open door of the shower across the bathroom.

Jason covers her body with his as holes blast through the bathroom door, aimed at the shower. The tempered glass shatters. Jason jumps up and turns the door handle, kicks the bathroom door open with his foot, and shoots as he goes.

Viola curls up next to the tub, hoping he's not been hit.

"Viola, get dressed, luv. Can you bring me my knickers, please?"

She gets up, trembling, covering her breasts with her shirt, she grabs Jason's underwear in her other hand, stepping out carefully, trying to avoid the mess.

In the room, a man—a soldier—is dead. Jason shot him.

Viola tosses Jason his skivvies and returns to the bathroom, to gather the rest of their clothes. She shakes the debris from them. She tiptoes into the room, handing Jason his phone.

"You should call someone?" she asks. "Did no one hear that?"

"These rooms are all soundproof. The front doors are bullet-proof."

"Was the door locked? How did he get in? Did someone let him in?"

"These doors lock when they shut. We all have our own codes."

"Who has access to yours?"

"I'll bet they planted a camera and the camera has been moved. How convenient," he says. "We'll go to the meeting as planned. Say nothing about this."

"Are we leaving his body here?" She asks, staring at the soldiers hands.

"Yes. The person who wants both of us dead is in that board-room. They're waiting to hear the news."

"Won't they look surprised when we walk in since we're alive?"

"No, luv. We're all taught to mask our feelings. These men are great Uncles. They're our teachers. They're better than us at all of this."

"Why is our blood more important? Isn't it the same? Why kill us?"

An idea pops into her head.

"I need to use your phone, Jason."

"Viola, they'll be listening."

She picks up her purse that she dropped earlier.

"I'll use the phone Jeffrey gave me."

Here, take this and hide it, Luv." he says.

"Why do I need a gun?"

-..Chapter 68-. .-

Viola and Jason enter a massive boardroom. Many men are already seated around a giant table. Viola counts twenty-five people present, including the four guards and herself. Uncle John and Dean are there. Uncle Isak is at the head of the table. Viola doesn't see Uncle Mark.

I hope he's alive. Did they shoot him, too?

"Everyone, please take a seat," says Uncle Isak. "We have a special guest today. My great-granddaughter, Althea Eastman, with her mate, whom you all know, Jason. Please, Althea, come and sit."

Jason pulls out a chair so she can sit down. He pours water into a glass for her. She thanks him. He moves three seats over to an empty chair and takes a seat.

Dean sits beside Isak. Uncle John is at the opposite end, facing Uncle Isak.

"Well, you're quite the surprise for us," Isak says. "How far along are you?"

"I'm not sure. I believe Jason and I conceived on my last day in England on the fourth of July, if my morning sickness is in line with my first pregnancy timeline."

Viola scans the room, noting the distinct features of the various family from Western, Eastern, Northern and Southern parts of the world. The blue, green, brown and vibrant hazel eyes she noticed on one of the soldiers, *Henrik*. Viola is part of the North Eastern family with her electric blue eyes. Mary also has blue eyes.

"Do you know the baby's sex?"

"No." Says Viola. "The doctor could only hear the heartbeat while I was at the Complex. They don't have a good ultrasound there."

"Jason told us you received a note in a suitcase. Can you tell us what the message said?"

"Yes, sir, it said, when you're ready, there was a number to call. It said, trust no one. These men are innovative, brighter than the family leaders, you know. They're the top Uncles. Find the invisible watcher."

Several top Uncles look around the room at each other.

"What did they mean by the note?"

"I have no idea, sir. I know now that you are the top uncles. I'm uncertain of what an invisible watcher is. I would assume it's someone here," she says, studying the men's faces around the table.

"What did they say when you called the number?"

"A woman answered. She told me where to meet her. She said to bring my baby the following day, and she'd get me out. When I got to the meeting spot, we got into a black van. There were no windows in the back. She put a black cloth bag over my head. I felt a prick in my arm. That was it."

"Did you see her face?"

"She wore a blue scarf around her head and big dark sunglasses."

"You woke at the camp?" asks Uncle Isak.

"Yes, sir."

"Why did you not tell Jason everything?"

"Before she died, my mother instructed me to trust no one. She spoke in many riddles. I never knew who my dad was, or that Uncle Benjamin was my grandfather, or that I had brothers. Only Uncle Mark told me about our blood. I was a normal teenager, going to school, doing normal stuff."

"That must have been quite a shock for you."

"Yes, it was."

"What about Zack? Did he treat you well?"

"Does that matter? I want to move forward with Jason and have our baby together. Uncle Ardent told me if I came to the Plant, I could never leave, so I would say I've proven myself to Jason by coming, knowing this is where we will live with our baby for my remaining years. My choice. That's why I'm here."

They all look at one another, then at Ardent, who locks eyes with Viola.

"Ardent," Uncle Isak says, "would you care to elaborate on Althea's last comment?"

"I was testing her, sir. I wanted to see her commitment to Jason. She did choose to stay in England at first. She asked to come the next day."

"Why did you not bring her?"

"Her uncle requested that she go back to England. Who was I to deflect his order?"

The door opens. Uncle Mark walks in.

"Mark," Isak says, "did you tell Ardent to have Althea sent back to England from the Complex?"

"No, sir."

Ardent shifts in his seat, and Althea notices four guards, one in each corner, with their guns raised. Jason's seat has moved back slightly.

He will shoot every man in this room to protect our child and me.

"I did not feel it would be beneficial to have her here at the Plant," says Ardent. "She is a distraction to Jason."

"She is his mate," Uncle Isak says." A pregnant mate, whom Patrick almost murdered."

"Three times, almost... sir," Viola adds.

"Where did you get the poison we found in Patrick's body, Althea?" asks Uncle Isak.

"When Aunt Lara kidnapped me, she said that her last baby was injected with that poison and died, and that I would, too. I took it with me after Patrick shot his mother and took me away. I knew I might need a weapon. She told me that Patrick would rape me to have his heir."

Everyone's eyebrows lift.

"Aunt Lara was angry about Dean being Uncle Mark's son, his heir. Being the oldest in his line meant he was next in line, not Patrick. Dean's already the oldest in Doc's line. So, I don't get why it mattered so much. But Aunt Lara told my dad that my mom was with Dean, which caused her death, not Dean's, as she and Patrick had hoped."

They sit staring at her, listening—though Jason is staring at Ardent.

"Anything else?" asks Uncle Isak.

"I don't think Doc was included in any of these plans."

Zack thinks so. I don't.

"I know, Doc. Doc nor Uncle Benjamin were a part of those plans. The people are here in this room and in America."

Jason's eyes close.

Fan friggin tastic, I said something I shouldn't have.

"You seem quite sure for someone who doesn't know much about the family," says Uncle Isak.

"A gut instinct, Uncle. I've been through a lot in a short time and somehow have survived this far."

"Who is involved, Althea?"

"I'm sure they'll reveal themselves today after this conversation. I'm happy about it. I'd rather they show themselves than live in fear for one more day." She says.

"Do you not think of your unborn child, Althea?" asks Uncle Isak. "Protecting it?"

"Of course. If the person here is out to kill me, they will, unless we uncover them sooner rather than later. We're all going to die, Uncle. It's a matter of when. I'd rather die with my child than have my children watch over their shoulder or be poisoned or shot when I'm not around to protect them. It's all about how you choose to view a situation. The longer we wait, the more time we give others to plot and carry out their kills. That's what has already been happening."

"Do you trust anyone in this room?"

"No."

"Do you trust Doc?"

"I'm not sure. I said that I didn't believe he would harm my mom or me. Doc would never supply the drugs to kill my mother. I think someone else poisoned Doc's wife, too. It wasn't Doc, but they want us to believe that. It's too obvious how all the evidence points to him. It's on purpose. They want him removed, so they're no longer looked at."

He laughs. "We have our detective right here. You and Jason make quite the team."

"I only want to love Jason and our children. I don't want this drama in my life, Uncle. I want it over with."

"Your Uncle Benjamin raised you well."

"He did. He was the best. I haven't had time to mourn him yet. I want you, wise men, to figure out who is killing our blood to hide their shame and lies so I can be with my family to spread my uncle's ashes and say goodbye."

"Is Zack aware of this information?"

Jason's stare catches Viola's eye.

She's unsure of the question.

"Can you please be more specific with your question?"

"Do you trust Zack?" Uncle Isak asks.

"No."

"Do you think he's involved?"

She pauses, looking Uncle Isak in the eyes. She feels Jason's fixed glare.

"He might be, but Zack is not a leader," adds Viola. "He would only be involved if he was told to do something. My dad trained him that way. He's a sock puppet. He was poisoned at birth. They made him what he is. That is the person we need to uncover. That person is the one who is attempting to cover their tracks, and I think you all know who that person is. How can you not? They're possibly older than Doc and my Uncle Benjamin. It's a scientist, a doctor, or a leader with access and control, one who could obtain the serums injected into our children and the people they wanted to be silenced.

"Everyone, put your hands on the table now!" Uncle Isak orders.

They all put their hands on the table as Uncle pulls out his phone and punches in a number.

"I want Doc moved now." He hangs up.

"Ardent, is there anything you want to say or add to Althea's comments?" asks Uncle Isak. "It seems a lot of your line has been involved in recent affairs. John, yours as well. Did you have no intel of Patrick's deceit as it developed?"

"No, I did not," says Uncle John. "I agree with Althea. As she mentioned, we need to review who among us may have had access to carry out these suspicious family deaths. My wife and I would like to know who poisoned our daughter. It could also be a doctor or scientist. Why they'd want or need to kill is beyond me, though they must have a motive."

"Ardent," Uncle Isak says, pointing.

Viola stops. She stares at Uncle Isak's hand, turning her head to look at Jason. She taps her finger three times. She hopes he saw it. He is observant. Unfortunately, so are others in this room.

-..Chapter 69-. .-

"What's wrong, Althea?" asks Uncle Isak, noticing the change in her body language.

"I'm not feeling well. This is a lot," she says, breathing in deeply. She stands.

"Drink some water," Uncle Isak tells her.

"No, no, thank you." Viola peers around, pretending to be dizzy. She looks at everyone's hands, stalling at Jason's hands, then into his eyes. She turns to look at Uncle Isak. "Uncle, could I be excused?"

"I'm sorry, Althea, we must stay in this room until we uncover who among us has caused these atrocities."

Viola waves her hands in front of her face, pretending to fan herself.

"I feel hot."

Dean stands up.

Sit down Dean, says, Uncle Isak.

He does. Viola peeks over at Jason.

Jason has no idea what I'm doing.

She reaches down, bending over.

One, two, three—focus, focus. Face your fears.

"Give me one moment, Uncle. I'm sure this hot flash will pass," says Viola.

How can I make the killer show himself? I hope this doesn't get Uncle Isak shot!

Uncle Isak waves a few men back to their seats. He stands and walks over to Viola.

From her sock, she pulls the small gun Jason gave her in the room. She holds it in her Uncle Isak's face.

Soldiers in all four corners aim their guns at her.

Isak raises his hand to stop them.

Every Uncle is standing with their own weapons raised—Jason included, with two guns, one each on two soldiers. Dean points his at another soldier, and Uncle John at the fourth in the room.

Ardent is looking around at everyone. He walks toward Uncle Isak with his gun and joins Viola with her gun pointed at Uncle Isak. Viola sees Uncle Mark pointing his gun at Ardent. It's all too much.

Jason speaks, "Viola. It would be best to tell us what you know before many Uncles die."

"Uncle Isak has the same tattoo symbol on his finger as Zack," she says. "Even the dead guy in our room who tried to kill us before we walked in here today had that tattoo on the same finger. I don't have one. Jason doesn't have it. Do Jason and I have a different father than Zack? Maybe we were made to think we were my dad's? Uncle Isak, were you nervous about our line? Did you and Ardent make a deal? Doc knows the truth, doesn't he? Uncle Mark found out through Ardent, so Jason went to England. Are we a part of his line? The problem is somehow with me."

You could hear a pin drop in the room.

"Uncle Isak has been trying to change the old laws," says Viola. "He's slowly hiding the history of the family. I figured it out when I saw the female statue in the foyer. My mother also had a picture of her. She taught me about a cult that involves that woman. The hierarchy of her bloodline has always been through the female, not the male—because you never knew which man, or should I say brother, impregnated her with his seed. So, the law stands that the top of the bloodline rests in a woman. Is that why Uncle Isak told Dad to have Zack get me pregnant before I was with Jason? He knew Zack was his line, but it was a risk because of Zack's tendencies. Now, with Jason's baby, if it's a girl, she will be top because I'm the top. My mom's line is Uncle Isak's, but my direct line belongs to whom? Uncle Isak's, Uncle Ardent's, or Uncle John's? Is this true or not? If yes, it makes sense because the torch must be passed. Then, it would give a reason for Uncle Isak to obliterate anyone who knew. Or Uncle Ardent." says Viola.

No one makes a move.

"Did he make Patrick a deal, too?" she asks, "knowing his weakness for power. Did Uncle Ardent want to kill Dean because he's jealous of Dean's succession in Uncle Mark's line? My mom died. She was never pregnant with Dean's baby. She knew something. A fix for our bloodline. You're all freaking out at the possibility that our family can finally go and live our lives free. Uncle Isak knows that Zack's weakness is me. That might be how he got him to help with plans—I'm not sure. Just connecting the dots is all."

Silence follows her speech, then Uncle Ardent speaks, "I regret my agreement with Isak. I'll admit to my crimes if he admits to his. This has gotten out of hand. Innocent people have died. This is why I didn't want you here, Althea. I know who intends to be rid of you, even with Jason's heir inside of you. Your Uncle Benjamin was not on the target list. Someone else wanted him killed. Althea's mom was innocent, as were Doc's other children. My grandchildren, he says. And you," he says, facing Isak. "You kept allowing it. The killing of my line. Why, Isak? Tell me now, or my bullet sails."

Viola's hand with the gun in it trembles as she turns it on Ardent.

"Please don't make me shoot you, Uncle Ardent." Viola says with tears streaming down her face.

"I want all my guards to have your guns on Ardent. That's an order." Isak says.

The four guards in the room don't move. They're aware that they have the guns of other Uncles aimed at their heads.

Jason creeps up on Viola. She's frozen in fear—fear of her pulling the trigger and possibly killing a man who may or may not be directly responsible for killing everyone she loved.

"Dean, I need you here now," Jason says. Dean moves. He takes the gun from Viola. He pushes her behind Jason, who still has his gun aimed at Uncle Ardent.

Uncle John speaks, "Ardent, thank you, my brother, for being truthful. We need to know what exactly has transpired over these years. We will hold counsel. At this time, Isak and Ardent will need to be put in the Box until we figure out the mess they've made—or that we've made. We must assume that everyone with Isak's tattoos is loyal to him. They must be brought in for questioning. We cannot have this chaos getting out, affecting thousands of family members globally."

John walks to Isak, taking his phone from him. Viola watches him hit redial.

On speaker, "Who is this?" asks Uncle John.

"Who is this?" asks Jeffery's voice on the other end.

"Jeffrey, it's Uncle John. I need Doc moved again. Zack cannot be told his whereabouts. Do you understand? You will safeguard Doc, then have Zack arrested. He collaborated with his Uncle Isak, who is now detained for many murders, including your mother's. Am I understood? Once you have confirmation that Zack is secure, we need you here. I'll send the details. Speak to no one." John hangs up.

All the uncles move to one side of the room. Ardent and Isak are put up against the wall. With a nod of approval from Uncle Isak, Uncle John retrieves handcuffs from two of the soldiers and secures both men.

"Why do you have this tattoo, Isak?" asks Uncle John.

Uncle Isak turns to look at Althea.

"You're brilliant, like your mother. She was a gift to this family line. You are as well, Althea. I wish we had never tried to muck with genetics, but we did. It didn't work out for your father or

Zack. Doc was supposed to give you and Jason the shot. We found out recently that he never did. You have been given something else. You're both your father's progeny. You're not Dean's daughter, Viola, if that's what you're wondering. Your mother was never with him. Dean is lying. Do you know where your baby is?"

"No. And right now, Uncle, I want him far from you, from all of this."

Someone's gun hammer clicks.

-..Chapter 70-. .-

Jason shoots Uncle Mark's revolver out of his hands.

Uncle Mark grunts as his hand lifts, he closes his fist. Dark red blood trickles down his forearm.

Jason shakes his head. Upset.

Uncle John's gun is raised at his son, Mark, along with the guards.

"Take care of my children and grandchildren," Mark says to John. "Viola, I cannot apologize enough for what you've been through—all your loss, the terrible situations you've faced. Jason filled me in when we met before Jeffrey saved you. Please forgive me for being so strong with you during our conversation in England. Jason, Isak cannot live after all the damage he's done. Jeffrey was injected, too. I openly accept my punishment for changing Patrick into what he became. I didn't realize my mate knew about Dean," adds Uncle Mark.

Halfway down the conference table, a man clears his throat with his forefinger raised.

"Go ahead, Ryan," Uncle Isak says.

"Viola, my name is Ryan. I'm Doc's son. My son is Henry, the doctor who did a gender test on your blood for your baby at the Complex. There was no Y chromosome. You're having a girl."

A trill of gasps can be heard in the room.

"She will be at the top of the line." says Ryan.

Jason's gun is raised and pointed at Uncle Mark's head.

"I'm sorry about Benjamin and your mother," Uncle Mark says. "Uncle was the best of us brothers. He had the biggest heart. He was a solid leader. He was fair. He was good. I did not put that hit on him."

"I'm worried this isn't the end, Uncle Mark," says Viola. "Others are involved. It's not this big, this many years, without more fingers in the pie. I don't think Jason and I are safe yet. Whoever was involved will want to clean up their side of the street. We may see more deaths. I hope not. You're involved and guilty, Uncle Mark. It's why you attempted to kill Uncle Isak."

Jason's other gun moves to Dean. Dean nods, lowering his weapon. He tosses it on the table, knowing he's been caught.

"I admit I've made mistakes," Uncle Mark says. "Isak is aware of most of them, as is Ardent."

"You know we're not Dean's kids, don't you?" she asks.

Mark nods. "Isak was truthful," he says. "Your mum would only have heirs with your dad—her brother."

"Carly's last child is mine, the girl." Dean adds, his finger raised, "She is mine, not Jeff's."

Holy shit. I bet Jeffrey has no clue.

"Why did you lie, Uncle Mark, about Dean being with my mom, or for saying she was pregnant? Why let my dad go crazy? He beat her."

"We all lie, Viola." Uncle Mark says, wincing as he holds his bloody hand to his chest, applying pressure.

I lie too. Zack killed Mom. Why have I been asked to lie? Why protect Zack?

"Consider this room your jury, Mark. Speak or be silenced." Says Uncle Isak, in handcuffs, still commanding the room.

"Dean was trying to gain Priscilla's trust—and Althea's recently—to see what her mum told her before her death. Priscilla knew big things that would affect this family in the future. As a young boy, I taught Jason to want Althea and only Althea. I made a deal with Priscilla that she would bear a child with Dean for my line.

I was angry when she refused, after everything I had done to raise Jason! I'm indirectly responsible for her death. It was Lara who told Russell that Priscilla had been with Dean. Bobby's death was only partially my fault. I agreed with someone else to tell Doc that Dean's son, Bobby wanted to kill Jason. I only said that because I thought—Bobby had learned things. Things I couldn't make go away. I regret it the most. I'm sorry, Dean," Uncle Mark says.

"You lied about my son," Dean says, repulsed. "You're own grandson!"

"You killed my family, not Isak," Uncle Ardent says with disgust, lifting his gun aiming at Mark's head.

"Take Mark to the medic, then to the Box." says Uncle John.

The guards look to Isak who nods.

"Wait." says Viola."What happened to Aunt Lara's last boy? What was he given?" she asks.

Uncle Mark smiles. The smile that says, *I'm fucked! Now what?*

"It was a mistake. I thought it was the same serum Jason received as a newborn, but it wasn't."

The guards move. One grips Mark's arm, the other Dean's.

"Althea, we believe you are the experiment."

"I don't understand. Please, Uncle Isak, tell me so this can stop. I've been through so much. What did you do to me?"

"You were injected with a serum believed to target the problem with our blood. Your mother, we believe, figured out how to mix our bloodline with yours. You and your first baby survived when other women have died. The female fix worked on you. We know this to be true because with this pregnancy with Jason's seed, without Doc's injections, you're past the point when other women die. Your mother wanted you to be free. Doc worked on this with her when she lived with him. Doc was unable to replicate what she created. That's what he told us. He has protected her findings at all costs, along with your Uncle Benjamin. She suffered terribly with your dad because of the drugs I ordered him to be given, hoping to make a superior warrior. We—we created an animal. That's what

Ardent and I are guilty of. We injected our children. Your Uncle Benjamin's mate, my daughter, was born different. We tested her after she had your father. We found a germline mutation, which can occur during DNA replication during cell division, so we made another fix. We know that was also a factor with regard to your dad's erratic behavior. We gave Priscilla a fix before she was born to clean the line. Our family is skilled in science, more than the rest of the world will ever comprehend. When your mother had Zack, your dad's DNA was apparent."

Whispers drift in the room. Uncle Isak has clarified that Zack's birth mother wasn't Doc's daughter, Cindy. This family secret is no more.

"We didn't inject Zack early enough because Benjamin and Doc hid him." Says Isak. "We tried to alter his genetics after he was born. He's still... different. Mark knew all along that we were working on a serum. Mark stole it from the lab at Doc's in Canada when it was still in testing mode. Mark injected Jeffrey, not me. As you've seen for yourself, Jeffrey is a great warrior."

Jeffrey's a killer trying to climb his way out of his animal.

"It was my command to have Dean steal something from Doc's lab." Says Uncle Mark. "I thought Doc gave that serum to Jason to be the next warrior. I didn't know it was poison meant for Russell—in case they needed to take him out quickly. Against Lara's wishes, I injected my last son. Dean told Doc of his betrayal after Doc saw Dean stealing it on camera. That's why Doc pushed Dean out. Doc was never jealous that I was with our sister, Ella We all share two heirs each, aside from the eldest. Doc knew Ella and I were in love. He knew I was with her on and off through the years."

Dean glares at Uncle Mark with disgust.

"So if Doc didn't kill my mother, who did? I've blamed Doc all this time," he says.

"I'm sorry, Dean. Lara poisoned her sister, Ella, your mum. Lara was furious that I kept seeing her. I found out what Lara did. I kept the secret to protect her."

"Who did you work with to kill my son? At least tell me why after everything I've done for you." begs Dean.

"I'm sorry, Dean," says Uncle Mark. "Bobby was angry. We believed he was about to cause a serious problem for us. He wanted Viola's dad in prison for sending him what he considered pornography of a minor. Bobby called me, not Doc, knowing I was his uncle. He threatened to call the police to tell the papers about the family. I told Bobby that would only get him and the family into trouble. I wanted to move Bobby to the Complex, out of the Americas. He would have been the better choice to rule. Patrick found out that I was going to put Bobby in charge of the Complex, not him. Lara told him. She was angry about it. It all became quite a mess. I was forced to say that Bobby was involved. I didn't know he—It was my fault."

"Forced," says Dean in disbelief. "You're the evil behind all of this—my father. I'm no different from Zack. I'm a sock puppet straight off your filthy foot. If I had my gun, I would shoot you where you stand. You've ruined my life. You were responsible for my mother's and my heirs' deaths. Bobby was a good boy."

Tears stream down Dean's face.

Uncle Mark nods, tears in his eyes.

"I'm sorry, Dean. Everything kept escalating." says Uncle Mark.

The room is silent.

-..Chapter 71-..-

Uncle Mark and Dean are about to be escorted from the boardroom.

Uncle Isak speaks. "All weapons on the table now aside from Jason's and my guards. No one will shoot anyone and no one leaves this room until we resolve the matter at hand."

Viola can't look at Dean, who is hunched over, weeping like any father would who lost a son.

I feel terrible for Dean, even though he made his own wrong decisions. Poor Bobby. Please, someone, change the subject. Nothing will change what has happened.

"So am I... cured?" Viola asks Uncle Isak. "Is my blood—can I have children outside of this family?"

"We're not sure, but we believe so. Russell killed your mother before she could do her final analysis."

Why are you protecting, Zack? He killed my mother. He needs to go to prison, and you know it.

"Priscilla knew Russell was planning to kill her. When we met, she told me everything." Says Isak. "Your mother had me read her journal before you ever did. We added the part about the man being a cousin since your dad had already questioned her about being with Dean. We knew there had to be a significant reason for that. We didn't know why. She couldn't understand why someone would tell Russell that. She didn't want you to stray from our line if your fix didn't work and you died. She agreed with me to change her words because she feared that if she was wrong and you got pregnant, the line would die with you. That's why she pushed for you and Jason to have heirs. She knew you wanted children. You told her."

"Viola," Jason says. "She asked me to set you free. She knew you wouldn't come into the fold, being brought up like you had been. I didn't tell you because she wasn't sure if it would work. She told me you wanted children. I promised her I would give them to you. I'm in love with you. I always have been."

The first time I had an ultrasound. Doc gave me something when I was pregnant with Zee. What was it? Was that my fix? The one I worked on in the basement at Blár Leif Bookstore?

"Did Doc give my baby, Zee an injection, Uncle Isak?"

"We believe so, yes."

"Did they check him for Zack's genes?"

Doc's son Ryan lifts his finger.

"Yes, Ryan," says Uncle Isak.

"Doc said he has fifty percent of Zack's DNA, but his genetic code differed. He's fine. Althea's baby, Zack, is the successor."

The room is silent.

"You know where my baby is, don't you, Uncle Isak? You want him safe."

"Your Uncle Benjamin made a deal before his death, Althea," Uncle Isak says, avoiding her question.

Uncle Mark snorts.

"Uncle Mark, you're the liar," Viola says. "Your mate told me you were weak and pathetic. Uncle Isak doesn't need to die for his mistakes, but you must go to prison for the rest of your miserable life. Mom told me it's the female heir, not the male, who's top of the line. You wanted me dead so Carly could have the top female heir. That's why Patrick kidnapped me. You didn't stop there. You made Dean believe he would have the top female heir with Carly, so that he would do your dirty work for you. Carly believes it, too. So, they slept together. This is your last chance to make things right. Take the hit off Doc, Jason, and me."

"The hit is on Zack, not Jason," Uncle Mark says. "Zack messed up my family the most."

"The Pit," she says.

A few heads turn.

How many of these men have had their heydays there.

"Sorry, Viola. Some things will go to my grave," says Uncle Mark.

"Take the hit off of Zack. He's been through enough."

"He's done the most damage." Uncle Mark adds.

"I doubt that. You chose to go to the Pit. Blame yourself. You chose to bend your children's minds to have the top heir—Zack's a product of the family's unorthodox practices. We can treat him. We can fix him—if this family is so scientifically advanced as you say we are. Zack is a full-blood heir, my mother told me. Dean knows it, too. Zack needs to be fixed."

"Jason will raise your baby," Uncle Mark says.

"They both should."

"It's out of my hands," Uncle Mark replies.

She puts together the pieces. The anger in Uncle Mark's eyes glaze.

"Carly?" she says. Viola knows she's right. "Uncle John, call Jeffrey. Carly is going to kill Zack. Please stop this. Jason, do you have her number?"

Jason's guns are still raised. She watches his eyes move. Viola goes into his pants pocket, gets his phone, and scrolls down.

"Which name do you call her? Never mind, I see it."

She hits *Doris*. Carly picks up.

"Jay, what's up?"

"Carly, it's Viola. You're on speaker. I'm with all the top uncles. Your dad wants you to drop the hit on Zack. If you don't, your line dies."

Everyone looks at Viola in surprise.

"Let me speak with him, Viola."

Viola shakes her head at Mark. Jason points one of his guns at Uncle Mark's face.

"He's got five guns in his face now, Carly. He's not getting out of this. I know you were planning with Patrick to kill me, weren't you? But you didn't. Why? If you stop now, Carly, you can be saved for your kids' sake. If you kill Zack, all deals are off."

"You're a female legionnaire, Viola. I need to hear my father say it."

Viola hands the phone to Carly's top uncle.

"Carly, this is Uncle John. I command you... to back off. The hit is off on Zack or whoever else your father asked you to get rid of. You have four children to think of."

They hear a shot. The line drops. Uncle John's face goes pale.

"Was Zack there?" Viola asks out loud.

"She was supposed to take him to a safehouse." Says Jason.

Uncle Isak asks to be put on the system. John sidesteps to hit a button on the table, and Uncle Isak calls out over the intercom system, announcing that all soldiers will report to the Top Commander-in-Chief, Jason Eastmann.

Jason orders the soldiers to take Uncle Mark, Uncle Isak, Uncle Ardent, and Dean away to the Box at the bottom of the house.

Jason speaks to the room, "I need everyone to place every weapon you have, on the table now, and stand against the wall closest to you. You will remove all of your knives. If not, you will be executed where you stand. Your phones will be checked. We will search your rooms. Only then will you be permitted to leave. You will be discovered, so please do the honorable thing. Step forward so you don't delay this process, making it longer than it needs to be."

One man steps forward—a cousin with a lean build, whose older than Jason with the same tattoo on his index finger as Uncle Isak. As more guards enter the conference room, Jason confiscates the cousins' phone. Jason enters a code to gain access. His eyes close

for a moment. Jason stares at the cousin. Soldiers remove the man
to take him to the Box.

-..Chapter 72-. .-

In the mansion's control room, at the Plant, Jason embraces Viola.

"Uncle John is the next in line behind Uncle Isak," he says. "Because of John's family's involvement, I must question him first. At the moment, he will not be put in the Box. We need to keep the facade going to find out who all in the family are involved. Jeffrey called me to tell me that Doc was missing. Someone must have called or messaged him. Jeff said we should hunker down at the Plant to uncover the truth. I told him Carly and Zack were together in England—that Jeff needs to track her or Zack. One of them, I believe, was shot."

"What do you think Jeff will do?" asks Viola.

"He'll follow the facts. He won't strike until he knows for sure. He knows, as I do, how people lie to save their arses. When he does uncover the truth—that's it."

"I've witnessed Jeff's 'That's it,'" she says.

A bell rings, and Jason looks at a camera to see who's at the room's entrance. There's a guard outside the door.

"Stay here, luv."

Jason hands her a piece of paper.

"Why can't I come with you? Do I have to stay in here alone?"

"The control room is the safest place in the building. I can't trust anyone at the moment, Luv. Don't worry. I'm locking you in. I'll be back within the hour. You can see me on that screen, and here's the code for that panel, should anything happen and you need to—"

She touches his chest, her eyes divert to the wall, and a keypad he motioned to.

"What's going to happen, Jason?"

"There's no way what was said in the boardroom won't get out. There are too many people and witnesses. You're not safe. They know who you are. I'm going to have the family members and the soldiers line up. I need to question them individually. I need to try to crack the men who bear Uncle Isak's tattoo."

The doorbell goes off again.

"I'll try not to be too long, luv."

She nods. He leans in to kiss her, and leaves.

The minute Viola sees Jason on the camera departing with the guard, she turns to face the overwhelming amount of equipment in this massive control room. Video screens show every inch of the property grounds. There are other screens, too, many of them flickering images of unfamiliar places, but she recognizes two locations: the outside area where she walked, the boardroom Jason mentioned. She wonders who was sitting here in these chairs watching—watching her. She can't waste any time. She scans the equipment until she finds the radio. Next to it is an antenna tuner and amplifier.

It sure looks old. I would have much preferred to use Uncle's in his hidden room in Telega. Here goes nothing!

The tube amp with plate and load knobs are pretty much like the one at Uncle's home in his bunker. He had Viola tune the amp so many times she used to dream about doing it wrong and blowing the tubes.

I hope these tubes are good.

Viola flips a switch on the amplifier, the tuner, and the transceiver, keying in one of the frequencies she learned when she was younger. Turning down the wattage on the transceiver, she reaches over to the amplifier to set the frequency band, the plate, and the load.

It feels like yesterday when her hands guided her fingers across the knobs and dials of Uncle's equipment in the secret room behind his study's bookshelves.

Viola keys the radio, then glances over to the wattmeter, making fine adjustments to the amp's plate control, waiting for the dip. She hits it. She unkeys, her hands shaking, realizing time is slipping away. Jason could come back at any moment to check on her. She increases the transmit power slightly on the transceiver. She peaks the plate control once more, then the load. Viola's pulse quickens. She confirms she's switched to the dummy load, increases power to transmit wattage on the transceiver, and tunes again. When she's dialed in, she switches to the antenna.

She noticed the antenna array while walking on the property with Uncle Isak. With full power, especially now during the current solar cycle, they will hear her. She's sure of it. She hopes.

Propagation is as good as it's gonna get. Please be there.

I'll use a one-time pad.

When growing up, she didn't like the endless hours spent reciting digits of pi. The countless strings of random letters were only slightly more bearable, always in groups of fifty. Viola's friend Jes detested Calculus. *"When will we ever use this?"* she'd say.

I remember thinking the same thing about radio communication.

Viola looks at her hands.

Here I am using this skill I was forced to learn.

Mom explained to Viola why she had to recite each letter in perfect order so many times. She told her she would use this knowledge to communicate when there was no other way to pass a private message.

Her mind jumps to Jason.

I hate that I might hurt you again. I hate it. Come with me. They want you, too. You have too, or they might not let me see my son again. I wish this could be over, Jason. I wish we both could be free. I know why Mom taught me everything she did. Why she had to keep me in the dark until the time was right, I can do this! I get it, Mom. I'll create the fix for Zee. I'll finish it. I'll try.

Viola keys the mic, "Dandelion, Dandelion, forty-seven, forty-seven. Dandelion, Dandelion, forty-seven, forty-seven. Twelve, five, twelve, five, twenty-three, fifteen, nine, twenty-five, twenty-five, twenty-one, nineteen, three, twenty-one, seven, nineteen, twenty-five, one, three, four, twenty, sixteen, nine, fourteen, twenty-two, sixteen." She pauses, repeats the transmutation as she was taught to do: "Dandelion, Dandelion, forty-seven, forty-seven. Dandelion, Dandelion, forty-seven, forty-seven. Twelve, five, twelve, five, twenty-three, fifteen, nine, twenty-five, twenty-five, twenty-one, nineteen, three, twenty-one, seven, nineteen, twenty-five, one, three, four, twenty, sixteen, nine, fourteen, twenty-two, sixteen."

On one post it note in Mom's handwriting inside of the Green Book at the cottage, it said, "trust The Rise." On a second post it note, Jill promised that *they* would be listening and to look for the Orchid.

Viola tells herself that no further transmissions would be beneficial. She turns off all the equipment. She waits.

-..Chapter 73-. .-

Jason enters the control room an hour and a half later.

"How did you figure it out?"

"Figure what out, Jason?"

Oh no, he saw me!

"About the tattoos?" he asks.

Viola releases a breath.

"It was the first thing I noticed after Zack kidnapped me. I saw that tattoo. I wanted to identify him if I ever escaped. It stood out. Do you know why they have it?"

"No, no one with the tattoo will talk," says Jason, scratching the stubble on his face.

"Ardent is more involved than he's letting on, Jason. It's a gut feeling, and Jeffrey might be. I think Ardent told Jeff to put the tattoo symbol on the infirmary door—or it could have been Uncle Isak. It was removed the next morning when I checked."

"I'll be able to pinpoint if it was Uncle Isak or Uncle Ardent with phone records," he says.

She looks at Jason. "Jeffrey was told to do it. Whoever was talking to him knows what that symbol means. Suppose it was Isak—fine. That worries me, too. I think Uncle John is the ringleader, not Uncle Mark."

"What makes you say that luv?"

"In the boardroom, on speaker phone, he told Jeffrey in a panic that Uncle Isak put the hit on his mom. But it wasn't Uncle Isak. Uncle John's trying to place blame, to have Jeffrey kill off whoever needs to be next, to sweep his floor. I bet he had Carly sleep with Dean and try with you. Poor Jeff. Uncle John wasn't surprised that Uncle Mark tried to shoot Uncle Isak. I can't be sure. He's hard to read. Patrick's dead and Dean's been arrested, and soon-to-be Carly if she's not already dead. I hope Jeffrey doesn't lay down more bad cards, or those four kids of Carly's will be orphans."

"They won't be. Catherine and Mary are good people. Garrett too. They'll make it, as maddening as all of this is. The family will pull together. People put aside their judgments whenever something tragic happens, at least long enough to help each other out. It would be best if you focused on yourself right now, Viola. You've learned a lot today."

She knows he means about their blood and the possibility that she can leave after her baby girl is born. Her only fear is for her children. Now that everyone knows who she is, her children will be a target, and she will not leave this family until she knows for certain that they, too, are cured of this family blood curse and safe. She will keep her word with Uncle Isak as long as he keeps his word.

"Jason, we're together. I'm committed to you, to us, our children." She touches her tummy. "I'm happy we're having our baby. On my walk with Uncle Isak, he told me he wanted Zack fixed because he was similar to Dad. Zack viciously killed animals when he was four. They did tests. They uncovered something. Uncle Isak wanted Mom and Dad to try again. Doc created a fix. But then he was livid when Dad beat Mom up. Uncle Isak found out about it. Dad should have been in prison or taken out, but he said that he didn't want our line to end. Pure blood. That is his crime, and Ardent agreed to it, and some fixes that turned out badly for others. Uncle Isak told me that after Mom healed from Dad's beating and they had me, he begged her again. Doc and Mom were already working on a fix. They injected me. They wouldn't know the results til I grew up. Isak wanted them to try again for another boy. Mom and Doc fought against it. Uncle Isak wanted an undamaged male heir. But that wasn't true. They wanted to try out a new warrior fix on you."

"He told you that?" asks Jason.

"No, his eyes told me, when I questioned him. Jason, I don't believe my mom wanted to be with Dad again or have another child with Zack's tendencies. Mom did mention one time that an Uncle Ardent lived in Telega the year you were born. I think Ardent gave you that serum against Doc's wishes. It all worked out since your DNA didn't grab Dad's abnormal gene."

"How do you know this?"

"I've worked with Mom all my life on our blood. I saw samples with your birthdate. I told Uncle Isak I was going to be straightforward today. He said it was time. I believe he meant it. I can't be sure. I think he wants to correct his wrongs."

"You're incredible, luv. Uncle Benjamin is the only one who doesn't make sense in any of this. I assume Uncle Benjamin argued or crossed a line. I'm not sure why Patrick murdered him."

"Zack," Viola says.

Jason's face falls. "I don't think—"

"Zack wanted Uncle Benjamin dead, Jason. He made a deal with Patrick. There's no saying no to Zack. He's playing me and plotting your death. He's obsessed with me, even though I'll never be enough for him. He has to have me. Zack doesn't care about the titles. He loves his life the way it is. He won't want to be a top Uncle. He may have made a deal with a top Uncle—I think it's Uncle John. Do you think he made any deals with Jeffrey? I can't figure out Jeff's involvement."

"Viola, Jeff is mad for Carly. That's about it."

"Yeah, but Carly? Not so much for Jeff. She wants the top heir. Carly will kill me. The only thing stopping her—I wonder. *Hmmm.* She might be in love with Zack."

"What makes you say that?"

"I know she's been with Zack, or does she do them both, Jeffrey and Zack? They share a lot. There's something there. Zack offered to share me with you. He said you wouldn't. I sensed Carly was mad that she couldn't seduce you. It surprised me that she would try, especially if she were with Jeff. I think she was more involved in this than we know."

Jason's eyes fill.

"I'm sorry, Jason. I know you and Carly were close growing up."

"We were, but there were always whispers when I came around. I was treated differently."

"Carly knew all of Patrick's plans," says Viola. "She said things without thinking at the Complex. I didn't give it much thought until now, trying to piece together this puzzle. She said something the day Patrick shot his mother. She told me Patrick went to the States to take Uncle out. She said Patrick wanted you to find his body. She was either in a room when it was planned, or Patrick told her on the way to Aunt Lara's place to kidnap me."

"It's so hard to believe," says Jason.

"Carly wasn't all that upset about her mother. Initially, I assumed she was in shock. I was more upset than her. Her mother had been angry about Carly and Patrick cheating. Carly asked me if her mom had said who she was with, so maybe she's been with more family members. Aunt Lara mentioned Uncle Mark being pathetic. I know it has to do with the Pit. You saw his eyes. Zack has stuff on Uncle Mark." Says Viola.

"We need a way to bring this all out before his trial. Everyone who is involved needs to get talking." Says Jason.

"Is it a real trial?"

"A family trial."

"And prison. Is that somewhere only for our bloodline?"

"Yes. I'll need to tap phone lines, luv."

"Zack has a lab at his club, Jason. He might be the one creating the poison. He has tranquilizers. I can't believe I haven't thought of that 'til now. He said that Henry was on his side. I think Henry might have been with Patrick, too." When she sees Jason's exhausted expression. "Jason, this is so much. Can we lie down?"

"Not yet, luv. It's all unfolding at a rapid pace. So many of these uncles and cousins are corrupt."

-..Chapter 74-..-

"**D**oc knows everything, Jason. We need to speak with him before he's taken out. Uncle Mark is hiding deeper secrets. There is a pile of shit here—years of crap. I wish that you and me could find the baby—find Zee and leave before one of these people kills us. They need to sort out their direct family lines. I want to start ours, make it new, you and me. Would you be willing to cut strings to be with me?"

Yes or no, Jason. Please say yes. If not, the Rise might not let me see Zee again. Please choose me.

Jason stares at Viola.

"As a kid, I watched you, more than once, alone on your stairs, playing with your wooden stacking dolls."

"Mom's nesting doll."

"When you were making food for yourself, cleaning the house, you were so peaceful. I told your mum I wished I had never had to bring you into this. I wished we could let you be. You were so happy, so innocent. I already knew far too much of what was going on. It's been this way since I was a lad."

"Zack said you were in. What does that mean, Jason?"

"He was phishing, luv. He told me about your conversation with Dean when he called me an hour ago. I told him you have no clue. That you were right pissed that he stepped in. You were hoping to get Dean to spill it. He laughed. He thinks you're cleverer than everyone combined. He's chuffed to the bits with you."

"In American English, please, Jason."

"He's quite proud of you, luv."

"He wants me. He wants you dead to get me... someday."

"I know," Jason says, looking away, and back to her eyes. "He sent a message to the cousin in the boardroom—the one who stepped forward. Zack wanted us tranquilized. You were to be taken from here, for him."

The shiver up her spine, shoots out her eyes. She can't stop it—the thought of being with Zack... him raising Zee. Her eyes scream fear.

"What do you want to do, Jason?"

"I want to get far away from here with you. We'll start anew with our family. You, me, and the baby."

"I can't leave without Zee."

"I meant him, luv. Our baby girl hasn't arrived yet. I have a plan."

"Oh, thank goodness," she says, taking his hand. "Can we leave now?"

"Pull out your mobile phone. I need you to call Jeffrey first."

Jason squeezes her hand. She pulls him to her, wrapping her arms around him, wanting to cocoon what's left of his shattered heart, knowing what he knows about Zack. She whispers in his ear, "Did you know Uncle Mark has a TV in his office?"

"Does he?"

"I feel like we're on one of those daytime TV shows I watched while I was kept in England. Who is sleeping with whom? Who is lying? The sneaky bad guy no one suspects is the one pitting people against other innocent people."

"And yet you still want to watch the show the next day to see what will happen, luv. We escape having to face ourselves by watching others' messy lives—in TV dramas, in the news. Every family has stuff. We'd rather not face our own, so we focus on other people. It can't change if we run away."

"I know what you're saying, Jason. We can run, but we'll have to face our family again, whether we like it or not, if we want to help the rest of them, and I want to help change all of this. But first,

I want our children to have an opportunity away from this chaos until I have to come back."

———

Viola calls Jeffrey. She mentions that Patrick told her on the way to the Complex that Uncle John approved of his mother's death, not Uncle Isak.

Viola tells him that she and Jason will stay put until things ease up, allowing the top uncles to clean their houses. She'll contact him again when she can.

"Carly played us all," Viola says to Jason. "I can only hope Jeff doesn't kill Zack when he finds out about his affair with Carly."

"He won't, luv. I've tracked Carly to Zack's apartments before. I know it's been happening for a while."

"Why didn't you tell me?"

"It's none of my business unless someone innocent could get killed. Jeff only recently told me about his feelings for Carly. Zack knew nothing about them. I saw how those guys lived their lives. I stayed to myself. You choose one road or the other. I was moved from my mum to England. I was told my mum wasn't my mum. My birth mum and dad were both working all kinds of angles in the family. I was pulled in every possible direction between Isak and Uncle Mark. Endless shite. I worried the most about you because I knew it would happen to you once you reached of age."

"It feels strange that I've lived for seventeen years not knowing about you."

"I know I didn't attend a regular school like you, but I still saw how the world seemed to work on a day-to-day basis. I made my own decisions. We'll leave now. I've a colleague outside of the family who will help us. Doc's been moved again. Jeffrey doesn't know where he is. I needed you to start Jeff on a new mission, so he doesn't try to track us until I'm ready."

"I'm so happy we can go at last—I hope no one can find us."

"They won't. Are you sure about your feelings for me, Viola? I can try to get you out if that's what you want."

Jason is key.

She takes his hand, placing it on her stomach.

"Our daughter and I are both certain."

I can't leave for good until I make the fix for Zee. The rise will never let me go until it works for both sexes.

-..Chapter 75-. .-

Viola loves Jason, but it's not right—to her, it's not. She wants to feel different and accept all of this, but she can't. She knows this is why Mom never brought her up in their traditions. Mom didn't want Viola to agree with this way of living—not after being raised like she was. She wanted Viola to finally fix their blood to get out of it. Priscilla wanted Viola to escape and read the Green Book, to learn about her famous ancestor, a man from the Eastman-Newton line in the 1600s who was raised outside of the family.

To hide him and protect him, our ancestors sold him to a couple who were farmers. The farmer was dying, and he wanted a son to continue his surname, Newton. Shortly after the farmer's death, his widow remarried and handed off Issac to her mother to raise him so she could remarry and have children with her new husband.

When Issac was a teenager, Isaac Newton was told about our bloodline. He refused our ways. He remained private. Knowing our curse, he never married, though he did attempt to find the cure.

What deals did Mom have to make with the Rise to lead Viola to the Green Book, to help her understand the formulas Isaac was working on? It became clear to Viola the moment Uncle Mark explained their bloodline to her. She couldn't believe it. Her brain couldn't accept it. Viola will need to retrieve the Green Book again. The Rise will help her. She understands that now.

I won't be a coward. I won't be selfish.

Mom's note in the book told her that the women in their line had all sacrificed, lifetime after lifetime, and they gave in to this way of life once they had children. They stopped trying to fix their blood. Viola's mother's horrible youth changed her feelings about her mother's oath, then Stephen changed them permanently.

Mom knew she had to help me change mine. She had to train me in case I couldn't get out. How can I walk away from these innocent, unknowing children like I once was? We're held captive by our blood. I know I can fix it. I'm going to fix it. Then I'm vanishing for good with my children.

Jason smiles as the wall inside Uncle Isak's command room opens at the Plant.

"Stay close, my luv. Uncle Isak has a secret route, an underground passage out of here. We must leave all phones behind but bring Jeffrey's number. We will still need him—and this."

Jason pulls out the Magellan NAV 1000, one of the first GPS systems built—the one The Rise left in the cottage nightstand for Viola. Jason told her in the forest that he'd keep it for her. He knew every item she packed to take to Siberia would be thoroughly checked. The day she drove away from the cottage, she watched him from the car's back window, knowing that she had led Jason and his two men at the cottage on a wild goose chase.

"We'll send Jeffrey our GPS coordinates once we arrive in the United States." Jason adds.

"The latitude and longitude," she reiterates, thinking of the pain this information will cause.

Jason and Viola wear construction hats with bright lights to guide their steps. The underground passage is long. The family has undoubtedly owned this property for many years. Jason explains to her how there are many tunnels and how they were used to transport at one point one hundred and sixty thousand convicts sent from England, and Wales.

"Forty thousand so called convicts from Ireland and Scotland were sent to Australia along with anyone considered a threat to

British rule. Whoever else the church or the King said were mental health patients, which in most cases were undesirable poverty stricken families the State wanted removed. It started in 1788, and continued til the 1860's."

"When did our family come here?" she asks.

"It was listed in some journals that a number of our family oversaw this atrocity, in order to branch out and settle here," Jason adds.

"I have a million questions."

"I know, luv."

"Why agree to send me to Siberia for training when I could have continued in Telega?"

"Uncle Mark felt it would be safest for you to train in a private lab. He made a deal with Uncle Benjamin the same day we burned your mum's journal. I didn't have a say in the matter."

"At first, I thought he might have wanted to see what I would work on. You know that I'm skilled in the sciences, don't you?"

"I do," says Jason.

"I think I know where that facility is. Do you think Uncle Mark wanted me there, knowing Patrick would kill me before I set foot in that place."

"I'm not certain," Jason says. "Uncle Mark is the one who decided you should remain in England."

"What happened to make him change his mind?"

"I'll find out. Maybe Patrick killing Uncle Benjamin changed him."

"Carly had many opportunities to kill me. I'm not sure why she didn't."

"We know Patrick and Carly both wanted you dead. That was their original plan."

Viola has an idea.

"Who decides which men sit in those meetings at the Plant?"

"There is a hierarchy," he says.

"Who are the top uncles? And which cousins are allowed there?"

"Their titles are in Old English. Great, Great Grandfather is *Faoweroa Faeder,* who is King. Great Grandfather, *Bridda Faeder. Feadera* (Uncle). *Faeder* (father), then their firstborn sons would be the cousins you saw. They're called Successor, the one that follows."

"What about the other children?"

"They're taught like the family you met in Ireland and Paris, unaware of the truth about our blood. They're only told if they move up in rank or need to know. It's for their protection and ours, Viola. I've told you before: The more people who find out, the greater chances our secrets could get into the wrong ears. In previous generations, we have been hunted."

"I read about it," says Viola. "So many of us in one family line wiped out."

"We worked with that line to bring them back." Jason stops, takes her hand, and turns to face her. "Are you afraid to tell me what you know? You don't have to be, luv. I'll never lie to you, not ever again. You are my all. My priority."

"I read about that story. The men in our line convinced the church that women were witches."

"I bet you've read more stories than I have."

"Maybe."

Jason tightens his grip on her hand directing Viola's feet, staying in step with his own in the dark. The lights on their hats peer into the nothingness.

-..Chapter 76-. .-

Their helmut lights glows in the vacant tunnel. The Green Book and the hidden journals, written in Latin by the East-mann heirs, cross her mind. Mom told her where to find it. It was buried with another fallen heir, Luci—the English title of the book, *Puritanically Stripped*. Mom left the book open to the page Viola was to read in the living room at Bell Park Community. Viola memorized the page—the brave Modir—mother in Old Norse.

Luci, our Eastmann ancestor, of Norse descent, died in 1588 when the men from our line stormed the castle where she lived. Luci, a private nurse to Queen Elizabeth I, could have escaped, but instead of fleeing, she waited for the men to give her children—her off-spring—the chance to escape in an underground tunnel. She was brutally raped by an army of men. They took her naked, broken body to a field where they tied her arms like a Shoy-hoy—a scarecrow up on a wooden cross. She was left in the field for vultures to peck away at until all that remained were her bones.

The following summer, the Queen's favorite flower, Mead-owsweet, magically grew beneath Luci's remains, and a rare orchid bloomed under her feet. Word spread, and people came to see her grave. Only her name was unknown, so the people called her Lady Jane after the beloved, innocent sixteen-year-old Lady Jane Grey, who was forced to marry and forced by her father to become the Queen before Elizabeth I. Jane was Queen for exactly nine days before she was arrested and set to be executed. It was treason for anyone to speak against her execution. The Queen Mary herself was said to regret the innocent Lady Jane's death sentence. She must have known how vicious the men are who were vying for power. The fearful agree with the rules.

Queen Elizabeth loved Meadowsweet so much that she placed it on her chamber floor to fall asleep with its sweet fragrance. It said that the Queen commanded that the flowers be planted in the field in memory of yet another innocent young female. The queen's ladies-in-waiting assumed she meant Lady Jane. From a page torn from the Queen's journal, glued into a family journal we know it was in memory of a brave nurse and trusted friend of the Queen... Luci.

Viola recalls her eyes trailing the statue of Luci's strong legs in the book from her obvious daily treks through the vast mountains and fields, gathering herbs for the queen, for her medicinal tinctures.

Mom told me Luci sacrificed herself, like many females have in her line, lifetime after lifetime. History repeats!

After she and Jason pass through a narrow barrier, they hear a noise above them.

"It's a lawn being mowed," says Jason. "We're getting close if we can hear sounds above us. It'll be another five-minute walk down."

Viola's helmet light shines on a sizable object ahead. As they reach the uncovered front of an outfitted Jeep, Jason pulls on a dusty green army tarp, and dust particles float in a triangle of light in front of her face. Jason uses his arm to sweep through the front seat, and the back, before he tosses the tarp into the back seat.

"Why are you doing that?"

"Spiders," he says, using his fingers in front of his light to mimic a crawling spider.

"I'm not afraid of spiders, Jason."

"I am," he replies, making her laugh.

"Is that why your face was green walking through the old shower stalls at the cottages?" she asks, and he leans in to kiss her.

"Maybe that's what it was," he says, before he resumes his task of checking the tires. "You know, luv, I was thinking earlier, had you not tried to run off with Zee, you would have gone to the Lab in Siberia sooner. Patrick would have killed you—or tried to anyway. As you've learned, one of his men planned to make your death look like an accident the moment you arrived. I'm baffled why he didn't. I've thought a lot about everything happening the way it has up to this point. I was stunned the day you ran. I thought you were taken. It did cross my mind at our place in England that you weren't breastfeeding Zee when I brought in your bags. That struck me as odd."

"Did you put it up on your board with the strings?"

"No. I assumed it was what normal people do in America."

"Some women prefer to breastfeed, while others don't or can't. I knew then that I might move Zee. Aunt Ruth gave me a note before my trip to see you. She didn't say when exactly to be ready. I weaned him, in case. I prefer to breastfeed for much longer after reading about its health benefits. I will with this wee peanut," she says, touching her bump. "Jason, I regret lying to you—"

"Don't," he says. "It worked out for the best, better than I thought it could... for us, though not everyone."

Viola, confused by his comment.

"How can you say that when we're running for our lives?"

"I'll tell you soon enough. We must go. We have a plane to catch."

He picks her up and sets her in the passenger seat. Then, he walks to the other side and jumps into the driver's seat.

"This looks old," she says, looking at the instruments and feeling the roughness of the leather seat.

"It is. The seating was replaced from canvas to leather years ago. It's a Kubelwagen. Ferdinand Porsche designed this. Uncle Isak claims that Coco Chanel herself rode in this jeep."

"How would he know that?" she asks.

"A family member was her driver. It's in the family journals—quite an interesting read."

"I read about how she saved innocent people during the war."

It's loud, far too loud to continue their conversation.

Viola thinks of Zee, her son, and what she's willing to say and do to save his life. She recalls her mother asking her with tear-filled eyes. "

What is one life worth?"

Viola tries to imagine what living in Coco's era would've been like. Priscilla showed Viola copies of letters explaining a secret code many women used during the war. It's rarely talked about why most women oppose war. Is it because their boys are killed, and their girls are raped. And for what? There is no freedom when a singular dictator is willing to kill innocent children for his own piece of his temporary pie. No one will ever own the land. Mother Nature dictates the rules. She gave us life. She can take it away, and she will, if we continue our greed and destruction of her.

When Jason hands Viola her passport, her insides shudder. How sad that she'd rather live underground than out in the world. Viola feels safer hidden away. Perhaps this is how many families felt during wartime, hiding from people who had nothing to do with their lives, yet decided to create an imaginary reason for mass murders and persecutions over land, religion, or power. Viola read about soldiers who didn't think it was right to kill innocent children. Yet they were ordered to do it, and they did.

Viola thinks of Patrick's followers, who have invented titles at the Complex, and the men at the Plant. They remind her of the people under the big top tent at the circus in Mom's children's book.

"If they would only stop clapping!"

Viola contemplates getting Zee and running away from her family circus. But now she knows the truth about their bloodline, and after her years of training, how to find the cure. Will she break her promise to her mother to never stop until the cure is found? Too many of her female ancestors sacrificed themselves trying to create a fix for their blood. The Green Book said they started in the 1300s.

That's six hundred years ago. The book said that Gisele was the first *Modir*. (Mother.) There was a clue in the Green Book—a riddle.

After Zee is safely in Viola's arms, she's going to travel where her mother wanted to take her before she died. Her Mom was like Luci. Viola is, too. They are the women in this family who realize birth is the greatest gift, and they're willing to do what is right for the greater good, for their children's futures. Even if it means dying for their children. After all, that's the risk every woman takes with every pregnancy.

Thank you for your sacrifices, Mom.

Viola swore an oath, but it's her choice. She's committed to ending this blood curse, even if it means sacrificing the freedom she longs for. She will free her children. She will free every child trapped in her bloodline.

"We'll leave the Kubelwagon here," Jason says, turning off the jeep, snapping her out of her thoughts.

He jumps out and pulls on the same army-faded tarp he rolled from the back seat to recover the vehicle.

"We're going to take a private plane, then a commercial flight, luv. It will be my first. We're not permitted to do so. We always use our own planes to stay under the radar. But this time I need to leave a trail."

He turns off the helmet lights as he removes their headgear, setting them both in the back seat.

In pitch black, in the tunnel, Viola stands on the front seat of the old jeep, waiting for him to lift her over.

"Jason!" He clicks on a mini flashlight to see her face.

"What was in that compartment in the closet at the cottage?" she asks.

"I have its contents at Uncle's house," he says as he lifts her over the door. He covers the jeep with the tarp. He takes her hand.

"Uncle Isak knows our plan, doesn't he? Can we trust him?"

They walk in silence. When Jason drops her hand, Viola hears metal scraping.

Jason grunts. The angle of his flashlight points up, capturing the outline of a few steel rod stairs and a door with a wheel attached to it. Viola hears water splashing.

"We'll be coming out next to a waterfall, luv. We'll walk a few miles. I radioed before we left. A driver is waiting for us."

Another grunt, the steel door is pushed open. The glare of sunlight bounces off it, and the sun and the moist mist make her eyes water. The sound of water crashing on rocks fills her ears with a loud white noise.

Releasing her thoughts, Viola inhales the fresh air with deep pleasure.

-..Chapter 77-..-

Jason and Viola arrive at the Philadelphia International Airport on their private plane. They're met and escorted by a man who Viola assumes is a private secret service. Once they're in the main airport with hundreds of other civilians, Viola excuses herself, while the man and Jason continue to talk. She motions to Jason that she's headed toward the visible sign several feet away, 'Restrooms.'

As Viola is about to turn in, she sees it... The blue orchid on the beige bag, along with a woman's purse around a man's arm. He moves the bag with the orchid painted on, so it's no longer visible. She thinks he looks embarrassed. Like any man might look who is waiting for his wife to come out of the ladies' bathroom, holding her bags. He stands against the wall, wearing an Eagles hat pulled down to cover his face. Viola doesn't miss the dimple in his chin.

She catches her breath as she opens the door. She walks in slowly. She heads to the end of the bathroom, passing by numerous open stalls. Her heart stops as she taps five taps on the last locked door.

Dit dit dit dah. Dah. Morse Code for VT, her code sign with mom for Viola Ted.

The bathroom door unlocks, and her eyes fill immediately with happy tears when they meet the crystal blue eyes of Zee. She covers her mouth, careful not to make a sound as Jill hands her son to her. They stare at one another. In his mouth, sucking in rhythm on a binky. His hand reaches for her nose. Her chest feels like it's exploding, shooting out endless amounts of invisible sparkle dust. She's overcome with joy. She hugs Zee to her. She inhales his baby's smell like she smelled him yesterday. She holds him pressed against her. Her cheek on his forehead, vowing to never part from him ever again, like she promised him would happen the next time they saw one another, before she handed him to Jill in the back of the van.

Jill hands Viola her baby bag, leaving the stall. Viola steps out holding Zee.

"J'ai besoin du *Livre vert.*" (I need the Green Book.) says Viola.

Jill doesn't respond. Viola knows that she heard her. Jill leaves the bathroom, and Viola glances around for a camera. She sees it covered. Jill already took care of it.

Viola waits one full minute, touching Zee's soft, dark hair, feeling a shadow in the corner her heart, fill with light. She departs the bathroom and moves toward the gate. The sign behind Jason is blinking, "*On Time*" *Destination, Buffalo, NY.*

Jason gawks at her. She smiles. His facial expression doesn't change. Her hand reaches out. Jason takes the passport from her. He turns around and proceeds to the flight attendant. Viola watches him purchase a ticket. The flight attendant peers around to see Zee.

Confirming, "Zachary Stanton." she says.

"Yes," Viola says.

-..Chapter 78-..-

I n Uncle Benjamin's hidden room in Telega, Jason and Viola listen in to various conversations. Both are wearing earphones. They're surrounded by wires, phone lines, live video feeds.

When they see Jeffrey's cell phone dial a number, Jason hits the record button.

"Hello, SHEC Services."

"Janic, how's the Pit these days, brother?"

"Howdy, Jeff, ripe as usual."

"Zack around?"

"Nope."

"Did he say when he'd be back?"

"*Nyet.* (Nope) Are you stopping by?"

"Hell, no, Carly would kick my ass out of the house. Have you seen her there recently?"

Janic laughs. "No."

"Has my father Mark been there?"

"Sorry, Jeff, I don't keep track of all the clients in this place—their names, anyway."

"No worries, Jan Tan."

"Ha, ha, real funny, Jeff. No one told me not to wear shorts in the tanning bed, and that I should spend no more than ten minutes on my first time. I plan to kick Zack's *zadnitsa* (butt) the next time I see him for telling you about that."

"Cheers, mate."

———————

Three days later, a call comes into Jeffrey's cell phone. Again, Jason hits record.

"Have you found them, Jeffrey?" Uncle John asks.

"Yes."

"Where are they?"

"They took a commercial flight from Philadelphia to Buffalo with an infant checked in."

"So, you think they have the baby? You don't think they went to Benjamin's?" Uncle John asks.

"Maybe. Zack closed it up along with his uncle's other homes. It's off-grid."

"When can you get there?"

"I'm close. A few hours."

"I wonder if they have him... Zachary. Monitor, stay out of sight."

————————

Jason dials Zack's cell phone.

"Jay, where are you?"

"We're at Uncle Benjamin's."

"In America?"

"Yes, Zack, but we're leaving. We won't be back. Someone tried to kill Viola and me in our room at the Plant. I want you to keep my house in England."

"How's Viola?"

"Good. We're having a girl."

"Fuck... Congrats. I cannot wait for Zee to meet his sister." says Zack.

"We have him. We picked up Zee a few days ago. I pulled a few strings. We're sneaking him out with us. I'll reach out to you, but not this year. I couldn't leave and not tell you. There may still be a hit on you once Uncle John finds out Carly faked it."

"Yep. She's good at faking." Zack huffs. "Jay, tell Viola I love her. Send me pics of Zee."

"Will do. Patrick wanted the top heir with his oldest daughter. We found out Carly's youngest daughter is Dean's biological child. Dean made it known at the Plant that his heir was next in line if Viola dies. It's Carly who took out the hit on Viola. They know we're having a girl. They want Viola out, boy or girl."

Zack is quiet.

"Zack, are you there?"

"I'm killing them all," Zack says. "Does Jeff know?"

"Viola told him. We think Carly may be playing him to kill our line off for her. Then he'd later be merked for doing it. She and Dean, or whoever, would have the top heir."

"It's not my kid, if that's what you're asking. I can't see Jeff turning on us."

"For Carly, he would. Look at what we've done for our sister," says Jason.

"Hmmm," says Zack.

"I'll take care of us," Jason says. "You be careful, Zack."

"I will, Jay. You'll raise my boy right."

"You have my word. Hold on, Zack."

Jason walks with the mobile phone to the back door at Uncle's place in Telega.

Viola calls out, "Hi, Daddy Zack."

Baby Zackary is cooing as he plays with a blue toy truck. He's bundled up for the chilly weather.

"Zack, did you hear that?" asks Jason.

"Hell yeah. Aw, man, I'm glad you got him back, Jay."

"Isak got him for us. He's locked in the Box at the Plant. Isak wants us to continue."

"I'll get him out."

"He's probably banking on that, seeing Uncle John's up to no good. Do it soon before they axe him."

"I will today. I'll miss you three."

There's dead air. Ten seconds of silence, when Jason clears his throat.

"You'll see us again in this life or the next. I hope my plan works. No one knows we're here."

"It's perfect," says Zack. "I would've never guessed."

"It was Viola's idea."

"*Hmmm*. I'm not surprised. Take care of her, Jay."

"Take care of yourself, Zack."

"Bye, Jay."

Jason hands Viola the cell phone. She hits end, then taps out a text to Jeffrey with the satellite coordinates of a specific location. Her eyes meet Jason's. She taps out another text.

"Hey, Jeffy. It's Viola. I'm sorry. Stay good. You're worth it!"

———

An hour later, Jason and Viola watch Jeffrey on the live camera feed walking around the white house that Zack took Viola to a few weeks ago. The cottage, that Zack said, was only for family.

Baby Zee is asleep in Viola's arms as she sits in Uncle Benjamin's recliner chair that Jason dragged into Uncle's hidden room for her.

"Jason, what does SHEC services stand for? Zack has a ball cap with those letters. Janic mentioned it on his phone call with Jeffrey."

"It's the name of Dad's... Zack's Crematory company, luv."

"Zack's place! It's nothing like a crematory."

"You were in a separate basement level of the business."

Viola's at a loss for words. The room with the large fire place behind a wall of tempered glass at Zack's black pit hole, enters her mind.

Their heads turn at the same time to watch on a screen as Jeffrey picks the lock at the white house's back door. Jeffrey pulls out his gun from the front of his cargo pants.

Once inside, he checks the kitchen, the spare bedroom, and they watch as he opens drawers in the master bedroom. Jeffrey pulls a book from a nightstand dresser, flips through it, flipping back to the inside front cover for an extra beat. He tosses the book on the bed.

"What book is it?" Viola asks.

"I don't know, luv," Jason replies.

They watch Jeffrey go into the bathroom. He flings open drawers, pulling out a pill bottle, reading it, slamming it down. A deodorant stick on the side of the sink, falls over. He studies the contents inside the cabinet before he pulls back the shower curtain. Jeffrey's right hand grips his chest. His left hand reaches behind him to lower the toilet seat lid before he sits down. Seated, he stares at the shower.

Viola releases a breath. Jason turns the camera off.

When Viola and Jason landed in Buffalo with Zee, they went to the white house to retrieve the coordinates, and also so Jason could set up several cameras for proof, when Jeffrey would uncover the truth for himself.

———————

An hour and a half has passes. An alarm goes off in the bunker. Jason sees on a camera from the backyard, towards the woods, a movement.

Jason texts Viola's mobile phone. *"Jeffrey has arrived. Here we go."*

Jason hits record when he sees that Jeffrey is making an outgoing call from his mobile phone.

———————

"Hi, babe," says Carly.

"Hi," Jeffrey says.

"Where are you?"

"I'm in Telega. I was at the white house where you meet Zack at in America to fuck. I saw your shampoo and conditioner in the bathroom, and your mint toothpaste."

"Oh. I stayed there with Patrick a long time ago."

"Is that why I found Zack's pill bottle, his deodorant, and a book that you wrote a personal message in. I saw what you wrote. Were you ever going to tell me, Carlene, about you and the Anaconda?"

The phone is quiet.

"It wasn't often, Jeff."

"Is your daughter mine, Dean's, or Zack's heir?"

"She's yours. Zack refuses to have kids with anyone but Viola. I was only with Dean one time."

"Really?" he says.

"I never meant for it to happen, Jeffrey. Patrick took me to the Pit. He took off. I was left with Zack. It happened. After that, I saw Zack now and then—if I was in America or he was in England. It's nothing, I swear it, Jeffrey. You know Zack!"

"I stopped all of that for you, Car. I sold my share of the club. I don't remember you batting an eye lid when I told you. You should've told me then."

"I stopped, too. I told Zack I'm with you now."

"Why Zack?"

"I'm sorry, Jeff. I never thought Father would allow you and me to be together again. I don't—I don't know what I'm doing."

"Tell Zack that Jason, Viola, and the baby are at Uncle' Benjamin's in Telega. I'm watching Viola and the baby out back. They're playing as we speak."

"Are you serious?"

"I can't believe it myself. I took a picture to prove it. I told Uncle John I found the plane tickets. It looks like they picked up the baby in Philadelphia two days ago."

"Why go back to her Uncle's place?" asks Carly.

"All her things are still here—typical Viola, face the fear. The problem is if Uncle John knows, he's told others. You know who I'm talking about."

"Can you reach Jason? Warn him before something happens. Zack wants Viola and the baby."

"She's having a girl, she told me," says Jeffrey.

Carly gasps.

From inside the house, Jason texts Viola's mobile again. Viola looks at it and quickly lifts Zee, taking him into the back door of Uncle Benjamin's house.

"Shite," says Jeffrey. "Viola just rushed her and the baby inside."

"I'm sorry, Jeffrey. Can you forgive me? I want to—"

"Car, I'd better go. If Jason comes out the door shooting—"

BOOM!

A loud blast distorts the phone line.

Jeffrey covers his head.

"FUCK," yells Jeffrey.

"Jeff... Jeffrey, what happened?"

"The bloody house blew up!"

-..Chapter 79-. .-

The phone on the coffee table at Jason's house in London buzzes for the third time.

"Car, what's up?" Zack hears her sniffling on the line. "Car, I hate waiting. Talk."

"Jeff knows about us. He found the white house. My things are there."

"So what?"

"Jeff's at your Uncle's."

"WHAT?" Zack jumps to his feet. "Why?"

"Uncle John found out they're there. There's more I haven't told you. There's someone else involved, Zack. But it's too late."

"Who else is involved, Car... FUCKING TELL ME NOW!"

"I was on the phone with Jeff. Viola rushed inside with the baby. Jeff thinks a wire must have been tripped. Jason knew someone was there. Jeffrey said that Viola and the baby barely got inside. Zack. The whole place blew up. There's nothing left of it."

Zack drops the phone on the area carpet. He picks it back up. He hits the end button. He dials Jason's number. Busy signal. He dials again—same thing.

"*NOOO!*" he screams.

Zack tosses the phone on the couch. His neck strains as he yells at the top of his lungs. He picks up a lamp, and throws it across the room. His fists clench. Like a madman, leaving the scene of a crime, he resets himself. He grabs his passport, money, and keys from a table. He rushes to take a framed photo of him and Jason from the living room. He stuffs it in a bag, lifts his coat off a chair, and flips a switch in Jason's house before heading out a side door into the garage. He pushes on a dent in the concrete wall, and an underground tunnel appears as the garage wall slides open.

It closes behind him.

-..Chapter 80-. .-

Five Days Later

Uncle John is seated at the head of the boardroom table at the Plant with what's left of the Top Uncles, the next-in-line Uncles, and first cousins.

Doc's son Ryan, from the Americas, has arrived with his eldest son, Henry. Alexander's son, Mikhail, has arrived from Asia. Uncle Mark's son, Garrett, has come from Siberia, and the men in the room are surprised to see Jeffrey is with him.

Eight guards with guns surround them to ensure the prisoners, Uncle Mark and Dean, are not harmed before their trial.

"Gentlemen," Uncle John says, "It's a sad day for all of us. You've all heard the news about the deceased—Jason and Althea Eastmann, along with Zack and his son and successor, Zachary. We believe one of Isak's loyal guards let him out of the Box. Isak has fled. We're not sure of his current whereabouts. We ask that if anyone has information, they let me know directly. Ardent will remain in the Box until we can find Isak and corroborate their stories. Mark and Dean are both here to tell us about their involvement in recent family scheming that has led to family members being murdered. Both men have admitted to serious crimes. We vote today to determine their sentencing. Is there any other business or code of conduct to be discussed?"

Garrett raises his index finger.

"Yes, Garrett."

"I'm deeply saddened by everything that transpired in this family. We are supposed to be a unit. We were raised and taught to be good people. Honesty amongst siblings, at the very least. It's how we've thrived and survived for centuries. I'm thoroughly disgusted that you, Uncle John, dare to allow my father and Dean to sit in this room after all their crimes are known to the hierarchy. They should spend the rest of their lives in prison without a trial. They are responsible for the deaths of our loved ones and for ending our ancestral purebred line over the resentment of a title. They're an embarrassment to this family. To set things right, I motion for Jeffrey, the eldest son of Mark and Lara Eastmann, to be reinstated and marked as Uncle for our line from this day forward."

Ryan raises his index finger.

"Yes, Ryan." Uncle John says.

"As acting Uncle in my father's absence, I second the motion."

"Mikhail, as acting Uncle for your father, Alexander, until his prison time is through, do you vote Aye or Nay?" asks Uncle John.

"Ani, "(no), Mikhail says, in Korean, glaring at Jeffrey.

Uncle Mark raises his index finger. Uncle John nods for him to speak.

"Until the trial concludes, I'm Uncle for my line," Mark says.

"Samuel has chosen not to be involved in family affairs," Uncle John says with a sigh. "Benjamin is deceased. Doc is in hiding. Alexander remains in prison. Ardent is the Box. Isak is at large. Therefore, this motion is left up to me as chief."

Dean looks ill. He raises his index finger. Ryan stares across the board room table at his brother.

"Yes, Dean," says Uncle John.

"I'm still officially acting Uncle for Doc's line in his absence—not Ryan, sir."

Ryan raises his index finger.

"Yes, Ryan," says Uncle John.

"Dean lost that privilege when he openly admitted he is Uncle Mark's top male heir, not Doc's. Might I add, also for putting a hit out on my father?" Ryan says with a disgusted look on his face.

The room looks to Uncle John.

"Ryan is correct about acting Uncle. We've yet to uncover any plots, Ryan, regarding a hit on whomever. We'll need proof before we accuse. As chair, since we are certain Mark and Dean will spend a lengthy amount of time in prison, I motion for Jeffrey Jonathan Eastmann to be reinstated," John says, looking directly at Uncle Mark. "I secure the motion for Jeffrey Jonathan Eastmann to be marked as acting Uncle. As chief, this is my decision, Mark, until your sentence has concluded."

Uncle Mark stands. He slams his fist on the table.

Jeffrey rises, pulls out a gun, and shoots his father between the eyes.

All the family members freeze in shock. The guards raise their guns.

Uncle John raises his hand, halting them as the bell at the entrance rings.

Mikhail shakes his head, with no expression on his face. Uncle John gets up to stand, but Ryan stands first. Since he's the closest to the door, he opens it.

Uncle Isak walks through with Zack, their guns raised.

"Guards," Uncle John says, "arrest both of these men."

The guards point their guns at the men sitting around the table instead.

John looks around, then at Isak.

"What is the meaning of this, Isak?"

"I might ask you the same thing, brother. We're aware of your recent taped phone conversations. It was you who put the hit on my entire line. It was your grandson Patrick who shot and killed Benjamin. You were the master schemer, having Mark, Lara, Dean, and Patrick set things in motion. You got Carly involved and, as you can see, she didn't complete your mission for her to kill my great-grandson Zackary here. Carly admitted to her crime. She also admitted to her involvement in her mother's death. And that she hid Patrick's gun in their room after he shot Althea at the Complex. We have reason to believe Carly has fled to avoid prison.

I cannot understand why you would take out the most important people in our crucial research—our only pureblood heirs. Our legacy, centuries old. Do you have anything to say for yourself?"

"Truth be told," Uncle John says. "I'm tired of you being in the King's chair, brother, making all of the major decisions, deciding which scientists have access to the latest biotechnologies. You don't openly include all the lines. We in this room are of the same blood. We all come from the beginning family. Who decided who would sit at the top?"

"Henry," Uncle Isak says, "you worked directly with the top scientists and Doc before he went in hiding regarding our top-of-the-line blood. Do you have any input for Uncle John regarding the bloodline all being the same?"

"The blood has changed through the years, as different cousins blended their genetics, and as you all know, environmental pollution alters our DNA and can damage how genes are regulated, leading to mutations. Jason's blood, from the direct line, has a unique immunity. This protein defends the body against many common infections, even immunodeficiencies and autoimmune disorders, while protecting the body's cells. It's a scientific breakthrough. We've pinpointed the microbes. Doc added the fix to Althea. Doc's last check on her blood showed that the fix had been successful. Now, with their deaths, we're at a loss without more analysis and testing on their blood. No one else in the line has this exact blood. We know it's due to the direct line. It's the cleanest."

"What about your handling of your grandson, Russell, Isak?" John says. "He was severely damaged by whatever concoction you gave him at birth, and you lied about it. So did Ardent, hiding his predatory animal behavior, allowing how many murders to occur. His sister Priscilla went through horrible beatings because of your weakness to put that animal to sleep for the greater good, all in the name of science."

"Priscilla wanted heirs. It was her choice to remain with Russell. It was because of you, John, that my beautiful granddaughter was murdered. Your lie about her being with your grandson, Dean. We both know she would never be with him or anyone but my grandson."

"Let's talk about Stephen," John says.

Zack's eyes shift to Isak, and back to John.

"We had no clue Stephen had the tendency he had." Uncle Isak says. "We know it was you, John, who put the hit on Jason and Althea here in their room at the Plant. You made that call. You set up the camera so your hitman could access the room code. I can't believe you allowed Mark to live after finding out about him and—"

Uncle John's gun lifts, but Zack shoots the gun out of his hand.

In the same instant, Uncle Isak shoots John between the eyes.

Dean leans over and grunts as he struggles to wrestle a gun from a cousin's grip, who has it raised toward Uncle Isak. The gun goes off, hitting the ceiling above Isak.

Uncle Isak, Zack, and the guards turn their guns on the cousin sitting next to Dean.

Dean grabs the cousin's gun, he looks across the table, locking eyes with his brother Ryan. In the next movement, Dean turns the gun on himself. The barrel is in his mouth.

"NO, DEAN!" Ryan yells across the table.

Dean's finger presses the trigger. The palm of Ryan's hands are glued to the sidearms of his chair. He stares as his older brother's head falls forward onto the table. His blood oozes away from him in an expanding circle.

"Guards, please remove the bodies," Uncle Isak says.

Uncle Isak points to the cousin sitting next to Dean's body.

"Take him to the Box."

Zack's gun lifts, he shoots the cousin before the guards move.

Uncle Isak, doesn't flinch.

The doorbell chimes.

Jeffrey remains standing, with his gun raised.

Zack moves to open the door, and Uncle Ardent walks through. Ardent smiles at Henry. His eyes investigate Ryan's. They follow Ryan, stopping. His mouth opens. He stares at Dean's head on the boardroom table surrounded by the thick fluid and the gun on the table in Dean's hand.

Mikhail slides his chair back. He walks over to Isak, who whispers in his ear. Mikhail helps Ardent to a seat.

Two guards remove John's body. Two more guards remove Mark, and two remove the cousin. Ryan turns his head as the guards lift Dean's body.

Once the boardroom door closes, Isak sits at the head of the table. Zack and Jeffrey remain standing guard with their guns drawn, ready to shoot anyone who moves.

"We have much to discuss, my brothers," Uncle Isak says. "We need to clear the air, as my beloved great-granddaughter, Althea Gisele Eastmann, so plainly reminded me not but a week ago. We will be truthful."

He glances toward Dean's vacant chair.

"We will forgive and move forward, stronger than ever as a unit bound by blood. Enough of this petty rubbish to be top of the line. We are all the same line. I motion to strike any further discussions of a top of the line title as of today."

Everyone in the room raises their index finger, saying, "Aye."

-..Chapter 81-. .-

After the meeting concludes, Uncle Isak speaks to Mikhail with his eyes, as they glance toward Ardent. Mikhail stands to help a distraught Ardent out of the room.

Zack slaps and hugs Jeffrey's back before they walk out together.

Ryan and his son Henry remain seated as the room clears.

Isak shuts the door.

"We needed Dean," Isak says as tears idle in Ryan's and Henry's eyes. "I'm sorry, Ryan. Dean saved my life. I didn't see that coming."

Ryan nods as wet lines slip onto his flushed cheeks. Henry's hands cover his face. A stifled sob escapes.

"Ryan, can you see what Dean was working on?"

"Yes, sir. I had—my brother followed. I know where he keeps his papers. We may have a problem with his goons."

"I'll speak with Zack about that," says Isak.

Ryan nods, focused on his hands in front of him on the conference table.

"I trust Doc is safe," says Isak.

"Yes, sir."

"I need Henry to keep a close watch on Zack. Zack's liable to go crazy with them gone. I want you stationed back at Doc's lab with your dad, Henry. I need you closer to Zack. Let me know if we need to sedate him for a while."

"Yes, sir," Henry says. He averts his eyes after peering at the blood on the other side of the table.

"Henry, I need your solemn oath. There can be no mistakes." Isak says.

Henry raises his finger, showing the same tattoo as Isak's. Isak does the same.

"We need time for this next phase to work as planned."

"How much time, sir?" Henry asks.

Isak looks him in the eyes. Henry exhales.

"I understand, sir."

All three men hold their index fingers up, saying, "Aye."

They stand as Isak leaves the room.

Ryan and Henry stare, both distraught.

"I shouldn't have said that to Dean," says Ryan. "It's my fault he..."

Henry moves swiftly to embrace his father before he can fall over.

-..Chapter 82-..-

Tuesday, March 16, 1993

Two birds are in flight toward the sun above the clear, turquoise-blue water. There's a flutter in Viola's tummy as she watches a dripping wet Jason step out of the ocean. His muscular legs leave footprints on the sand as he walks in front of white painted wooden steps leading up to the wrap-around porch of the beach house. He strolls toward Viola in his swim shorts with a smile that, in this moment, makes her forget all her yesterdays.

This private island paradise is one that her mother had spoken to her about going to in their make-believe boat. Here, Viola can feel her mother's spirit and the spirit of the women before her that the family hid... for a while.

Did mom sit in this chair years ago?

Viola looks at the old domed-lid chest made of oak and strengthened with iron banding, sealed with tar, to keep the water out. Jason pulled it from the shallow ocean floor with Tae.

Following a few weeks hiding elsewhere, Tae met Jason, Zee and Viola at a private airport. Tae brought them to the island. Only Tae and two other female divers know the importance of this secret location in the Mediterranean Sea.

While Zee napped in a secure room in the house, Jason put on scuba gear that Tae brought, to retrieve the hidden chest under the shallow coastal water. He was shocked when Tae dove in next to him without any scuba gear.

The chest was buried under what appeared to be a trap door, which is actually a chamber to equalize the pressure inside. A sea woman, Gerta, drowned re-burying it years ago. The family didn't have to search for her. Her body washed ashore. It was decided then as a safety precaution, that two females would come to this private hideaway to retrieve the chest together. Viola being very pregnant, this time, Tae brought extra scuba gear for Jason.

Viola waited for Jason and Tae on the shoreline. Jason set the chest on the sand, taking off his mask, wearing a confused expression. Viola nodded to Tae, who then explained.

"Like you Jason, I was trained from infancy. I grew up in South Korea. My mother was one of the 'Haenyeo', or what people since the eighteen hundreds called 'a daughter of the sea.' Female free divers have been around for centuries in my family. We dive for many meters, holding our breath longer than an average untrained person. Our community is led by the females. We harvest seafood primarily, and our father's raise the children, tending to the household."

"I've never heard of such a thing." He said. "How can hold your breath for that length of time without—"

"We have an enhanced pulmonary function, a rare genetic variant that evolved over time. My position in the Eastmann family is hiding important information where it can't be found, for the greater good, and from what I hear, you're position is not that different."

"How so?" he asked.

"You hide important people with important information to continue our species."

"You're one of us?" he asked.

"Yes. I'm from your bloodline."

"How is that possible?"

Viola remained silent, along with Tae.

———————

Later that evening, after Tae left with a supply boat, Jason asked, "How is Tae South Korean, not caucasian?"

"Did you know, Jason, that I read it was a German anthropologist who in 1795 made up the word, caucasian? He thought that the Caucasus Mountains was the origin place of the "white race". Those mountains are located between Europe and Asia."

His eyebrows raised.

"There's no proof to any of it." she added. "I'm just explaining where I read the word came from."

Jason's expression was blank. Jason and Viola agreed to never lie to one another again, but also agreed not speak of certain things that might endanger someone other than the two of them.

Viola thinks back to the moment she saw Tae at the private airport. Seeing Tae's face, she knew that Tae's mother's is Lee. Viola's mother Priscilla had a picture at their townhome in Telega. Viola's mother was standing with Lee who was holding a small mother of pearl jewelry box. In mom's letter, Viola recalls reading that Cindy used to babysit her mother, and so did Lee. But in the photograph, Viola's mother and Lee appeared to be close in age. Viola started to piece it together after Uncle Isak told her they added things to Mom's book because they knew *others* would read it.

Mom was giving me a clue. Lee and Mom were two of the six growing up. Aunt Lara told me her sister was one of them and she was Mary's mother. And Jill is Polina's mother. That makes four.

The last pages in the Green Book at the cottage reminded Viola why the Haenyeo, and specifically Lee's existence, is a secret and sacred oath among the women in the Eastmann family. Lee and Tae's lives are a living vow, a covenant.

"The last time I saw Tae, I was four years old, Jason. Tae told me that she remembers that day and that she and Mary went to the ocean. I was sent to a lab. Tae said that Lily and Camee were sent to a forest."

"Should you be telling me this information Luv?"

"You saw their names at the cottage, Jason. I know you've set up your strings, which means, you already know some things."

"I do." He said.

"Having Tae here... Jason, I'm trusting you not to ask or speak of Tae to any of the men in our family. Her identity—"

"You have my word, Luv."

"Thank you."

She leans in to kiss him.

Tae's been in touch with Polina. Viola told Tae that Polina had already made contact when Viola was kept at Uncle Mark's office in England.

I'll need to leave the island after our baby girl, Priscilla's born. I'll need to meet with Polina.

-..Chapter 83-. .-

E arly the next morning, Viola sits in a chair on the verandah, thinking about the time she questioned mom for being forced to learn so much more than her friends in Telega.

Her mother opened an old book in the basement at the *Blár Leif Bookstore*. The hollow clicking of Aunt Ruth's stilettos were coming down the cement stairs. Priscilla showed Viola the old markings, spreading out the art work, and it's story: the Story of Cleopatra VII.

"Cleopatra was no different than you and I," said Mom. "She knew multiple languages and used her intellect more than relying on her beauty to form strategic alliances. Cleopatra did what she had to do to protect her children's children future. It's written that her father learned from his youth about the insatiable desires in his family to have what rightfully didn't belong to them... to rule. He knew that an envious ruler only tears apart society. And this is what happens again and again when the unknowing pleasure-seeking ego rules."

"But you told me that I can't have children," nine year old Viola said.

"Vee Bee, do not interrupt your mother," said Aunt Ruth.

"It was Cleopatra's father who taught her how to be successor." Mom said. "He sent Cleopatra away to come back, to lead. He understood in 64 BC what we also understand. He wrote about his conniving brother's behaviors. When Cleopatra was born, her father realized her future brothers envy would be amplified by the false greed, the destruction that would ensue, and what would become of their dynasty."

"What does Cleopatra's story have to do with me?" Viola asked.

"The word hedonistic comes from the greek word *hedone* which means pleasure. Life's not about wasting time on guilty pleasures. Yet many people focus on immediate gratification rather than think about the future consequences of overindulging. Like many of the wealthy King's in history, who lost their crowns, we too are lost if we fail to grow up and achieve individuality. Envy leads to everything evil. We know from a young age which children may start wars."

"How can you know that, mama?"

"We test them. We pay attention to our children's behaviors. The ones who start jumping trees. The story of the two trees, the reflection of the tree on the sea, is Mother Nature's warning and no one, no thing can direct the wind. We can choose to adjust our sails, to travel in harmony with the force of nature, or we're against it," said Mom.

Aunt Ruth placed her hand on Viola's shoulder.

"There will always be two trees and sometimes you'll stand in the middle of them, in the chaos and choose to remain calm in the eye of the storm, Vee Bee. Each individual is born with talents to create, to connect, to heal. Or they destroy themselves and everything around them."

My grandmother, my dad, Zack, all jumped trees. Freud said that "all family life is organized around the most damaged person in it."

And we'll spend most of our time trying to steer them away from destroying the good. Is life on this planet one big test?

Viola watches the movement of the sea, to let go, to remember that day in the basement at *Blár Leif.*

"In the beginning, Vee Bee, the earth was mostly covered by the ocean. All living things including humans depend on water for survival. It's written that a family friend in the late 1800s in England, a Henry Fleuss, spent his life working on the first practical scuba diving suit. It would be well into the 1940s before Jacques-Yves Cousteau and Emile Gagnan would discover that using a regulator with high pressure tanks would allow deep seas exploration."

"Why would they spend their life working on that?" Viola asked.

"Hydration, hygiene, food, agriculture, sanitation systems." said Mom.

Aunt Ruth leaned in to point to an article.

"Read out loud to me what Jacques-Yves Cousteau said here."

"The future of the world depends on the water," said Viola.

"They understood the importance of their purpose on earth. This is your mother's scrapbook. I gave it to her and I want you to keep it, Vee Bee. You will add to this, any of your new findings and the future articles of every invention people are working on. This is how we educate ourselves. Knowledge is how we advance our species generation after generation," said Aunt Ruth.

Viola is hypnotized by the sway of the vast ocean.

"We're responsible for clean water," she says, thinking about the water in Zee's baby bottle when she gave it to him, at the Philadelphia airport. Viola wishes she never had to wean him, wishes they never had to part in the first place. Viola spoke in French, telling Jill to retrieve the Green Book. Viola must figure something out—an equation that she overlooked when in a hurry to read its entire contents. Viola also knew it was imperative that Jason not know Jill's identity.

I didn't lie to him. I did, if not telling him is a lie.

She blinks three times, wanting to release the guilt.

When Viola walked up to Jason at the gate holding Zee, Jason didn't say a word.

He's a better person than I am. Thoughtful.

Before the explosion at Uncle Benjamin's, before they secured themselves in the underground bunker, Jason asked Viola what belongings she wanted from Uncle's.

He's always thinking about me and what I want.

When they arrived on the island, Jason handed Viola back the silver penny Uncle Benjamin had given to her when she became a woman in their family.

Viola regrets her angry words that day when she thought Uncle Benjamin was not on her side.

Jason strolls out onto the porch with Zee in one arm. In his other hand, he carries a few envelopes, placing them on the table in front of her, handing Zee to her.

His eyes glance down at the smaller worn sealed envelope on top.

"It's from Uncle Benjamin. That's his hand writing." she says.

Viola didn't want Uncle's letter when Jason tried to give it to her at the cottage. She ignored him.

"You weren't ready to read it, luv. I planned to give it to you once we spread Uncle Benjamin's ashes."

"When will we do that?"

"When it's safe."

"I hope that someone let Uncle Isak out of the box?"

"They did, luv."

"How can you know for sure?" she asks.

"Uncle Isak's sent several messages over the HF radio at the Plant. He's fine."

Viola grins ear to ear, recalling her own HF transmission at the Plant.

"Uncle contained... pick up in two."

The Rise understood the urgency of the first part of her message. Uncle Isak was imprisoned, she feared for his life.

The main reason for her transmission was the second half. It was to let *them* know that she had completed *their* mission and it was now time for *them* to deliver on Jill's promise... to reunite Viola with Zee.

-..Chapter 84-. .-

After lunch, sitting on the porch with Zee on her lap, Viola peers over at Jason.

"What was in that compartment in the closet at the cottage?"

"Some photographs, a handkerchief and a jewelry box. it contained... a ring." he says.

Was the jewelry box made of mother of pearl? The same one in the photograph in Telega with mom and Lee?

"Did you bring them here, to the island, Jason?"

"Might I ask Luv, at the cottage... what was buried in the dirt?" he asks.

Her breathing slows.

I'm tired of all of these secrets. With him more than anyone else. Will this ever end?

"I dug six feet and found nothing," he adds.

"Forgive me, Jason. I can't tell you."

The Rise knew Jason would track Viola's footprints. Jill left the GPS for this sole purpose. Viola already had the map of where Jill said to rebury the Green Book. The blue orchid flower petal in the book came with a riddle on a square sticky note. Viola buried it much closer than Jason would consider looking. She buried it directly underneath where she buried the blue orchid Jason brought as a wedding gift from Aunt Ruth.

Jason watched as Viola planted the orchid in front of the cottage, behind bushes, away from the scorching sun, so it wouldn't shrivel up or die from being left inside the the room when they departed. Viola hid the Green Book in plain sight.

Viola thinks back to her conversation with Uncle Isak at the Plant. Isak spoke quickly. Viola listened as they walked outside the gates when she first arrived. She questioned why they tried to hide Jason from her. Uncle Isak wouldn't answer. Isak told her that she must run.

"It's imperative for all future generations in our bloodline, that you survive." Isak said.

Does he think I know the cure or does he want my offspring?

They made the deal for Viola to have time with her children, away, hidden. Viola would only agree to his terms if Jason could go with her. She wouldn't have asked had she not received the note at the Complex.

"Change of plans. Jason is key."

Uncle Isak said no. He tried to explain Jason's high rank in the family. Viola told Isak that Jason would go with her, or she would vanish with her children for good.

Isak stopped, slowly taking her by the shoulders.

"You don't have a say in such matters, Althea. Jason is too important in our line. He has many missions to complete. He cannot disappear with you."

"Then I'll disappear, Uncle Isak!"

"If I allow Jason to go with you, we'll require your full cooperation in the future, Althea," he added. "You will agree to a female heir with Zack, or they'll be no further negotiations. You are key."

She blinked twice.

I never want to be with Zack again. Once I fix Zee's blood. There's no need to continue any of this.

Uncle Isak reluctantly agreed with most of her other terms and to let Jason go with her, before they walked back through the gate at the Plant.

From the grand house's wrap-around porch surrounded by the opulent sea, Viola glimpses a sun halo around what Zee in sign language calls *a ball of fire.*

Viola, conditioned by her upbringing, quickly corrects him.

"The sun's not fire, Zee. It's a ball of super heated plasma. Hydrogen and helium held together by it's own gravity."

Cecilia Payne-Gaposchkin discovered it. She wrote about it in her thesis in 1925. Viola remembers her mother's words about the sun when Viola asked the same question.

"No one knows everything about the sun and no scientist knows what gravity is exactly. Compared to the vast universe, earth is a spec of dust. What we do know, Viola, is what the story in the book of Treowth says, about the two trees. Men and women were born to create new life together. This planet has a built-in capacity to renew itself, to continue life on earth. But that's only if humans don't destroy the earth with wars and nuclear weapons."

Five year-old Viola asked, "If nuclear weapons destroy the earth will the sun stop shining?"

"No. But if the sun stops shinning organic life as we know it will cease to exist. Well, the tardigrades or water bears as you like to call them, my little sprinkle, might survive the freeze."

"I'm glad the water bears will survive." said Viola.

Mom tickled Viola's side.

"This curious, instinctive feeling inside of you is your connection to nature, my little sprinkle."

Viola eyes water, staring at the ring of light in the sky.

The ring.

Something moves in Viola's stomach. Her hand bring's Zee's chubby fingers to her round belly as she feels a kick.

"Did you feel that kick, Zee? Soon, you'll meet your sister."

Viola pats Zee's hand.

Jason leans down, placing his hand over hers and Zee's for the next kick. Jason's lips brush Viola's lips, leaving her lightheaded, before he lifts Zee up and onto his shoulders.

Jason didn't tell Uncle Isak about the ring. The camera at the cottage... he made sure the Rise saw that he had it.

"After you open your letters, luv, your dragonflies await your lovely fingertips on the shoreline."

Jason's eyes are focused on the unopened letter from Uncle Benjamin next to the flat sealed package on the table in front of her.

"It's time, luv."

"I don't want to, but I'll read them." she says.

Viola rubs her tummy, her frown turns upright, watching Zee's face light up on Jason's shoulders. His fingers pull on Jason's curly head of hair.

On the private airplane when Viola asked Jason, he told Viola that Henrik at the Complex was Viola's invisible watcher.

"Jason, do you know if Henrik was the masked man who helped me out of my car wreck in Telega?"

"I thought your mum took you to see Dean after your crash?" Jason says.

"No. She didn't. She was at Dean's lab when I woke up."

Viola recalls the man in the ski mask, in the black car who took her to Dean after her car accident.

In the Green Book there was a golden head band with three rubies.

The book spoke of the "Daughter's of the Sea," as well as another family that this particular crown belongs to. A family who have helped the women in the Eastmann clan for centuries.

The man in the black car in Telega had the same image tattooed on his bicep of what Viola realizes was a golden crown with three triangle points, and three jewels set in the shape of four pointed stars. When the man in the black mask cut the seam and tore off his arm sleeve, Viola glanced at the tattoo before she wrapped the tattered fabric around her bloodied injury.

"Was it Henrik who shot the old nomadic woman with a dart, Jason?"

"If he did, I don't think he killed her, luv. Nor did he kill the other soldiers who were shot by the darts. They all woke up. Henrik most likely shot them to stop the men from killing innocents. And from what you told me, he saved the nomad woman from being killed by one of Patrick's men."

Zee giggles.

"I'll leave you to read, my luv. Zee and me have a playdate on the sand."

Jason slowly twirls around, placing his large hands behind Zee's body to steady him.

-..Chapter 85-. .-

Viola opens the larger thin envelope mailed from America first. She unfolds the paper, knowing it's not the Green Book, and it's not a letter. It's a newspaper article from a few months ago. Scribbled in pen, in a recognizable writing style, there's a note from Jill.

"Embrasse le petit bonhomme pour moi." (Hug the little man for me.)

The Telega News

Sunday, January 3, 1993

In the early morning on January 1st, a group of girls in Telega, NY, drove to the police station after witnessing what appeared to be a kidnapping by a man dressed in black, wearing a green mask that fit the description of the mask worn in an attempted kidnapping on July 31, 1971. The suspect was driving down Main Street in a silver car with no license plate. After a twenty-one-year hiatus, is the man in the mask back, or is he a copycat?

Viola covers her mouth.

"I need Jill to get a message to Aunt Ruth. Zack must be stopped once and for all. I can't live here and not care about what's happening on the other side of the world. I can't! I'll ask Aunt Ruth to make Uncle Isak a new deal if he'll imprison Zack."

She hears Zee's trills echo. She watches them, down in front of the steps on the sandy beach. Jason set Zee at the water's edge for him to dip his fingers. She hears Zee's high-pitched laughter.

"Has a dragonfly landed?" Viola calls out.

Without thinking, Viola dipped her hands in the pristine salt water last week, lifting them toward the sky, while sitting half on the white sandy beach with her legs in the ocean. She spoke to the sifting breeze.

"Show me a sign, Mom. Are you still here like you said you'd be?"

To her surprise, a dragonfly landed on her finger—and then, on her other hand, another. It was a magical moment.

"Was that you, Mom...Uncle?"

Her heart's filled with love and despair as she thinks of Telega. She thinks of Zack.

"I worried that he'd be a little crazy or a lot crazy."

She hears her mother's voice.

"You can't fix crazy."

On the outdoor veranda, Viola places the article on the coffee table, not wanting to read any more of it. She lifts the letter from Uncle Benjamin, sucking in a breath as she opens the envelope.

Monday, July 6, 1992

My sweet Vee Bee.

Forgive me for not being honest with you. I was born and raised to respect my superiors, and I, like you, have sworn my oaths. I can never explain too many things, and truthfully, there is no need, as they are my past, not yours. We are a family of scientists, with six hundred years of knowledge hidden and dispersed across the world. As you're aware, in science, specific remedies don't work as expected across all mammals. There will always be trial and error, and most often, their effects differ significantly between females and males. You've done this research yourself, as have I. I'm proud of you. I was proud of your mother.

After Stephen violated you, I knew with my entire being that I, along with your mother, would find a way to set you free, so you could live, as your mother called it, "utenfor flokken." (Outside the herd.)

Our studies have shown that a man who rapes, is seeking power, or he's angry, or he seeks revenge. Stephen wanted to infect your brain because his was infected. Stephen was deliberate in his harm. He was a talented scientists, and like your abilities mimic those of our ancestors, his did as well.

Your findings are astounding. Doc told me that we are close. We believe the fix for the female blood condition in our family is now complete. Something is amiss with the fix for the males in our bloodline. You're being sent to Siberia for a purpose—more than one. You must not work on the solution while you're in the lab in Siberia. They're taking you to this lab, to watch you, to see what you know. A contact is in place. Henrik will reach out to you when you arrive. He will assist you. Jason has been informed and will explain; however, should Jason rise before he can tell you, Auntie is also aware, as are the hidden, whom you will travel to meet to collaborate with on this final project after your next baby's birth.

I want you to keep this lucky coin. In our bloodline, you are Lady Luck, my dandelion. Keep it in remembrance of me in your younger years. You mean the world to me, Vee Bee. You are and have always been the light in my eyes. Don't allow anyone or anything to change your shine, not even me. No thing is worth holding space for hatred inside. This lifetime is short, patience is a virtue. We are past a six-century-old hurdle. Go forward and stay true to you. If your mother were alive, you know she would tell you to face your fears. I believe you've faced more than most and there are more to face, still.

I've made mistakes. I know I have. I did what I felt I had to do to continue my line. You will, too, Vee Bee. Tell me who said, "Experience is merely the name men gave to their mistakes."

With tears rolling down her cheeks, she smiles.

"Oscar Wilde said it in 1891. Not much has changed Uncle," she says.

Now that you'll have children, Vee Bee, you'll find it difficult not to feel responsible for their happiness and their sadness as I have for my children. They must grow to be responsible for themselves to be happy in self. That is what I want for you. Never forget: Jeg er ansvarlig for meg selv. (I am responsible for myself.) I love you very much. In faith, Uncle.

Viola folds up the letter.

"I am responsible for myself, Uncle. Forgive me. You only ever wanted to see me happy. I thank you, Auntie, and Mamma. I'll find the hidden. Jill and Mary are helping. So is Tae."

Viola stands. Tears trickle down her cheeks.

She recalls Uncle Benjamin telling her, *"Each lifetime, man takes from the previous inventors and adds the next missing piece to an unfinished puzzle."*

"That's what I'll do. I'll finish what our ancestors started. Uncle was on my side!"

His written words sound in her head.

"Patience is a virtue, Vee Bee."

William Langland wrote this in 1360, although Uncle told her it comes from deeper roots in a Latin collection of proverbial wisdom, The Distichs of Cato, from the fourth century AD. Uncle read its meaning from the Family Bible, how suffering produces patience.

"Maintaining a positive attitude is hard, Uncle... I'm trying." Viola says to the gentle air.

She walks across the porch, down to their private beachfront to join Jason and Zee.

Viola's eyes lift toward the sky, thinking about her high school friends, Jes, Abby, and Sandy, sitting at a table in the cafeteria when they shared their five-year plans with each other. Of all people, Sandy said, *"Patience is a virtue,"* after Jes mentioned her desire to become a professor of education.

Viola inhales the sea air, holding her protruding basketball size bump.

"How long will it take me to fix this, Cilla? I'm no longer me. I'm an us. I've got you littles to think about. You're my responsibility. You're in my tree."

She can see the back of Jason's head on the sand. The lower half of his body is in the water. Jason's hands are buried. His left hand is playing peek-a-boo with Zee, popping out and back into the sand before Zee can grab it.

"My five-year plan Cilla, is to end this blood curse for every child in our family. If it takes another five years, so be it. I'll create the fix, and you and Zee will be free."

Then I'm free, too.

Zee's eyes are wide when he sees Viola. He points toward Jason's visible toes, floating above the shallow water on the edge of the beach.

"Fieye Mamma, Fieye."

A dragonfly sits on Jason's big toe, that's sticking out of the water. Viola's stomach flips, doing a happy cartwheel inside.

"Your fly is a dragonfly, Zee. *En øyenstikker.* The dragonfly's presence tells us that our ecosystem is healthy. They eat hundreds of mosquitoes every day, helping to balance nature."

Viola has spoken to Zee in sign language, Norwegian, German, French, Russian, Korean, and English since he was born.

"No Mauve Pappa," Zee says, pointing.

"*Ingen bevegelse* means 'No move, Pappa!'" says Viola.

Zee grabs Jason's thumb, which has poked up from the sand. Zee squeals with joy.

Viola sits on her knees next to Zee. She grabs Jason's index finger, with a coy smile, she's enamored by the grin on Jason's face, who's still watching the dragonfly perched on his big toe. Jason's chin dips as the dragonfly takes flight, joining with another dragonfly nearby.

His head tilts toward Viola. His bright blue ocean eyes meet hers.

"Thank you, Jason, for saving us."

"Thank you for saving me, luv."

-..Chapter 86-. .-

The Next Day

Jason bounces Zee on his knee, sitting at the kitchen table in the house.

"I'm going for a swim." Viola says, after rereading some papers from the chest in the living room.

Viola wants to reset her thoughts by submerging herself in the ocean like her ancestors said they did in the book from the sea titled, "Tsewa" to silence the noise of the mind.

As she goes down the steps to the beach, she's unable to see her feet from a growing Cilla, inside, waiting to face her reflection, to draw her first gasp of air.

Viola recalls the french Auntie who was shot and murdered in front of Viola when she was four years old, by an Alexander in the family. The woman spoke to Viola and Polina about the meaning behind this word.

"In the Amazon Jungle this word "tsewa" means 'gift. The gift is..."
Polina poked the dead mouse on the table with a pencil she had in her hand.

Viola giggled.

"Faites attention!" (Pay attention!) The woman said.

Viola heard what sounded like the pop of fireworks outside of the room.

Viola sighs. The horizon billows with a grey hue, hinting at what's to come.

"Jill told me the six girls from the photograph share the gift." Viola whispers to the scurry whistling of the wind.

She counts in her head as she was taught to, when she needed to let go of her thoughts.

One, two, three...

Viola forges forward into the sea.

Jason mentioned yesterday, a gale-force wind was heading their way. Intense Mediterranean storms are known to be fierce in Malta during certain months.

Viola's been feeling a storm brewing inside. A desperation to come up with the sequence to uncover the remedy for Zee's blood. She attempts to push her angst aside.

Viola taps her stomach where her cotton nightgown now clings to her skin from the ocean water.

"I'm going to enjoy this day, this life with Jason, Zee, and you too, Cilla."

She continues walking.

One, two, three...

Viola's vision aligns with the water's swell. A gentle, blurred pulse, matches the breathing of the sea.

A wave comes seemingly out of nowhere, crashing over Viola, dragging her under. She screams, swallowing the salt water, with her arms flailing. She swims up, reaching for the surface.

As she inhales her first lungful of oxygen, an insight suddenly crystalizes in her mind.

———

Restless, in bed, Viola wakes in the dark from a dream.

She glances at the nightstand to the digital alarm clock Jason brought to the island. The numbers emit red light showing the time, 11:11. The outline of the white shell bracelet in front of it that Jason and Zee made for her, glows in a burnt orange color. The twisted pattern reminds her of a drawing on one of the maps that was inside of the chest pulled from the sea. Her mind is racing.

Viola thinks about her mother showing her the pattern on the shell of the cone snail species.

The left side always repeats. The right side, nobody knows for certain.

"Why does a planned smooth take off end with a bumpy landing? "Mom asked.

Ten-year old Viola shrugged her shoulders.

"Stephen Wolfram's 'Rule 30' teaches us how simple rules can create the unpredictable behavior we see in nature. *There are no shortcuts. All travel is a risk. But without taking that risk, we won't find the answers we're looking for."*

"What are we looking for?" Viola asked.

"You'll know when you see it, my little sprinkle. We must never stop. The only way out, is in."

Mom explained to Viola how minor decisions, and early environmental changes can greatly alter the long-term life of an individual, group, or a social system development.

She was talking about our family. We can change it for the better. We have to want to and not everybody wants to.

Viola can't explain her recurring dream. Since she was a little girl, most of them involve her being in the ocean under water or on a beach at the water's edge. Was it a premonition or something completely different? A precognitive phenomena? A sixth sense?

How can I know what this is without ever learning about it?

-..Chapter 87-. .-

Unable to drift back off to sleep, Viola uses a log roll technique to get out of bed. In one of her long white cotton nightgowns, barefoot, she slowly makes her way out of the bedroom. She gazes from the kitchen window at the moon shining on the ocean. She's amazed by the celestial canvas of stars. She thinks of Zee with his fists crossed at his chest. His arms exploded outward, when they sat around the fire pit a few nights ago. He did it again, raising his hands in the air, wiggling his fingers.

In sign language he said, "Boom boom twinkles."

Viola recalls the drawing and an inscription about a cure for a virus. Earlier, she was careful, turning page after page and had stopped at that drawing. She pointed, asking Jason where the location was on the map.

"The Amazon Jungle," she says under her breath.

A sequence flits through Viola's mind. She couldn't figure it out initially when she pulled out the papers and maps from the chest.

Familiar footsteps approach.

"It's almost midnight, Luv, are you alright?" asks Jason from behind her.

Viola reaches for him, glad he's woken up. He comes around to face her.

"Yes. I can't stop thinking about that drawing on the map."

"The stone corkscrew tower?" he says.

"Can you please bring me that map, Jason."

Jason leaves, returning with the map. He turns the kitchen light on.

Viola stares at the map and the stone corkscrew tower.

"It's a coiled fossilized worm. This worm's polychaete mucus and it's silver nanoparticles uh—I can't explain it, Jason, but I swear that my eyes have looked at this diagram before. A long time ago."

"When were you in the Amazon Jungle, luv?"

"Never. But polychaete worms can be found in salt water habitats across the globe. This stone corkscrew tower may have been a polychaete worm found in the Amazon, but they've been on earth for five hundred million years. I read that there are fossils dating back to the Cambrian period when there was no land plants or animals. I saw this exact symbol when we were in the infirmary at the Complex."

"The day you were shot?" he asks, amazed.

"No."

Viola stares past Jason.

"Sorry Jason, my brain is trying to dig through old archives. Um. When you were lying on a medical bed unconscious, I watched Dean put a vial in one of the cabinets. It had this symbol on it. I remember looking at the symbol and thinking it looked familiar. I didn't know why. When I dreamed about it earlier, I knew what it was."

She glances at him dumbstruck.

"What is it, luv?"

Her eyes look up and to the left.

"This worm has a remarkable regenerative ability. It can be used to create a heritable genetic modification. I know the sequence."

With fear etched on her face, she glances back into Jason's eyes.

"Why did Dean have it? Was he supposed to bring it to the Complex for me? We need to retrieve that vial, Jason."

He moves closer, with a serious look.

"We can't love, I'm sorry. We can't leave this island. Not now."

Jason's hand slides up her arm. His face goes pale.

"What is it, Jason?"

He lifts Viola's right arm, taking her other wrist, he moves her forefinger along a tiny hardness, The size of a single piece of rice, can be felt, two inches below her armpit.

"What is it?"

"During World War II, scientists were working on a dog tag, a tiny transponder that could be easily inserted under a soldier's skin. Usually under their right arm."

"Are you telling me that I've been dog tagged? Am I being tracked?"

Jason is silent.

"Oh no. They know where we are. We're not safe, Jason."

"I wonder who implanted you, and when."

Viola's thoughts rush to Polina, when she stuck Viola with a needle in Uncle Mark's boardroom, with the hope that she wanted to track her whereabouts. But her needle went in at the bend in Viola's right arm, not higher. She thinks of Janic, while she was asleep in the loud truck from the Nomad's camp, headed to the Complex. Her mind quickly reverts to Dean.

"Dean was standing over me in the private family airplane when we arrived in Buffalo from the Complex. When I woke up, he was hiding something behind his back. I felt strange. I knew something wasn't right."

"If that's the case, luv, you should be safe, since Dean, Uncle Mark and Uncle John are deceased."

"They are? Why didn't you tell me, Jason?"

"Are their deaths something you need to know?"

Her lower lids fill, threatening a downpour, thinking about Dean.

"I've been listening to the radio set to RX only in the bunker room, luv."

Viola finds it odd that Jason calls a rock-site installation under this house a bunker. It's nothing like Uncles. Would it withstand a blast like the one at Uncle's in Telega?

"I'll need to reach out to someone," says Jason, "to be sure that no one else in the family was working with them. I'll have to leave you."

"What makes you think they were working with someone else."

"Maybe not, luv, but my gut tells me they were."

"Why can't you send a message from here, Jason?"

"I can't send a message from the bunker here, or we'll be found. It's only for listening purposes, or in case of an emergency."

"I think, in this case, we—"

"Have you forgotten, luv, that we're both supposed to be dead?"

Viola eyes shut and open. She nods her head.

"Sorry, Jason, um, when does the next boat of supplies arrive?"

"In another week. I'll go to the mainland, luv. I'll buy a disposable mobile phone and contact Henrik . I'll have Henrik check the Complex for the vial with the symbol. Come with me to the ensuite. I'll rid you of this."

"The on sweet?" she says.

Jason wears a playful grin. "The master bathroom, Luv."

––––––––––

Jason removes the device, placing a bandage on her arm.

His brow furrows.

"What is it, Jason?"

"This isn't a transponder."

"Huh, it's a coated biomarker," says Viola. "Why would Dean want to track my health data?"

Viola takes the slender needle from him, thankful the device is not a transponder.

"If that vial is still at the Complex, Henrik will get it for us. No one can track us here. You, me, Zee, and Cilla, after she's born, are safe. Please don't worry, luv. I promise, no one will find us."

You read what I did in the book about the gift. You saw the drawing of the parrot looking at its reflection in the mirror. You know the truth about me, don't you Jason?

Viola brings her finger to Jason's cheek. In three movements, she traces the capital letter R.

His confused stare, confirms it.

He doesn't know.

"I wish you could promise that we'll be okay, Jason? I'm going to pretend this is our Lagoon and no one will ever find us and we'll stay here for the rest of our lives. I know we can't, but I wish—"

Stop! Stop it. Stop thinking.

"I can promise to love you for every moment we're alive," Jason says, taking the biomarker from her other hand, slipping it into his housecoat pocket.

His eyes wide with concern, soften.

Viola knows this look. She can feel it on her face.

Jason's fingers trail down her nightgown to her stomach.

"I think Cilla's asleep," he says.

Jason reaches up to rub the back of Viola's neck and shoulders.

"Let's go to bed, luv. Allow me to erase these bad dreams," he says, with a wink.

She releases a breath she didn't realize she was holding. Viola relaxes, giving into his strong touch. A smile plays on the corners of her mouth.

"When you put it like that, Jason Stanton. That sounds really good to me."

Jason grabs her by the waist. With one hand, he unties the silk bow of her nightgown that's resting on the small dip at the base of her throat. The twinkle in his eye fills Viola with a tingly feeling all over as his finger tips drag over the fabric covering her breast.

Her heart pounds in her chest. She can hear the blood roaring in her ear drums. She restrains herself from untying his robe, not wanting to change the course of his plans for her. Viola leans in, placing a kiss just below his ear. She moves her head back. His eyes hold hers.

"I love you, Jason."

With a low moan, Jason claims her mouth, forcing a faint gasp from her parted lips.

Viola decides to copy Zee's earlier game. She steps on Jason's bare feet with her own. In a throaty melodic sounding laugh, Jason walks them from the master bathroom toward the bed.

About the Author

MERSAIDEE SOULES ™ is a member of The International Thriller Writers Novelists, Inc., a member of Women in Film USA and Toronto, IBPA, Author's Guild, Canadian Author's Association, and an ASCAP/SOCAN member.

Mersaidee grew up in the Eastern part of Canada. She was born in a small town in the province of Ontario. She currently lives in the Southern United States with her family.

Visit Mersaidee's website to learn more and watch the trailer's for: A Viola Ted Saga ™. A limited edition merch can be found exclusively in the Book Store & Shop section.

www.mersaideesoules.com

Sign up and stay tuned for important dates and for her companion book releases for:

A VIOLA TED SAGA ™

To see the questions from book two, please go to Mersaidee's website and sign up to join her book club.

Acknowledgements

To my husband, my life partner. I love you so much. You R my heart.

To my incredibly talented, creative children. Never stop being curious. Dad and I believe in you and we love you for who you are.

Papa. Thank you. PM, Mom, Dad, Mom D, I love you.

Thank you Aunt Kathie and D, for the phone conversations and unconditional everything.

To my 'no matter where, no matter what,' Karen, (who's not a "Karen!) Let's write our next books and continue to empower each other.

To all of my wonderful family (there are a lot of us) and to my extended family, you know who you are, I love you.

To my friends, beta readers, and Dimple Kumar for your awesome grammar catches. Hug to you.

To my Mississippi friends, Tennessee, California & Canadian buds. I love you to bits...

To Hope, for helping my kiddos with the hefty school workload.

Thanks to the wonderful and talented Angelica R and to Dom Chung for your amazing photography.

Thank you to my film maker friends, helpers, actors, book models for this saga.

Matthew Ladner, you are uber talented. Thank you for another off the charts amazing book cover. I love your positive energy, your kind spirit and your bad ass never ending creativity and a hug to you James.

Dana, Thank you for not changing my voice and for being an incredible human being. Double hugs to you! And additional Editing, S.P. & S.H. xo

Brandon Adams, not only are you the music man, you're also an amazing audiobook editor/producer. Thank you so very much!

Taryn Caan, thank you for your incomparable voice narration on my audio books. You're wonderful.

I would like to thank everyone at ITW, and special thanks to Dr. Bebee. Glenn Payne for your trust and endless drive. Peter Markham for your cinematic teaching, and passion about the details that make all the difference.

To my cherry blossom good mother to the Yorkie clan, (big hugs) and a shout out to my sis cousin, Erin, for every 'Happy Friday' message! Love ya soooo mucha.

The countless strangers and mentors, thank you for your encouragement.

S.P. My gratitude for you is an ineffable feeling; no words can express it!

And Thank YOU for purchasing book two in:

A VIOLA TED SAGA ™

When it's my time to fly, we'll fly together again:

Dad, Cindy, Jamie, Aunt Ida, Uncle Bob, Grandad Eddie, Grannie, Cuz Tanya, Uncle Sam, Tim Johnson, Tom Booth.

I'm grateful for the many strengths that dyslexia gives me. To you, the creative person working toward your goals ...

"To thine own self be true." William Shakespeare, *Hamlet*

If you're in crisis, call or text the Suicide & Crisis Lifeline in the United States at **988**.

You're not alone! Get help now! Call the National Sexual Assault Hotline RAINN. **800.656.4673**

Choose to be the change, otherwise... It's always the same.

Much love, Mersaidee